RISE OF A WARRIOR
BLADE OF ICE
BOOK ONE

JESSICA WAYNE

B.A.D.
PUBLISHING

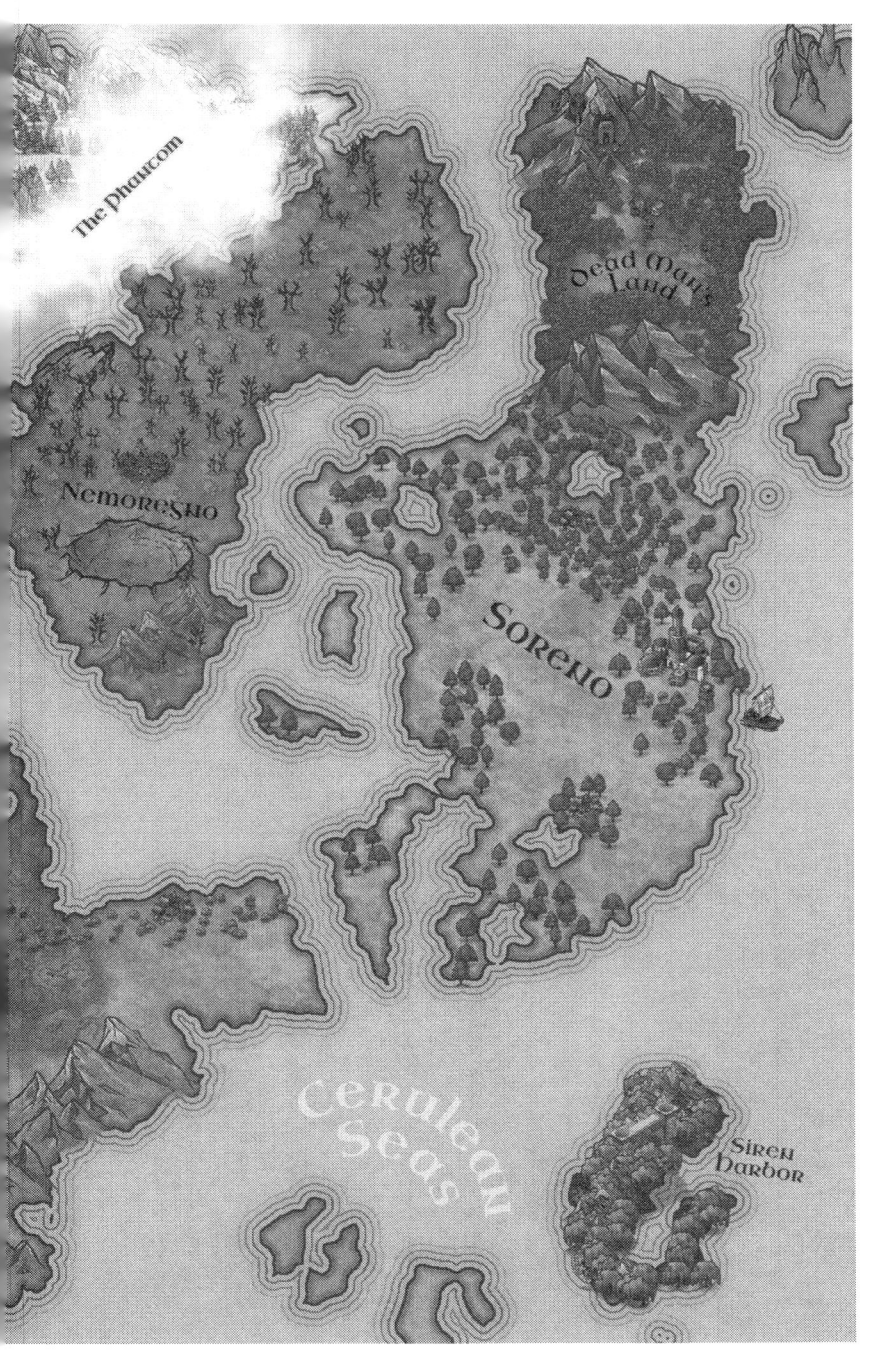

B.A.D.
Publishing

RISE OF A WARRIOR
Blade of Ice, book 1
By Jessica Wayne

Copyright © 2023. All rights reserved.
This book is a work of fiction. Names, characters, places, businesses, and incidents are products of the author's imagination or used fictitiously. Any resemblance to actual persons, living or dead, places, or actual events is entirely coincidental.
No part of this book may be reproduced or transmitted in any form by any means, electronic or mechanical, including photocopying, recording, or by any information storage and retrieval system without written permission of the author, except for use of brief quotations in a book review.

Edited by McKenna Lay
Proofread by Tasha Lewis
Proofread by Dawn Y.
Cover Design by Covers by Christian
Hardcover Design by TwinArtCoverDesign
Interior print art by Samaiya Art

*To anyone who has ever been underestimated.
Never let them tell you how bright your flame can burn.*

A sheltered princess. The head of her guard. An icy world of forbidden desires, treacherous secrets, and mortal danger.

Every second of my life has been leading up to an arranged marriage with the king of a neighboring land. It is my duty to secure an alliance, to be seen and not heard, and to birth an heir.

But my heart has always belonged to another.

Fort is everything my family forbids me from wanting.

He's lethal. A blood-stained blade rather than a shield to hide behind. Yet he watches my every move. An unshakable shadow that eliminates threats before they truly exist.

When my world crumbles around me, it's Fort left standing. Together, we must flee the only place I've ever known, so I can survive long enough to unite a now broken realm.

The longer we're together, though, the hotter the flame between us burns. And when we finally give in, I know there's no turning back.

Even if it is my future husband I must beg to aid us in this fight.

Passion.

Treachery.

Hatred.

Death.

In this twisted war for the throne, I have discovered it's my blood that is the prize to be won. And those hunting me will not stop until the final Navalis Royal has fallen.

CARLEAH

Music from the orchestra drifts out of the ballroom as I hastily fasten my coat. Wine dances on my tongue, and a giggle escapes my lips as I look back at the man behind me. His light hair is disheveled, his tunic askew, but he watches me with a hunger in his hazel gaze that makes me feel like a woman rather than a sheltered princess of barely eighteen.

"Come on!" I urge with a laugh, reaching out to pull him with me.

He takes my hand and lets me drag him outside. Snow crunches beneath our shoes, but my laughter will not be heard thanks to the party noises still drifting from inside.

I do not know the man's name, but to be honest, I don't really care. He's a distraction. A way to get my mind off of the destiny that is now hurtling my way at lightning speed.

We reach the edge of the frozen lake as it glistens beneath the bright moonlight. Overhead, an owl hoots, and somewhere in the distance, a wolf howls. It's home. A beautiful, perpetual winter paradise.

The man spins me and slams my back into a large tree as his hands go to my waist, his mouth on mine. The kiss is fast, hard, but lacking any real passion—at least on my end. Though the wine making me dizzy helps me pretend that there is.

I wrap both arms around his neck and let him bury his face against my pulse. His tongue grazes over my throat, and I let out a soft groan even though I feel nothing.

Sheltered.

Spoiled.

That's what they all think of me. I'm the youngest royal child and the only girl, which means eventually, my family will marry me off. Likely to the future king of Soreno, if I had to guess. Which, essentially, means my path has already been chosen.

My life laid out for me.

So, that in mind, I'm determined to live as much as I can before the doors are shuttered permanently against any actual adventures. I will be a wife. A mother. A queen. And passionate kisses outside of a party will be nonexistent.

"We should go somewhere more private," he urges as he slips his hands beneath my jacket and grazes the tips of his fingers over the open back of my dress.

"This is just fine," I say with a laugh as I try to

redirect him to my mouth. I grab his hands and pull them back to my waist, but he forces them up again.

"No. It's not. Come on, I know a place." He starts to pull me away, and the first shred of fear ices through the wine buzzing in my veins.

"I'm not leaving," I reply with a forced smile. "This is my party after all."

His eyes harden. "A party you were quick to leave, princess. Come on—" He starts to tug me again, so I try to pull him back in. I press a quick kiss to his lips in an attempt to cool the situation, despite the heaviness in my chest.

My gaze darts back to the castle. "Actually, I'm quite cold now. Maybe we should—"

A low growl emits from just behind him, and my gaze widens fearfully when I note the massive wall of angry man stalking from between the trees. *Fort.*

He wears a black coat the same shade as his obsidian hair along with dark riding pants. His leather boots move near soundlessly in the snow, making him appear more like a living shadow than a living, breathing man.

But it's not the sight of him moving from the trees and across the snow, his large hand wrapped around the hilt of his blade, that has my heart pumping faster. It's the fact that his amber gaze is *murderous*—and trained directly on the stranger.

"Fuck off, asshole," the stranger orders. "We're—"

I don't even have time to tell him just how stupid it is to taunt the head of our guard before Fort reaches forward and grabs him by the back of his coat. He flings him off of me and to the snow before whirling on me.

His gaze travels down to my lips, then my throat, and the swell of my breasts, exposed, thanks to my partially open coat. Nostrils flaring, his eyes find mine again, and a muscle in his jaw tightens.

"We were just having fun," I insist. "The party was—"

"Yeah! Just fun." The man scrambles to his feet and tries to run.

I could have told him it was useless, but I don't even get the chance to. Fort rips out a short blade and flings it, sending it soaring end over end until the hilt slams into the man's back. He falls to the snow—silent.

"Did you kill him? What the hell, Fort!" I try to rush forward to make sure I didn't get the asshole killed, but Fort's hand tightens around my jacketed arm. Heat burns through the contact even as I cannot directly feel his hand on my flesh.

Every inch of my body reacts to him, a pull I've only ever read about until this moment. Cheeks flushing with more than the wine I indulged in earlier, I feel every bit a woman now, pinned beneath the gaze of a man who has always seemed larger than life to me.

My gaze travels over Fort's sharp jaw and locks with his amber gaze. And when I let myself sink into it, I'm momentarily frozen by the carnal ferocity reflected in his eyes. I open my mouth to speak, but nothing comes out. What does one say in a moment like this? When the entire world has tilted on its axis? When everything suddenly becomes so clear and incredibly complicated, all at the same time?

Fort leans in closer, the stubble of his jaw scraping deliciously against my cheek as he inhales deeply. When he pulls away, he lets out a low growl that is more animal than man before he releases me. Then, he turns and stalks away, stopping to sheathe both his sword and the blade he threw before lifting the now groaning party guest from the snow.

Even though Fort cannot speak—he's never uttered even a single word—I can feel his anger.

And in my wine-induced haze, I cannot help but wonder if perhaps that emotion stems from something far more than his sworn duty to protect me.

CHAPTER 1
CARLEAH
TWO YEARS LATER

In the beginning, there were giants.

Massive human-like creatures who stood watch over the realm, ensuring our world remained safe from those who sought to steal our peace. They were our greatest protectors and our most loyal allies.

The giants supported the King of Navalis, and beneath his rule, there were no wars.

No conflicts.

But if history teaches us anything, it's that peace does not last forever.

"Carleah, are you listening to me?"

I glance over at my mother, a sheepish grin on my face. "Of course." I turn away, studying the world outside my gilded cage. A world covered in snow, which serves as a backdrop to the bright red cardinals playing in the cool air.

Here, up high in the Navalis Mountains, our kingdom

is a secluded reminder of the peace that once existed in this realm. Because, outside of this place, the greed of men still reigns. The only reason it doesn't reach us here is because my father wears our crown.

Legends of giants may be what some believe led to our serenity, but I choose to see those for what they are: legends. Stories told to children so they will not venture too far into the woods.

The truth, as I see it, is that, as long as a Rossingol sits on the throne, our kingdom will not suffer the fall as so many others have.

Soreno is the only other land in this realm that still maintains its hold on all that is good in this world. The others are traitorous places where men take what they want. War and bloodshed are the only things they understand.

A crimson bird lands in the pale snow, its tiny feet leaving footprints on the surface.

Oh, how I long to be a bird. A creature capable of flying wherever it chooses. A being with no forced marriage hanging over her head, nor regal duties to tend to.

What must that freedom be like?

My mother clears her throat again, so I turn away from my window and fully face her once more.

She arches a pale brow and crosses her arms. The ice-blue gown she wears is the same color as nearly every dress in my wardrobe. It is the color of our kingdom, a mark of our family. "Then tell me what it is I said."

My cheeks heat. "I was not listening," I admit.

"I figured as much." She reaches out and cups my cheek with slender fingers. "My love, you are an adult now, which means your marriage is on the horizon. You must know these things if you are to be as great of a queen as I know you are capable of."

I let out a sigh. "I am sorry, Mother. Truly. I haven't been sleeping well, so my focus is not what it should be." I leave out all mentions of nightmares plaguing me, never mentioning the winged horse I see every night when I close my eyes because my mother will not take either well.

In her eyes, I must be perfect. Because, to Molly Rossingol, perfection means I will make a good queen when I take my place in Soreno. The mere thought of it makes my stomach churn.

"I remember those days. When I turned twenty and my marriage to your father was mere weeks away. I had been so terrified of what was to come that I barely ate or slept."

"But you had wanted to be married?"

"Absolutely." Her smile morphs to one of romance, and she pulls her hand back to press both to her chest. "I'd wanted to marry him from the moment we met. We'd known each other since we were children, you know." She stands and moves through the room to set the book she'd been reading to me aside.

The story of my parents is one told even in the city. It's a true fairy tale. As children, they'd known each other —with him the future king of Navalis and her the daughter of a member of his guard. They'd been betrothed at birth and fallen madly in love as teens.

Love that is still just as present now as it was back then.

Which is why I struggle with my betrothal to Patrick. He is kind, that much is true, but there is no connection. No passion between us. I recall the stolen kiss last year beneath the fragrant blooms of our garden—when his family had made the two-month-long journey by ship to ask for my hand.

My parents had accepted, ecstatic, the idea of linking the two kingdoms of our realm far too fantastic a concept to ignore. So I had forced my smile even as I felt nothing for him. No excitement, no sparks—just the moist lips of a man I really wish I did not have to marry.

Hell, secret kisses with random men who attended our parties over the years were more exciting than the one I shared with my soon-to-be husband. And even those lack the enjoyment they once held. Nothing has been the same since Fort stalked out of the woods that night two years ago.

No one comes close to making me feel what he did that night. And he did it without his lips pressed to mine.

If I'm being honest, there's even more to it than lack of passion, though. My mother's marriage may have been arranged, but she was born here in Navalis, and here she gets to remain. I am the first Navalis royal forced to leave their home and reside in another kingdom.

Because I am the first royal daughter born since the separation of our realm and the legendary disappearance of the giants. Therefore, my marriage to Patrick will solidify a connection between Navalis and Soreno.

My throat tightens. What a burden to carry.

"Child, what is it? You are a million miles away," my mother says as she gathers her skirts and crosses toward me. "Are you ill?"

"No, Mother." I gently bat her hand away. "As I said, I'm just tired," I lie. Truth be told, sleep is the last thing on my mind. No, what's on my mind is a deliciously tall man with dark hair and brooding amber eyes.

Her soft smile returns. "Very well, my love. Go and rest."

"Actually, I think I will take a walk instead." I stand. "Stretching my legs and getting some fresh air might help."

"Do not forget tea just after lunch," she says pointedly.

"I won't." I kiss my mother's cheek then leave her sitting room behind. As I walk, I pass portraits of my brothers and me throughout our lives, as well as those of our parents and the ancestors that came before us.

They are the ones who settled these lands, who dared to live in perpetual winter when all others fled to the warmer climates. It was they who—according to legend—befriended the giants and brought peace to the entire realm.

Even if that peace did not last long thanks to the greed of men.

Whenever I'd felt scared as a child or overwhelmed into my adolescent years, my father would remind me that our family did what others claimed couldn't be done.

We tamed the wildlands of the north.

We reside where giants used to live.

And to him, that makes us giants as well.

"Good morning, Carleah," Genevieve—my handmaiden since I was born—stops me just before I reach the front door. As usual, her grey hair is pinned atop her head, not a strand out of place. The dress she wears is a pristine white, the same color all those who work within the castle walls wear.

I'd once begged her to add a bright ray of color to her ensemble, but she'd refused. I'd been too young then to realize that the white gown is something she is proud to wear and that adding any color at all would have been an insult to her status.

"Morning," I greet cheerfully.

"And where are you off to?" She arches a grey brow, studying me with even more scrutiny than my own mother.

"For a walk."

"Without your coat?"

I look down at the pale sleeves of my gown then gesture toward the coat hanging by the door. "Of course not. I just hadn't reached it yet."

She clicks her tongue at me. A soft *tsk, tsk, tsk* as she reaches out and retrieves my heavy fur coat from a hook near the door. "You would freeze to death if it weren't for me."

"That I would." I laugh because I know it makes her

feel good to look after me. With the wedding and my departure on the horizon, she's been treating me more and more like a child. And while others might have taken offense to that, I see it as what it is.

She's going to miss me.

Just as I am going to miss her.

"You know, occasionally, you need to look down at what's around you. Otherwise, who knows what you might miss?" She smiles wistfully at me, and it doesn't take much for me to understand to what she's referring.

She's the only one I've fully confided in. The only person who knows the true desires of my heart. "I don't miss him," I tell her. "It's hard to miss what you've never had."

Genevieve finishes helping me into my coat then reaches out and cups my cheeks. "You really should talk to your father, child. He will understand."

"He will not," I tell her truthfully. "Because he is adamant that my marriage to Patrick is my only future."

Her pursed lips are visible evidence of just how much she disagrees with it. "You've done so much for me and Leopold. I only wish the same happiness for you."

"Introducing you to your husband was hardly a challenge."

"It is when I'd been longing after him like a love-struck young girl but too terrified to actually speak to him. Sound familiar?" She arches a brow.

Genevieve is older than even my mother, so the idea that she was ever a love-struck young girl—especially a mere five years ago—is not an easy thing to imagine. "I merely presented you with an opportunity," I reply.

"And I wish I could do the same for you." She releases me. "You have to tell him," she says. "Before it's too late."

I reach out and take her hands. "No good will come of that, Genevieve. You and I both know that." After releasing her, I slip into my gloves. "In a month's time, I will be married to Patrick and living the rest of my days in Soreno."

Genevieve doesn't further argue, though she steps out of my way. "You will regret it if you do not tell him," she warns.

"I know."

She clears her throat then smiles sadly. "Now, get going on that walk before it's time for lunch. You have—"

"Tea," I finish. "I remember."

Genevieve smiles, wrinkles forming at the corners of her hazel eyes. "Good." She squeezes my arm, moving past me.

I slip outside, breathing in a deep breath of cold air as I do. Two guards stand just outside the front door, and as I move down the steps, they follow, granting me enough space to give the illusion of solitude.

It's something I'm used to by now, though, since my entire life has been this way. After all, they cannot let anything happen to delicate Carleah. I swallow back my groan and try to focus on the world around me rather than the fact that I long to be seen as far more than a princess in need of protection.

The snow crunches softly beneath my boots as I walk. Just ahead, an ice-covered lake sparkles beneath the sun, a tall pine beside it. My mind drifts back two years, to the night I'd snuck out of my party in the company of a man I'd wanted to merely pass an hour with.

At least, until he tried to pressure me into leaving my home for someplace more private. When Fort had stepped through the trees—I shiver, recalling the way he'd ferociously stormed forward, blade drawn, and ripped the man off of me.

It was at that moment that I saw Fort for the man he is and not just a protective shadow.

Fort rescued me.

And I've been unable to get him out of my head ever since.

Metal clashes against metal in the distance, and my pulse quickens. There's a lightness in my chest, and I gather my skirts, changing my route and following the sounds of training.

Because, if they are training, then *he* is out. Excitement dances in my belly, but I keep my pace easy so as not to look too eager to the guards following closely behind. When I round the corner of the castle and into sight of the training arena, though, it becomes even more difficult to do just that.

Because I see *him*. Shirtless and in the ring. One hand is tied behind his back, the other gripping the hilt of his blade. He's larger than any of the other men, besting them in both height and muscle mass. Fort is a force to be reckoned with.

A warrior with no equal.

Which is why he's the head of our guard even when he is barely eight years older than I am and a year younger than my eldest brother, Alex. Tradition dictates that the son first in line for the throne is to lead the guard. But when my father saw how capable Fort was, he placed him at the front in Alex's stead. Though, given Fort's muteness, my brother handles the orders while Fort takes charge of training and on the battlefield.

Fort's obsidian hair gleams beneath the bright sun, and while I cannot make out his amber eyes, I know they are focused in concentration. Sweat shines on his bare back even as his breath comes out in puffs of air, showcasing the contrast between his body heat and the chill 'round him.

Fort steals my breath in a way that I wish Patrick did.

And he does it without ever having spoken a word to me.

He moves with a precision that no one else in our kingdom is capable of. Including—to his dismay—my eldest brother Alex, who is currently sparring with him. They've made a game of trying to level the playing field, hence the arm tied behind his back. But I know, even one-handed, Fort will best every man here. As he's done it, over and over again.

Alex swings his blade, but Fort drops down and sweeps his leg out, bringing my brother to the snow with a muted *thud*. He then jumps up, presses a knee to my brother's chest, and grins.

Lust unfurls in my belly as I imagine it's *me* he's looking down on.

I shiver.

"Fort kicked his ass again," I hear Henry, one of the guards behind me, whisper to Stephan. "Pay up."

Stephan groans. "Fine."

"You dickhead," my brother groans, pulling my attention back to the ring.

Fort's smile widens as he drives his sword into the snow then reaches down to lift my brother from the ground with his free hand. He doesn't speak. Not that he ever has. When my father took Alex on his first stag-hunting trip when he'd been nine, they'd stumbled across Fort. He'd nearly been frozen to death and completely alone.

Healers claim he's a mute.

But I believe the boy saw things that the man cannot face.

There's a darkness in his eyes that I've never seen in any others. A weight he carries that I've longed to shoulder ever since that night, two years ago, when he'd come to my rescue.

My brother's white hair shakes as he clears the snow from it. Then he catches sight of me. "What the hell are you doing out here, Primrose?" I inwardly cringe at the nickname granted to me by my siblings.

When I'd been barely four, my family thought I'd run

away but, instead, found me toddling through a patch of blooming primrose flowers.

It stuck.

"Out for a walk." I offer him a smile. "Hello, Fort."

He offers a quick nod though doesn't fully look in my direction.

"Are you taking in the sights and sounds of the world before you become an old, married hag?" My second eldest brother, Bowman, calls out from where he stands, blocked by some of the soldiers.

I laugh as they clear a path so I can walk to him. "Please, do not call me a hag."

He wraps his arm around my shoulders, tossing back his pale hair, which is far longer than Alex's. "Cannot hide from what's to come. As of this time in one month, you will be married and living in a land with no snow." He mimics pity. "How horrible that will be."

I don't tell him that I'm petrified to leave this place. That the idea of living in a kingdom where there is no snow, and the weather is warmer than I even dare to imagine, sounds absolutely horrendous. But, my marriage to Patrick secures an alliance with his father's kingdom. It secures the continued safety of my people because we will be tied—forever—to our greatest ally.

And even if my heart wants someone else, the security of my home and those I love is far more important.

"Yes, well, you won't know what to do when you're rid of me." I swallow hard and look to Fort, who has his back to me as he sharpens a blade. The ridges of muscles on display make my mouth water, and lust pools in my belly.

"We already don't know what to do with you," Alex says with a laugh. "You're more trouble than you're worth, Primrose." He winks, and I smile.

My brothers are wonderful, happy men, who have done nothing but care for me my entire life. I was a shock to my parents, who believed they'd had their final child—my brother, Ethan—who was born two years before me.

And it was an even bigger surprise when the doctor announced I was a girl.

While my brothers have always treated me with nothing but kindness, it's Bowman who taught me archery when the others weren't looking. He's the only one who believes having skills to fight are necessary regardless of what your position is.

"I keep your lives interesting," I retort.

"That, you do, dear sister." Alex reaches out and pulls me in closer to plant a loud kiss on the top of my head then faces his men with a smile. "Now, you had better get going before the stench of these worthless fighters rubs off on you."

The men around him throw their heads back and laugh. As next in line for the throne, Alex spends nearly every waking moment at my father's side or here in the training ring. All of these men respect him, but it's more than that. They consider him their friend as much as they see him as their leader.

I start to ask if I can stay, but Bowman steers me

away. "Come, Primrose, let's get you away from these animals."

As I move away, I take one last look at Fort, who is now turned in my direction, his gaze raised to mine. I lose my breath as I stare back at him. He watches me intently, as though I am the only other person in the entire world. I let my gaze travel over his sharp jaw and sweat-slicked, muscled body.

And when he tears his gaze from me, turning his attention back to his blade, I imagine it is my flesh he is stroking tenderly.

CHAPTER 2
CARLEAH

Bowman reaches out and gently nudges the bow higher. "Keep your aim true, Primrose. Otherwise, you'll end up hitting what you don't want."

I grin over my shoulder at him. "Like the time you nearly shot Father?"

He pales. "I was only just learning.'

With a chuckle, I face my target once more—a burlap sack stuffed with straw and painted with a bright red circle. I feel the weight of the bow in my hands, the taut string against my finger, and when I release the arrow, I embrace the slight sting in my cheek from the fletching as it leaves the bow and sails toward its target.

It hits right in the center, so I turn and beam at Bowman. "See?"

He grins proudly. "I suppose you haven't lost your touch."

I lower his bow, offering it to him before I cross over

and take the arrow from my target. He follows behind, moving at my pace. Bowman is the only break I get from the guards constantly following me around because he's the only one who dismisses them. Granted, it's because our parents would likely punish us both if they were to discover he's taught me to use his bow at all.

And if they'd discovered he's also taught me some basic self-defense and how to cut, dress, and cook an animal?

I cannot even imagine the horror.

"Mother has kept me quite occupied with her classes."

"And just what has Mother been teaching you? How to smile pretty and stand up straight?" Bowman questions as he plucks the arrow from my fingers.

Trees loom overhead, their dark green needles dusted with this morning's fresh snowfall. "You're not too far off, Brother." I let out a sigh. "She has been teaching me how to behave like a queen," I say. "How to stand silently by and allow Patrick to rule as a king must." I roll my eyes. "I swear, it's as though I'm being taught how not to have an opinion."

Bowman chuckles. "Dearest sister, I cannot even imagine you not having an opinion."

I laugh. "And what are you going to do?" I ask, turning my attention away from my bleak future and toward his. "When I'm gone, you know Mother will be after you and Alex to get married next."

Bowman visibly pales. "No, thanks." He rapidly fires

three arrows, moving so quickly I barely see him draw new arrows from the quiver strapped on his back.

Where Fort excels at hand-to-hand and swordsmanship, Bowman is far better with his bow than anyone else in the kingdom. Something he continues to showcase every year during the Navalis Trials, a competition that tests the strength, resilience, and skill of whomever chooses to enter.

"You don't wish to be married?"

"I do not," he replies.

"Why?" I question as I follow him to retrieve his arrows this time.

Bowman stops and takes a deep breath. "What future do you think I have here?" he asks. "Ethan and Diedrich can leave; they can travel, because they are not expected to stay put. But me? It is customary for the man who is second in line for the throne to lead the guard."

"But Fort leads it."

"Exactly. Which means I am meant to simply wander around after Alex?" he scoffs. "I want to see the world, and marriage will only cement my future here." He yanks his arrows free, so we turn and begin walking back toward where we've tethered our horses.

"If your future is here, then how do you plan to change it?"

He turns toward me, a look of pity on his face. "If I could change yours, I would."

I force a smile. "Mine cannot be changed, Bowman. Nor should it be. Marrying Patrick is what's best for everyone."

"Is it? Or is it best for our parents?" He shakes his head. "I cannot imagine you marrying that damned worm is best for you."

I snort. "Worm?"

"Don't tell me you haven't picked up on that. He's a coward."

"Hey," I say, choking on a laugh. "That is my future husband and king you're talking about."

Bowman laughs and shakes his head. "I'm going to ask Mother if I can go with you to Soreno."

Hope warms my chest. "Do you truly think she will allow that?"

He arches a pale brow. "Is that something you would be okay with?"

I don't answer. Instead, I throw my arms around his neck and cling to him.

Bowman laughs. "Is that a yes?"

"Absolutely. But only if that will make you happy."

He pulls away from me and sets his bow against the tree. "I long to see the world beyond this place. So, yes, going with you to Soreno would be a way to accomplish that goal." He undoes the top of his leather skin and tips it up, drinking deeply. "Besides, who will keep you out of trouble if not me?"

"Who else will let me be someone other than a meek woman?"

"You are anything but meek, Primrose."

"Not in their eyes," I reply then hold out my hand.

Bowman removes his quiver and offers it to me. I slip

it over my shoulder, take his bow, then retrieve an arrow with my back still turned to the target.

"You are more than they can see, sister," he says softly. "Do not let anyone tell you how bright your flame can burn."

I take a strong, steadying breath, letting his words resonate deep within my soul. Then, I whirl and release.

One arrow.

Two arrows.

Three.

Until all three shafts are sticking from the very center of the target.

"Very good, Carleah!" Bowman cheers. "You'd give me a run for my money."

"I learned from the best," I reply as I take a deep breath and cross the distance to retrieve my arrows.

∽

GLEAMING white marble floors are smooth beneath my feet as I leave my room. Lunchtime tea over with, the rest of the day is mine.

My home is silent around me, which is not unusual given that, this time of day, most everyone is off tending to their own responsibilities. I start down the hall toward the stairs, my feet padding silently against the cool marble as I go.

I'm just passing Ethan's room when I notice movement out of the corner of my eye.

Stopping, I gently push the door open.

The brother that is closest to me in age looks up from his book and grins, light blue eyes shining. "Primrose, what are you doing wandering?"

"Just out for a walk," I say as I push into his room. "And what are you doing in here?"

He runs a hand through his shoulder-length white hair. "Reading before Alex pulls me into the ring just as he did Diedrich." He grins at me, a sly smile that tells me he's supposed to be prepping for training and is, instead, stealing these moments. It's not a surprise, though. Ethan always has preferred books to blades. He's a scholar at heart.

I take a seat on the edge of his bed and reach a hand out. "What are you reading?" He crosses over and sits beside me, offering me the thick tome. "The History of Elves," I read the title aloud then smile because it's so fitting for him. "A little light reading, then?"

"You know me," he chuckles as I offer him the book. "It's a good one."

"I know," I reply, nudging his shoulder. "I've read it twice."

He laughs. "Of course you have."

"Wait until you get to the part about the mythical sirens and their underwater kingdom." I wink at him, and he rolls his eyes.

"You all mock. But one day I'm going to travel the world—not just this realm—and discover all of its secrets."

I lean against my brother, feeling more relaxed than I have since holding the bow this morning. "I know you will. And I don't mock. I believe there is more out there than we could possibly imagine."

Ethan takes my hand in his and pats it gently.

We fall into companionable silence, with only the sounds of the birds outside his window. Try as I might, the image of Fort watching me has haunted me. I want so badly to take Genevieve's advice and tell him how I feel.

Maybe she's right and things will turn out well.

Or, if she's wrong, I will have confessed my love to someone who I can never have. Then, if he feels the same? I'll be forced to stand at Patrick's side while my heart remains with someone else entirely.

"What's on your mind, little sister?" Ethan questions.

I sigh. "I'm at a crossroads," I tell him. "And I'm not sure what to do."

"Is this about Patrick?"

"How can you tell?"

Ethan laughs. "It's all over your face."

"I don't want to marry him." I scrunch my nose and speak candidly. While Bowman has always shown me things others would have thought inappropriate for my title, Ethan's words of wisdom have always guided me through the darkest of times. He's wise well beyond his twenty-two years.

"If it helps, I don't want you to marry him either."

"Really?"

"No. You'll be leaving," he says. "And I don't want you to go." Ethan nudges my shoulder.

"Mother believes the alliance is well worth the sacrifice. My hand in marriage for the promise of our allies always supporting us."

"No real man will ever barter with you for their love, Carleah." Ethan wraps an arm around my shoulder.

"They believe Patrick is a real man."

"I'm sure he will be—one day." Ethan presses a noisy kiss to my temple, and I laugh.

"I will miss you when I'm gone."

"And I, you, little sister."

I turn toward him. "Can I ask you something?"

"Anything," he replies as he reaches down and takes my hand in his. Emotion claws at my throat. How am I to live without moments like this? Without those I care about most in this world?

"How do you decide which path to take when faced with a fork in the road?"

Ethan looks down at me. "Easy. You follow your heart, Primrose."

"That does not sound easy." I look away. "And if following your heart means doing something that no one else might approve of?"

"Follow your heart," he repeats, squeezing my hand. "And the rest will fall into place."

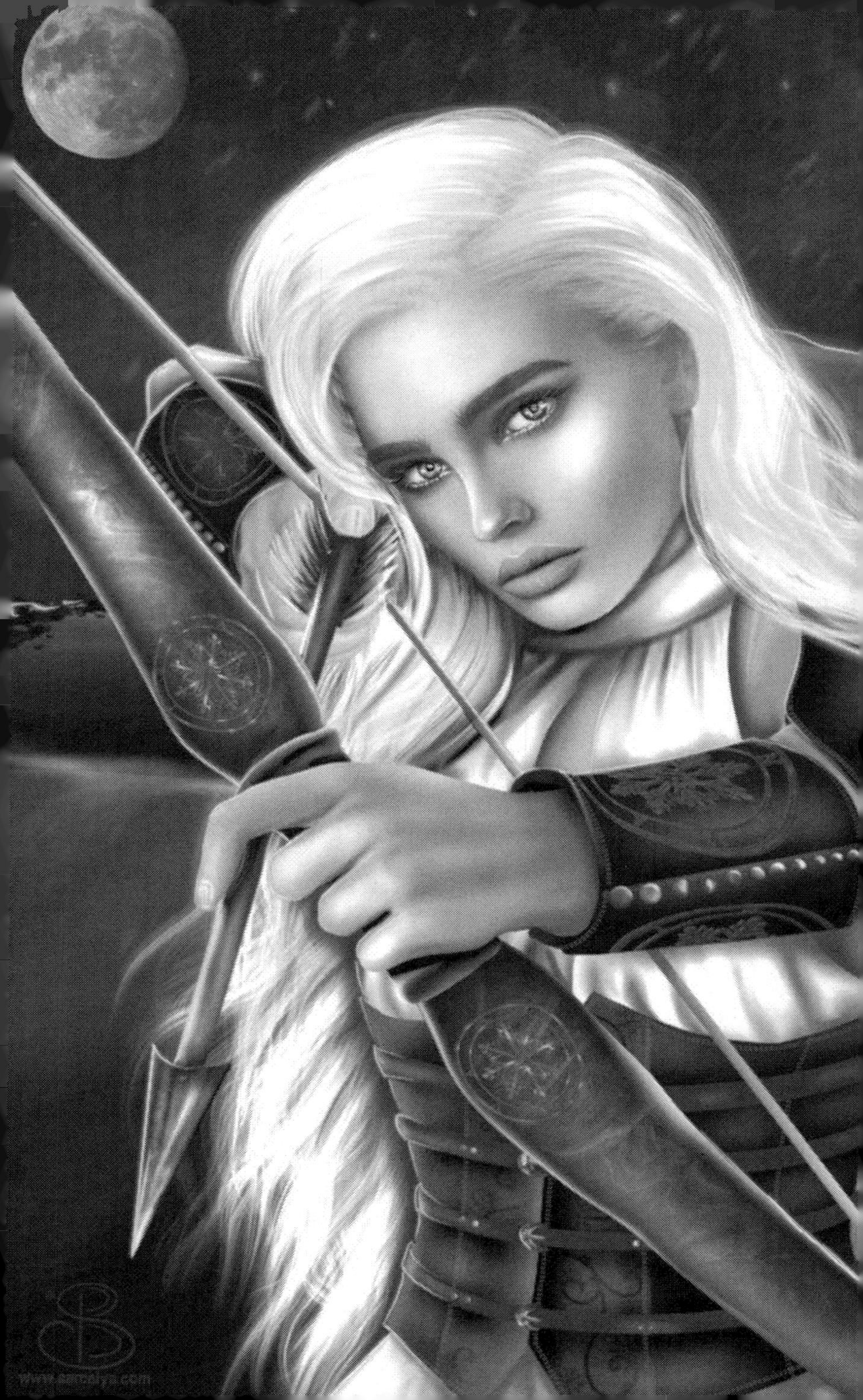

CHAPTER 3
CARLEAH

"*Follow your heart, Primrose. And the rest will fall into place.*"

Ethan's words of wisdom give me strength as I prepare to do just that. Either things will happen, or they won't. But at least, by going to my father first, I can hopefully avoid learning how Fort truly feels until I know if it's even a possibility.

I take a deep breath and knock on the heavy wooden door. "Father?"

"Come in," he calls out.

I push the door open. The King of Navalis looks up from his desk to where I stand in the doorway. A wide smile spreads over his lightly wrinkled face as rosy color dusts his cheeks. A short, grey beard covers the lower half of his face, and a golden crown sits atop his silver hair. "My dearest daughter. Come. Come in!" He gets up from his chair and moves into full view. His ice-blue tunic is belted at his waist with a golden band, and he's wearing his black riding pants with boots up to his knees.

He looks every bit like a king—and my hero whenever I'd been too afraid to fall asleep.

"I was curious if you'd like to have some tea with me," I offer as I move into his embrace. I breathe him in, the heady scent of pine filling my lungs. Somehow, my father always smells of the forests that surround our kingdom. He claims it's from his afternoon walks, but I think the land is as much a part of him as he is of it.

And as such, he always carries the scent of our kingdom with him.

"I am always open to tea with you, Carleah." He pulls back and kisses my forehead.

I smile and loop my arm through his as he guides me down the hall and toward the stairs. They're narrow and built in a spiral, so as we walk, I reach out with my free hand and let it glide over the stone.

When I'd been young, I'd asked why they were so narrow. Especially after seeing Patrick's expansive staircase on one of our trips to Soreno, years ago. My father told me that they were designed so soldiers could fend off attackers as the royal family was ushered to safety.

It always seemed barbaric, to sacrifice people for security.

But after I brought that up, I was told, without royals, the kingdom would fall into anarchy as they fought to establish a new leader. And somehow, that seems even more horrific.

"What is on your mind, Daughter?" My father pats my hand.

"Thinking of the staircase."

He chuckles. "You are always thinking."

It's meant as a joke, but when I'd been a child, I had tutors constantly telling me that I spent too much time asking questions and not enough time simply absorbing information. Ever since then, I cannot help but feel the sting of his words. "I find that if I don't think, my mind remains empty."

"Knowledge is power, my dear. But you do not need to fret an attack." He pats my hand again. "We are perfectly safe." We reach the bottom of the steps and continue down the hall and toward the library.

"Of course. I wasn't worrying about that." I smile up at him. "Just that I will miss this place."

Something passes over his expression that I recognize as pain. Mainly because I feel it, too. "Yes, well, Patrick will be kind to you. He will make a good king someday."

"I believe so as well." And I do. I simply wish it wasn't me destined to be his queen. Maybe after tonight, it won't be.

We step into the library, and my gaze instantly falls to the massive hearth that stands as tall as I am. Flames dance vividly before me, casting shadows off the walls boasting shelves full of books that have been in this library for generations.

I've read nearly every single one of them. Devouring one book a day in some cases. That is until my regal training began. Now, I'm lucky if I manage a book every week.

My gaze raises to the high shelf where my mother's romance stories reside. So much love between those pages. Perhaps I will grab another before I leave this room tonight. Make it a point to lose myself in a heroic story of passion, heroism, and victory.

"Your Highness," Gerald, my father's butler rushes over, head bowed. "What can I get for you?"

"Peppermint," my father says.

"Of course. My lady? The same?"

"Yes, please, Gerald, thank you."

He smiles. "Of course." Then he ducks out of the room as my father guides me toward a chair. I take my seat, and he takes his just beside me so we're both facing the flames, a small, round table between us.

"What is on your mind now?" my father asks. "Still the staircase?"

"No," I tell him honestly. In a lot of ways, I can be more open with my father than I can my mother. I simply hope this doesn't backfire horribly. "Everything is changing."

He reaches over and pats my hand. "Yes, but change is good."

"Most of the time." I smile at him, though it's not heartfelt. "Patrick's kingdom is so different."

My father chuckles. "It is, but perhaps you will enjoy the heat."

I bite my tongue because I'm not ready to argue just yet. Right now, what I truly want is a possibility. But the moment I speak out, that illusion will be shattered one way or another. Either he will support me, or I will be married off to Patrick.

Expected to lie in his bed, bear his children, and stand at his side, the silent support every king needs from their queen.

"Mother is nearly done with my training," I tell him. "Then she says we begin wedding preparations."

My father's face pales slightly. "I still cannot believe you are getting married. You are barely old enough to walk in my mind."

I chuckle. "Father, I am plenty old enough."

"Not to me, you're not." He squeezes my hand. "If I had my way, you would remain here as an old spinstress."

I don't smile. Don't laugh. Because that would be my wish, too. "Then have your way," I say quickly. "Let me stay here with you guys."

My father arches a brow. "And be an old spinstress?" He barks out a laugh. "That would be a horrible future for you. Besides, marrying Patrick is going to be good for you because you will make a wonderful queen."

Hope deflates in my chest. "What if I don't want to marry him?"

"Change is frightening, Carleah, but once you're on the other side of it, you'll realize it is precisely what you wanted."

"I—"

"Here is your tea." Gerald interrupts, carrying a

silver tray boasting two steaming porcelain cups. He sets them down between us then bows and leaves once more.

"Fort is training hard." The words are out of my mouth before I can stop myself.

My father arches a brow. "Is he, now?"

My cheeks heat. "Yes. He and Alex were in the ring earlier. In fact, they'd tied one of Fort's arms behind his back."

"And what were you doing near the ring?" He blows softly on his tea.

"Out for a walk. I heard the racket and went to investigate."

His knowing smile fuels my embarrassment. "Always inquisitive, aren't you?"

"It doesn't hurt to know your surroundings," I reply, keeping my tone cool.

He chuckles. "My daughter, out with the soldiers. Don't let your mother hear of it. She won't let it go."

"That's true." I smile then take a sip of my tea.

"Fort is a good man," my father says softly. "A strong warrior. Loyal and compassionate."

"He is."

"I wish things were different, Carleah. I truly do. For your sake and hi—" The door opens, and Alex strolls in, a serious look on his face. It's so out of place that it catches me off guard.

"Father," he greets. "Can we have a word?"

"Is it necessary right now?" he asks.

Alex looks to me, his expression far more serious

than I've ever seen. "I'm afraid so. Carleah, please leave us."

Carleah. He never refers to me by my name.

"What is it?"

"Not your concern," Alex replies. "Go, Carleah."

I start to argue, to insist, but we all know that will go nowhere. So, I stand and kiss my father's cheek. "Tea next time."

"Yes, my daughter." With a forced smile, he nods, so I turn and leave the room. Alex doesn't look my way when I pass, which only stirs my anxiousness. So much so that I find it difficult to keep my gaze trained at my feet and put one foot in front of the other when all I wish to do is turn around and beg to be included in the conversation if only to put my mind at ease.

It could be a myriad of things.

Perhaps something happened in the city bordering our kingdom. There could have been a fight that needed to be broken up; a farmer might have lost some livestock under mysterious circumstances.

But even as I think those things, my logical mind pushes them out.

My brother had been genuinely upset.

So what could have caused it?

Thoughts so focused on what's behind me, I pay no attention to what's in front, and as I round the corner, I slam into a solid body. I fall, stumbling backward until large hands grip my waist and pull me upright. Heat spreads through my body, lust hammering in my veins as I look up into the breath-stealing amber gaze of Fort.

He stares down at me, hands still on my waist, gaze trained directly on my face.

I lose my breath.

My pulse quickens.

And as I so often do only in his presence, I find myself completely speechless.

Lust spreads rapidly through me as his hands momentarily tighten their hold on me. My lips part, letting out a soft gasp that unfortunately seems to snap him out of whatever trance he'd been in.

Fort blinks rapidly and releases me, taking a couple of steps back.

"I'm all right," I blurt. "I apologize. I was not paying attention to where I was going."

He offers me a nod. Then he moves down the hall as my entire body warms to the lingering heat of his hands touching my waist. Large, heavy hands that held me for far longer than they needed to.

I shiver.

That is the kind of passion I wish I felt with Patrick. The kind of passion I long for in my life partner.

But, unfortunately, it seems as though destiny has something else in mind for me.

∽

EXHAUSTED, I lean against my window frame. The sun is beginning to sink just outside, casting my world in soft shades of pink and orange. It's absolutely stunning, and I soak in the moments before I'm expected to go downstairs to dinner.

Alex hasn't come out of Father's study yet, which means my conversation with him will likely have been long forgotten.

Something moves in the corner of my vision, so I redirect my attention.

Nearly completely out of my line of sight, a man stands with his back to me. He's shirtless, his flesh slick with sweat much as it had been when he'd been training. He brings an axe up and swings it down with power that flexes every visible muscle.

The wood beneath him splits in two, so he moves it to the side then grabs another and places it on top of the log.

Even as I cannot see his face, I know it's Fort.

Because I have memorized him.

Lust heats my body, and my pulse hammers until all I can hear is the heavy thundering of blood in my ears. How can he not hear it?

The throbbing between my legs becomes impossible to ignore, so I clamp them together in an attempt to ease the ache. Fort and I might as well be so close we could be touching for the effect he has on me.

I stand and move from the window, needing space even though I'm on the second floor and he's outside of our walls.

I'm drowning in thoughts of him. In the passion I believe we could share if only he'd look my direction.

After ensuring my door is locked, I lie back on my bed and close my eyes. I imagine the way Fort's hands gripped that axe, the way his fingertip trailed down the blade after he'd finished training.

I picture the way he'd looked at me in the hall.

The way his gaze had dropped to my mouth while his hands had held my waist.

And then I picture the way it would have felt if he'd carried me up to my room right then. How it would have been if he'd stripped me from my dress and laid my naked body down before covering it with his own.

When I can no longer take the throbbing between my legs, I slide the skirts of my dress up and glide a finger over my wet heat. It had taken an entire year to get comfortable enough to bring myself the pleasure I've read about.

I do not shy from being sexual. I do, however, despise the notion of any man but Fort touching me. Because I crave no one else the way I desire him.

I moan, pleasure shooting through my body. I curl my toes and begin to move my fingers faster, all the while imagining Fort doing things I've only read about in novels.

The pressure in my abdomen builds, higher and higher, until my orgasm tears through my body. I call out, just a throaty sigh not loud enough for anyone passing by my door to hear, and I continue my gentle strokes until the pleasure has completely consumed me.

Until my body is weary, my muscles liquid.

It's only then I slide my hand out and push to my feet to clean myself. By the time I pass by the window, Fort is gone, but the stack of wood remains

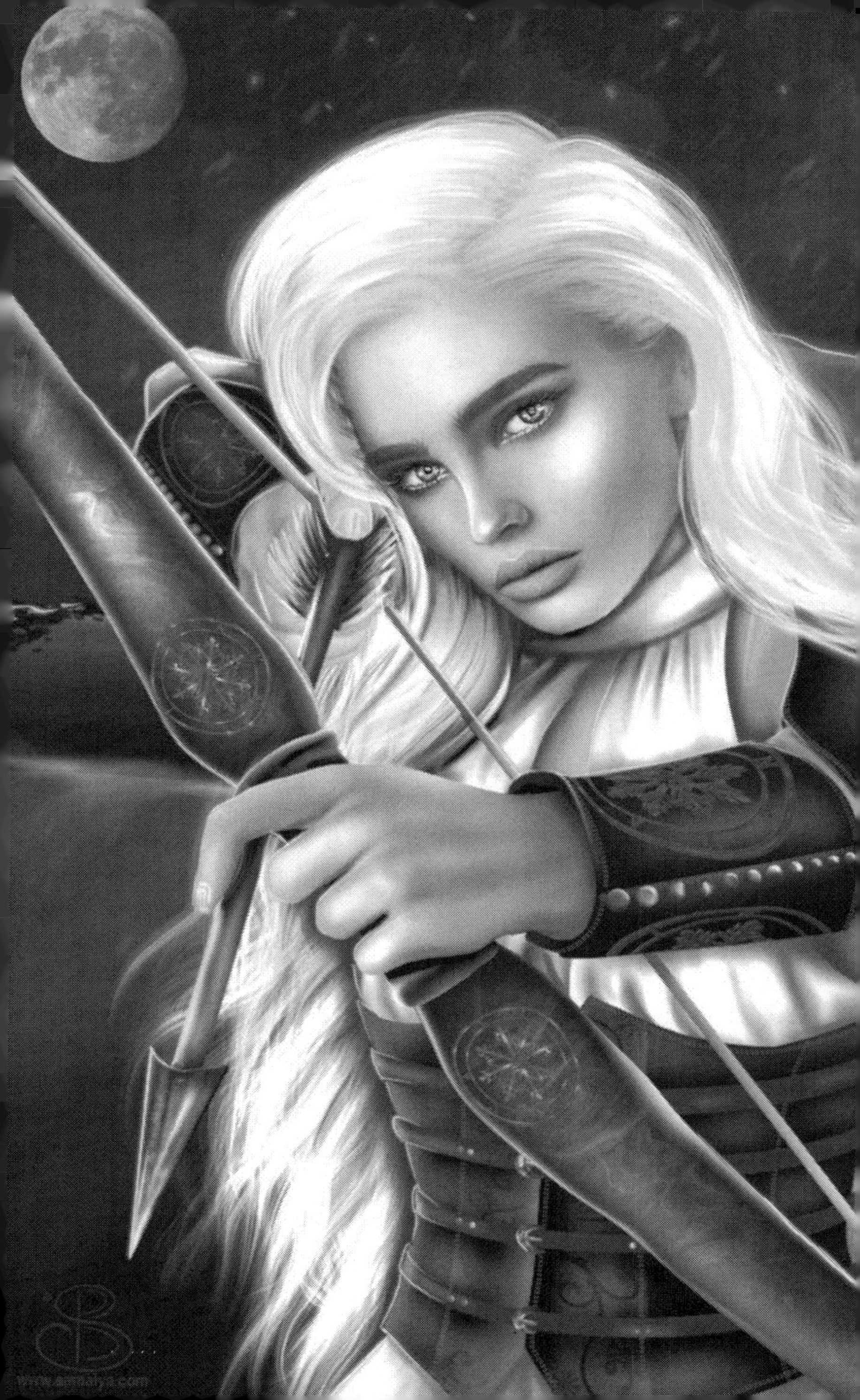

CHAPTER 4
CARLEAH

"Fort kicked your ass!" Bowman accuses as he gestures toward Alex with his fork.

"I beg to differ," Alex argues, a smile on his face. The stress from earlier is not gone, though, as evidenced by the hollow gaze he, my father, my other brothers, and even my mother share as we sit around the dinner table.

I stick a piece of meat in my mouth then chew and swallow it down, barely noting the flavors as they dance on my tongue. Given that everyone here is on edge, my mind is still far too wrapped up in what could possibly be wrong. And since no one seems to care enough to fill me in, I can only speculate.

Fort chose not to join us for dinner tonight, and while that worries me, given Alex's earlier conversation with our father, I'm trying really hard not to focus on it —or him.

"Primrose, you saw it, what do you—" Bowman

trails off, eyes widening as my mother's head whips toward me.

"What did you see, Carleah? Were you out with the soldiers again?"

I glare at my brother who sinks back down in his seat, guilt etched in his expression. If only Mother knew what I'd done in the privacy of my room mere hours ago. I clear my throat. "I was out for a walk, Mother, and passed by the training field."

"Carleah Donnah Rossingol."

I stiffen. Nothing like her using my full name.

"She was not there long," Bowman chimes in, trying to save the mood which has quickly changed from half-joyful jesting to accusations and scolding. "Just passed by."

"She shouldn't have been there at all." My mother's gaze never leaves my face. "You are a betrothed woman, Carleah. I swear! I am going to have to instruct your guards to prevent you from going anywhere near that ring. What will it sound like if your future husband catches wind of you watching half-naked men as they fight?"

"I feel he should applaud me for taking such an interest in my brothers since they are the reason I was out there." The lie tastes horrendous. And based on the looks I get from my father, Bowman, and Ethan, they see straight through it. Which is fine. Because it wasn't for them, anyway.

My mother shakes her head. "You must be more careful. You are to be a queen."

"Yes, Mother. I have not forgotten." My throat burns with emotion that I must keep shoved down. Anger has no place inside a princess—per my mother's instruction. And it certainly does not belong inside a queen.

Keeping my emotions neutral is something that has been ingrained in me for as long as I can remember. So, I force an emotionless mask in place and dip my chin in a respectful nod. "I will not let it happen again." *Rather, I will not get caught.*

"See to it that it doesn't." Her expression softens. "I am merely watching out for your best interests."

If you were doing that, you wouldn't be shipping me away. "Since we are on the subject of promises and protecting those we care about, who will tell me what is going on?" I ask, taking a piece of bread and placing it into my mouth.

"What do you mean?" my mother questions, though I don't miss the quick gaze she shoots at my father.

"Today. Alex came to see Father." I let my gaze travel from my mother to my eldest brother, then over to my father, Bowman, Diedrich, and Ethan. Every one of their expressions shifts to hide something. "Why? What is going on?"

"Nothing you need to worry about, Primrose," Diedrich promises me. "Isn't that right?" he asks Alex.

"Of course." Alex smiles. "Nothing that cannot be handled swiftly. Though, I will miss you when I leave for my trip."

"Trip?" I sit up straighter.

"Fort and I are taking some of the more seasoned

soldiers out for a training exercise. But don't worry," he adds with a grin. "We will return before you're married off."

I swallow hard. The idea of both of them leaving at once—of Fort not being here for me to see each and every day—it hits harder than it should and I have to fight to keep my mask of neutrality in place. "When will you return?"

"One week at most. Likely only a few days, though." There's a look shared between him and my father that has my stomach churning.

They've never done this before.

There had never been a need to train outside of the ring. The army of Navalis has left to aid Soreno before, but only at the request of their king. "Are you going to Soreno?"

"No," Alex replies.

"Then why must you train away from the ring?"

"Carleah, it is not your place to question a king," my mother warns. "If your father and brother wish for you to know, they would tell you."

"They told you," I say, my tone shaky. "So why can I not know?"

"Carleah—" my father starts.

As I begin to lose the fight with my control, I take a deep breath and stand. "I wish you safe travels, Brother. And I look forward to your return." With a nod at my family, I turn and leave the dining hall on shaking legs. I take the steps two at a time, not stopping for a breath until I've reached the solitude of the upstairs landing. Then, I lean back against the wall.

I likely have nothing to worry about. Perhaps, they're merely doing as Alex says and changing their training routine.

But if that's true, then why do I feel this fear gnawing at my gut? Why does the voice in my mind tell me that my family is hiding something far more sinister?

Images of the blood-stained snow in my nightmares assault me.

Of a winged warrior horse.

My heart begins to race. Kneading my chest with the heel of my palm, I try to loosen the knot. It does nothing to ease it, though. In fact, with each passing moment, the knot grows—nearly smothering me.

Bootsteps echo down the hall, so I quickly wipe my eyes and start toward my room. When Fort comes into view, I stop. So does he. There's a moment between us. A silence that feels heavier than the weight of all of my fear. And then, he drops his head in a nod and continues down the hall, disappearing into his room at the very end.

I stare after him, considering the very real possibility that this could be the last time I see him. What if something happens and he doesn't come home? What if I never get another chance? Will I spend my life regretting being afraid?

"Follow your heart, Primrose. And the rest will fall into place."

Gathering the skirts of my dress, I rush across the

distance before I can give it much more thought. Then, I raise my fist and knock softly. Part of me hopes he doesn't hear it because what I'm about to do is—the door opens and Fort stands on the other side.

He's shed his jacket, tunic, and boots, now wearing only his riding pants, which are partially undone at the top. I drink in the sight of him. Of the taut skin stretched over ridges of muscle. He towers over me, which somehow makes this even more reckless.

I push into his room, grateful that he takes a step back to let me through, then shut the door behind me. Fort eyes me, his gaze narrowed.

"You're leaving tomorrow?"

He nods.

"Is it dangerous?"

No response.

"Why the hell can no one tell me what is going on?" I turn away from him and stalk toward the window to look out. The trees are tall, casting shadows over the snowy ground. "I deserve to know."

I turn back around, surprised to see Fort standing only a few steps from me. He's silent as he moves, a trick I cannot figure out.

"Is it dangerous, Fort? Don't lie to me."

He swallows hard and nods.

I close my eyes, fear clawing at my throat. "I care about you. I need you to know that."

A finger runs over the side of my face, and I freeze, not even daring to breathe. Aside from that night by the lake, and earlier when I'd run into him, Fort has never touched me. With my heart in my throat, I open my eyes and stare up into his.

His full lips are parted as he stares down at me, barely banked heat in his gaze.

"Do you know that?" I manage. "That I care about you?"

He nods then drops his hand.

"I—if you don't—to hell with it." I reach up and grab the back of his neck then pull his mouth down to mine. Fort stiffens for a brief moment, but less than a heartbeat later, he comes to life against me.

It's not just a finger caressing my face anymore. Now both of his muscled arms snake around my waist. Fort holds me to him, his tongue slipping into my mouth and sliding against my own. I moan, a soft plea for more. For all of him.

His large hands slide down to my ass, and he lifts me, pinning me to the door and stepping up between my legs. I feel his hard length pressing against me, so I tighten my legs around his waist so that I can feel more.

All of him.

He is an *animal* as he ravages my mouth. And in this moment, I have found everything I've ever craved. Fort turns and carries me to his bed. The mattress dips beneath our weight as he covers my body with his.

My hands grip the strong muscles of his shoulders. I slide them down over his arms and snake them around his body, digging my nails into the flesh of his back. Fort growls against me as his hand slips down my side and grips my breast through the fabric of my dress. His thumb caresses my pebbled nipple, and I moan, arching up into him.

A door slams out in the hall, and Fort pulls away, leaving me cold and more turned on than ever. His dick is hard, a tent in his damned pants. And his chest rises and falls rapidly as he stares at me from a few feet away.

In this moment of silence, it feels as though more than I could have ever hoped to say out loud is spoken.

I clear my throat and climb off of his bed. As I pass, I press my palm to his chest and look up into eyes holding the same carnal heat as I know he'll find in my own. "Please come home," I tell him then open his door and rush out before I can convince myself to stay.

~

THE STARS just outside my window are alive tonight. Twinkling and shining down upon our snowy wonderland.

Yet, I feel none of the joy I usually do when looking up at them. How can I when, every moment that passes, the dread curling in my stomach grows with the knowledge that my brother and Fort will be leaving tomorrow?

I reach up and touch my fingers to my still-swollen lips. The feel of Fort pressed against me—how can I ever get that out of my head?

Will anything ever change, or will I truly be leaving Navalis for good in a month's time?

Thirty days.

Twenty-nine nights.

A tear slips down my cheek, but I angrily wipe it away. No more crying. If it happens, then it is because this is my destiny. As the first daughter born to the Navalis royal family. To *any* Navalis royal family since the time of the Great Break. The moment in history when the giants were so angered by man's constant warring that they broke apart the continent, separating kingdoms by oceans and monsters.

Or so legend says.

Someone raps softly on my door, and my heart leaps at the thought it might be Fort. But just in case it's not, I pull my robe closed over my nightgown then cross over and open my heavy wooden door. Guilt weighs with disappointment when I see that it is Alex who stands on the other side, the lantern in his hand casting shadows over his face.

"May I come in?" he asks.

"Of course." I step aside and let him through then close the door softly and take a seat in one of the two chairs in my room. He sits in the other.

He's still wearing the same clothes he had on at dinner, which likely means he's been in the study with our father, discussing whatever it is they seem so bent on keeping a secret from me.

"You were upset," he finally says.

"I am tired of being treated like a child," I say. "If I am old enough to be married off where I will be forced to share the bed of a man I do not love for the sake of our kingdom, then why can I not know what is happening around me?"

Alex's lips flatten into a taut line. "You're right." He blows out a breath and leans back in the chair.

I gape at him, dumbfounded. *Did he just say I was right?* Alex has never offered up any information when I've pressed him. In fact, he is quite adamant that I do not know anything of any substance. "I am?"

He looks at me. "Yes. You are going to be married in a month, which means you will be a woman."

I don't mention that marriage won't change the fact that I've been a grown woman for years now. Because he seems dangerously close to telling me everything I want to know, and the last thing I want is to derail the conversation.

"We've heard whispers of an army camp that has moved through the Phantom between us and Nemoregno."

"What? That's impossible." I brace my hands on the arms of my chair.

The Phantom is a barrier created by clouds that separates us from the rest of the realm. We cannot see out, and no one can see in. In fact, attempting to cross it might as well be a death sentence.

There are miles of Phantom between us and Nemoregno. Miles where you can see nothing but your own hand in front of your face. It is why Patrick and his family travel around the continent and arrive by ship.

"No one crosses the Phantom," I say.

"No one has ever crossed it," he corrects. "Before now."

"They are not from one of our villages?"

He shakes his head. "They wear crimson armor and carry a solid obsidian banner boasting the golden skull of a boar."

Crimson armor.

Obsidian banner boasting the golden skull of a boar.

I gasp. "It can't be. They are rumored." The Tenebris were the soldiers of legend who nearly destroyed our realm. Some stories say they crept from the depths of the underworld while others believe they were conjured by the greed of humans.

They are said to be the reason the giants broke apart our realm.

Alex touches my hand. "They are nothing more than humans using our legends to drive fear."

"And if they are not?"

"Then where are the monsters they ride with?" he questions. "Our scouts saw nothing but human men."

I consider his words. The legends speak of monsters who travel with the Tenebris. Creatures that were banished to Dead Man's Land, a land surrounded by jagged rocks and spelled to keep the creatures imprisoned. It lies between Nemoregno and Patrick's kingdom.

Still, legend or not, these soldiers spell danger for Navalis.

And that alone seems impossible.

"Do we know why they are here?"

"There is talk about them looking for the entrance to the cave of the sleeping giants."

I try to laugh, to feign humor, but my insides are churning with unease. "All of this is straight from the pages of a fable. The giants are a bedtime story told to frighten children from venturing too far into the woods."

But my brother does not smile, nor does he return any agreement. "Fables have root in truth, Carleah. Isn't that what you just said?"

My stomach twists. "Tenebris are not giants. It is easier to believe they are simply men who were made out to be larger than life. You speak of giants, Brother. Of huge creatures taller than the mountains themselves. You do not believe such things, do you?"

Alex groans and rests his head in both hands. "I do not know what to believe anymore. But this is a very real concern for more reasons than just that. If they encroach too closely, they become an actual threat to our home. The kingdom has not faced any conflict on our own soil in well over a millennium."

"But our warriors are strong. Capable. And this is our home. We have the advantage."

Alex reaches over and covers my hand with his. He squeezes gently. "Our warriors are trained," he says. "But they outnumber us."

"The crimson soldiers? You're sure?"

He nods. "According to our scouts."

I climb off my chair and sink to my knees in front of him. "Please do not go, Brother. Please send someone else. Anyone else."

He smiles down at me. "The only other person I would trust to go in my stead is Bowman. And he is not the swordsman I am."

"Please," I beg. "None of you go."

Alex takes my hands in his then presses a gentle kiss to the top of them. "What kind of leader would I be if I did not stand with my men? If I sent them into danger without me? What kind of brother am I if I allow such a threat to put your life at risk?"

"The kind that lives," I choke out. "You and Fort stay. If it is truly so large of a threat that you are worried, then doesn't it make sense to stay here? To protect our home."

"We are merely going to meet with their leader. Once we know more, we will return. It is not a fight we seek, Sister. And with the code of honor in place, we will be safe unless war is declared. In which case, we will have ample time to return."

"That's only if they respect the honor code," I say as I pull my hands away and stand to pace. "If they don't—"

"They will. All men do. It is law in our land."

"The Tenebris are not men," I retort. "And they are not from here. Alex, what if you don't come home?" A tear slips down my cheek.

He stands and crosses over to me to brush it away. "Little sister, have I ever let you down?"

I shake my head, unable to speak.

"Then why do you believe I will fail now?"

"I have this feeling," I manage as I press both hands to my stomach. "This dread in the pit of my stomach. Nightmares—"

He smiles. "I believe that's called cold feet."

I shake my head. "It's more than that. I understand what my duty is to this family, what my purpose is."

Alex's jaw tightens. "You are more than a purpose,

Primrose. We want you to be happy. To wed a man who can keep you safe."

"I know." I close my eyes and take a deep, steadying breath. "My point is I do not fear marriage to Patrick. Even as miserable as I will be, I will know you all are safe. But this, everything I've been feeling, feels like something else. Like a warning."

Alex moves forward and leans down to press a kiss to my forehead. "I love you, Sister, but this must be done. We have no other option. I will go and discover their true intentions, then I will return home."

"Do you vow it?" I ask as he pulls away and retrieves his lantern. "Do you vow to return home to me?"

Alex's smile is hopeful. "I do."

I try to return it, but I know my expression is hollow at best. "Then you'd better not break it."

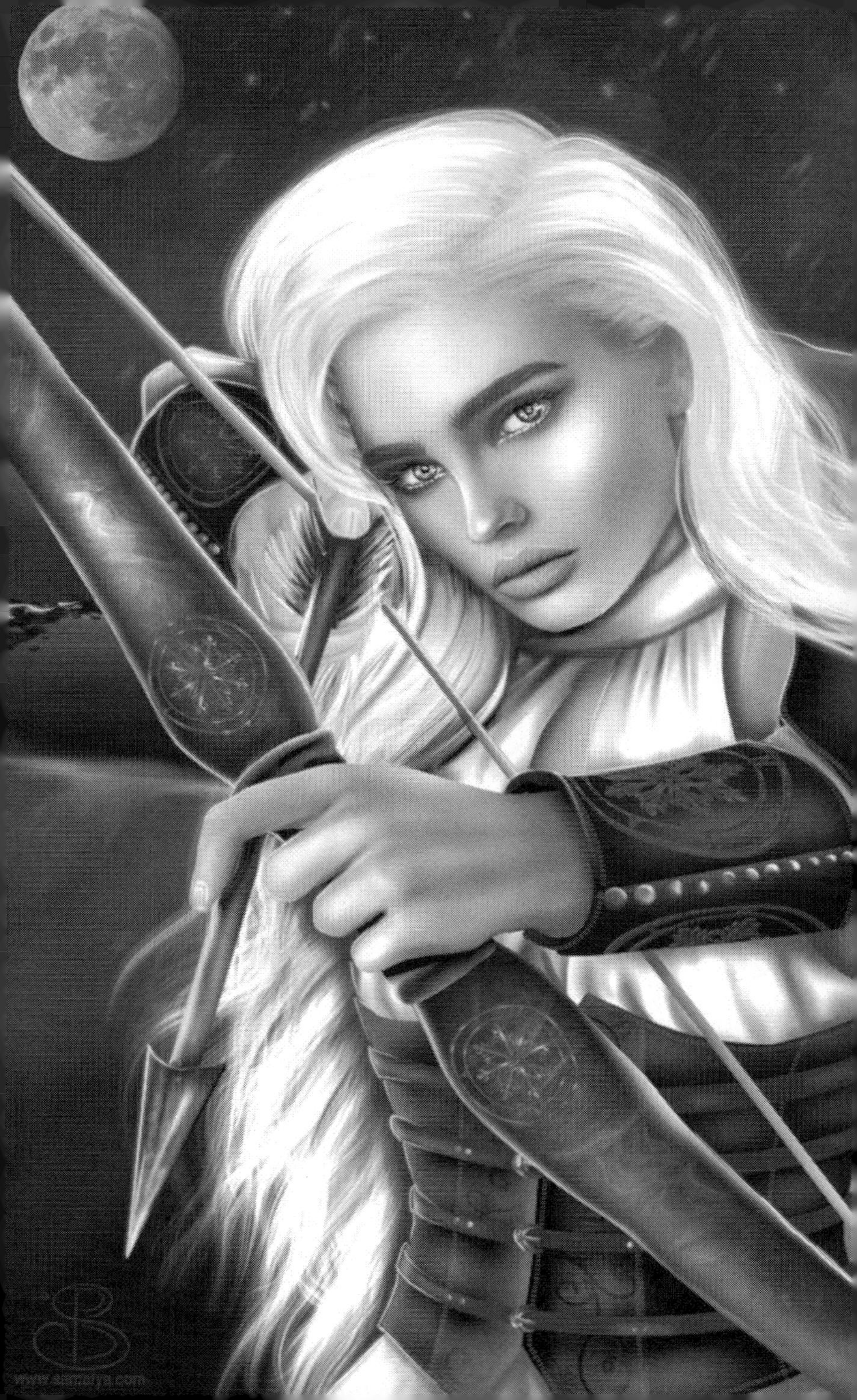

CHAPTER 5
CARLEAH

The castle without my brother and Fort feels empty. Hollow. I managed to make it three days before it became enough to drive me outside. It doesn't help matters that I've yet to get a single solid night's sleep since they left.

Nightmares of death haunt me every time I close my eyes.

Images of the winged horse carrying me away from all those I love as my home burns to ash.

And I'm not the only one feeling their absence.

My father has been holed up in his study with my other three brothers, and even my mother has put off the final days of my training as she prepares the staff for the arrival of my soon-to-be husband and his family.

A date that is still nearly a month away.

It's clear she's distracting herself, and after spending three days pondering what Alex told me the night before he left, I can understand why.

An army encroaching on our land, with crimson armor and a banner boasting the sigil of the Tenebris, speaks to a threat unlike any we've seen in a millennium or more. And that threat ended in bloodshed and heartbreak.

Just a story, I try to remind myself for the thousandth time, but once again, it doesn't fully settle. Alex had been afraid. I'd seen it on his face even if he'd refused to fully admit it.

And my eldest brother showing any fear at all does not bode well for anyone.

I reach out and run the tips of my fingers down the long face of my mare. The guards linger behind me, two whose names I do not know, though they remain silent as I continue showing my horse affection. She longs to go for a run, but I've been forbidden from leaving the grounds.

My mother says it's because she may need me. But I know it's because of where Alex has gone.

My mare whinnies and nudges me with her nose as I brush her obsidian hair.

The white star on her face and stockings on her feet are the only breaks from her midnight coloring and earned her the name Snowdrop. "I know, girl. My emotions are all over the place." I pet her gently then wrap both arms around her neck and hold on. She returns the gesture, hugging me with her head in a way that makes her feel more friend than animal.

Which, I suppose, she is.

"There you are, girl!"

I release Snowdrop and turn as Genevieve rushes in. Instantly, I'm flooded with worry. "Is something wrong?"

"You're going to be late for your dress fitting! The tailor is already here."

The worry leaves, though annoyance remains. "That's *today?*"

"Do you never listen to me, girl?" she scolds, as she takes me by the arm and guides me out of the house. "I told you yesterday that your appointment with the tailor had been moved up."

As I run through my mind, I try to recall that conversation, but I'm coming up blank. Still, I know from experience that letting Genevieve know I was not listening when we spoke will lead to even more trouble. "Yes, of course. I'm sorry. It completely slipped my mind."

"Worrying about your brother and Fort, are you?"

I swallow hard. "About my brother, yes."

She smiles at me. "It's okay to worry about Fort as well," she says. "He has been around your entire life after all. Basically a brother," she adds with a pointed look at me.

No. Not a brother. My feelings for him are anything but familial. Which, given the grin on her face, means she knows it and is simply jesting me. "I want all of them to come home safely," I reply as she guides me toward the castle. It stands, a solid fortress, against a backdrop of snow and mountains.

A fortress that is far more smothering now than it was before.

The guards move behind us while six more stand just outside of the house where they've been ever since Alex and Fort left with half of our army.

My mother rushes outside, relief on her face as soon as she sees me. "There you are. I thought we were going to need to send a search party out for you."

"I had my guards with me, Mother," I say. "Besides, didn't you tell me there was nothing to worry about?" I ask her. As far as she and the rest of my family are aware, I do not know the true nature of Alex and Fort's trip. And they've made no move to tell me anything to the contrary. Not even Bowman. Still, I've continued to press, hoping that one of the fissures left behind by Alex's absence will cause my mother to crack and confide in me.

"There isn't," she replies as she loops her arm through mine. "We are merely ensuring your safety at your future husband's bequest."

It's a lie. And that alone has my heart beating faster. "Mother, if something is wrong, I can handle it."

"Nothing is wrong," she assures me. "Now, let us enjoy this afternoon as we put you in your wedding gown for the very first time." With a smile that is clearly forced, she guides me up the stairs and toward my room.

As soon as the doors are opened, I'm hit with the sight of a gorgeous, white satin gown lying on my bed. Covered in embroidered gemstones the color of ice, it steals my breath.

I may not wish to marry Patrick, but I will look every bit a queen when I do.

"This is lovely," I whisper as I step forward and run my fingers over the satin bodice. It's smooth beneath the tips of my fingers.

"Not nearly as lovely as the princess who will wear it."

I look back and smile as Sarah, our kingdom's tailor, steps forward and wraps her arms around me. Growing up, she was here more often than not, mending my brother's torn trousers. "It is wonderful to see you."

She sniffles as she pulls away and cups my cheek. "And now you're getting married! I cannot believe it. You are every bit a gorgeous woman." She looks back at my mother and Genevieve. "When did that happen?"

My mother smiles, her eyes a bit misty. "I wish I knew."

A moment passes between us, one where she is not a queen and I am not a princess, but rather we're mother and daughter. The way it used to be before I reached an age when she was no longer needed to tend to every one of my scrapes.

"Let's get you into your wedding dress," she says softly, and the moment ends.

The satin is like a flower petal against my skin and molds to my body like a glove. The long train is secured at my lower back with a button so it flows around me like an extra skirt. A deep neckline plunges between my breasts, revealing enough to show me as a woman, but not enough that there is no mystery.

All in all, I know I look beautiful.

But that is where my excitement ends.

"My love, you look wonderful." My mother clasps her hands together and sniffles. "Like a queen."

"You do," Genevieve agrees.

"Even better than I could have imagined," Sarah comments. "And it fits perfectly."

"It does feel nice," I reply. And because I don't want to hurt her feelings, I add, "It's absolutely perfect, and I cannot wait to wear it during my wedding."

The tailor beams at me. "I am so—"

A high-pitched scream echoes through the house, and adrenaline surges through my system, sending my heart beating so fast I can hear little else.

My mother spins on her heel and rushes toward the door.

"Wait!" Genevieve tries to stop me, but I follow, hot on my mother's heels as I take the spiral staircase with far less caution than I usually do. My heart is in my throat, that feeling of dread that's been haunting me for days tenfold now.

Something is horribly wrong.

My mother's grief-stricken cry fills my ears. *Alex! Fort!*

I quicken my pace, nearly falling on my face as I round the last corner and emerge into the foyer. There are people everywhere, household staff wearing bright white, gathered in a circle.

I shove my way through them, determined to get to the center where my entire world crumbles around me. My body goes cold, heart shattering as I take in the stomach-pitting sight before me.

It can't be.

"No." I rush forward and sink to my knees beside Alex's body. His chest is covered in crusted blood, his face splattered with it. Both eyes have been closed, though the bloody smudges on the lids tell me he died with his eyes open.

My brother *died.*

"You promised," I whisper as I rest a shaking hand on his arm. "You promised me you'd come home." The words are strangled and barely above a whisper. I take his hand in mine and hold it to me as my mother rests hers on his chest.

"My son!" she screams, tipping her head to the ceiling. "No! Please, no!"

Bowman, Diedrich, and Ethan burst into the room and rush over, all of them wide-eyed. Bowman looks angry—the harsh line of his jaw a contrast to his misty eyes. Both Ethan and Diedrich are shattered just as I am.

And my father. He pushes into the room, mouth ajar, eyes wide and brimming with tears. "No. Not my son." He nearly trips over himself to fall to my mother's side.

I tear my gaze from my brother's body and take in the man kneeling a few feet away. Fort will not look at any of us. His tunic is stained with blood, his sword coated in it as it lies at his side. He breathes heavily, chest rising and falling with the weight of his exhaustion.

"What happened?" my father demands.

Fort simply shakes his head.

"Dammit, boy! Speak!" my father bellows it, and Fort winces.

"Stop, Father! He cannot!" I yell and climb to my feet to rush over to Fort's side. His shoulder is gashed open, a gnarly injury that looks mere moments away from festering. It's not deep, but if it's not tended to, he could lose his arm.

"What happened to my son?" my father chokes.

I kneel before Fort and take his hands in mine, not paying any attention to the blood staining my white gown. I sniffle and try to momentarily curb my grief. "Fort. Look at me."

He refuses.

"Please, Fort." I squeeze his hands, and finally, he looks up at me. His amber eyes are full of pain. "Just nod or shake your head, okay?" he nods. "Were you attacked on your way to the crimson army?"

His gaze narrows, confusion momentarily beating back his grief.

"Alex told me where you were going." If anyone is shocked, they say nothing. "So, were you attacked on your way there?"

Fort shakes his head.

"Then on the way back?"

He shakes his head again.

Anger churns in my gut. So they did not respect that code of honor. "They attacked you before the meeting?"

He nods.

"They attacked you without a meeting first? They broke the code?" my father demands.

Fort nods once more.

"I will *slaughter* them," my father growls. He turns to Bowman. "Get the army prepared."

"Father—"

"No argument, Bowman. You are now Navalis' next king. Start acting like it. The moment we bury your brother, we are going to march out and go to fucking war."

I've never heard my father so short. So angry.

Bowman's cheeks redden, but he doesn't argue. He turns and leaves the room with Diedrich following. Ethan, however, remains rooted in his spot, frozen in place, his gaze on Alex, tears in his blue eyes.

I turn back to Fort, barely managing to keep my head when all I want to do is march off into battle right alongside them. "Were there any other survivors?" I ask, voice barely above a whisper. I run my thumbs over the tops of his blood-crusted hands.

Fort lets out a broken sigh then shakes his head.

"They're all dead?" my father chokes out.

"How could you let this happen!" my mother screams at my father. "You said it would be safe! You said they would respect the honor code!"

My chest tightens, and I start to pull away, but Fort's hands tighten on mine, so I remain, though I look up at my mother. "You did know, then. What they were doing."

She doesn't answer, just chokes out another sob and lays her head on Alex's chest.

"You all knew. And you kept it from me." I sniffle to

keep my own tears from falling. "You all lied to me. Told me it was going to be okay."

"It should have been okay!" my father bellows.

Fort's shoulders shake with rage as he pulls away from me and clenches both hands into fists against the stone. The remaining pieces of my heart shatter as he throws his head back and lets out a tortured battle cry that's blended with heartbreaking anguish.

Not once in my entire life do I remember him making a single sound.

I look over at my brother, at the way my mother cradles his broken body, and think of all the happy times.

The laughter.

Him calling me Primrose and taking me to the stable when I'd been learning to ride.

Alex has always been the glue to our sibling bond. A constant shelter in my world of snow-capped joy.

And now...he is gone.

∾

"Come, girl," Genevieve reaches down to pull me up from the cool stone as Bowman and Eric lift Alex's body. My father helps my mother to her feet, though she can barely stand, one arm banded around her abdomen as she sobs.

At some point, Fort must have been taken to the infirmary because he's nowhere to be seen. All while I sat on the ground as the day made way for night. Shadows dance along the wall as the torches flicker.

Everything feels so surreal now.

So different.

How am I supposed to go on? How am I supposed to marry and leave my family when my brother was ripped from us so violently?

"I am so sorry, Carleah," Genevieve whispers as she wraps her arm around my waist and takes me up to my room. "Alex was such a good boy and an even better man." She sniffles, tears slipping down her cheeks.

"Everyone loved him," I reply. My voice is hollow and doesn't even sound like my own. "I can't believe he's gone. What does this mean?" I ask her.

"Shh now, girl. All will come to light." She pats my hand and guides me into my room. My copper tub is already full of steamy water, but where it would otherwise seem inviting, all I can think of is the fact that my brother will never get the chance to bathe again.

He will never see the fresh blooms in our wintery flower garden or have the ability to take the throne that should have been his.

I collapse as grief strikes me down to my knees. A tortured sob is ripped from my chest as my shoulders begin to shake. Genevieve is right there, at my side, her arms banded around me. I turn into her, thinking of all the things my brother will miss.

His wedding.

The birth of his children.

Meeting his nieces and nephews.

"It's not fair."

"I know, girl." Genevieve strokes my hair as we sit.

When my crying has stopped, she cups my face and wipes my tears with the pads of her thumbs. "I'm sorry. I lost it—"

"Hush now. I am not your mother, and therefore, this is spoken out of turn. But you need to understand something. You are a human, girl, and you are allowed to *feel*. Never apologize to me."

I try to smile, but my expression does not change from the brokenness I'm feeling on the inside. Genevieve gently brushes strands of my white hair out of my face, her sympathetic smile doing nothing to hide her own grief. She loved my brother too.

Even as I want to curl in a ball and disappear into happy memories, I allow Genevieve to help me stand, remaining still as she undoes the blood and dirt-stained wedding dress I was supposed to wear on the day that should start my new life.

Instead, I wore it on the last day of my brother's.

~

HOURS PASS BY IN A BLUR, but my heart remains broken. I pace down the hall, waiting for Fort to return from wherever the hell he went. My mother and father are with my brother's body while Diedrich and Bowman are readying the soldiers for war.

Ethan has made himself scarce, likely burying himself in a novel as his way of coping.

Alex. A tear slips down my cheek, and I quickly wipe it away.

Bootsteps echo on the stairs, and I turn just as Fort hits the landing. His flesh has been cleaned, and since he's shirtless, I can see the bandage covering his shoulder. He stops when he sees me.

"Are you all right?" The words come out as a whisper, barely even audible really, but Fort shakes his head. He drops his gaze to the floor and moves past me.

I follow, not caring whether he wants me to or not.

He opens the door to his room but doesn't shut it. I walk through and close it behind me then lean back against it as Fort goes to the window.

"My father shouldn't have yelled at you like that," I say. "He's—" I close my eyes and swallow back a cry. "We're all grieving."

Fort turns back to me, his eyes full of pain.

I rush over and wrap my arms around his waist, but he makes no move to return the gesture. Still, I hold on. Alex was his best friend. They were as thick as thieves. And he'd been forced, not only to watch him die—but carry his body who the hell knows how far.

"If I could hunt them down, I would," I tell him.

Fort pulls back and cups my face. He stares into my eyes and shakes his head.

"They killed him," I say. "And they hurt you."

With a deep breath, Fort pulls away from me and crosses his arms. He keeps his gaze trained on the floor.

"Fort. Look at me, please."

But he refuses, shaking his head.

"Do you want me to go?" I choke out.

He nods.

"But I don't want to be alone," I choke out. "They all lied to me, Fort. Every single one of them—but you and Alex."

Fort swallows hard then looks up at me and holds out his good arm. I cross over toward him, burying my face in his chest and clinging to him as my shoulders shake with the force of my sobs. Grief weighs me down, a stone falling to the bottom of an icy lake.

And as Fort wraps a single arm around me, guiding us over to the bed, I lean into him as though he's the only thing in this world that can keep me firmly on my feet.

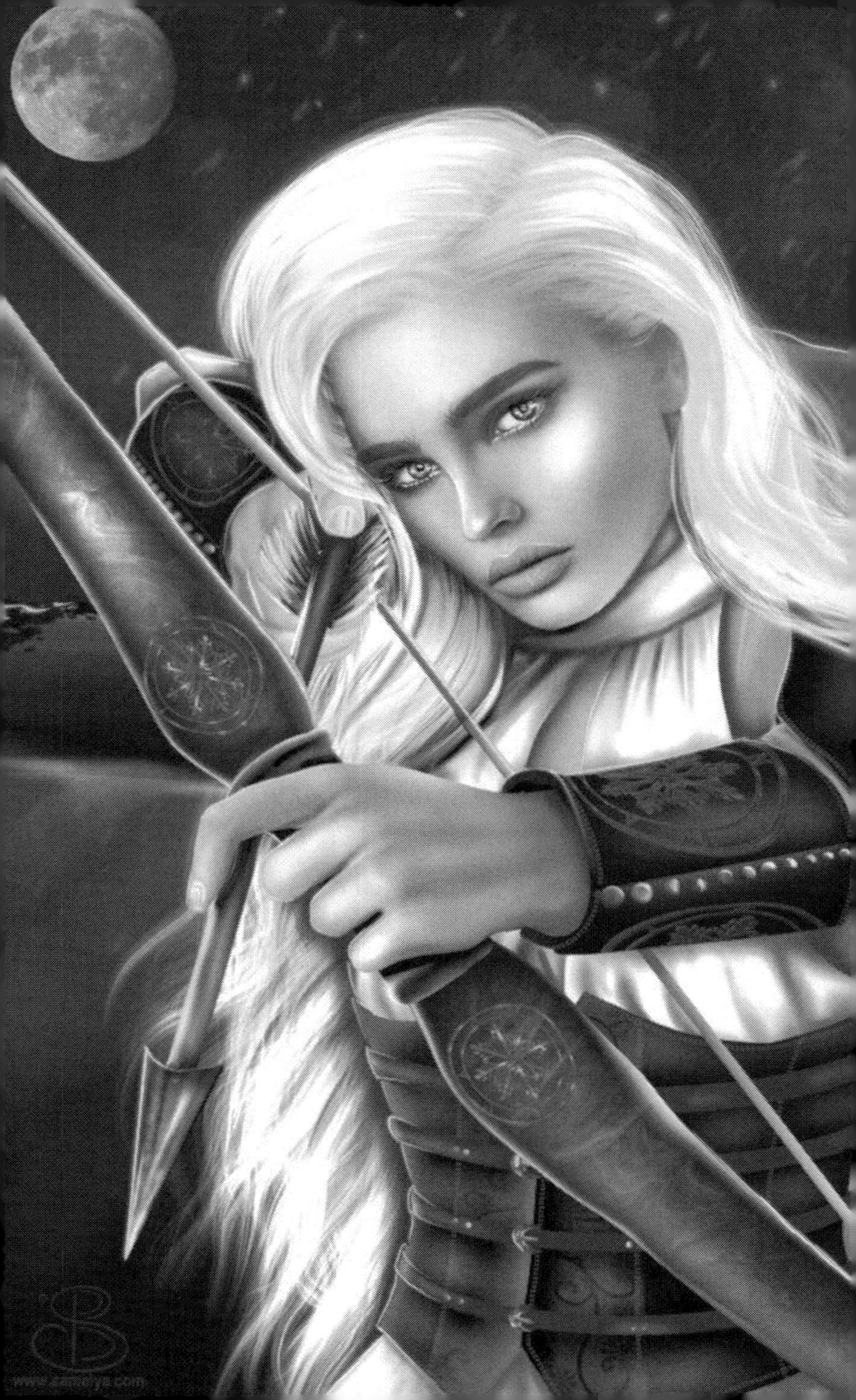

CHAPTER 6
CARLEAH

"Today we lay to rest a great man. Alex Harry Rossingol was a seasoned fighter, a loving brother and son, and the future king of Navalis."

Wearing a black gown that falls to the snow at my feet, I stand alongside my mother as the Clergyman speaks of my eldest brother. He lies before us, the wooden coffin open so we can see his pale flesh.

I wish it were closed.

Wish that it was not our way to sit and stare at the dead. My brother is no longer there. His soul has left, leaving behind nothing but a shell made up of pale flesh and bone that will remain long after the rest of him is gone.

Cool wind whips at my braided hair and hits my wet cheeks.

"Alex was taken too soon, but he will be embraced by

ancestors in what awaits beyond this place, of that I am sure."

The entire kingdom has gathered. Every man, woman, and child from the village amassed in a crowd on the outskirts of the burial grounds. Fort and my brothers remain beside the casket, ready to close and lower it into the ground where it will remain for the rest of eternity.

My gaze rests on Fort now. I haven't spoken to him since I cried in his arms the night he returned. When I'd woken a few hours later, he was gone, and despite my best attempts to check on him, I haven't been able to figure out just where he's been going.

He refuses to look any of us in the eyes, as though he feels guilty for not being able to protect Alex. No matter how many times Bowman told him that he was thankful that he brought our brother home, he still carries that weight.

Now, he stands cradling his injured arm against his body, his good one dangling down near the casket. Dark circles line his eyes, and his black hair is longer than it has been since I've known him.

He's broken. Just as the rest of us are.

The Clergyman nods to my father, who stands and retrieves a handful of dirt as the clergyman closes the lid over my brother's face. I close my eyes, my throat burning with emotion. When I open them again, it is to see my father setting that handful of dirt over the top of the casket. My brothers and Fort each grab a handle carved into the side and lift then carry him over to the hole where they gently set him inside.

Then, they each repeat my father's gesture and put a handful of freshly dug dirt over my brother's grave.

My mother is next, and I follow on legs that might as well be numb. Ironic since I've been anything but for the last two days as we've prepped for my brother's funeral. I've been unable to feel anything aside from the pain that has shattered my soul and the bone-deep anger at the fact that none of them felt so inclined as to tell me the truth.

Not one single member of my family aside from the one we're burying in the ground.

The dirt is cold in my hands, even through the thickness of my gloves, and I drop it onto the casket then turn away as a villager begins shoveling dirt and snow onto the top of the wooden box.

Each step that carries me farther from my brother feels like a step away from the woman I was before he was killed. Even with all my questions, and all the knowledge I'd amassed by reading and listening—I know that I'd been naïve. Despite my best efforts, I might as well have had the ideals of a child.

Now, I understand, though. I understand that the world is closer to the wars and ugliness that I have experienced in fiction. My family shielded me from it for so long that I feel incredibly unprepared for what's to come.

And ever since Alex's death, I've poured over books I once believed to be mere legends. I've learned of the Tenebris and their thirst for blood and chaos. Of the giants, who were our only allies. Of Elves that supposedly reside in the highest of mountains.

If the Tenebris are trying to revive the ancient creatures, that does not bode well for anyone. Because legend says that whoever wakes them will have the power to save or destroy us all.

I can only speculate which side the soldiers will be on.

Genevieve takes my arm and guides me toward the carriage that awaits. We're surrounded by armed guards, their presence becoming my new normal. They follow me when I stroll through the gardens.

They await in the hallways outside of our bedrooms.

They stand guard on the front steps of our castle.

All waiting for the crimson soldiers who slaughtered my brother and those of their ranks.

I sniffle.

Bowman climbs in next, followed by Diedrich and Ethan. They say nothing to me, though, not even as the carriage begins to rock with the movement.

All I can think about is how Alex would be trying to make us all laugh. How he would be smiling and chattering on about what comes next.

A tear slips down my cheek.

Bowman wraps an arm around my shoulders, and I lean against him.

"Are you okay?" I ask him.

"No," he replies.

Bowman never wanted to be king. He'd longed for a life of adventure, of sailing the Cerulean Seas in search of faraway lands. Once, he'd joked about becoming a pirate. About tracking down the feared Captain Neo and trying to join his crew.

Then, he'd had plans to come with me to Soreno. Now, he will live and die as the king of Navalis. Whether he likes it or not.

The carriage comes to a stop, and the door is opened. Bowman releases me and climbs out first then reaches up to help me step down. Genevieve is already there, her carriage having arrived just before mine, so she takes my arm once more and leads me up to the castle.

The halls are empty.

"Thank you, I will go up to my room alone."

"Are you sure? I can help you dress for dinner," she says.

"No, thank you. I would prefer to remain in my room for the evening." The idea of sitting at the table and listening to my family speak of Alex makes me nauseous.

Her expression softens. "Girl, you should spend time with your family."

"They lied to me," I snap then close my eyes and take a deep breath. "They kept things from me that I should have been made aware of."

"Alex told you, did he not?"

"But they didn't know he'd spoken to me," I remind her. "So, as far as I am concerned, they lied." I close my eyes and sniffle. "I wish to mourn my brother in the quiet of my room. Please have someone bring me dinner."

She purses her lips but doesn't argue, so I continue up the spiral stairs alone.

By the time someone knocks on my door with dinner, night has fallen just outside my window. I watched the light fade, half-expecting murderous soldiers to explode from the tree line.

"You may enter," I call out, still lying in my bed with the covers over my lap.

The door opens, and my father moves into my room, holding a tray in his hands. When I see him, I straighten a bit then smooth the covers over my lap. "I thought you might be hungry," he says softly as he sets the tray with two plates of roasted meat, potatoes, and carrots onto my lap.

"Thank you."

He takes a seat at the foot of my bed, his back to me. "Alex told you of where they were going?"

"He told me of the crimson soldiers," I reply. "Of how there are whispers they are searching for the entrance to the cavern of sleeping giants."

My father sighs. "Yes."

"But all of that is a fable, correct? A scary bedtime story of an origin beginning with magic?"

"Some believe it is not myth," he replies. "My concern is of the very real threat the army poses to us. Tenebris or not. As of now, they remain far enough that our scouts have not warned us of an impending attack. But after what they did to your brother—"

"After they ignored the code of honor and slaughtered him and his men in cold blood?" It comes out quite a bit harsher than I meant.

My father turns to me and arches a dark brow. "They should have adhered to the code."

"Not all men follow the same code."

He sighs and stands. "It stands as a way to keep order in the realm. If there were no code, if men followed no honor, it would be anarchy."

"If they truly followed a code of honor, there would be no war." I put the food aside and stand, retrieving my robe from the chair beside my bed. "There would be no need for battles—or swords—because honorable men do not spill the blood of other honorable men!"

He shakes his head and looks at me as though he pities my outlook. "Am I not honorable to you?"

"Of course you are."

"I have spilled the blood of others, Carleah. Many times. I have entered into wars with Soreno. I have fought to remain their ally so that they may be ours when the time comes."

"And where are they now?" I choke out as a tear slips from my cheek. "Where are this honorable king and his son, whom you seek to marry me off to, when we need them the most?"

"They are on their way here," he replies. "For your wedding, and they are traveling with a large enough fighting force that, combined with ours, will ensure our survival. But it's a two-month trip by ship from Soreno. Which means they will likely not arrive until just before you take your vows."

I swallow hard. "You're still marrying me off then?"

"Yes. We need the alliance now more than ever. Daughter, I wouldn't ask you to marry Patrick if I didn't believe he was a good man; this you must understand."

"I don't," I reply. "Because marrying him may be best for our lands, but it is not what I want."

"Carleah—"

"Does it not matter to you? That I love someone else?"

My father's expression morphs from one of annoyance to one of pity. "Fort is not for you, my daughter."

"And why the hell not? You married the daughter of a guard. Why must I marry a future king?"

"Because Fort cannot protect you the way Patrick can," he says softly as he reaches out and brushes my hair behind my ear.

Tears burn in my eyes as I stare at him. "How can you say that? He's the strongest man here, likely the strongest in all of the Third Realm.'"

"Fort does not have the army Patrick does, Carleah. You have to trust me that residing here is not what's best for you. I know it hurts, but this infatuation with Fort will fade with time."

"Infatuation," I repeat with an angry shake of my head. "Because I am a child who has no idea what genuine affection feels like."

"No," my father says sadly. "You are not. But Patrick will keep you alive. You will grow old, have children who will sit on the throne of Soreno, and with him at your side, I can finally rest easy that you—" He trails off. "That you will be happy."

"I will be happy here," I plead. "Please don't make me leave, Father. Please."

"I have no choice, Daughter."

I turn away from him, determined to hide my hurt. "Then I suppose we will see if they ever arrive," I snap. "As far as we know, they're dead just as Alex is. The crimson soldiers could have destroyed their ships and we have not yet received word." My words are sharp, my tone harsh, but I'm tired of this foolish notion that I cannot handle the severity of our situation. Tired of being forced into a future I don't want. And if they wish to treat me like a child, perhaps it's time I start throwing a fucking tantrum like one. "If they are dead, there will be no marriage. No alliance. No aid coming. Alex believed we were outnumbered. Is that the case?"

My father's jaw tightens. "Yes."

"But we have the advantage."

"Yes," he repeats. "But an advantage only takes you so far, Carleah. Our best hope, despite my initial reaction of hunting and killing every last one of them, is to remain where we are, prepare for a fight, and hope the King of Soreno and his forces arrive in time."

"You all should have told me." I turn toward him. "I could have handled it."

My father crosses the floor and cups my cheek. "I see how strong you are, Carleah. That was never the question."

"Then what was it? Why keep this from me?"

"Telling you of the danger would have only dulled the light I've seen shining within your eyes since the moment you were born. You are a true gift, my daughter. A blessing to our people and this kingdom. I could not bear to see the fear clawing at me radiating from your face. Not even for a moment."

I swallow hard, emotion eating at me. I'm hurt. Angry. Depressed. "Please do not make me marry Patrick, Father. I beg of you."

"There is nothing I can do, Carleah. You must marry Patrick. Of that, there is no other option."

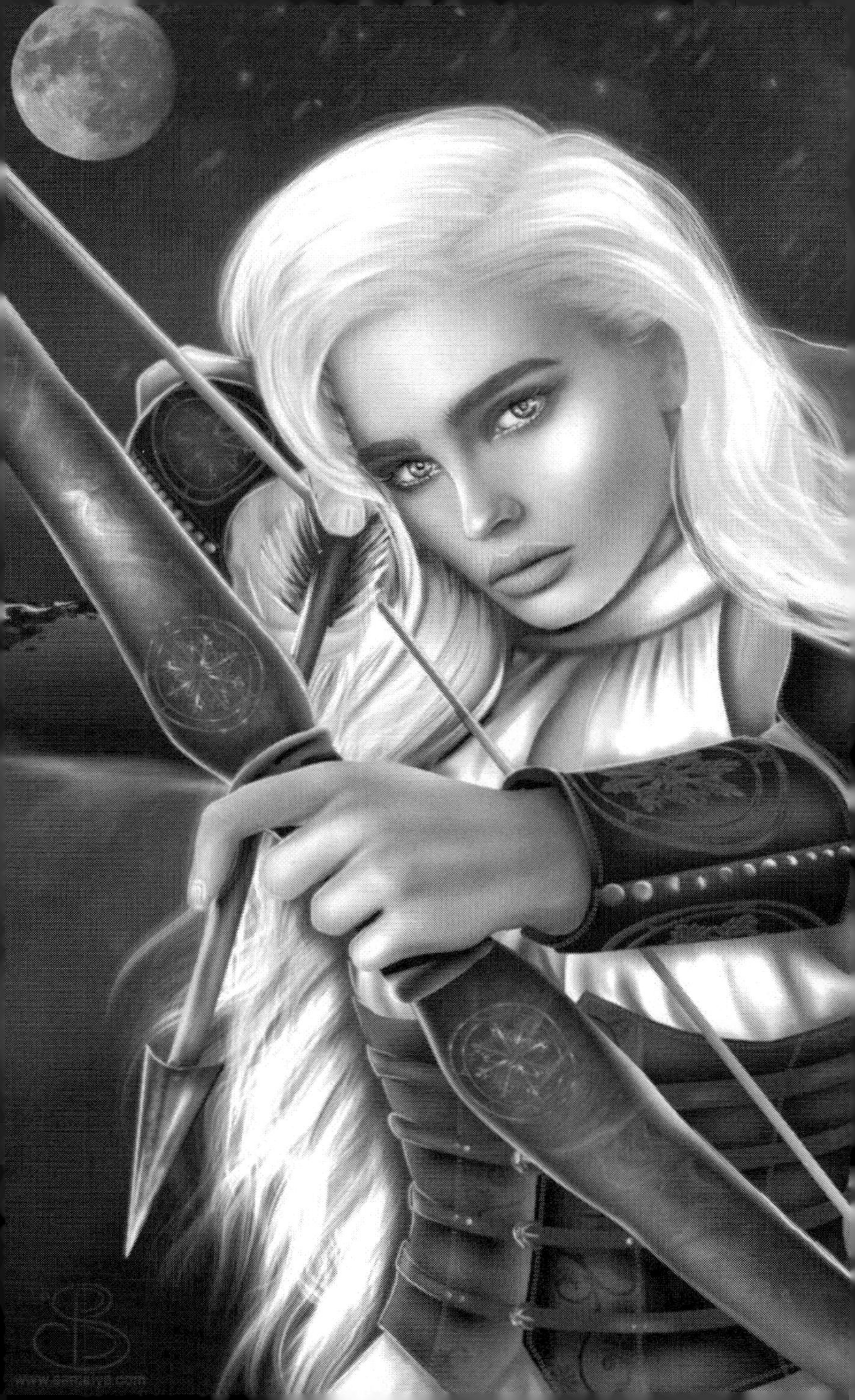

CHAPTER 7
CARLEAH

A scream echoes through the halls of the castle moments before my door is thrown open. Two men rush in, their crimson armor gleaming beneath the light of my dying fire. Fear claws at my gut. It tears at my heart as I jump out of bed, grabbing my robe as I go. I cover my body, holding it up over my nightgown as I plaster myself against the far wall.

"Princess," one of the men growls. "A sight for sore eyes."

"Get away from me!" I scream. "Help!" They rush me at once. On instinct, I grab the lantern beside my bed and swing. It shatters against the helmet of one man, and he stumbles back.

"Fuck! It got in my fucking eye!" He falls backward on my bed.

"You little bitch!" the other growls. I cannot see his face aside from what little of his eyes are revealed through the slit in his helmet, but I can tell he's snarling.

"You'll pay for that. He never said you had to be unharmed."

I dodge him as he comes for me, ducking down and grabbing the hot poker beside my fireplace. I swing, slamming it into the side of his head, then turning—poker in hand—I race out into the hall.

My foot catches, and I go down hard, slamming into the stone beside a body. As I'm pushing myself up, I catch sight of the deceased's face and let loose a scream. Genevieve's eyes are frozen open, a gaping wound in the side of her skull.

"There you are!" the man yells.

Tears in my eyes, I push to my feet and race down the stairs, keeping the poker in hand.

The dead are *everywhere*.

Our staff, the butlers, soldiers. Men in crimson armor race through the halls. The front door is open, and I start toward it, but the man who followed me down reaches the bottom at the same time as two crimson soldiers step into my home.

"Get her!" he bellows.

They run toward me.

I sprint toward the kitchen, trying not to see the faces of the dead as I go. My father has to be here. My mother. My brothers. They'll know what to do. I race into the kitchen and start toward the servants' entrance. It begins to open, so I duck into a corner and hold my breath as silent tears stream down my cheeks.

"Where is your daughter?"

My blood chills.

"Gone," my father snarls. "Far away from every single one of you fuckers."

A loud crack fills the room.

I cover my mouth with a shaking hand as my other one clings to the fireplace poker.

"I've taken your wife. Give me your daughter, or I will torture and kill every one of your remaining sons until one of them tells me where to find her. Either way, I *will* find her."

"You won't fucking touch her," my father replies.

I've taken your wife. Grief tightens my throat, it weighs down upon my chest, but I take a deep breath because there is no other choice but to keep my head on.

I remain where I am, attempting to conjure any scenario in which both my father and I walk away from this. Where my brothers survive. And then it hits me. There is none. If these men are here for me, and my life will spare my family, then what choice is there?

I have to save those I love. Even if it costs me the breath in my chest.

"Which son should I start with?" the man demands. "The youngest perhaps?"

Ethan. That does it. "I'm here!" I jump up into view, keeping the poker hidden behind my back.

My father's familiar gaze lands on me—and falls. "You should have remained hidden," he whispers.

"You can't kill them. Please don't hurt my father or brothers. No more death and I will go with you."

The man removes his helmet. His face is scarred, his eyes nearly black in the dark of our kitchen. When he smiles, I note two gold teeth. "The daughter of Navalis, it is quite the honor."

I swallow hard. "Let my father go."

He looks at my father then shoves him forward. I reach out, my fingers brushing his as the man brings his blade up and severs my father's head from his shoulders.

The scream catches in my throat as his expression freezes, and the life vanishes from my father's eyes. His head lolls off to the side and slams into the marble floor with a sickening *thud*. "No!" I fall to my knees in his blood, but I don't remain there for long. The man starts forward. "You murderer!" I scream then bring the poker up. I swing it as hard as I can, but the man catches it and wrenches it from my grasp.

He grins. "You have fight in you. That makes this immensely more satisfying." He tosses the poker to the side, grips my arm with bruising strength, and rips me out into the cold.

It envelops me, freezing me to the core as I trade one gruesome scene for another. My mother lies dead, Ethan beside her, a blade just out of his reach. Diedrich lies away from them in his own crimson snow. The tortured cries wrenched from my chest are so horrific that even I don't recognize them as my own.

"You killed them!" I fight, thrashing against his hold. I kick, scream, and punch, all while he laughs.

"Keep it up, Princess. You are only wearing yourself out."

I let my entire body go limp, and he throws me to the ground beside my mother's body. I try not to look at her, try to stay focused on finding a way to escape, but all I can see is the lack of life in her eyes.

The man kneels, his knee pressing into my back. He lets enough of his weight press down on me that I'm gasping for a single breath. "I heard you were rather spirited," he spits out. "Won't matter, though. You belong to *them* now."

I squirm, my hands gripping at his legs, but he laughs in my face and presses down further. "How does that feel? To be such an insignificant little pest?" He flips me over, pressing his knee into my chest now as he eyes me with amusement.

"I will kill you," I choke out, never having uttered and meant those words in my entire life. But I do now. Now that the bodies of my loved ones lie beside me.

"Unlikely."

I spit on him, and he rears a hand back, cracking it against my cheek. Pain shoots through my face, and I taste blood. The coppery tang fills my mouth as my vision wavers. He slaps me again, and my ears ring.

"How did that feel, little bitch? Keep it up, and I'll make things far worse than they need to be." He stands and bends to retrieve me but freezes at the same moment an arrow protrudes through his eye socket.

He falls forward, and I try to move, but I'm not fast enough. The soldier falls on top of me, the weight of his body and metal armor suffocating. I buck, trying to get him off, but he barely budges.

"Shit! Carleah!" The body is ripped from me as Bowman and Fort come into view.

Bowman's face is splattered with blood, Fort's contorted in rage. He carries two short blades—one in each hand, while Bowman holds his bow at the ready, another arrow already poised.

"They killed them," I cry out as I tremble.

"I know," he growls then looks down at me. "Mother fucker. You're practically naked! Did they hurt you?" he demands. "Did they touch you?"

"Does my innocence truly matter right now?" I demand as my mouth chatters. "They're dead, Bowman! They're all dead!"

Fort rips his tunic from his body and offers it to me. I slip it over my head, and the fabric falls down to my upper thighs.

"Father," I choke out. "They killed him. They said if he gave me to them, they would spare you all—" My shoulders begin to shake. Whether from the skin-numbing cold or grief, I'm not sure.

"Calm yourself, little sister. We will get these fuckers. But we need to go. Can you walk?" my brother asks.

"Yes."

"Shit, you have no shoes. Your toes will blacken and fall off. Fort, can you carry her? I'll keep my bow rea—" He trails off as his eyes widen.

"Bowman?" I question.

Fort looks behind him then rips me out of the way as Bowman falls forward, faceplanting into the snow. An axe sticks from his back, and I scream. "No! Please, no! Bowman!"

Fort rears back and sends one of his blades flying. It

slams into the attacking soldier, and he falls to the ground.

"No, no, please no." I try to pull the axe from my brother's back so I can flip him over and get his face out of the snow, but my shaking hands fumble to keep a strong grip on the handle.

Fort sheathes his sword, retrieves Bowman's bow and the quiver that fell beside him, and slips them over his shoulder. Then, he reaches down and tries to rip me away from my brother. From my family.

"No! Please, Bowman. Wake up." He tugs again. "We can't leave him, Fort!"

"Carleah!" A deep, gravelly voice stills me, and I tilt my face to look up at Fort. He stares down at me, his amber eyes wide and pleading. "We must go," he says.

I'm struck silent because...his voice—

"Please," he says. "They are gone. I cannot watch you die, too."

All fight leaves me because he's right. If I die, then the entire royal family is wiped out in one night. There is no one left to tell our story. To seek vengeance for what was stolen. So, I nod and let Fort lift me into his arms.

He sprints toward the tree line, the snow crunching beneath his boots. His body is cold, so I wrap my arms around his neck and try to warm him with my own. The deeper we move, the farther I get from my family. Even now, though, I can see their blood staining the snow around our home.

Fort moves through the trees near silently even as my

body begins to shake violently. The cold numbs my body, but every muscle spasms with my tremors.

"Hang on, Carleah." The screams grow louder as we get closer to the village. I start to turn, but Fort tightens his hold. "Don't look. Please."

But I do. And instantly wish I'd heeded his wishes.

More dead litter the snowy ground. They're everywhere. Whole bodies with gaping wounds, pieces of bodies—limbs—strewn about. Like monsters ravaged them, ripping them apart and leaving the rest for scavengers.

"They slaughtered them," I whimper. "The entire city."

Fort doesn't respond as he carries me toward the door of a house at the very edge of the city. It's ajar, a woman's body holding it partially open. I swallow hard as Fort steps over her carefully then creeps into the house.

He carries me just inside then sets me down and immediately moves before me, his short blade in hand. He gestures to a spot just behind the door. "Stay there," he orders.

I nod and slip out of view. As I crouch down behind the door, I cover both feet with my hands, trying like hell to warm them. It's then my gaze falls to the dead woman's feet. They're sticking just in sight, and although it makes my stomach churn, I slip the soft-soled leather boots from her feet and quickly put them on.

By the time I've finished lacing them, Fort returns. He studies my feet then looks at the bare ones between us.

"Good thinking," he says then reaches down and pulls me to my feet. "Follow me."

We move cautiously up the stairs and into a bedroom where Fort creeps toward the window and peers outside. "Check the wardrobe. Find something warmer to wear so you don't freeze to death."

"What if they check this house?" I move toward the wardrobe, pulling it open to reveal an array of dresses just inside. I don't bother looking at the fabrics or making a choice. I just grab the closest dress to me and place it on the bed.

"They have already checked this house," he replies as I slip his tunic over my head. "We need to hurry, though, before they double back for the bodies."

I shiver as I pull the dress on. "Can you lace it?"

He nods, so I turn and show him my back. The dress is far too long, the bodice too large for me, but it will keep me far warmer than the nightgown I wear beneath it.

As soon as I am laced, I retrieve two warm coats then offer one for him as soon as he's slipped his tunic back over his bare chest.

He puts the coat on, so I follow with a smaller fur.

By the time I've buttoned it in front of me, he's already back at the window.

Voices carry toward us though I cannot make out what they are saying. Fort doesn't appear too worried yet, though he continues watching.

Someone screams outside, far too close for comfort. He whirls on me. "Shit. We need to go now." He rips a fur blanket off of the bed and wraps me in it. As soon as I'm covered, he picks me up again, cradling me in his arms as he creeps down the stairs. He moves so smoothly, so purposely—something that should be impossible for a man who is carrying another person. Especially given his wounded shoulder.

But I don't bring it up because, frankly, I'm too damned grateful that he can and is carrying me.

Once we reach the door, all of my thoughts vanish, until I can hear nothing but the pounding of my own heart.

Fort looks outside, keeping his—and my—body hidden behind the door, then sprints out and into the trees once more. He runs, once again sprinting far faster than I would have thought a man could move while carrying another body.

He doesn't look back, but I do.

My gaze is trained on the city slowly growing smaller as we slip farther and farther into the trees. These men stole my brother. Then they came and took the rest of my family.

They took my home.

And I silently vow to return and take vengeance for all that I've lost.

By the time I turn back toward what's ahead, we've nearly reached the edge of the city. Somehow, the high stone border has never seemed as imposing as it does today. But before I can ask him how he plans to get over it, Fort stops.

"I need you to get on my back. Can you do that and hold on?"

"Yes."

He sets me down then turns and drops to his knees, so I open up my blanket, managing to cling to the edges as I wrap both arms around his neck. Fort stands, and I slip my legs around his waist. He slips the bow up and over my head, backs up, and sprints toward the wall.

My heart hammers in my chest as I wait for impact, but then—Fort's hands close over a vine hanging over the wall. He grabs it and uses his feet to propel us up the wall.

He climbs with speed, and we reach the top of the wall in mere moments.

The second his feet hit the ground on the other side, he races toward the trees for cover. It's not until we're tucked away inside the tree line that he kneels again so I can climb off of his back.

"Are you all right?"

"Not even a little," I growl as tears slip down my cheeks. "Where are we going?"

"Away from here. We need to regroup, figure out where to go."

I grip his arm. "Promise me something."

"Anything," he replies.

"Promise me that we're going to come back and make them all pay." Angry tears stream down my cheeks as my adrenaline begins to wane and exhaustion settles in my bones.

Fort doesn't say anything, but he does offer me a single nod then gathers me again and races further into the trees.

Behind me, the continued screams of my people begin to fade until there is nothing but the echo of it etched into my mind.

Forever.

~

Rays of gold glint on the snow-capped ground as Fort walks over toward a riverbank. He sets me down carefully. My entire body shakes, every single inch of my skin cold as the snow we walk on.

"I'm going to grab some wood for a fire, okay?"

"I can help." Without giving him the chance to argue, I shove the blanket to the ground and move through the snow with him, gathering twigs as I go. He snaps branches from the nearest tree then gathers some dried pine needles from the ground just beneath it.

Fort clears a spot in the snow with his boot, so I offer him my branches. Moving quickly, he piles the wood up and stashes some dried needles between them.

"I don't suppose you have any flint?" I ask, half-joking.

That is until he reaches into his pocket and pulls out two black rocks. "Always."

"How often are you making fires in the woods?"

"Likely more often than you'd think," he replies as he strikes them together. Sparks fly into the needles, and they begin to smoke. Fort leans down and blows gently, stoking the flames to climb higher.

Within seconds, the needles are engulfed, the wood crackling along with them.

I kneel and hold out my palms to the fire. My fingers are frozen, but thanks to the dead woman's shoes, I can feel my toes again.

"How are you?"

"Cold. Angry. Grieving." I turn to him. "You?"

"The same."

We fall back into companionable silence while I let my mind run over the events that have brought me to the middle of the Navalis woods alongside Fort. And when those prove too painful to focus on, I consider the risks we face.

If the soldiers don't catch up to us, it's entirely possible we'll freeze to death before we reach the next village. I've never viewed snow as dangerous before. It's always been a beautiful constant in my life, but right now I long for heat.

For something other than ice.

Silence stretches on between us, so I sit back on the fur blanket and close my eyes.

"Did you see them die?" I ask. "My mother, Ethan, and Diedrich?"

Fort doesn't say anything.

I open my eyes and stare into his amber ones. "Answer me."

Fort sucks in a deep breath but doesn't respond. His silence is something I'm used to, but I won't allow it. Not anymore. Honestly, the fact that he's hidden his voice for so long angers me, but it pales in comparison to what we're facing, so I shove it down...for now.

Finally, he begins to speak, "The scouts alerted us to the arrival of the crimson army. A large group of them was heading around the mountains, so we missed them. As soon as we knew, Bowman and I gathered what we could and went to the stables. Someone had let out all the horses though; they were gone."

"Alive?" I think of my horse. Of my little Snowdrop.

"As far as we know, yes. Their stalls had just been opened. So, no, Princess, I did not see them die. They were dead by the time we found them." He coughs and hisses.

"What is it? Are you hurt?" I get to my knees, fear icing me even more than the frozen water surrounding us. I move his jacket and tunic to the side and note fresh blood pooling in the fabric of his shoulder, right over the injury he sustained when bringing my brother home. "Dammit. Did you pack any medical supplies?"

He nods. "Some."

"Give them to me."

He hesitates.

"Do you want to bleed out?" I snap.

Finally, Fort leans back and reaches into his pocket to withdraw a tiny leather satchel.

After opening it, I breathe a sigh of relief to see a needle and some thread along with a couple of bandages and a tiny vial of iodine. I shove his jacket off of his shoulders then grip the bottom of his tunic and draw it up over his uninjured arm first. I pull it up over his head then slide it down over the injury.

It sticks to his torn flesh, so I have to tug.

He doesn't make a single sound.

"Stay still." I straddle him, trying to get close to his injury.

I thread the needle then shove it through his torn flesh. He winces but remains silent as I continue closing the opening in his shoulder. Jagged flesh is crusted with blood, already torn from the stitches he ripped out, likely when he'd been carrying me.

Once it's closed again, I douse it with iodine then put the supplies back in the satchel and climb off of his lap. He pulls his tunic back on and slips into his jacket, so I offer him the satchel.

He sets it beside him, and I grip a corner of the blanket and wrap it further around me. "They're all dead," I whisper. And even though I saw it, even though I'm speaking it, I still cannot believe the words to be true.

"Yes. But you are not. And they would want you to remain alive."

Tears blur my vision. "My entire family. Everyone I've ever known. And why?" I turn to him. "Why were they killed?"

Fort hesitates for a moment. "Those men were not trying to kill you, Carleah. You understand that, don't you?"

I swallow hard as I fight to remember anything but

the sight of my slaughtered family. Then, I remember what the man said just before Bowman killed him. *"You belong to them now."* Who did he mean? "They died because of me," I say. "Because those men were coming for me? But why?"

"I do not know. But we need to keep you away from them. At all costs." He looks over his shoulder at the trees. "We need to keep moving."

"You need to rest your shoulder. You could tear—"

"I'd rather tear my shoulder open a thousand times than have something happen to you." He kicks some snow over the fire then reaches down and pulls me to my feet.

"Fine. But you need to let me walk. They aren't right behind us, and you may need your arm for more important things."

He clenches his jaw. "For a short period of time, fine. But I can move faster if I don't have to keep your pace."

I would be insulted if he weren't telling the truth.

Fort shoves the first-aid kit into his pocket then lifts the blanket and wraps it around my shoulders. We fall silent once more and begin to walk, each step carrying me farther and farther from the only place I've ever known.

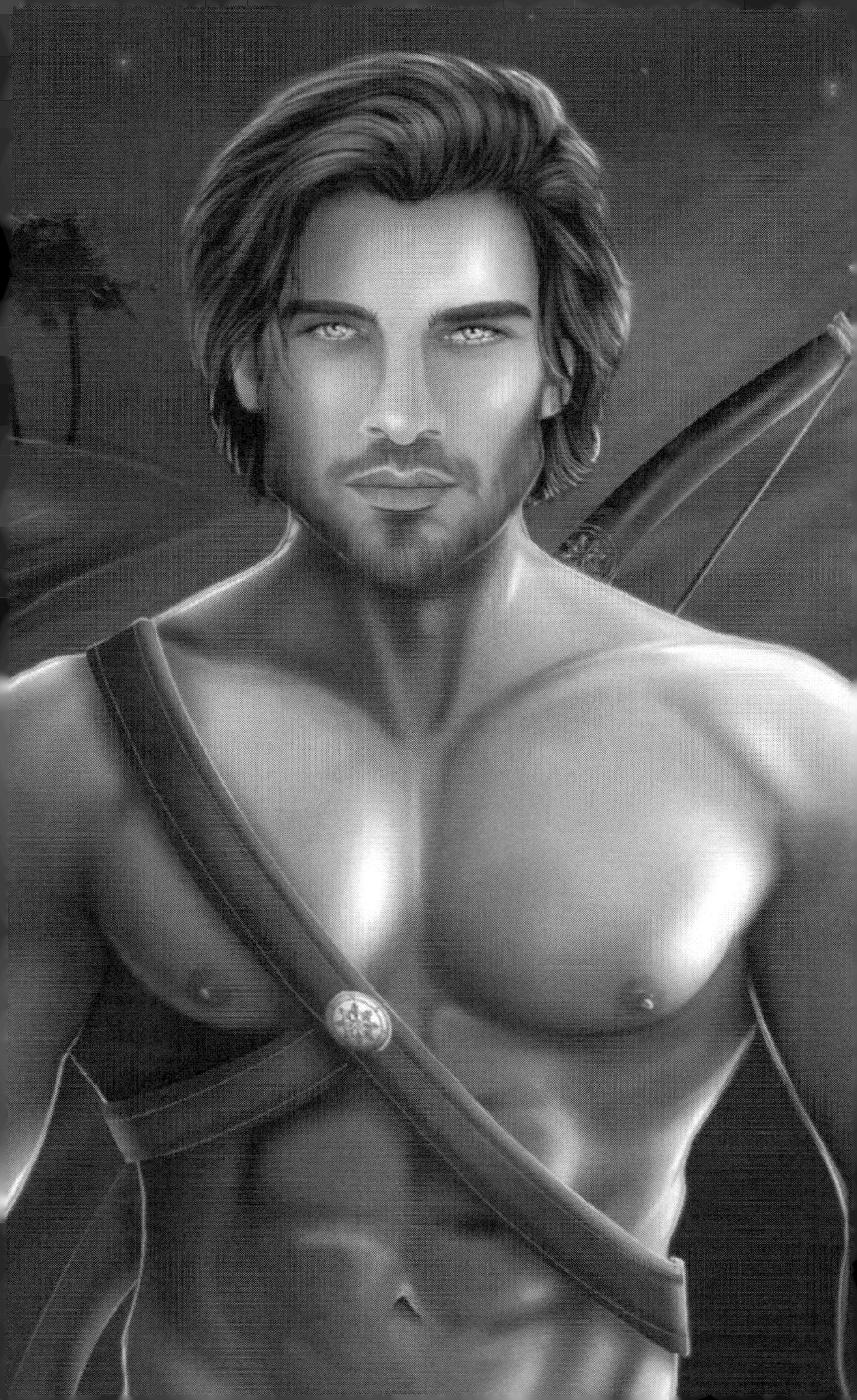

CHAPTER 8
FORT

Between our combined body heat and the exertion of walking while carrying Carleah for the past few hours, my flesh begins to thaw. After a morning of walking, Carleah was so exhausted she'd nearly fallen over in the snow. She'd argued, but eventually, I'd won the battle and carried her.

Not too long after, she fell silent, her breathing steady.

And in the quiet, I've had time to think.

To consider all of the ways I failed the one family to show me a single bit of kindness since they found me damn near frozen to death in the snow. Images of the dead run through my mind on repeat, reminders of how weak I am.

No matter how old I get.

How proficient I become with my blade.

I am still not enough to protect those I consider family.

Alex was the first to fall. Those bastards agreed to our neutral meeting then surrounded us and started killing before the first words were spoken. I'd barely gotten us out of there, only to have Alex bleed to death before I ever got him home.

And now the rest of them.

I thought we'd lost Carleah as well. When that man crumpled on top of her—my arms tighten around her. She could have been crushed. And when we'd discovered that she'd survived but was nearly naked in the snow—I've never felt rage like that before.

A thirst for blood.

She stirs against me, but she does not wake. The sun is high in the sky though I know dusk is not far off. So far, I've heard no signs that we are being hunted, but that only brings me more fear.

The Tenebris are not typical soldiers.

There is something wrong with them. Something *evil*.

They live for the fight, for spilled blood, and they fight with a ferocity I've only ever seen in one other place: Nemoregno. Most men, when forced into battle, will hesitate before killing those who are unarmed. But these crimson warriors did not.

Their blades struck without pause, and they relished the blood they spilled. Every horrific memory from my childhood, everything I ran from, came to fruition and destroyed the only people to have ever shown me kindness.

Ahead, a path curves up the side of the mountain, so I

start toward it even as I know my legs are going to burn with the incline. We're nearing the edge of the kingdom, though, and I need to know where we're going before I go anywhere near the Phantom.

The very idea of attempting to cross it makes my skin crawl.

I hold Carleah in place as we ascend, climbing up to a plateau covered in bright green pines.

A stream weaves along the ground, leading to a waterfall that carries it down the other side of the mountain. I scan the area for the best vantage point then settle on a smaller pine with bushes nearby. It's then I stop and stare down at Carleah in my arms. I expect her to wake, for those gorgeous blue eyes to flutter open and steal my breath.

But she doesn't.

I start to set her down, and the moment I shift her in my arms, she wakes, thrashing in my arms. "No! Let me go!"

"It's me," I remind her.

She falls still, eyes blinking rapidly as she stares up at me. Carleah's gaze has always fascinated me. When she'd been young, her eyes were a pale blue like her brothers and mother.

But as she got older, the blue grew brighter until they began to burn like twin azure flames. Hers is a gaze that has captivated me for years. Even more so since the night I rescued her beside the icy lake near her home when she'd damn near been abducted.

Seeing that man's hands on her. The way he'd had his mouth on hers—it altered the way I saw her. Given our eight-year age difference, we'd never spent much time together.

But after that night—it was like I was seeing her every-fucking-where.

And then that kiss in my room, the night before Alex and I left—

"Sorry. Nightmare." Her tone is clipped as though she's angry with herself for having one at all.

I set her on the ground then pull the blanket free and lay it down. She sinks down onto it, so I flip one of the sides up and cover her legs.

"I am going to gather wood for a fire. We will camp here tonight and should reach Miserico before nightfall tomorrow. We can re-supply there."

"Let me help." She starts to stand, but I shake my head.

"No. You rest. Please. It won't take me long." I retrieve Bowman's quiver, my hand closing over an arrow as I slip his bow off my shoulder. The heaviness in my chest grows, and it's all I can do to keep my rage in check.

Losing my head will do me no good now, so I take a deep breath and then head for the trees.

∼

THE FIRE CRACKLES between us as night blankets the sky in

bright stars. We eat the rabbit I killed in silence, neither of us having spoken since my return with the wood.

Carleah's expression is hard, her emotions masked. She's treating me differently than before, though I expected as much when she realized that my lack of speech all these years was by choice, not hindrance.

I've grown used to catching her lingering gaze on me, but now I imagine I'll be lucky if she sees me as an ally when all this is over.

"When we reach Miserico tomorrow, we can try to get on one of their supply ships. That way, we avoid Nemoregno and No Man's Land."

"You do not think the crimson soldiers have taken that village, too?"

"I don't know," I reply honestly. "It is entirely possible."

"Then is it wise to go there at all? Should we not just press on?"

"We don't have the supplies to do so," I tell her. "Aside from Bowman's bow, I have no weapons. We won't survive Nemoregno." The very thought of stepping foot in that place makes my heart race and my palms sweat.

I know better than most what resides beyond the Phantom.

"And if the soldiers have overrun Miscerico? If they've slaughtered everyone as they did our city?" Tears stream down her face, but she angrily wipes them away.

"Then I will go in and steal what we need just as I did before we left the city."

She doesn't respond and still doesn't look in my direction. Carleah just continues to stare into the flickering flames as if they alone hold the answer to our survival.

Until finally, she turns toward me, those bright blue eyes narrowed on my face. "Why did you never speak to me? Did the others know? Did they keep that from me, too?"

My chest tightens.

"Unless it was my entire family that you lied to," she snaps. "Was it all of us? Or was it just me you fooled?"

I stare back at her. "When your family found me, I'd been so exhausted that speaking was not an option. They'd asked me countless questions, and I physically couldn't respond." I swallow hard, the memory of the terrified young boy I'd been surfacing. "The questions stopped rather quickly, and I was able to move forward without being expected to answer. So, I clung to that. And vowed never to speak again so that I could live my life free of where I came from."

"Why was answering their questions so horrific?"

Because the truth would have gotten me killed. "I didn't answer them then, and I have no plan on answering you now, Princess. The past is just that—the past. We have enough risk to our present to speak of such things."

"You're afraid then?"

"Excuse me?'

She clears her throat. "In my experience, men will refuse to speak for two reasons. Either they are protecting someone else, or they are protecting themselves. I cannot imagine that you would have remained quiet and stayed with us for so long if you'd been protecting someone else. Which leaves fear for yourself."

Or both. "I am not afraid. I just have no interest in reliving a past that no longer affects the man I am."

She laughs, but there is no humor in it. "Our pasts mold us, Fort. To pretend otherwise is naïve."

"You believe we are our pasts then? That we cannot be more? Because, in that case, you are little more than a princess who has lived high above the rest of the world, tucked safely in her tower."

Her gaze turns molten, and that heat spurs my own. "I didn't say that we *are* our pasts, you ass. I said we are shaped by them. We get to choose where we're going, but that destination is *always* going to have something to do with where we've been."

I can still taste her on my tongue, feel the way her body molded to mine when I pressed her against my mattress. And the very fact that I am thinking like this now makes me a bigger bastard than I ever thought I was.

"Ass?" I arch a brow. "You've been on the road less than two days, and you're already speaking like a soldier." My words are meant to bring humor to our bleak situation, but she does not smile. Instead, she turns her gaze back to the fire.

"Why talk to me now, then? If you are so against answering anything about your past."

My answer is an easy one. It shouldn't be, I should have considered the consequences. "Your life was in danger. I had already failed your parents and brothers. I could not fail you, too."

A tear slips down her cheek as she pushes her rabbit aside. "Will you tell me what happened to Alex?"

My chest constricts. "You do not need to know."

She clenches her hands into fists in her lap. "Everyone tries to shield me, to protect the gentle-natured princess, but am I protected now?" she demands, throwing her arms out to the sides. Her blanket falls, revealing skin bared from where the dress dips too far in front. My mouth dries.

It shouldn't.

It's wrong to be attracted to her—especially in this moment—but her beauty is so much more than surface. It *radiates* from her.

I really am a bastard. I swallow hard. The truth is I never agreed with keeping her in the dark. When it comes to someone's security, I believe they deserve to know when their life is in danger. And her life has been in danger more times than I can count over the last nineteen years. Since the moment she drew her first breath, enemies have been coming for the first-born daughter of Navalis.

Enemies that have been far closer than she will ever know.

"Our scout discovered the army on their usual patrol. We'd believed we had the upper hand, but as it turns out, our enemy had spotted him, too."

"How long ago?"

"A month."

"A *month?*" she chokes out.

"We sent scouts ahead, had them keep an eye on the army while we sent word to Soreno just in case. Before we got word back, the army moved closer."

I look over at Carleah, who is watching me intently. Alex may have given her a partial story, but he'd left a vast majority of it out.

"For two weeks, they sent a handful of men toward our borders. We managed to head them off, offering them their freedom in return for an oath that they would never return to our city."

"You offered them freedom because of the code."

Her tone is irritated at best. "Your brother lived by that code," I remind her.

"And he died by it," she retorts.

She's absolutely right, and her words mirror my own thoughts. Yet more guilt crushes down on me. If I'd spoken to Alex sooner, if I'd vocalized my concerns, would it have saved him?

"One of their men managed to sneak through undetected. We didn't find him until—" I take a deep breath and recall the day I followed Carleah and Genevieve to town. I'd had to stay out of sight per her father's orders, but I was there. Watching as they strolled out of a shop, laughing and carrying a bag of wares they'd purchased.

I'd been so taken by her beauty, by the sheer radiance of her joy, that I almost missed him lurking in the shadows, his gaze also on Carleah.

"He got close to what mattered, so I killed him—after I tried to extract what information I could."

"Extract? You tortured him?"

I know what answer she's searching to unearth. "I broke the code," I reply. "And it is that death that sparked their retaliation. I am the reason Alex was killed. Because, in their eyes, I struck first."

Her gaze does not turn accusatory, though I can see her processing the information. Putting the pieces together, just as I have. "How did they know you'd tortured him?"

"Where there is one roach," I say, "there are always others. One simply needs to know where to shine the torch. I was so focused on protecting what mattered that I didn't bother to look for more roaches."

The guilt that has crushed me since Alex was killed feels even heavier looking at the pain in her eyes. "Do you believe that they would not have attacked if you hadn't tortured that man?"

"No. One day, they would have gotten through. It was merely a matter of time."

"Because they wanted me." She shakes her head. "The man who killed my father told me that I 'belonged to *them* now'," she says. "Whoever *them* is, I can assume the Tenebris were either sent there to retrieve me or were paid because they were already on their way."

Carleah has *always* been far more intelligent than anyone ever gave her credit for. Perhaps I saw it because I was busy listening, paying attention rather than trying to speak or direct.

Truthfully, it's one of the very reasons I forced my distance over the last few years. Because she is far more beautiful than she should be to a man like me. A man with no family, no home, and no future aside from serving the crown of Navalis.

"Did your parents never tell you of the true reason for your betrothal?"

"Yes. Because they were looking to form an alliance with Soreno."

"That is true," I say hesitantly. "But it is more than that. You are the first daughter to the crown, and there are those who believe taking you will grant them all of Navalis. Men have been after you since you were born, Carleah."

"What?" she chokes the word out, horrified by the meaning.

"You were a treasure to be had, and with every other attack, abduction—we were able to fend them off. To protect you. Your parents were sending you to Soreno—to our allies—because it was the only way anyone saw you being able to survive."

Her horrified expression contorts with rage. "Why the hell did no one tell me this?"

"They did not wish to scare you."

"No, but they could all stomach selling me off! Tell me, what did Patrick's family bargain in exchange for my hand?"

"They offered you protection."

"In exchange for what, exactly?"

"Your hand," I repeat. "They wished for their son to marry you and agreed to be your shield against those hunting you."

She crosses her arms and shakes her head. "I very much doubt that was all."

"That is all I know, Carleah, I swear it."

"And how am I to believe you? How am I to know you are not lying—or leaving things out to 'protect me'?"

"Because I never agreed with their silence. I believed you should have been made aware of the danger to your life."

"Yes, and if only you'd been able to speak on my behalf and make your opinions known," she sneers. "Or, better yet, tell me yourself."

"I nearly did." When she doesn't respond, I continue, "Do you remember the night of your eighteenth birthday? The party when you'd snuck outside?"

Her gaze widens just slightly. "When you'd come from the trees?"

"To rip that son of a bitch off of you? Yes."

Her brow furrows. "I remember."

"They'd had a carriage waiting to steal you away, and you nearly walked right the fuck into it."

"No. I asked him to go outside."

Jealousy fumes inside of me even though it has no place. "You may have asked, Princess, but I assure you; he had every intention of taking you away and no one would have been any the wiser as to where you had gone."

"How do you know that?"

"Because he told me. Right before I cut his fucking throat," I snap. I wait for the horror on her face, for the disgust that the body count I'm confessing to is beginning to get larger, but I see none.

"I went outside with a man who was planning to kidnap me? And they *still* didn't think it was important to tell me my life was in danger?"

"They assigned you a silent guardian. One you wouldn't see lurking in the shadows," I tell her. "Just in case."

"And who was that?"

"Me."

Now her glare turns icy. "You've been following me around since I was eighteen?"

"Only when you went to town," I tell her. "Or when your family hosted events. When it would have been easy for you to sneak off or for someone to grab you, I was there."

"You've been following me," she repeats then shakes her head. "Unbelievable. So they thought I was in so much danger I needed the head of their guard stalking my every move, but not enough to actually tell me anything."

"Had you not been sneaking around with strange men, it wouldn't have been an issue." The words are out of my mouth before I can stop them.

"I deserved to live, Fort. And since no one else was helping me do it, I had to take matters into my own hands."

It's a dig at me. I feel it in her tone, see it in her eyes. "By letting strange men accost you in the woods? Smart."

She grins, but there is no humor in it. "I never thought you a prude."

"I'm not." In fact, had someone not slammed a door when she'd been in my room, ripping me from my lustful stupor, I would have buried myself in her before the night was over. Of that, I am sure.

"Hmm." She turns her attention back to the fire. "Tell me what happened to my brother. I want to know everything."

Denying her the truth will do nearly as much harm as telling her will. So, I opt for the latter. Especially since it will also change the subject. "We received word from their messenger that they were willing to meet per the code. When we showed up, they surrounded us. Our men were cut down before they ever had the chance to draw a sword. Your brother and I fought our way out of the circle, but we were both injured. Him more than me."

A tear slips from her eye, but I continue anyway. If she wants the truth, she will get it. The ugly, raw, unhindered truth. I'm already in far enough as it is.

"He'd been run through with a blade, but I managed to get him away from the fighting. We were halfway back to Navalis when he bled out."

She whimpers. "He suffered?"

"He did. But the chill numbed the pain after a while, and he no longer hurt by the time he drew his last breath."

"I told him not to go," she whispers. "I told him I'd had a bad feeling."

Alex's mumblings as I'd carried him begin to make

sense. "He told me that he'd vowed to return home. That he needed to get back to fulfill his promise. So even though he didn't survive, I made sure he made it back."

She chokes on a sob. "And you carried him home."

"I did."

"How? When you were injured? How did you manage to make it back?"

Since telling her the truth will only lead to more questions, I lie. "Adrenaline, I'm sure."

"Adrenaline," she repeats then covers her mouth with a shaking hand.

Unable to stand her pain, I get to my feet and cross over to kneel at her side. "I am so sorry that I couldn't protect him. That I couldn't protect any of them."

With her knees drawn up and her face buried in the blanket, I cannot see her expression. "It is not your fault," she whispers as she finally lifts it so I can see her. Red, tear-stained cheeks, swollen eyes—fuck, what I wouldn't kill to see her smile. "Even with what you did, they would have attacked. At least, Alex was saved the pain of knowing what became of the rest of our family."

I hate that she must cling to that peace. That Alex already being in the ground when the rest of her family cut down is what brings her a sliver of comfort.

"Thank you for saving me," she says. "But the lies—"

My chest tightens like a fist around my heart. *If only she knew.* "Going forward, I will never lie to you again."

She doesn't respond right away. "So we make it to Miserico, what then?"

"We gather supplies and hopefully get on a ship."

"To Soreno."

"Yes."

"Then, what, you leave me to my fate of marriage and hope they allow you to join their guard?"

"Is that what you want?" I ask.

"Does it matter?"

"To me, it does," I reply. "I am not your father, Carleah. And I will never force you to do something you do not wish."

Her gaze holds mine, something passing between us that feels oddly like a connection. "No. It is not what I want."

"Then what do you want?"

Her gaze hardens, her hands clenching into fists. "I want what I made you promise. I want to take back my home and get vengeance for my people."

Even as I knew that would be her answer, the worry it brings is suffocating. Though, I certainly cannot blame her. After all, it's what I would want. What every single one of her brothers would have chosen in her stead. "Then we need an army. And the only place we get that is—"

"Soreno."

"Yes." I hate the idea of seeing that prince put his hands anywhere near her, but if it is vengeance she seeks, he is the one who can help her get that. Marrying him will ensure her kingdom's survival.

Her eyes widen. "But—they're on their way to Navalis now. What if they get there and are ambushed!"

"Our guards raised the crimson flag," I tell her. "It's a

warning to all ships coming in that we are in danger and they need to re-route. As long as the Tenebris didn't lower it before they saw, your betrothed will be fine." The words are meant to be assuring, but all they do is twist in my gut. The man she is going to marry might be a prince and a future king, but he's spineless. A fucking coward.

There's no way he will ever be able to protect her. Not like I can. But then I remind myself that, while I might be a shield, I am also only one blade. Patrick has an army behind him. The safest place for her is behind his high stone walls.

"It has nothing to do with him being my betrothed," she replies. "And everything to do with the fact that you're right. If we're to take Navalis back, we need his army."

"Who will rule Navalis then? Patrick?"

She pins me with an icy glare. "No. Only a Rossingol will sit on the throne."

"And you believe your husband will allow you to rule separately?"

"I do not intend to marry him, Fort. I am going to simply ask for his help."

The idea has no merit. "That man will not raise a finger to help. Especially if you break the engagement. That was a promise between your father and his."

"Well, my father is dead. As is his promise. I *will* rule my kingdom, Fort. And you can either help me take it back or let me go alone."

I reach out and touch a finger to the bottom of her

chin so I can raise her face and look into her eyes once more. Her skin is smooth beneath the tip of my finger, and I long to feel more of it. To taste her again.

But she is not for me.

Still, I will not leave her side until the moment I draw my last breath. "I will die to protect you, Your Highness. My sword is yours." I bow my head. "Queen Carleah of Navalis."

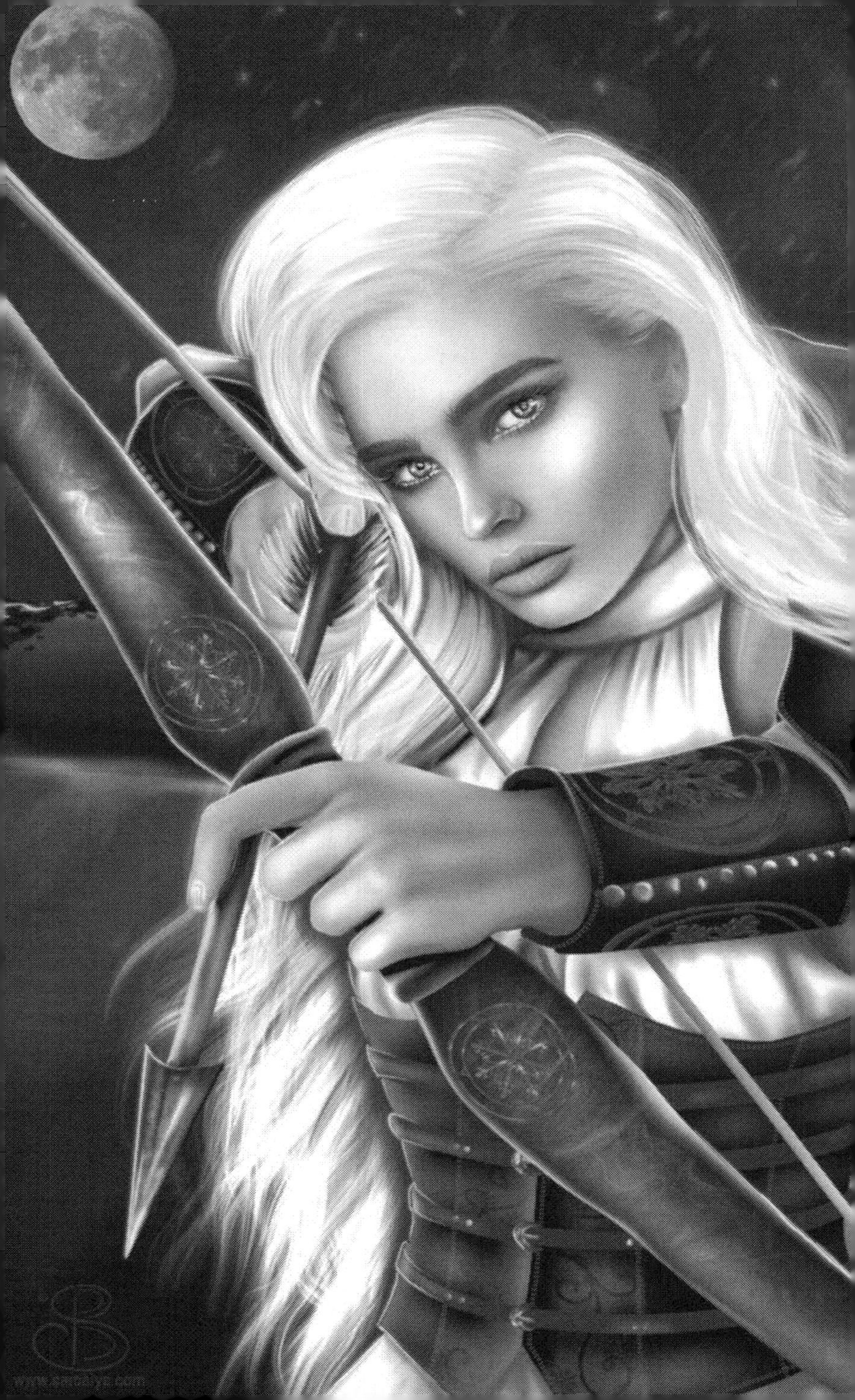

CHAPTER 9
CARLEAH

Queen *Carleah of Navalis.*

The words fill me with unease. Never, in a million moons, did I believe I would be taking the throne. Truthfully, I never wanted it. Because the crown falling to me means my entire family is gone.

Stolen from me in the dead of night by Tenebris soldiers.

My throat constricts, but I refuse to shed any more tears.

Not until I am able to walk back into my home, using the bodies of dead Tenebris soldiers as stepping stones.

My family had been my entire world, their presence filling every moment of my days. I've never known anything else. Yet, with all of Fort's confessions, I have to wonder if I ever knew them at all.

My entire life they'd lied to me. Kept things from me.

Grief wells in my chest, a constant ache, as Fort withdraws his hand and sits beside me. He offers me the partially eaten rabbit.

"You must eat," he says. "We need our strength."

I take a bite, but it's flavorless on my tongue. Fort's declaration about Soreno runs through my mind. What am I supposed to do if I cannot count on our greatest ally to stand at my side?

Navalis has gone to the aid of Soreno at least half a dozen times since I was born and even more before that. Will they truly turn their backs on us in our time of need simply because I will not marry their son?

I finish eating what I can then set the rabbit aside. Fort takes it and stands. "I'm going to take this into the trees and bury it. So we don't attract wild animals. Are you okay for a few minutes?"

"I think I'll manage," I deadpan. Irritation laces my tone because I'm damned tired of being treated like I cannot take care of myself.

"I didn't mean anything by it."

"Sure you didn't. Go. I'll be fine."

He hesitates a moment but clearly thinks better of continuing the conversation because, seconds later, he disappears into the tree line.

I stare into the flames, taking in the sight of them dancing before me. A shiver runs through me, the bite of cold steadily nibbling away at the exposed flesh of my face and neck.

No matter how hard I try to burrow down, it still reaches me.

I have only been camping once in my life.

Bowman took me when I'd been thirteen. We'd snuck out and into the trees just beyond the castle. That was the same night he taught me to track and dress a rabbit. It is honestly one of my best memories.

But even though I know I'm not alone, it feels so damned lonely being here without him. Without all of them.

A branch crunches, and I whirl as Fort steps out into the firelight. He looks so battered, so beaten, yet he's still the strongest person I've ever met. I should be angry with him for lying about his ability to speak. But I cannot muster up the strength.

Because, in the grand scheme of things, it doesn't matter.

In one single night, my carefully woven reality was ripped away from me, leaving behind ashen ruins and a heart of broken glass. Casting out the only person I feel like I can count on would be foolish.

"Are you cold?" he asks.

His question makes me realize I am trembling. "I'll be fine."

Fort's expression shifts to concern, and he stares at me for a moment before crossing over. "That blanket is large enough to lay on the ground and fold over the top of us."

"Of us?"

He nods. "If you would allow me to warm you with my body heat, too, I believe we can keep the cold at bay until we find proper lodging."

I swallow hard. For years, I wanted to lie close to

Fort. Wanted to feel his broad chest pressed against me, and now that it's happening, I feel horrible. Guilty. Because in this ocean of grief, him being near gives me hope that I won't always feel so destroyed.

"It's all right if you are not comfortable, I can—"

"No, I'm fine. Please." I stand so we can smooth out the blanket.

The chill hits me instantly, and I shiver, my nipples pebbling to tight peaks beneath the coat and oversized dress I wear. I wrap both arms around myself and do my best not to fall over from sheer exhaustion as he moves the blanket closer to the fire then lies down on it and raises an arm for me.

My gaze holds his as I sink to the fur beside him, rolling to my side and scooting back so my back is to his chest. He's a solid warmth behind me, a muscled mass that I've seen honed to absolute perfection.

His arm bands around my waist, and he pulls me to him then throws the other half of the blanket over us. Fort's breath is hot on my neck, his arm heavy as he tightens it and pulls me closer.

Within a few minutes of silence, the cold has mostly subsided, leaving my body toasty warm even if my face still stings from the chill.

"Better?" he asks.

His hot breath whispers against my skin. "Yes."

"Get some sleep. I will keep watch."

"You need sleep, too."

"Do not worry about me, Your Highness. I am quite adept at missing sleep."

I roll over and bury my face in his chest. I breathe him in, the now-faded scent of eucalyptus filling my lungs as I do. "Wake me in a few hours so you can get some sleep. You're the one who was running all damned day."

Fort chuckles. "Yes, Your Highness."

"Please don't call me that."

"Why not?"

"Because I am more than a title," I say as I pull back to look into his eyes. We're a mere whisper apart. From here, I can make out flecks of green in the amber of his eyes, a gorgeous combination that momentarily stuns me.

"I know you are more than a title," he replies. "But I am your guard, and as such, there is a level of respect I must pay to you."

"That's not respect," I reply. "It's duty. And you owe me nothing." I want to bring up the kiss. To bring up the heat between us back then and point out that respect was the last thing on both our minds when his hands had been on my body, but I don't.

"I owe your father everything," he tells me.

"In case you can't tell? I'm not my father." I lay my head down and close my eyes.

"I assure you, Carleah, I *know* you're not your father."

Moments tick by in silence as we lie in the fading light of our fire. An owl hoots in the distance, though I hear no other signs of life—animal or insect alike. It's eerily quiet. Shouldn't it be louder out here?

"I was so horrible to them," I whisper.

"What?"

Again, I pull back enough to look up at him. "I was angry that they'd kept things from me. So, instead of celebrating my brother's life with them after the funeral, I mourned his death alone in my room."

"Carleah." He reaches up and runs a finger over my cheek. "They understood."

"Perhaps. But it doesn't erase the horrible things I said to my father, nor does it make up for the fact that I argued with him. And now—" I trail off, swallowing down my grief. "Now they're gone, and I'll never get to see them again."

Fort moves in closer. "If it's any consolation, they were not angry."

"You were there?"

"I was," he replies. "And they all understood why you wanted to be alone. Bowman actually told your parents that it was well past time they filled you in on everything. He told your parents that he was going with you to Soreno, to watch over you in your new marriage."

His words bring me a strange relief, as if some of the guilt I carry is lessened. "He did?"

Fort nods. "Your mother wasn't too happy about it, but your father agreed."

"He told me he was going to ask. That it was his way of seeing a world beyond Navalis. But after Alex died—"

"Bowman refused the throne, said that Ethan was better for it."

The ghost of a smile passes over my lips. "I imagine my mother loved that."

Fort chuckles. "She was not overly thrilled, but your father agreed that, if Bowman chose not to sit on the throne, then Ethan could take it."

"I'm glad he died believing his dream was coming true. And I know how twisted that sounds."

"Not twisted," Fort replies. "Your family loved you, Carleah."

"I know they did," I reply, my throat raw.

Silence consumes us once more, giving me time to imagine that I am lying in my bed, surrounded by all those I love.

Wrapped in these furs, I focus on the happy memories with my family, and not on the secrets they kept from me.

I focus on nights spent around the dinner table.

On mornings drinking tea and watching the sun rise.

And I think of my mother, and how she always smelled of floral blossoms.

And my father, whose laugh could bring joy to even the most dire of situations.

I begin to drift away on those memories, letting them guide me to a peaceful rest, and in the distance, I swear I hear the humming of a lullaby. Slow and sweet, familiar and warm.

∼

WHEN I WAKE, there is nobody pressed against me. I sit up and rub my eyes, clinging to the blanket. My head throbs, and every muscle in my body aches from exertion. Never would I have considered my body soft, but two days of moving constantly is a stark reminder of just how void of physical activity my life was.

Fort has his back to me as he works with something, the fire still burning in front of him.

"Are you okay?" My throat is raw, my chest tight, but today, the grief is a little lighter.

He turns to me, his gaze narrowing on my face. In the depths of his eyes, I see pity, and I know I must look horrible. "I'm fine." He turns toward me, holding an arrow in one hand and a piece of our fur blanket in the other.

"What is that?"

"Makeshift shoes," he says as he holds up another.

"I have shoes."

"They are not fit for the weather. You were shivering all night."

"I'm sorry—"

"You don't need to apologize," he replies as he kneels beside me.

I stare at the small fur booties tied together with leather laces I know he must have pulled from his tunic. "You made me more shoes?"

"The blanket was plenty big enough, and your feet were frozen. Besides, they're just to cover the ones you already wear, for more warmth. May I?" he asks, gesturing to the blanket.

"Sure."

He lifts the blanket from my feet, and the cold air hits my exposed warm skin with a sting.

Fort works quickly, slipping the fur around my boot and securing it with the laces. By the time he's done, both of my boots are covered and protected from the chill. Pieces of tree bark are secured to the soles, on the outside of the fur, to keep my makeshift shoe coverings dry. "This should help keep your feet warm until we can get you better boots."

"Thank you." I look up at him, and our gazes hold.

Fort nods. "We should get going."

Fort looks away first and stands. He turns to the fire and kicks the snow over the top. It hisses and sizzles, turning to smoke that disappears on a light breeze.

I get to my feet and grab the blanket then wrap it around my shoulders.

Fort is watching me carefully when I meet his gaze again. "Can I carry you?"

"I can walk," I insist.

"I know, but we can move faster if I carry you," he explains. "And right now, speed is our friend."

I purse my lips. "You're going to exhaust yourself."

"You clearly have no idea how we trained," he interrupts. "I am going to have you climb on my back, though —if you think you can hold the blanket over us?"

"I can do that."

"Great." He reaches down to the snow and grabs something. When he straightens again, he offers me a handful of winterberries.

The crimson orbs are about the size of the tip of my finger, so I am able to eat them quickly. The fruit is a delicate mixture of tart and sweet, and the flavor brings fond memories of afternoons spent making jam in the kitchen with Genevieve.

"Thank you," I say as soon as I've swallowed them.

"You're welcome." He stands and retrieves Bowman's bow and quiver. After hanging them on a low branch, he kneels in front of me. "Your chariot awaits, Carleah."

With the ghost of a smile, I grip the blanket and wrap both arms around his neck. He stands with far more ease than should be possible, given the weight of me on his back. Then, he retrieves the bow and quiver, holding them in front of him as he begins walking.

"Are you feeling better this morning?" he asks, his breath coming out in a puff of air.

"I ache," I tell him.

"As would be expected. The bruise on your face is looking particularly painful."

"My face?" And then I remember the soldier's hand cracking across my cheek. "Oh. I suppose I'd forgotten."

"Can you not feel it?"

"My head hurts," I admit.

"I wish I could bring him back to life so I could kill him again," Fort growls. The sound of it vibrates through his back and into my chest. "I wish I could slay all of them for you."

"They will get what is coming to them," I say. "One way or another."

Minutes tick by in silence as Fort carries me. No matter how far we walk, he remains steady in his movements, never faltering despite the fact that he's carrying me.

"Are your feet warm?" he asks.

"Warmer than they were yesterday," I reply. "Thank you."

"It is my job to care for you," he says.

More obligation, then.

"Regardless, I appreciate your kindness."

Fort falls silent, so I rest my cheek against his back and close my eyes. The scents of the forest surround me, reminding me of the way my father always carried a piece of the kingdom with him. Will it be the same for me when we reach the border and leave Navalis behind?

∼

"We need to seek shelter before nightfall, and we cannot risk a fire this close to Miserico. Not until we know whether or not the Tenebris are there as well."

He walks through the snow until I hear the rustle of water traveling over stone. We emerge from the trees, and he stops near a spring. After setting me carefully down near the water's edge, Fort kneels and cups the water with his hand before putting it to his lips. I watch his throat bob as he swallows it, enjoying the sharpness of his jaw in the dimming light.

Seconds tick by before he looks over at me. "It's fine to drink."

I shake my head to clear it. "You were tasting it for safety?"

"It could be tainted."

"Then you shouldn't be drinking it." I kneel beside

him, dipping my hands in the freezing water. After putting it to my lips, I draw the cool water into my mouth, savoring the satisfaction it brings me. Then, I dry my hand on the outside of the fur and sit back on the ground. "Your life is no less important than mine."

"I beg to differ," he replies.

"You're wrong."

A muscle in his jaw tightens, but he doesn't argue further. Good. Because he wouldn't win, anyway.

"We need to find somewhere to sleep. Somewhere well off the road. This close to the edge of the kingdom, there tend to be bandits."

"Bandits?" I nearly choke on the word as my gaze travels the tree line. I've heard of them, of Alex and the others being dispatched to deal with the occasional issue, but with the other threats—the Tenebris and freezing to death being at the top of my mind—I completely forgot.

Fort nods. "The world is vastly different out here," he explains as he turns his back to me. "Climb on."

I do as he instructs, keeping the blanket firmly in my hand and wrapping both arms around his neck. He carries the bow and quiver while I cling to his back, and we head toward a large mountain range just ahead. There, the stream disappears into the stone. Fort sets me down near the edge of the grey rock then palms an arrow and hands me the bow and quiver.

Instinctively, I withdraw an arrow and ready it as he creeps toward the small cavern—and disappears into the darkness.

I wait, heart in my throat, until he moves back out. "We'll sleep in there tonight."

Honestly, I'm relieved to not be out in the elements. Being shielded from view is a pretty damned good thing, too.

Fort opens his fur coat then grips the bottom of his tunic and tears, shredding the lower half of the fabric from his body—enough to reveal a slim strip of tanned flesh and hard muscle.

Warmth churns in my belly, so I force my gaze to his face as he scans the ground then retrieves a stick from atop the snow. He wraps the top of the stick in fabric then drives the base into the snow and reaches into his pocket for flint.

After rubbing both pieces together, sparks hit the fabric, and it begins to smolder. He blows softly, igniting flames on the newly crafted torch. "Ready?" he asks.

"As I'll ever be," I reply, though I continue clinging to the bow even as I follow him into the darkness.

We have to stoop through the entrance, him far more than me, but once inside, there's enough room for us to build a fire and still rest comfortably. Still, I barely liked being trapped in the castle whenever the storms had been too strong to venture out. So this feels far more confining than I care for. But I don't complain because it's a hell of a lot better than the alternative.

"You're sure this is safe?" I ask, studying the cavern space.

"The dirt is not disturbed, which means it is not an animal's home. I can gather some berries for dinner, but once night falls, we will have to ensure the torch is fully put out so we don't draw attention to ourselves."

"Okay."

"It's better than being out there," he replies. "We're tucked away."

"Except if they find us, we're trapped," I counter as I try to concoct an exit strategy should we be discovered. Unfortunately, there is none. We're just going to have to hope that luck is on our side.

Fort reaches out and grips my arm. "They are less likely to stumble on us in here than if we were to make camp out there. I'm going to go retrieve some berries then brush our tracks away from the entrance. If the torch burns out before I get back, do not panic."

"I won't," I reply. "I'm not afraid of the dark." Though the idea of him not coming back, of me truly being the last person standing, is gut-wrenching.

"Carleah," Fort says softly. I look up into his eyes. "I will return."

Alex's similar vow assaults me out of nowhere, and my eyes sting, but I look away so Fort cannot see.

"Carleah—"

"Go," I say. "I'll be fine."

He doesn't say anything else, just hands me an arrow then takes the bow and quiver with him as he crouches down and leaves the cavern.

Holding the arrow tightly in my hand, I stare at the torch, willing it to burn slower. With no oil on it, though, the fabric-wrapped wood will not last nearly as long. Minutes longer, if I had to guess.

I may not be afraid of the dark, but being left alone is apparently a new fear of mine.

The light at the entrance of the cavern fades with each passing moment, so I distract myself by spreading the blanket out on the far end of the cavern. That way we'll hear bootsteps before they manage to see us.

Even the smallest advantage could mean our survival.

The torch continues to burn until it fades to a soft ember, and then—

Bootsteps just outside the cavern have me planting my back to the far side where I'm just out of view, even though I know it's likely Fort. Still, when he rounds the corner and I see his face, relief floods me. I relax back against the cavern wall as he clears his throat and sets the berries down in front of me.

"Dusk is beginning to fall," he says. "We should make sure we're settled by then."

"I got the blanket set up," I say.

"Good. You put us out of direct sight of the entrance."

"Not just a foolish princess," I retort.

"I never thought you were," he replies as he sits down on it first.

I take a seat beside him and take the berries he offers.

We eat in silence in the flickering embers of our dying torch. And when it burns down to nothing, Fort shuffles around so he's lying on his side. I do the same, pressing back against him until I can feel his body against mine.

Because I'm between him and the cavern, I pull the blanket up over us.

"Are you all right?" he whispers against my neck.

"Fine. Why?"

"You aren't speaking."

"And that means I am not all right?" I ask. "You went years without speaking, and did I constantly ask you if you were okay?"

He chuckles. "No, I supposed you didn't. Then again, silence was normal for me. It is quite the opposite for you."

"You speak as though you know me," I say as the shadows from the dim light outside fade completely away, casting us in pure darkness.

"Carleah, in some ways, I know you better than I know myself."

"Why? Because you followed me around without my knowledge?"

He's quiet for a moment. "Yes."

"Observing someone doesn't mean you know them," I retort. "For example, I observed you for years, and I still know nothing about you." It's my way of trying to get him to open up, a non-invasive way of asking for more, but he doesn't bite.

Instead, he wraps an arm around me and whispers, "Goodnight, Carleah."

I wake to a hand over my mouth.

I squirm, fighting against the hold. Did they find us? How did they—"Easy," Fort whispers. "It's just me."

I still, and he pulls me up, tucking my body behind his. Panic abated—for now—I can hear the muffled sounds of voices just outside our cavern. The faint sound of him nocking an arrow fills my ears.

After a few, silent, heart-pounding moments, the voices quiet. Fort scoots to my side, leaning back against the cavern wall with me.

"I'm sorry I woke you," he whispers. "But I didn't want you to wake up and make noise while they were outside."

"It's okay," I whisper. "Are they gone?"

"I'm not sure. I will remain awake until morning, you try and get some sleep."

But my heart is racing far too quickly for rest, so I sit in the dark, my head leaning back against the cool stone, and wait for the sun to rise.

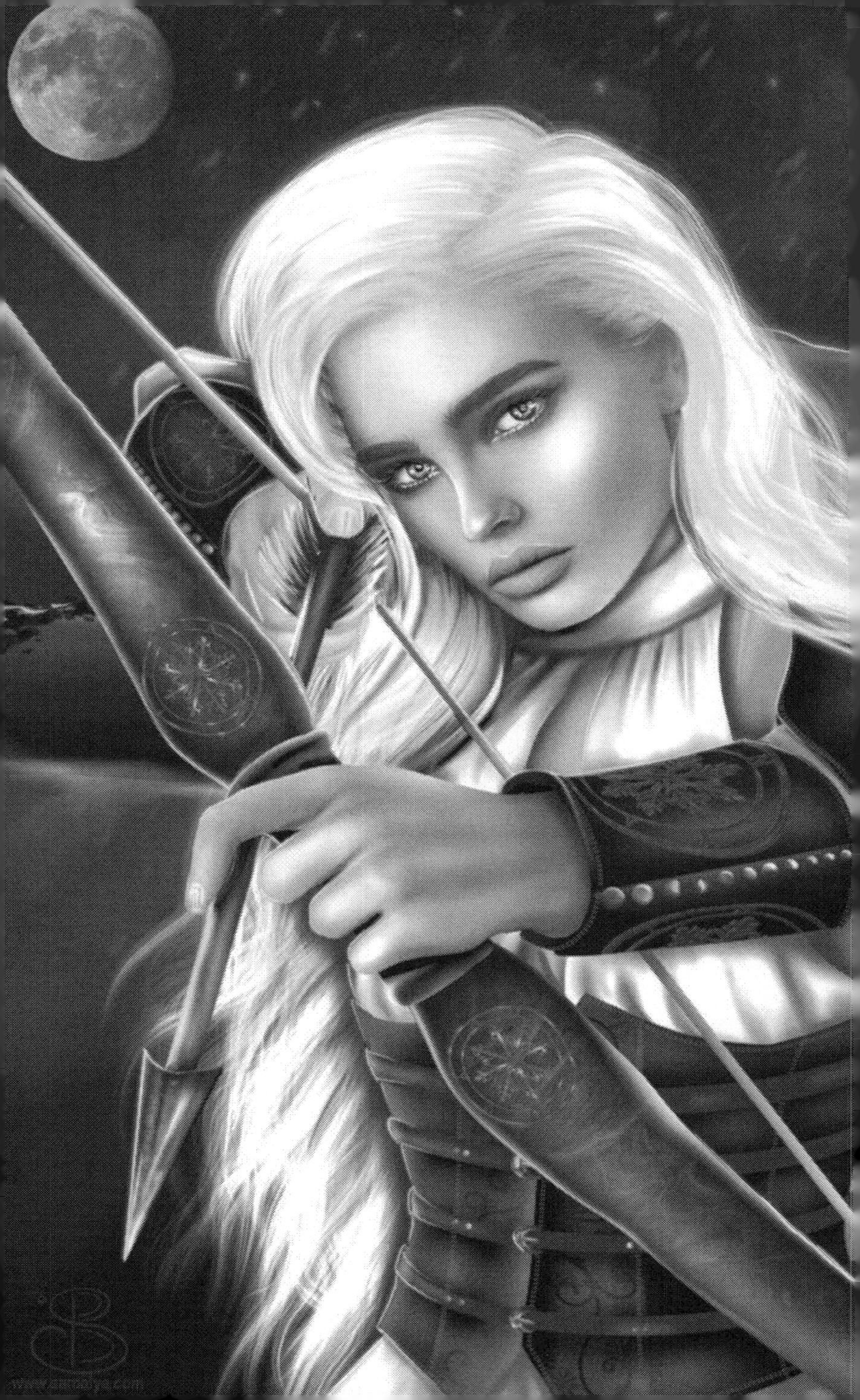

CHAPTER 10
CARLEAH

I've never seen any of the villages in our kingdom, aside from the city that resided just outside our castle. So, while I'm not entirely sure what to expect of Miscerico, I was not prepared for the normalcy before me.

The village is bustling with activity, with shops wide open and men, women, and children strolling through the street as though they haven't a care in the world. It's a twisted type of relief to know that the world has carried on for so many others while hundreds of lives were lost less than two days ago.

Snow falls down on top of us, heavy flakes that stick to my eyelashes and onto the fur of the blanket wrapped around my shoulders. Fort kneels beside me, one hand wrapped around the hilt of his short blade, the other bracing on the ground as he studies the scene before us, likely seeking anything that feels odd.

"I see no crimson armor," he says.

"There are a lot of people out and about," I add. "They do not look afraid."

"No," he agrees then straightens, so I do the same. His gaze narrows on me, and he chews on his bottom lip as his eyes flick up to my hair. "We need to hide your hair."

"What?"

"You will be spotted instantly. We need to keep that from happening. At least until we're absolutely sure the village is not compromised"

"I can keep the blanket over me."

"Not good enough." He looks around, studying our surroundings, then turns back to me. "Do you still wear your nightgown? Beneath the dress."

"Yes."

Fort kneels at my feet. "May I tear some of it away? We can wrap your hair in it."

When I don't answer right away, he smiles. "Or I can pull some mud from the creek bed."

I drop the blanket and grab the skirts of the dress so he can easily access the nightgown beneath it. The bite of the cold air against my bare ankles is uncomfortable, but it's a hell of a lot better than mud smeared in my hair.

Fort withdraws his blade then slides one hand up the inside of the skirt. The backs of his knuckles graze against my skin, and I fight the urge to lean into his touch. I've grown to crave it these last few days, as though, if he's touching me, then not all is lost.

He makes quick work of slicing part of my nightgown off then pulls my skirts back into place and stands. I turn my back toward him, and he uses the cloth to tie over the top of my hair. The rest he pushes down beneath my coat and pulls the hood up over the top.

Then, he moves around in front of me. "Shit, hang on." Fort steps in closer and slides his fingers over my forehead, shoving strands of white hair beneath the fabric as he goes.

I close my eyes, hating myself for being so enamored by the contact, even as I hope he never stops touching me.

Fort steps back. "You look—almost normal."

"What a compliment," I shoot back as I reach down and pull the blanket up over my shoulders.

Fort doesn't respond though the corners of his lips twitch. He tugs the hood further back into place. "You ready?"

"For fresh clothing and a warm bed? Absolutely."

He sheathes his blade, but keeps his hand resting on the hilt as we make our way out of the tree line and down the slope toward a large wooden gate ahead. It's wide open, allowing people to come and go as they please.

As we walk, I keep my gaze on the trees, watching for any crimson. But I see nothing. In fact, as we move past the gate, I sense nothing but genuine joy coming from the occupants.

Which both relieves and angers me.

How can they be so at peace when their king is dead? Their queen?

"They likely do not know," Fort says softly.

"Know what?"

"About what happened... If no one escaped, no word would have reached here."

It eases some of that anger, but not the ache.

A man wearing green trousers and a yellow coat steps from the stables and crosses toward us. He holds up a hand, so Fort stops. "Hello, travelers!" he says. "Can I help you?" His kind smile is complimented by soft, grey eyes that I get the feeling miss absolutely nothing.

"We need lodging. And to speak with your representative."

The man smiles at me, so I return it. "My wife is who you are looking for. She runs an inn above the tavern and is the king's representative for our village."

Fort dips his head in a nod. "Thank you."

"Absolutely. Have you traveled on foot then? No horses to see to?"

"I'm afraid not," Fort replies. "Bandits got us last night." He lies so smoothly, so easily, that the man's expression contorts to anger on our behalf.

"Damned bandits. We try our best to keep them away from the village, but they get people every now and then. I'm sorry you fell victim."

"Thank you." Fort takes my hand and pulls me toward the tavern.

"Thank you!" I call out.

"You're most welcome, my lady!"

"They don't know," I whisper to Fort.

"They will after today," Fort replies. "They're lucky we got here first. We can convince them to leave."

"You're going to get these people to leave their homes?"

"It's that, or they die," he replies, then stops walking and turns to face me. "You did not see them that night, Carleah. They slaughtered without mercy. Men, women, children—" He shudders. "I've seen a lot of bloodshed in my life. But never men who cut down innocents for the sake of conquering."

"They will pay for what they did," I tell him. "Every life they stole, every drop of blood they spilled." Something burns inside of me, a rage that is both unfamiliar and welcome at the same time.

Because it means I am still standing.

"They will," he agrees then starts walking again. I fall into step beside him, and together, we climb the steps of the tavern—a building that was spotted easily enough, thanks to a large foaming ale burned into a sign that hangs from the porch.

The door opens and Fort grabs and spins me as two drunk men stumble out. They fall off the steps and to the ground in a loud *thud* of laughter and belches. The stench of beer and stale food drifts out, but my stomach growls in response nonetheless.

Fort eyes the men warily then takes my hand and pulls me inside. There are at least a dozen wooden tables throughout the lower floor, nearly all of them full of people. Some patrons are hunkered over their tables, playing dice or cards, while others are engaged in happy conversations.

A few men turn toward me, so I tuck in closer to Fort

and shield my face with my blanket. Soon, they will likely know who I am, but not until Fort has a chance to speak with the representative. Each village in our kingdom has one, and it is that person who brings the troubles of the village to the king then relays his solutions or laws back to the people.

"Stay over here." Fort sets me near the corner of the bar. "Don't move, okay?"

"Where are you going?"

"To talk to the barkeep, but she's surrounded by people, and I don't want to risk anyone noticing you yet."

"My hair—" I whisper.

"Is covered," he interrupts. "But that's only part of it, Carleah. You have eyes unlike anyone else in the kingdom. Should anyone get close enough to see them—" He trails off and purses his lips. "I will be quick."

Fort offers me a slight nod then crosses the inn toward a woman wearing a soft green gown, her bright red hair pulled back out of her face. I'm so focused on them that I don't see the man approaching until he's leaning into my line of sight.

"Eh, that's a pretty soft blanket you have there," he coos as he reaches out to stroke a finger down the area framing my face.

I move away. "Thank you. Please do not touch me."

"Where you from, gorgeous?" He completely ignores me, his sour breath fanning over my face and making my stomach churn.

"Do not touch me," I reply, far more sternly now.

"And why not? Pretty little thing like you needs some compa—" He stops speaking, eyes wide.

I shift my gaze up, noting Fort standing just on the other side of him, his expression contorted in rage. "Touch her again and I'll cut your fucking spine out where you stand," he snarls.

"We was just having a chat!" The man puts his hands up. "I'll just be going, then. Pleasure talking to you."

As soon as he's gone, I let out a breath I didn't know I was holding.

"Are you all right?" Fort questions as he shoves the arrow back into its quiver.

"Fine. He just caught me off guard."

Before he can respond, the barkeep moves into view behind him. "This way," she says quickly then rushes up the stairs. Fort and I follow, taking the steps quickly until we've reached the top. She unlocks a door and moves inside.

Fort steps around me, going in first, but I don't wait for his order before following him in and shutting the door behind me.

The redhead checks the window then crosses her arms. "What's this about, then?" she demands, her raspy tone leaving no room for argument. The woman oozes strength; it's no wonder she was chosen as Miscerico's representative.

"You're sure this village is secure?" Fort demands.

"Yes. You're the first travelers we've had in weeks. So I know something is off." Her gaze flitters to me. "And given that this woman bears a striking resemblance to

Carleah Rossingol, I'm assuming it has something to do with the royal family. Especially given she is escorted by the head of their guard."

I am not surprised she recognized either of us. And since it seems futile to keep up the charade, I drop the blanket, remove my jacket, and pull the cloth from my hair. White strands fall freely now, and the woman's gaze widens.

She dips her head in a slight bow. "Princess," she says softly.

"Queen," Fort corrects.

The woman's gaze widens, and she straightens. "Queen? What happened?"

"My family was slaughtered in our home," I tell her. "Along with every man, woman, and child in our city."

The woman gasps, eyes filling with tears as she covers her mouth with shaking hands. "Dead? They're all dead? But how?"

"Tenebris soldiers," Fort tells her. "Or those bearing their armor and carrying their sigil."

"It cannot be possible."

"It is," I tell her. "And they will likely be coming here next."

"The king is dead?" she chokes out. "The queen? Your brothers?"

My eyes fill, but I blink the tears away. "All except me," I reply. My voice betrays the pain I feel, though I try to hide it. "We are in need of supplies so that we can make it to Soreno and seek aid. If you can help us, I will ensure it is paid back three times over."

The woman crosses the distance between us and takes my hands. She drops to her knees before me. "I am so sorry, Your Highness."

The entire thing makes me uneasy, so I tug her up to her feet. "Please do not bow to me," I tell her. "I am coming to you for help. It should be me on my knees."

"Never, Your Highness. Your family was good. Kind. We will see to it that you get what you need for your journey."

"When do your next supply ships leave?"

"Two weeks' time," she replies.

"Two weeks is too long," I tell Fort. "We can cross Nemoregno by the time we would even be leaving."

He turns away from me and mutters a curse.

"Would you like a bath? Some fresh clothes?"

"Yes, please," I reply. "Both. But we would like to keep my presence here quiet. If you are not already on the soldiers' radar, I do not want to bring danger."

"Of course," she replies.

"Thank you—"

"Phyllis, Your Highness."

"Please just call me Carleah. I do not sit on the throne yet."

"Carleah," she repeats. "I will get you what you need and ensure no one else knows of your arrival."

"Thank you," I tell her.

She nods then hands me the key in her hand. "I shall return shortly."

The door closes softly behind her, and Fort wastes no time flipping the lock and drawing the curtains tighter over the window. While he does that, I cross over toward the bed and take a seat. The mattress is plush beneath me, and it takes all of my physical strength not to lie back and fall asleep where I sit.

"I can see if she has more blankets to bring in. Then I will take the floor."

"What? No. Unless you want the floor. But you're even more exhausted than I am."

"It's improper."

"Improper?" I choke out. "Like the night before you left?" The words leave my lips before I can stop them.

Fort glares at me.

"Besides, we've been doing it since we left the castle. Unless it bothers you to lie beside me, I'd prefer it."

Fort's gaze darkens. "It does not bother me."

"Good."

There's a knock at the door, so Fort opens it again, and Phyllis slips in, her husband beside her.

"Your Highness," he says as he bows.

"I needed help with the water," Phyllis says as she carries two buckets over to a copper tub and dumps them in. Her husband does the same with the two he carries. "Micah is the only one I trust."

"Then we trust him, too." I offer Micah my hand so he sets a bucket down and takes it.

"We thank you for your hospitality."

"Anything for a Rossingol," he replies with a smile. "One more round of these and you should be ready for a bath."

Neither of them waits for a response before they leave to retrieve more water.

"Somehow it feels even more exposed being here than out in the woods."

"Because you're having to trust people," I tell him. "Which seems to be something you do not care to do."

He doesn't miss the dig. "Trusting someone who has the ability to destroy you is a foolish thing to do. Especially when they're above you in status."

I cross my arms. "And why is that? My family never gave you any reason not to trust us."

Fort shakes his head. "Your father may have been a great man, but he was still a king."

"Does that mean you don't trust me?" I cross over and jab my finger into his chest.

"I—"

Another knock on the door has Fort pulling it open. Phyllis and Micah return with four more buckets of steaming water, which they pour into the tub. "If you're needing anything else, please let us know. We will retrieve you some fresh clothing while you bathe."

"Thank you," I say with a forced smile.

They both bow their heads then leave, and Fort locks the door behind them before turning back to me.

"Don't bother answering," I tell him. "We both know you don't." I turn away, but Fort grips my arm so I face him again.

He's closer now, his amber eyes darkening. "I trust only you," he says softly.

"Why?"

"Because you need me right now," he replies coolly, despite the heat in his gaze.

"That's a lonely way to live, Fort."

"It's the only way I know how to survive." He releases me. "You bathe first. I'll keep an eye outside with my back turned to you for privacy." In demonstration, he turns away, and I cross over toward the tub.

I'm not a modest person. Having people around you all the time—even when you're dressing—erases any need of privacy. But being this close to Fort when I'm naked, this close to the only man I've ever *really* wanted, makes my cheeks heat as I undress.

My gaze on him, I slip one foot into the tub and groan. "This feels amazing."

Fort clears his throat. "Good."

"You should get in, too. We can turn our backs to each other, but otherwise, they'll have to drain the tub and bring up fresh water."

"I don't think that's a good idea."

"Because you're so offended by my body?"

"Hardly." He all but growls the word, and it ignites my blood. "It's just—"

"Improper?" I ask sweetly, repeating his earlier word.

"Yes."

"It seems foolish to start erecting barriers between us now, Fort. I promise not to grope you. I'll even keep my eyes closed until you're in the water." I hesitate. "Is it that you've never seen a woman's body?"

He chuckles, and honestly? It's a bit irritating. "It is not that."

How many women has he shared a bed with? How many have known him as a lover? And why do I care?

"Then come get in the damned tub, Fort. It's plenty large enough for the two of us if we keep our legs pulled up. Unless, of course, you want a cold bath, or desire to wait even longer for one."

Fort hesitates another moment, but I see the slump of his shoulders when he gives in. "Fine. But turn around and make room for me before I do."

My pulse quickens, the thought of him being naked along with me far more alluring than it should be. As I promised, I turn around and bring my knees up then cover my breasts and close my eyes. "Done."

I hear his bootsteps carry him closer to the tub. Then he's silent for a few moments. My heart races in my chest, beating so loudly I'm sure he can hear it. I long to lose myself in the connection between us.

Long to forget about our troubles as I lie beneath him.

But doing so when the entire kingdom is counting on me feels foolish. So, I remain where I am even as I hear his clothes falling to the ground.

The water sloshes as he climbs in, his much larger frame taking up a huge part of our large tub. His back slides against mine, warm, naked skin pressing against me.

"Good?" I ask.

"Yes."

The relief is evident in his voice.

"I told you it felt good."

"You were not lying."

I reach forward and grab a bar of soap from the table beside the tub to run it over the back of my neck and the parts of my body I can reach. Then, I reach back and offer it to him.

"Thank you," he grumbles.

"Want me to get your back? I promise not to look at anything else."

He's silent a moment, and I wonder if I've crossed some sort of line. But then he replies, "Fine."

"Let me know when you're ready." I lean back against him as he washes then hands me back the soap. His hand brushes the top of my breast when he reaches back, and I bite down a groan as a wave of pleasure shoots through me.

How pathetic that a simple touch can illicit such a powerful reaction.

"Okay. Turning around."

In the tiny amount of space I have, I turn toward him, soap in hand, and lose my ability to think clearly. I long to trace every ridge of muscle, to taste his skin and know that he is learning me in return.

"Everything all right?" Fort questions, ripping me from my fantasy.

"Yes. Sorry." I reach out and run the soap over his back, stroking tenderly as I go. I have no business imagining anything right now. And yet, I can't seem to help it.

Fort bows his head, dropping his chin down to his chest and letting out a soft sigh. Even after he's clean, I continue, letting the soap drop down to his lower back before bringing it up to the tops of his shoulders.

Between my movements, the warm water, and the fire crackling in the room, it's as though we're in our own little world. A place where we're safe from what hunts us, where we can just be Carleah and Fort.

"I can wash yours if you like," Fort offers.

"Yes. Please." I hold the soap out over his shoulder then turn so my back is to his again. "You can turn around."

The water sloshes as Fort moves, likely having to stand up before he turns around. I keep my eyes cast down at the knees I've got tucked up at my chest. When he settles again, one hand goes to my shoulder while the other runs the soap over my body.

I damn near lose it.

His touch is nirvana.

Paradise.

Like I'm standing in the eye in the center of a storm that has been brewing for so damned long I cannot remember a time I wasn't wrapped in it.

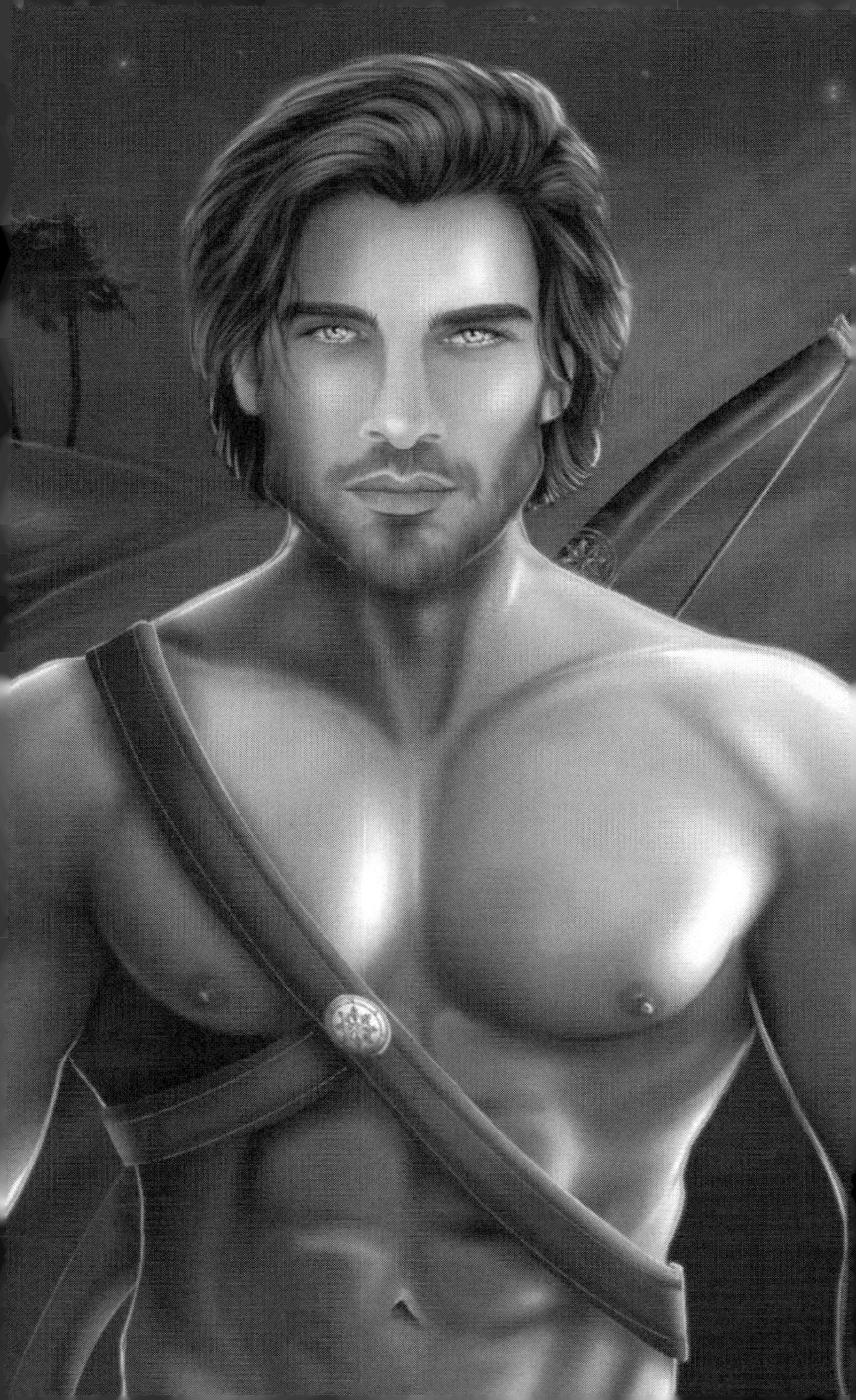

CHAPTER 11
FORT

My cock is so fucking hard I have to arch away in order to avoid Carleah discovering what the simple act of me washing her back is doing to me. But I've wanted this for two damned years. Ever since I ripped that asshole off of her, I've wanted Carleah naked next to me, her body writhing beneath mine. But I never acted on it because I owed her family everything, so soiling their daughter was never even an option.

But now—I close my eyes.

After that kiss. That small taste of the fire in her veins...

Fuck, I'm a bastard.

As I run the soap over her milky skin, I take in every inch of her back, forbidding my gaze from dropping any further, because if I see much more of her, I'm not sure I can keep my hands to myself.

Improper.

That's what I'd told her.

But the real reason for my initial refusal was because I'm not fucking sure how I'm supposed to keep remaining this close to her, and still deny myself the one thing I want more than anything.

I could lean forward and press my lips to the back of her neck, could snake my hand around and cup one of her perfect fucking breasts. And what makes it even harder is that I *know* she wouldn't pull away.

Even as the thought occurs, Carleah raises her head and lets out a soft moan that goes straight to my fucking cock. "That feels amazing."

Breathing ragged, I can't even bring myself to respond.

"Fort?" she asks.

Still, I'm speechless. Because a part of me *hopes* she'll turn around.

As though my thoughts were voiced aloud, Carleah turns her head and looks over her shoulder at me. Her lips part as her bright azure gaze drops to my mouth, finally sinking lower to my chest. Carleah is the type of woman who makes a person feel *seen*.

Her gaze rises back to my face.

And because I'm a bastard careening face-first into what will likely be my death, anyway, I lean in closer. My gaze holds hers and I search for any hint that she wants me to remain at a distance.

But I see none.

A mere breath before I can touch my lips to hers, someone bangs on the door.

Carleah turns away, so I climb out of the tub, grabbing my jacket to wrap around my waist as I do.

"Who is it?" I call out.

"Phyllis. I have fresh clothing."

I risk a glance back at Carleah, who has pulled her knees back up to her chest and has rested her cheek on them so her face is turned away from me.

Disappointment settles on me, but I pull the door open. Phyllis holds out a stack of clothing. "Thank you."

"As soon as you are dressed, come down, and I will feed you a proper meal. The tavern has been closed for the night, so you do not need to worry about being recognized."

"Thank you."

She smiles softly, dips her head in a nod, then turns away.

I shut and lock the door. Then turn around.

"Phyllis brought clothes."

"That is kind of her."

I carry the clothes over and set them on the bed before separating them into what is meant for me and what is meant for her.

As soon as I have two separate piles, I cross over and retrieve a towel from a shelf near the tub. After carrying it back to her, I avert my gaze and hold it out. Slender fingers brush mine as she takes it.

Water sloshes as she stands, and it takes every fucking ounce of willpower I possess not to pick up where we were cut off.

"You can open your eyes, Fort. I'm relatively decent."

I do then instantly wish I'd kept them fucking closed. She's out of the tub and standing directly in front of me, so our height difference puts her head at my chest. Giving me a perfect sight straight down to where the milky swells of her breasts are spilling from the towel. My mouth dries.

My cock twitches painfully.

I want to bury myself in her.

Fuck her hard until neither one of us can cares about the fate of the realm.

Instead, I raise my gaze to hers. "I'm finding it really fucking hard to keep my hands off of you."

"Then why do you?" she retorts.

"Because I don't want to be something you regret when the smoke settles and the world falls back into place."

Carleah reaches out with the hand not clutching her towel and presses her palm to my chest. I close my eyes, savoring the feel of her hand on me. "You will never be something I regret, Fort. And my world will *never* fall back into place. Settle into a new normal? Sure. It has to. But I am not the same person I was before the fall of Navalis. And I never will be again."

I cover her hand with mine. "I appreciate that you feel that way now, but I am not the person you seem to think I am, and I am not *worthy* of someone like you."

CARLEAH HASN'T SPOKEN to me since I pulled away from her and dressed. She sits beside me at the table, hands in her lap as she studies the tavern room around us. Sun still shines in through the window outside though the place is empty, just as our hostess had assured us it would be.

Carleah's long, white hair is loose around her shoulders, and the riding pants Phyllis brought her look far too fucking amazing for my own good and do very little to hide every single one of her delicate curves.

The combination of what nearly happened earlier and seeing her wearing what she is makes it very difficult for me to keep what little honor still remains in my blackened soul.

"Here you go." Phyllis sets plates of meat and steamed vegetables in front of each of us, and my mouth begins to water.

"And some ale to wash it down." He sets two frothing mugs down then slides one over to Carleah and gives one to me.

"Thank you both," she says softly then picks up her fork and stabs a piece of meat. She slips it between her lips and groans.

Once again, the sound goes straight to my cock, which doesn't seem to realize it can never fucking happen.

Seconds later, she tips her ale up and drinks deeply.

"How long has it been since—" Micah trails off.

"Almost three days," I reply.

"Three days." Phyllis shakes her head. "I am so sorry for what you've been through."

"Thank you," Carleah replies as she takes another bite.

I begin eating, too, enjoying the warm food as it slips down my throat and heats my stomach. The flavors are perfection, the ale delicious.

"There were no survivors?" Micah questions.

"Not that we are aware of," I reply around a forkful of carrots.

"You should get your people to leave, move farther into the mountains," Carleah tells them.

"You believe those soldiers will be coming here?"

"I do," she replies. "Because they know I escaped. And if they aren't looking for me yet, they will be soon."

"If the royal army was no match for them—" Micah trails off. "Shit, this is a right fucked situation, isn't it?"

"Micah!" Phyllis scolds.

The ghost of a smile plays at the corners of Carleah's mouth. "It is absolutely a right fucked situation," she agrees.

Micah beams at her, and Phyllis shakes her head.

"You said you plan to go to Soreno?" Phyllis asks.

"Yes. To ask for aid."

"From your betrothed?" Phyllis questions. "Surely he will not say no."

My hand clenches into a fist beneath the table at the mere mention of Patrick. "We can only hope Soreno will come to our aid as we have them in the past."

Micah nods. "We will all hope for their assistance, then."

Something about the way he says it alludes to the

same lack of hope I feel. Truthfully, I don't see much of a chance that they will help us take the kingdom back. At least, not so Carleah can rule. They will likely want it for themselves.

And when she refuses, I can only hope they will honor her wishes and let us go.

Otherwise, we might not ever leave Soreno. Alive, anyway.

"I still cannot believe it," Phyllis says softly. "I was just at the castle last month. Everything seemed so normal."

"My family liked it to appear that way," Carleah replies as she downs more of her ale. "They liked their secrets."

I reach out and place my hand on her lower back, my way of steadying her when I feel like she's teetering over the edge of saying something she will regret.

She clears her throat and forces a smile. "They never wanted anyone else to worry," she says carefully.

Phyllis returns her soft smile then turns to me. "You can see my brother in town. He runs a shop and can get you some extra clothing and fresh boots. The blacksmith will help with weapons, and Micah will get you both horses."

"You both have no idea how much we appreciate everything."

Phyllis reaches across and touches Carleah's hand. "There is nothing we wouldn't do for you and your family, Your Highness."

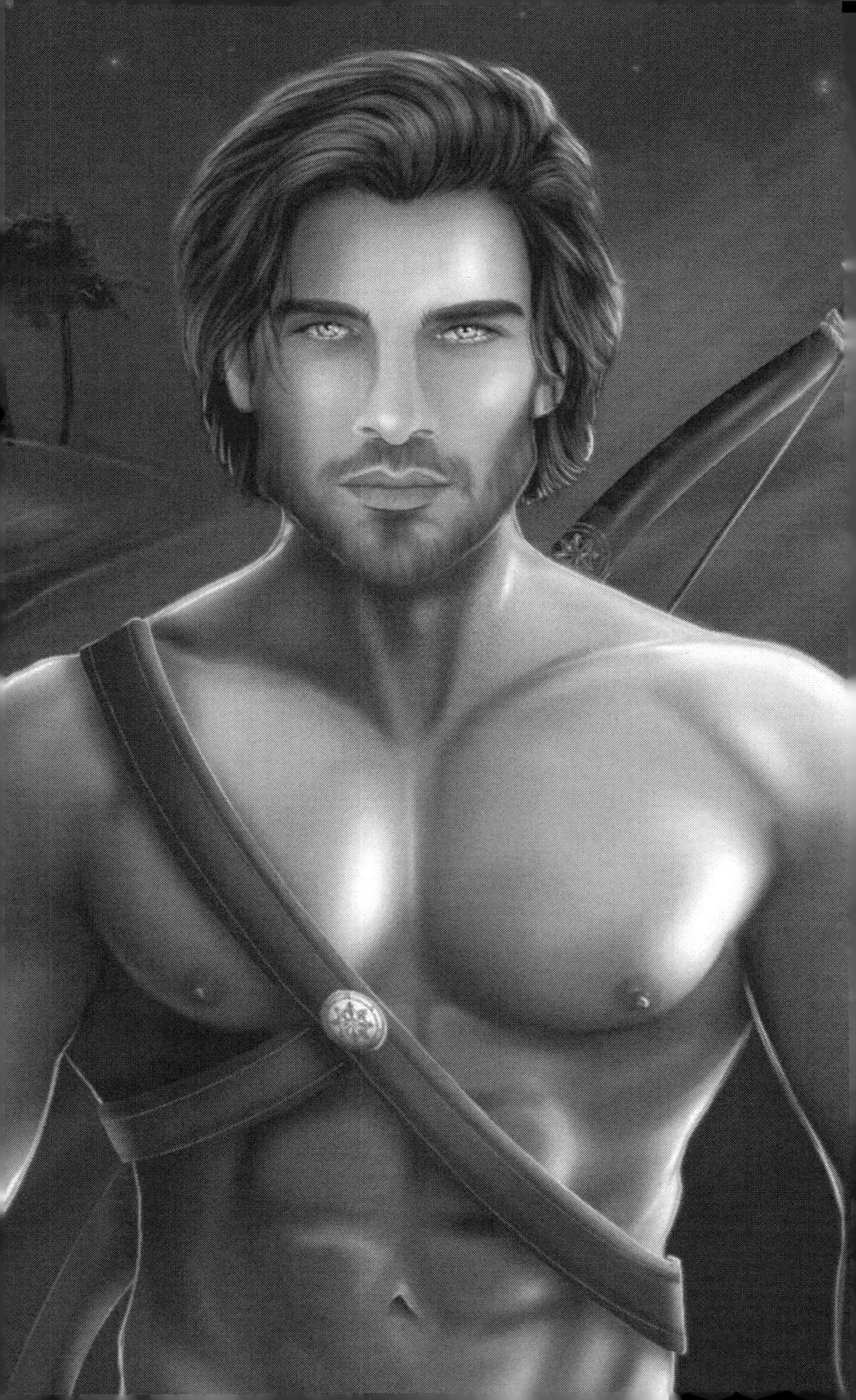

CHAPTER 12
FORT

Since we can't want to risk her being spotted, Carleah remained back at the empty tavern. I can feel her absence, though, and mere minutes after leaving her side, I am desperate to get back.

Still, we need supplies. And every moment we wait, the risk we'll have to flee without them grows. I step into a small shop full of various clothing, shoes, and saddlebags, alone. The aroma of leather clings to the air, filling my lungs and bringing about memories I wish could stay buried forever. My mother ran a leather shop.

She'd crafted boots, belts, saddles, reins—damn near everything. And she'd taken her time to teach me how to pay attention to the details when carving something because it's those details that really make the difference when we're looking at a larger picture.

"Can I help ye'?" A man asks, pulling me from my thoughts as he steps around the counter. His dark hair is cut short though his beard is long. His hands are stained with the leather treatment, but he smiles kindly at me.

"Yes. I need a pair of women's riding boots."

"Size?"

Shit. "I—"

The man chuckles. "How about I give you the size I sell the most of. Then you can come back and swap them if they don't work."

"That would be great, thank you."

He nods, then turns and heads toward a shelf. "Are you visiting long?"

"Just passing through," I reply.

"With your woman? Wife or sister?"

"Friend," I reply even though it feels like a lie. After what happened with us earlier, I'm not entirely sure what we are. She's pissed at me, that's for sure.

"Ahh, understood." He grabs a pair of leather boots from the shelf and offers them to me. "These look like they will work?"

I study the intricate designs carved into the sides, the gorgeous feathers that wrap completely around them. "Absolutely."

"Anything else you might need?"

"Do you sell women's clothing as well?"

"That I do. Is she petite-framed? Sturdy? In the middle?"

"Petite," I reply. About this tall?" I gesture to the area just below my sternum where the top of Carleah's head rests. "Pants, please. And a tunic if you have it."

"I have both. My wife prefers trousers as well when she's traveling. Makes it easier to ride."

"Yes."

"You're the couple who came into town and are staying at my sister's, right? She told me you were attacked by bandits."

"Your sister has been most kind."

"Phyllis has a soft spot for people. But she's a sharp mind."

Conversing with another person feels strange. It's been two decades since I talked to a person. What's stranger, though, is that talking with Carleah doesn't make me feel as out of place as speaking with others does.

Likely because when she'd been young enough that she wouldn't remember, I'd been so desperate for a friend that I would hum the lullabies my mother sang to me when I'd been a child. Confiding in Carleah then, when we'd both been young, had been as easy as breathing.

If only I could still spill my secrets in her company. Perhaps then, I'd feel lighter. Perhaps if she knew and still chose me, I would feel deserving of her affection.

"Will this do?"

I swallow down my thoughts. "Yes, thank you. Coats?"

The man smiles. "That I do. My sister told me to give you anything you needed."

I chuckle. "And we appreciate it."

"We care for our own," he says kindly as he retrieves

two heavy coats, two fur hats, and two pairs of gloves before setting it all on the counter. "This do?"

"More than. I wish I had money to give you now rather than later."

He waves a hand as though he's waving the thought away. "When my sister sees ya as deserving, I take it as such. Don't worry about the price. We do all right enough that we can help the occasional traveler out."

"You will be repaid as soon as we can," I tell him. "That is a promise."

"Well then, I look forward to the day our paths cross again." He offers me the stack of clothing, boots on top, then waves as I turn and leave.

As I step out onto the snow-covered street, my gaze falls to the tavern looming just a few buildings down from where I am now. The image of Carleah standing before me in little more than a towel, her gaze cast up at me as though I was the only thing in the world she wanted, settles in my mind.

It reminds me of a time when things were far simpler between us.

When I was her protector from the shadows and the head of her family's guard.

Ever since that night by the lake, when I'd pulled that fucking would-be abductor off of her and saw the swollenness of her pout, the way her eyes glazed over with lust when she'd looked up at me—I'd wondered what it would be like to run my fingers down her spine, over the milky flesh of her body.

To take her lips and be the very reason for the hammering of her pulse.

And that night in my room, when I nearly had, has driven me mad ever since.

I shiver. She will never know the restraint it took not to reach out and touch her today. To claim those lips with my own and distract the both of us from the bleak future we face.

But I am not good for her.

I am tainted by circumstance.

Corrupted by the blood in my veins.

And I will not put that on her. Not until she knows exactly what it is she's getting.

The blacksmith looks up at me as I approach. His face is stained with soot, his hands worn from working with steel.

"What can I do for you?" he grumbles.

"I need weapons."

∽

I STARE out the window into the night sky then down the ale in my mug. With what little alcohol I've allowed myself to have mildly tainting my system, and the immediate danger having passed, the events over the past few days assault me at record speed.

Morality. What a fucking joke.

If men still had morality, I wouldn't be on the run with the last remaining member of the royal family. A family that no one seems to realize is dead yet. This village is on the outskirts of the Navalis kingdom and is the last one we will rest in before we cross the border. I would have expected word to have reached them, and the fact that it hasn't means that, for whatever reason, the crimson soldiers want it hidden.

Another strange occurrence since men who conquer rarely remain quiet about it.

Morality. That word echoes through my mind again.

I once believed I possessed a moral compass. But my time with Carleah has disproved that damned theory. Because, if my soul contained even an ounce of morality, I wouldn't be imagining the way it would feel to crawl inside the bed with Carleah.

She's still sleeping soundly behind me, her back to me. The riding pants she'd worn earlier are discarded beside it, so my imagination has concocted just what those thighs look like with only the bottom of her tunic brushing them. Even now, across the room from her, I've considered what it would mean to rouse her awake with my lips. My hands.

I haven't done it.

But I can't stop thinking about it.

Carleah groans in her sleep, so I turn my attention to her, noting the harsh lines of her expression as firelight from the hearth dances over her.

"No," she whispers. "No." She begins to thrash in the bed, so I jump up and rush over, gripping her shoulders.

"Carleah, wake—" Her fist slams into my jaw, and pain explodes on the side of my face. "Son of a bitch," I groan.

By the time I manage to see straight again, she's staring up at me, eyes wide. "Are you okay?"

"You fucking hit me."

"I'm so sorry." Her gaze is sparkling with tears.

"It's fine." I rub my jaw. "Nightmare?"

She nods and sits up, keeping the blankets at her waist. "I keep seeing them dying, Fort. Over and over again. The image of my father—of Bowman." Carleah closes her eyes tightly, and some tears escape.

Not once in the time since we ran has she broken down. Honestly, it has shocked the hell out of me. Because even the most seasoned of warriors would have fallen apart at seeing their entire family ripped from them so brutally.

I take a seat beside her on the bed. "Do you want to talk about it?"

"What's there to talk about? You were there. You saw it all happen."

"Not all of it."

She'd been forced to face her father's murder alone, witnessed her parent beheaded when he'd reached for her.

"I'm such a fool for thinking I could save him."

"Not a fool," I tell her. "He was your father."

"The man told him that, if I was found, he'd spare the rest of them. I didn't think about it like I should have. I just leapt up and gave myself over." She angrily wipes her tears.

"I would have done the same thing."

"Except you would have saved him. We all know the

fighter you are." She rests her forehead down on her knees. But before I can respond, she's looking up at me. "Teach me."

"What?"

"Teach me to fight. Bowman taught me some basics and how to use the bow. But I want to learn how to use a blade. Please, Fort." She reaches out and closes her hands on my forearm. I stare down at them, blood pounding in my ears at the mere feel of her hands on me.

Her parents would have forbidden it. Hell, if they'd known that Bowman had been teaching her, they would have been furious.

But they're not here. And I have a chance to teach her how to keep herself alive. So if there is ever a time when she cannot rely on me—I pull away from her and cross toward the weapons sitting atop the chest of drawers. After my hand closes around a weapon I chose specifically for Carleah, I cross back toward the bed where she kneels, the tunic sitting just over her thighs.

Her hair's a mess, her eyes wild, and I drink her in, realizing just how fucking gone I am. I will slaughter kingdoms, topple empires, and slay entire armies for this woman. And frankly, that makes her far more dangerous to me than I am to her.

Because of what I am willing to do if only she asked.

I offer her the dagger—a silver blade leading to a glass hilt that is far stronger than any steel.

She takes it, eyes widening further as she palms the weapon.

"Crystal," I tell her. "From the Navalis mountains, so you know it's strong."

Carleah's hands close around the hilt, and she stares up at me. "Thank you. No one has ever given me anything like this before."

I sit on the edge of the bed again. "I will teach you to fight, Carleah. To protect yourself. Because even as I wish I could shield you further, there is no telling what danger we face. Not just in the Phantom or Nemoregno but Soreno as well."

"You don't think he'll help us."

"I know it's our only chance," I say. "But no, I believe that by going there, we are handing over our lives to men who would rather see their own blood ruling over the entirety of the realm."

Her lips part. "Do you truly believe that?"

"It's a risk," I reply. "You have no army to back you, no reason for them to fear retaliation."

"Then do we really need to go?"

I go against every one of the warnings in my head and brush a strand of hair behind her ear. Carleah's gaze drops to my lips then back up to my face. "We have no other choice. If we are to take back your home, then we *need* Soreno on our side."

"Our home," she whispers.

"What?"

"Navalis is your home, too, Fort."

No, I long to say. *It never was.*

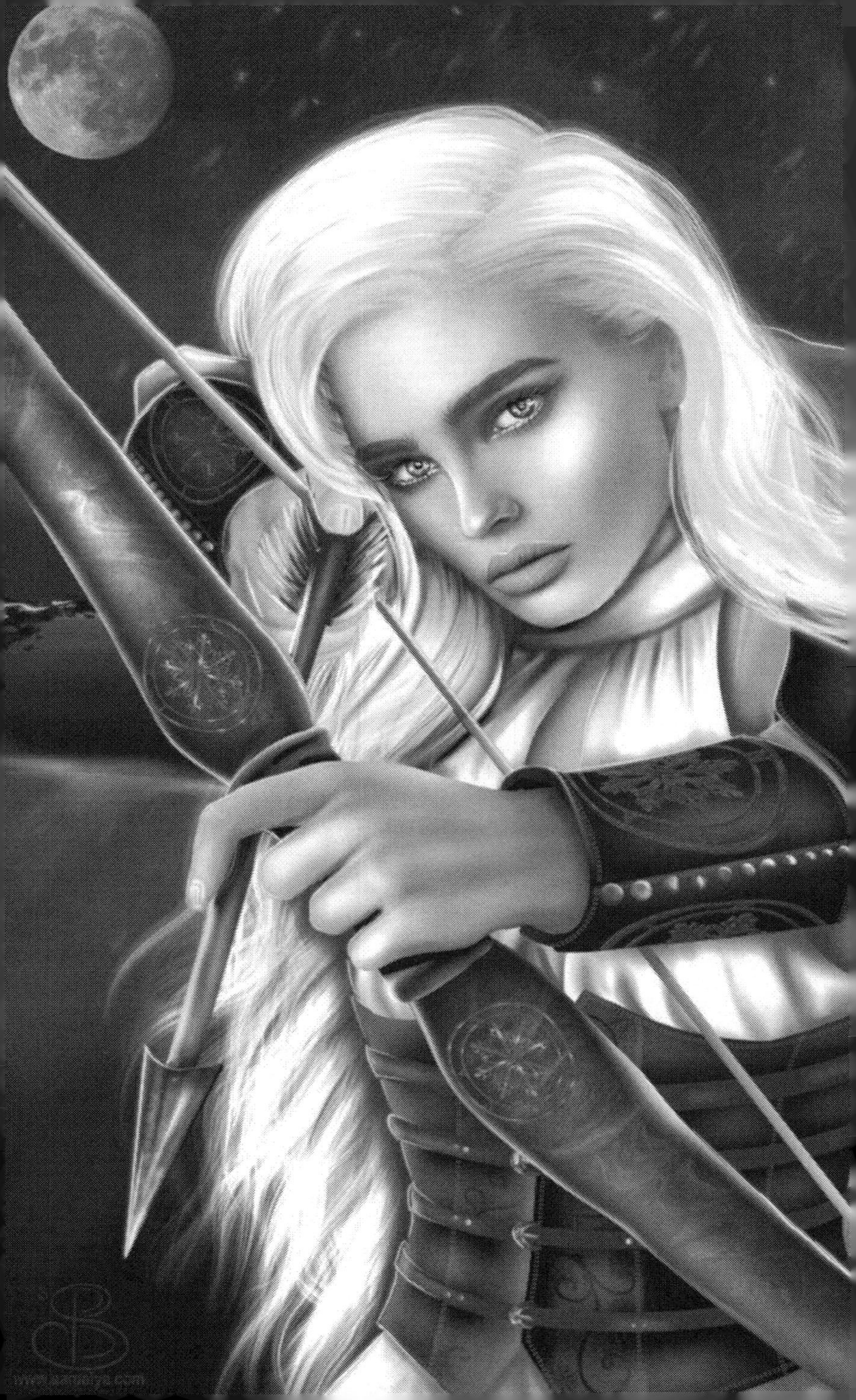

CHAPTER 13
CARLEAH

I wake with the first rays of dawn. Fort is pressed against me, his hand resting on my bare thigh beneath the blankets. Something hard presses against my behind, so I still. Warmth floods my veins and swirls in my belly. Surely that's not—

I nestle back into him, and his hand moves further up my thigh, gliding the tunic up until his arm bands around my stomach—beneath the fabric.

Every inch of my flesh is on fire.

My body burning beneath the flame of my need.

I barely breathe, terrified I will wake him and this moment will be over. Instead, I close my eyes and remain completely still. Even when his fingers dance higher, stopping just beneath my breasts.

Higher, I silently urge. *Let me feel you. Let me lose myself in whatever this is.*

He groans, arm banding even tighter around me as he pulls me against him. The length at my back presses into me, and the throbbing between my legs becomes too much to bear.

Fort's hand drifts higher, the palm of his hand brushing over my pebbled nipple as it settles on my chest, just beneath my throat. I'm completely exposed now, the tunic having traveled up with him.

Sun bathes the parts of my body that are exposed between the top of the covers and the hem of my tunic. I risk rolling just enough that, if he were to open his eyes, he would see me. It's that movement that jostles him, though, and his gaze flies open as soon as I'm on my back.

"Shit, Carleah—" He starts to move his hand, but I reach up and grab it.

He stills beneath my touch, throat bobbing as his gaze travels down over my breasts and belly. I grip his hand, guiding it down from my throat and pressing it to my breast.

He groans.

Pleasure shoots through me as his calloused palm rubs against my nipple. I moan.

Fort's grip tightens on my breast, and the length pressed into my thigh moves ever so slightly. "You're fucking killing me," he whispers, the hot hair fanning over the side of my throat.

"You want this, too," I say.

"Of fucking course I want this." He releases my breast and starts to get up. But just when I think he's leaving me behind, he climbs on top of me and settles himself between my legs. His hard length presses up against me with only the fabric of his riding pants between us. Then, with his hands planted firmly on the mattress on either side of my head, he leans in. "I've wanted to bury myself in you ever since that night by the lake," he whispers as he trails his lips over the side of my throat.

My heart hammers, and I turn my head to give him more access.

"When you came to my room, I wanted to fuck you, so fucking hard that neither one of us could remember just why we needed to leave the bed at all." Fort's lips brush against my temple. "I've dreamed of your body—of the way you'd look when you come on my cock."

I gasp, and his hand drops down to my thigh. He grips it, raising it and running his palm from the back of my knee down to my ass.

"And if a quick fuck is what you're looking for, Princess, then I can give it to you right now." He thrusts up into me, and pleasure rockets through my core. He groans. "I can feel how fucking wet you are already."

"I want you," I whisper. "I've always wanted you."

He drops his head down to my breast, the scruff of his short beard scraping deliciously against my tender flesh. "And therein lies the problem, Carleah." His hot breath fans over my nipple, and a soft moan escapes my lips. "I am *not* to be had. Anything with me would be fleeting because you are meant for a hell of a lot more."

"Then I'll take what I can get. Any of it. All of it." My body shakes as I arch up, trying to urge him closer to my breast.

His mouth closes around my nipple, and I cry out. I

grip his hair as he draws the taut peak into his mouth, nipping, sucking, tasting. Then, he releases me. "You deserve better," he says softly.

"You keep saying that. Keep saying that I should be allowed to know things that pertain to my life. That I should be permitted to make my own decisions, yet here you are, denying me a pleasure I've long since dreamed about because *you* think you know better."

He sits back, grabs my wrists, then pins them to the mattress. "I am not a soft man, Carleah."

"I don't want soft. I've had soft my entire fucking life."

His nostrils flare. "You've lost your refinement."

"I was never truly refined, Fort. As someone who followed my every move, I should think you know that."

His thumbs graze the skin of my wrists, right over the hammering of my pulse. "And what happens when you realize just who I am? When you discover that you deserve something more?"

"I may not know where you come from, Fort, but I *know* who you are. When are you going to realize that you deserve more than you're willing to allow yourself?"

He chuckles darkly. "You have no idea what I've seen and done."

I lean up as best I can with my hands still pinned beneath his. "I. Don't. Care. I want one person in my life to treat me like the woman I am and not the delicate flower I've always been seen as. You want rough? Fine. I'll take it. Use me however you need because I guarantee you're not the only one getting something out of it."

His breathing turns ragged, and his gaze darkens. "Fuck it. I'm already condemned." He slams his mouth onto mine, and my world floods with color.

Lust slams into me at full force, heating my blood as something inside of me comes to life. The world around us vanishes as his tongue slides over the seam of my lips, urging me to open.

An urging I answer with my own ferocity. His tongue glides against mine, and I struggle against the hold on my wrists so I can touch him. So I can feel his hard body beneath the tips of my fingers.

Fort grinds his length into me, and I moan against his mouth. My bare breasts brush against his chest, and the friction furthers my pleasure. Every single inch of my body is on fire. Every stroke of his tongue against mine merely grows the flames of desire I've carried for him.

If being with Fort means walking into the fire—I want to fucking burn.

And then he's gone.

My heart pounds in my ears as Fort rushes across the room toward the window, his blade already in his hand. When the hell did he grab a sword?

"They're all dead!" someone screeches just outside the window.

I feel the color drain from my face, and every ounce of lust I'd felt vanishes in a puff of smoke.

"The royal family is dead, and the Tenebris are coming!"

Fort turns to me. "Get dressed."

I nod and scramble from the bed, retrieving my

riding pants and tugging them on. Fort dresses quickly as well, and I'm just pulling on my boots when someone bangs on the door. My body feels numb now, as though I'm going through the actions but not truly present in this moment.

Because my thoughts are back with the city that fell. With my family on blood-soaked snow. Is that what will happen to these good people?

No.

I retrieve the dagger Fort gave me from the bedside table and tuck it into the top of my boot.

"Who is it?" Fort demands.

"Phyllis. You need to open the door. Now."

He does, though he keeps a handle on his blade.

Phyllis rushes in, cheeks red, eyes full. "You need to come downstairs. A man—"

"We heard him running through the village," Fort snarls.

"He's downstairs in the tavern. No one else but Micah is there, but you need to hear what else he has to say."

"We'll be down in just a few minutes. Keep everyone else out of the tavern."

"We will." She offers me a sad smile then leaves the room. Fort shuts and locks the door behind her.

He turns to me. "You can stay up here if you want."

"No," I snap. "I will be there."

He nods in understanding. "Then let's not keep them waiting."

After retrieving Bowman's bow and quiver, and Fort

putting on his boots, I follow him down the stairs. I made no move to hide my hair, though I did braid it down my back so it would be out of my face.

Fort's been quiet, likely wrapped in his own thoughts just as I am. If the Tenebris are truly coming, the people here are in more danger than they even realize.

The man's soft sobbing drifts toward us the moment we reach the middle of the stairs. By the time we've reached the bottom, my stomach might as well be full of stones.

He sits at a table with his back to us, though I can make out the all-too-familiar staining of blood against the tunic of his white shirt. His head hangs low, long hair matted and crusted with either mud or blood. My heart aches for him.

Fort and I move around into eyesight of him, and the man gasps and stares up at him. Recognition is instant because I spent more time in his shop than anyone else's in the entire city. "You survived?" he chokes out as he stares at Fort. Then, his attention shifts to me. The bookshop owner, who introduced me to worlds outside of my family's library, scrambles backward out of his chair before falling to his knees. "Princess. I—I don't understand."

His shoulders shake with violent force, so I rush over and sink to my knees before him. "Bartin," I whisper, tears burning my vision. I wrap my arms around him, and he hugs me in return, his sobbing deafening. Only when the trembling has stopped do I pull back to look into his familiar blue eyes. "You escaped."

"Barely," he chokes out. "And only because I laid still beneath—" He closes his eyes and begins to shake again. "Because I hit beneath Marjarie's body. They killed her, Princess. They slaughtered everyone."

"Marjarie was his wife," I say without pulling my attention from him. "I snuck out at night. But not before—" He swallows hard. "They killed your family, Princess. And I thought they'd gotten you, too. All the bodies were strung up on the walls of the city, their heads shaved and white hair on the ground beneath them."

Bile rises in my gut, and I push to my feet, turning away from everyone as I try like hell to get that mental image out of my head. My family strung up like the carcasses of dead animals. And if he thought I was dead, too, that means they used another woman's body in place of mine. Which is likely why they shaved the heads.

"Carleah," Fort whispers. He touches my shoulder, but I shake my head and turn.

"You can speak?" Bartin says.

"Yes. Tell me what they did with the city," Fort demands. "How many soldiers remain in the kingdom?"

"Hundreds. Maybe more," Bartin replies. "I saw no other survivors," he chokes out. "They killed...everyone."

"You said they were coming here. Outside, you yelled that the Tenebris were headed this way."

He nods. "I saw them. Marching. Just over the hill. I ran as fast as I could, but I don't know how far behind me they are."

"Shit." Fort turns away.

"We need to leave," Micah says. "Now."

"We cannot move the people that quickly," Phyllis argues. "There are children, elderly—and I won't leave anyone behind."

"Son of a bitch!" Micah exclaims, slamming both fists down on the table. Phyllis goes to him as Bartin hangs his head low once more.

I cross over toward Fort. "We cannot leave them here to die," I whisper.

"And I won't risk you by staying to fight. The people here are not trained soldiers, Carleah, and the Tenebris *tore* through men who had been training their entire lives for war."

"You are here. And you're the best chance they have to survive."

"Every second we remain here, you are in danger, Carleah. And, like it or not, *you* are their queen now."

"Exactly." I move in closer. "Do you think my father would abandon them for safer pastures? My brothers?"

"They were seasoned fighters," he replies. "I do not say it to be callous, Carleah, but they knew war. They could handle themselves in a fight. You—"

"Are not trained," I interrupt. "But I am damned good with a bow."

"That won't save you when they breach these walls." I see the fear on his face, and I know it's more about who I am to him than who I am to this kingdom. So, I take his hand.

"I am not leaving this place until I know they are safe. If that means I die here, then here, I'll die."

"Carleah—"

"What happens if we do run? You said yourself Soreno is a risk, too. So what happens if we leave these people to die, and then Soreno refuses us anyway?"

"You'll still be alive," he growls. "That's the difference."

I take his face into my hands. "We will survive long enough to get these people out of here." I say it with such conviction that even I feel a surge of hope.

"This is a fucking suicide mission," he snarls as he pulls away. He moves past me, so I turn as he stops just in front of Bartin. "How many were marching this way?"

"A portion," he replies. "Maybe two dozen?"

"We can handle that," Micah replies. "That's not nearly the numbers we were worried about."

"Those soldiers are not normal men," Fort replies. "It will take three well-trained fighters to take on one of them." He shakes his head. "Do you have any cannons? Any heavy artillery?"

Phyllis shakes her head. "The wall will hold, though, won't it?"

"I need to see who is able to fight," Fort demands. "If we're going to win an impossible battle, we need every capable hand holding a sword."

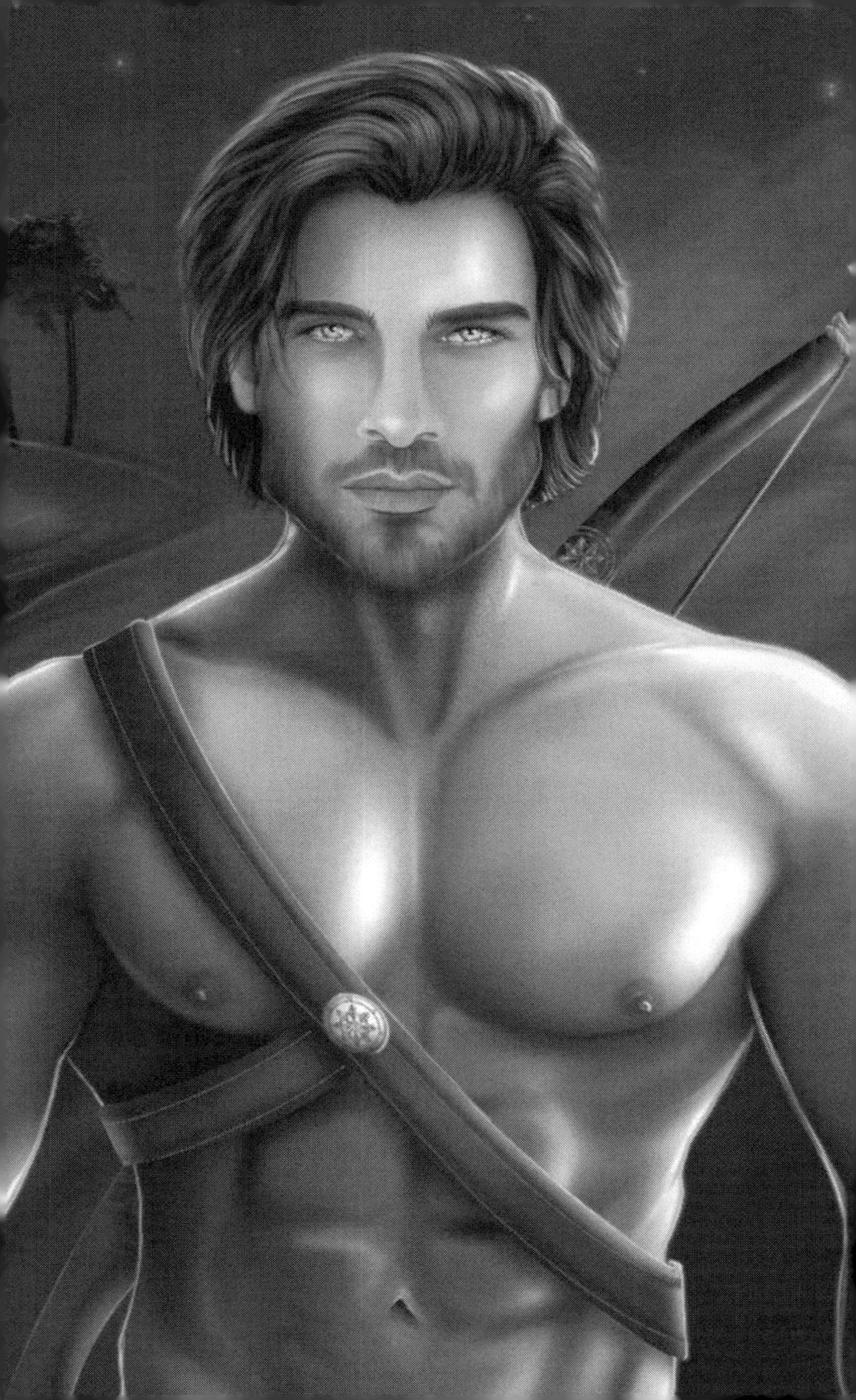

CHAPTER 14
FORT

This is fucking doomed.

I stand on the porch of the tavern, staring out at just barely fifty men and women, all holding weapons. They are untrained and without armor. Civilians who are rightfully terrified, I can see it in their eyes.

It speaks to our potential defeat that the Tenebris were so unthreatened that they sent such a small cavalry our way. If they did not feel the need to send more, then what chance did they believe we had at survival? Our only hope is that we were vastly underestimated.

And I guarantee they didn't count on me being here, too.

The last two hours have been a whirlwind of preparing the village for what's to come. We've boarded up the gate and done a perimeter check of the wall that surrounds the city. It was made to withstand a handful of bandits that would come and steal what is not theirs.

It was not designed to fend off an army, which is precisely what we need it to do.

Those who could not fight are barricaded in the cellar of the tavern at my back, though even at my insistence, Carleah is not one of them. I can feel her at my back as she steps out of the tavern. Know she's there even before the whispers break out in the crowd before me.

And as she comes to stand beside me, I imagine a world where we were not interrupted this morning. Where the Tenebris were not on our doorstep and we'd had a chance at a future where we could be—well—anything.

"You are all brave for being here," she calls out to the crowd. "The Tenebris are terrifying. I won't pretend otherwise because I would want the honest truth if I were in your shoes. But we have something they don't. An honorable reason to fight!"

The crowd nods and some cheer. But their hope does little to ease the dread in my gut.

"These bastards took everything from me. They stole my parents—your king and queen. My brothers—your future kings. They slaughtered people I'd known my entire life, ransacked a home I'd foolishly believed untouchable, and now they are here beating on your doorstep! But we are not going to let them in!" she calls out.

More cheering.

"We are going to fight for everything Navalis stands for. We stand for peace, hope, and honor while they fight to possess! But they cannot have what is ours!" she bellows.

She steals the breath from my lungs with her strength. She always has, but right now, it's amplified. Whether from the brief taste I got this morning or her willingness to sacrifice herself for the people counting on her, I cannot be sure.

But here she stands, in a place where so many others would have run. Where even her father would have taken a backseat—I'm sure of it. He was not the warrior others saw him as, not that I would ever taint Carleah's image of him. Bowman and Alex would have stayed. But the others? I don't think Carleah realizes just how fucking brave she is, even compared to the family she still mourns.

"So will you fight with me? Will you stand at my side and make these fuckers wish they'd chosen another kingdom to invade?"

"Yes!" the cheer is resounding.

"Then let us prepare!" She holds a fist in the air, and the crowd raises their weapons with renewed strength. They all turn and leave, rushing to the battle stations I gave them. We have rocks, oil, and fire to keep the Tenebris out of these walls. After that—"It's going to work," Carleah insists.

"You have your hope. I'll save mine until the battle is won." I turn away, but she grips my arm. When I face her again, she offers me a tight smile then releases me and steps off the porch.

I rush forward and grab her arm, tugging her into the

alley between buildings. My mouth is on hers before her back ever hits the wall. Carleah's fingers thread through my hair, and she wraps both legs around my waist as I pin her against the side of the tavern.

Her tongue slides against mine, and I lose myself in the moment. In a kiss shared between two people who, for all intents and purposes—never should have met.

In this calm before the storm, I take what is given freely because I'm not sure we'll ever have another chance.

I pull away and cup her face. "Stay the fuck by me. Understand?"

Carleah kisses me again then cups my face. "Always."

A horn sounds moments before someone yells, "They're coming!"

I set Carleah down, reach into my pocket, and withdraw a pale green scarf. Quickly, I wrap it over her hair, hiding as much as I can beneath the fabric. The last thing we need is for them to realize the princess they're searching for is right here under their nose.

Then, I move away and draw my sword.

Carleah readies the bow as we head straight for the stairs that will lead us to the platform that overlooks the ground on the other side of the wall.

Heart in my throat, I stare down at the men marching toward us, a black banner raised high. The golden boar adorning it shimmers in the light. The last two times I faced these assholes, they won.

But not this fucking time.

After a quick count, I'm grateful to see that Bartin

was not wrong in his estimates. Two dozen men march toward us, a small fraction of what assaulted even our army at the meeting. Two dozen we can handle.

They come to a stop just outside of the wall. "By orders of your new king, we will see the one who is in charge!" one of the men calls out.

"We only serve a Rossingol on the throne!" Phyllis yells back, a bow in her hand.

"Then you will die," the man replies. He steps back and offers a nod.

Six men rush forward with bows in their hands.

"Get ready!" I bellow.

Our archers—Carleah included—dip the ends of their wrapped arrows in oil. Bartin rushes by, a torch in his hand, and lights them.

I watch Carleah's throat bob as she raises her bow. Then, they fire.

The Tenebris soldiers throw up shields, but a handful of them go down as the arrows strike true. Angry roars from below signal that the fight is headed for the gate, but the archers do not let up.

They take another wrapped arrow and dip it in oil; then Bartin lights them.

They aim—and fire.

Unfortunately, the Tenebris are ready this time. They throw their shields up faster, and the second every arrow has fallen, their own archers set up...and fire.

Arrows sing through the air toward our people. Some move in time, ducking back beneath the wall. Bartin is not so lucky, though. An arrow plunges into his throat, and he falls—the torch with him.

"Move the fucking oil!" I bellow. Thankfully, they do, and Bartin's torch hits the ground with a muted thud.

I turn my attention back to the Tenebris who have rushed the wall.

"What the hell are they doing?" Carleah demands. "They can't—" She trails off when they rush backward.

"Get off the fucking wall!" I roar as I close my arms around Carleah and leap from the platform. Before we ever hit the ground, the wall explodes. Shards of wood splinter toward us, and I feel them in the back of my neck and arms.

Carleha's body shielded with mine, we land as soldiers rush through the now gaping hole. I draw my blade, and she rips out a dagger while palming an arrow in one hand.

I raise mine and rush forward, clashing with the first man. The Tenebris are faster, stronger than any regular human. So, I suppose, it's a good fucking thing that I am, too. I spin, driving the sword into his gut.

Then, I move backward, dodging an axe before swinging my blade and removing the fucker's head. Sweat beads on my body as I fight my way through them, my blade another extension of my body.

It's always been like this. Because, from the time I was old enough to hold one, I've been training. Preparing for a future where I would serve a master until my dying breath.

I bury my blade to the hilt in a soldier's stomach then

turn when Carleah grunts. The side of her head is bloody, but she's ripping her dagger from the throat of a man while Phyllis removes her own short sword from his gut.

The two women fight right behind me, both of them managing to hold their own, so I return my focus to the fight, doing my best to ignore the bodies at my feet. I rush forward, sliding down to my knees and slicing through the gut of a soldier as he prepares to slaughter Micah.

Phyllis's husband scrambles backward, not wasting anymore time before jumping onto the back of an enemy currently engaged with the blacksmith.

By the time my muscles are burning with use, warmed, and primed for a continued battle, the fight is over. The dust clears, leaving a sea of crimson on the snow that looks a hell of a lot too close to the way Navalis looked once they were done.

But then, there'd been no one left standing.

Of the fifty fighters we had, seventeen remain breathing. Which, while small, is a victory. I turn toward Carleah, who is watching me with a new curiosity in her blue gaze. Her face is splattered with blood, the scarf covering most of her hair coated.

I rush over and cup her chin, tilting her face to take a closer look at the wound on the side of her head.

"I'm fine," she assures me. "It happened when we fell."

I inwardly curse.

"You both need to get out of here quickly."

Carleah and I face Phyllis, who is helping a limping Micah.

"They will be coming back," he says. "When their men do not show."

"You all need to be gone, too," Carleah replies. "They will bring more."

"We will be," Phyllis assures us. "We're going to bury our dead then head for the mountains. There are some caverns there we can hide out in until this passes." She steps forward and takes one of my hands. "You take what you need and protect our queen," she says. "We need her."

I look back at Carleah. "Always."

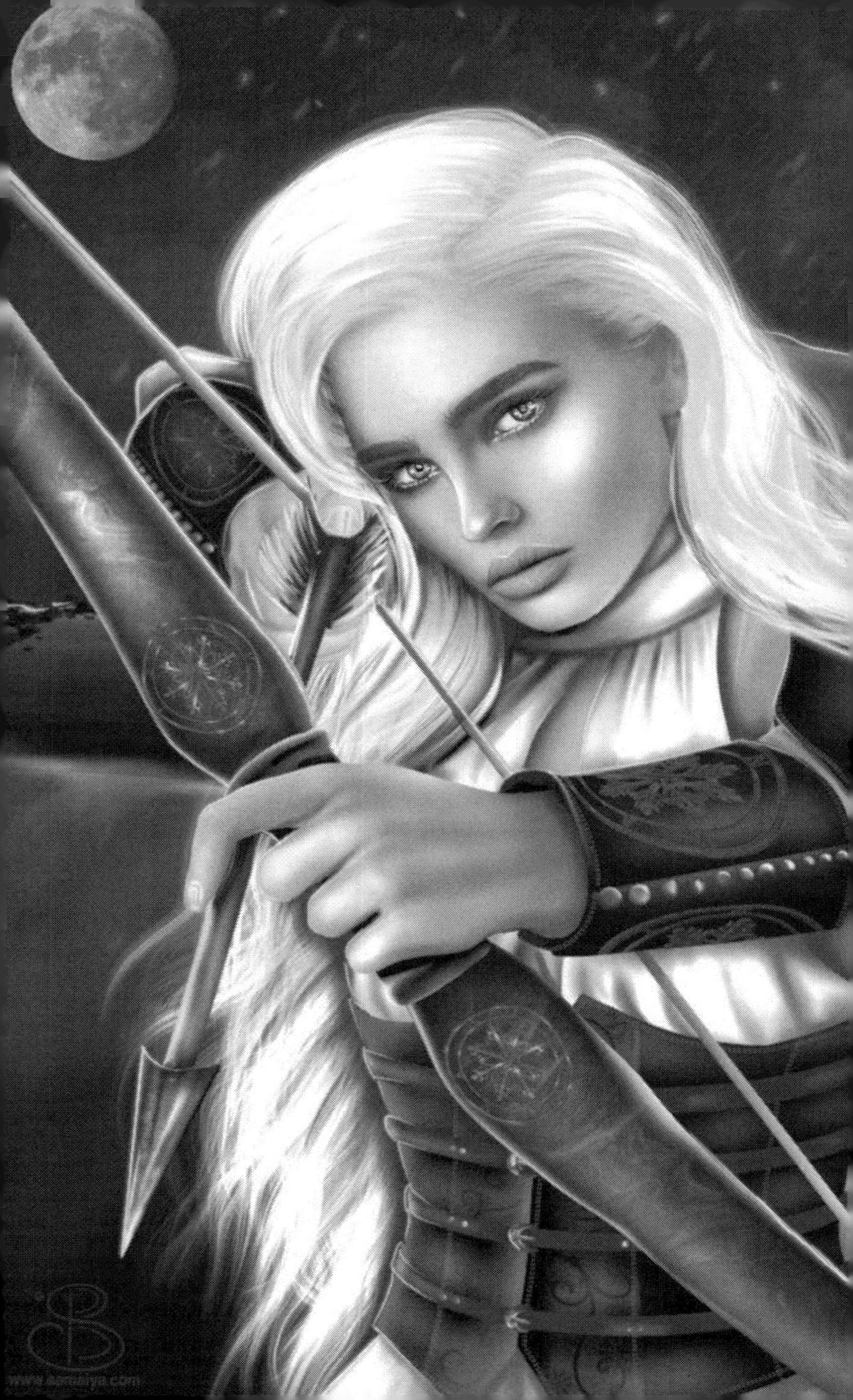

CHAPTER 15
CARLEAH

The sun is just beginning to sink before we stop. The Phantom shimmers just ahead, a thick barrier of clouds and mist that make it impossible to see through. My stomach twists into knots as I consider what it means to cross it.

I will be leaving Navalis behind until who the hell knows when. I take a deep breath and climb off of the back of the mare Phyllis gifted me. Fort dismounts his gelding, and together, we walk them toward a small stream.

We've both been silent since we began our ride, which has given me time to ponder my theory. One I sincerely hope is wrong, but I very much doubt it is.

"We can camp here then go into the Phantom tomorrow."

His shoulders are tense, his tone strained. "What are you?" The words are out of my mouth before I can stop them or come up with a far more tactful way of asking.

Fort turns toward me, snow dusting his obsidian hair. "What?"

I move in closer. "I've never seen a man like you before. You have always been taller than anyone—even Alex—until today. Those men...they were larger than the others. Faster. Stronger—" I trail off then take a step closer. "They were built like and fought like you."

A muscle in his strong jaw flexes, and he averts his gaze.

I recall thinking that I did not believe he was a mute, how I believed the boy had experienced things the man could not face. Now, I realize with horrifying clarity, that I was right.

What has he seen that puts such a darkness in his gaze? "Fort."

"Do you know why those men were stronger?" he asks. "Why they are larger than normal men? Faster?" Now it is he who moves in closer, his amber eyes dark with challenge. "Because Tenebris soldiers are not trained, Carleah. They're *bred*."

"Bred? Like animals?"

"Exactly like animals," he replies. "And...like me."

I suck in a breath and take a step back. I'd known there was something different about Fort. Something I couldn't quite put my finger on until I saw him fighting the Tenebris today. The way they'd moved was so routine, so similar to the same aptitude that Fort displays, I'd been unable to talk myself out of believing it were a possibility.

"You're a Tenebris."

"I would have been," he replies. "Had I not chosen a different path."

"This is why you were so afraid of my father learning where you came from?"

"Yes."

"And just where do you come from?" I question. "Or is it true that Tenebris simply crawl up from the ground?"

"Nemoregno," he replies.

"On the other side of the Phantom," I breathe the words because, of all the things I expected him to say, that was not on the list. "That's why you're so hesitant to cross it. Because you know what's in there and what's on the other side." Emotion claws at my throat.

"Precisely. I've seen the worst of men, Carleah, and they fucking thrive in Nemoregno."

"But you escaped. You were able to run away."

He snorts and shakes his head then turns away from me for a moment. I wait for him to look back again, but he doesn't. Instead, he continues staring at the stream.

"Fort. What aren't you telling me?"

"I didn't run away," he replies. "I was sent. To Navalis."

My blood chills. "What the hell do you mean 'sent'?"

Now Fort faces me, his expression a mask, making it impossible to discern any actual emotion from him. "As young boys, our strength was tested in what we called The Pit. Which is a fancy fucking word for a massive hole full of the skeletons and bodies of those who didn't survive within it. We're thrown in and expected to fight to the death. Only the strongest survive in The Pit. And the dead are left there to rot for all to see."

I'm horrified. Disgusted. Furious. But I do my best to hide it because Fort looks a million miles away as he continues speaking.

"The women there are born to be bred. Every year, men from the army will come to impregnate any who are over the age of seventeen, which is considered old enough to bear children. When they're done, they take any boys who have survived The Pit with them to be trained. The man who fathered me was the leader of Nemoregno, and because of that, I was offered the chance to prove myself worthy by stealing the first-born daughter of Navalis."

Every muscle in my body goes rigid.

My blood ices.

My heart pounds.

What he's saying is fucking *horrific*. Women as breeding stock? Men being shipped off when they are barely old enough to hold a blade?

"I see the horror on your face, Carleah. The disgust. And if you're going to hate me? Fine." He moves in closer and grips the front of my fur coat so I can't leave. Lips pulled back in a half-snarl, he continues, "My mother didn't want me to go into The Pit. She tried to help me escape, and when they caught us, my father had me tortured in front of her. Burned so fucking badly that I would never forget what I'd tried to do. When they took me to the healer, they slaughtered my mother and left her body for me to find." He stares down at me, eyes hard with anger. "Then, my father dragged me to the Phantom and told me that, if I didn't return with the daughter of Navalis, he was going to throw me into The Pit again—only this time, I wouldn't be allowed to leave it."

"You were sent to Navalis to kidnap me?"

"Yes."

"But you were a child."

"That's what you're hung up on?" Fort scoffs and releases me. "Remember how I told you people have been after you since you were born? I was one of those fucking people, Carleah." He slams a fist to his chest. "I was sent to steal you away from your family and take you home to Nemoregno where you would have been bred like a fucking animal as soon as you were old enough. Just so children born in Nemoregno would have some right to claim the throne of Navalis."

A tear slips down my cheek. He wants me to be angry, horrified. And I suppose, in some way, I am. But my horror is for the way the young boy suffered. The way it sounds as though so many suffer. "Did you know who the soldiers were that Alex was going to meet?"

"Yes."

"You didn't tell him?" I choke out. "That the men were not typical men? Did you warn him, Fort?"

"Yes," he says. "I broke the vow I made to myself and told him the night before we set out."

I consider the way Alex had spoken to me before he'd left. He'd been back and forth in his convictions, one moment telling me they were mere men, the next agreeing with me that all legends are based in truth. "Did he not take you seriously?"

"No," Fort replies. "He was convinced that they were merely using legend to drive fear into our hearts."

"He told me as much," I recall.

"And then he made me swear never to tell another my story because he feared your father would have me executed."

I gape at him. "What? No. Father wouldn't have done that. Not after everything you've done for our family."

Fort steps closer. "Yes, Carleah, he would have. Your father may have been a kind man, but he was hard. Unforgiving. And terrified of anything happening to you. He would have had me killed without hesitation simply because he would never have been able to trust me again." He takes another step toward me until he's close enough that I can see the flecks of color in his eyes. "I would always be the man sent there to abduct you."

"Were you ever planning on it?" I ask. "Was there ever a moment you considered taking me?"

"Fuck no," he spits out. "From the moment they killed my mother, I knew there was no way in hell I was *ever* letting them get their hands on you. My purpose in Navalis was to protect you because I couldn't stomach the idea of my father getting what he wanted. Then, it became more about not letting anyone get you because I cared for you. For your entire family. You were what I longed for. So, I kept my mouth shut, let the charade continue, and as soon as I was old enough, I worked my ass off to train an army that could one day protect you. And it failed."

"Fort." I step forward, but he moves away from me.

"How can you still look at me like that?" he demands angrily.

"Like what?"

"Like you give a shit. Did you not fucking hear me, Carleah? I was there to destroy your family by stealing you. That was my sole purpose in life."

"Sounds to me like you hate yourself enough for the both of us." I cross my arms. "You lied, sure. But you didn't do what they asked. If anything, your presence in Navalis kept me safe."

"You call this safe?" he demands, holding out both arms.

"Yeah, I do. Because of you, I am alive." I step closer. "Because of you, an entire village still stands." Another step. "And because of you, Fort, I stand a chance at putting these assholes into graves and getting vengeance for my family and my people."

"I should have gone to your father. Once I knew who those soldiers were. I will never forgive myself for listening to Alex. He might still be alive if I had. They all might."

I reach up and cup Fort's face. He leans into my caress. "No," I say. "They wouldn't because those men were coming regardless." I run my thumb over his scruffy cheek. "But if you're right and my father would have had you executed, then you would be dead, too. And I would be alone, suffering whatever fate it is they meant for me."

He reaches up and covers my hand with his. "You don't know that."

"I do," I reply, throat raw. "And so do you."

He opens his eyes. "I will die before I let anyone get their hands on you, Carleah. I swear it."

"I need you to swear that you will live. That you will survive this. Because I need you, Fort."

Fort's gaze holds mine. "I will do my best," he replies. "But if it's my life for yours, it's not even a choice."

"Then let's hope it never comes down to that." I pull my hand away then turn to survey the snowy ground where we're going to make camp. Fort crosses toward the horses and removes their gear, setting it on the ground beside us. Then, he offers me a bedroll.

After I lay it out, I take his and put it directly beside mine as Fort moves snow from the ground with the side of his boot and drops some dry branches he collected in the center. He sparks his flint together, and it's mere seconds before small flames are crackling before us.

He retrieves the heavy fur blanket we grabbed way back at the kingdom, covers me with it, and sits down at my side. I offer him a corner, and he covers his own lap then removes his gloves and reaches into the saddlebag beside him for a hunk of bread.

After offering me some, he begins to eat. The sun begins to sink overhead, casting us in shadows. Fort moves in closer, and I lean against him as I take a bite. So much to process in what he's told me. So much to understand, but at the core of it, I know Fort is a good man. And I believe every word he spoke.

"You said they burned you," I whisper. "Where?"

He's silent for a moment. "On the insides of my thighs," he replies. "They threatened to take my—" He trails off, and I snake an arm around his waist.

"You don't need to tell me any more," I whisper, trying to keep my tone level when there is so much fury burning inside of me. Tormenting a young boy? Burning him and threatening to remove a piece of him? I fucking hate Nemoregno, and I've never even set foot there. "It's okay."

Fort doesn't respond, but his arm goes around my shoulders, and a yawn escapes his lips,

"Tired?" I ask, looking up at him.

"Yes," he admits with a half-smile.

"Then sleep. I'll keep watch." I reach over and pull Bowman's bow and quiver closer.

"Carle—"

"No argument, Fort. I'll take first watch."

I expect him to argue. Instead, he lies down and tugs the fur up higher on his chest. "Very well. But wake me at the first sign of trouble."

I smile. "Rest easy, warrior, I can take it from here."

Fort closes his eyes, and his breathing evens out, so I begin to hum a lullaby that has been stuck in my head ever since I was a little girl.

"Do you know what you sing?" Fort asks me.

"Just something that has been in my head for as long as I can remember. Why?" He opens his eyes and looks up at me. "It's the tune of my mother," he says softly. "I used to sing it to you."

My heart flutters in my chest. "You sang to me?"

He moves an arm beneath his head and stares up at the trees. "When I first met you, you were nearly a year old. I'd been silently grieving my mother and unsure how to cope with being seven and without one. So, as my way of trying to keep her with me, I'd sung to you whenever no one else could hear me. Your brothers or parents were usually not far, so I had to be careful, but it was the only way I knew to carry my mother with me."

I *knew* his voice was familiar. "Then why did you stop talking to me? I could have kept your secret."

"When you were older, you started asking me questions in front of others. I was scared that they would discover the truth, so I put distance between us."

I feel oddly betrayed. "But you could be my friend when I'd been too young to remember; then turn your back on me and not even tell me why? No wonder I felt so rejected by you. I just didn't understand why. Like a one-sided joke, right? You just couldn't let me in on your secret."

"Carleah—"

"No. I care for you, Fort. I always have. And you dismissed me."

"It was one of the hardest things I'd ever done. You were my friend, despite the years between us. You were the only person I was comfortable talking to. The only one who didn't know enough to ask me questions about things I wished not to answer."

I swallow hard. "Then why ignore me? Why not interact when I spoke to you?" I ask. "You could have at least given me a wave. A smile, something." I recall the way he'd wave to me when we passed. Until I'd become betrothed. Then, it all changed.

He stopped *seeing* me.

"You were to be married. It didn't seem appropriate."

"That's an excuse. And a pathetic one at that." I look away from him. "We were friends before I was ever promised to Patrick, and we could have been friends after."

"Your prince would beg to differ," he snaps. Something in his tone has me taking pause.

"What do you mean?"

Fort turns away from me then mutters something and turns back. "I was approached by your precious Patrick," he replies. "Mocked by his guards for being unable to speak as he warned me to stay away from you. He said, and I'm quoting here, 'I see the way Carleah watches you. She's a foolish princess, and you are the thing she cannot have. Stay away, or I'll have your useless tongue cut from your mouth then tell the king you seek to tarnish his perfect daughter.'"

I gape at him, my blood turning cold as my heart burns with anger. "He *said* that to you?"

"Yes."

"Why didn't you say anything then? Why not—" I trail off and shake my head angrily. "You were going to let me marry someone who treated you like trash."

"It would have been my word against his, and I can guarantee that I would not have been believed after spending my life lying about being unable to speak."

I know he's right. Hell, I can see the way that conversation would have played out, and it would not have been in his favor. My anger deflates. "You should have told me. Then, I could have—"

Fort sits up. "Do you truly believe you had a choice?"

"Of course I did. My father—"

"Loved you," he interrupts. "I will not take that from you, but he was a king, Carleah. And you were in danger. No matter what you wanted, they were going to send you to Soreno. There was no getting out of that marriage for you. But had I told you what a miserable ass Patrick was, you would have gone into your marriage hating him. And what good would that have done you?" He reaches forward and brushes my hair behind my ear.

"I would have known the truth. And knowing is far better than being left in the dark," I tell him.

"I wanted so badly to break the silence between us. You have no fucking idea how hard it was to keep my distance. Especially when I realized how I felt about you. The very knowledge that you would be marrying Patrick was pure torment for me."

"Then why not say anything? Why not fight for me? We could have found a way to be together."

"Because I'm a liar, Carleah. A man bred to be a monster. And you—" He sighs. "You were light, Carleah. Bright, shining light that burned through the darkness etched in my soul. But you were the daughter of a man who took me in when he could have left me to die, and I knew that if I were to open up to you, to tell you how I felt, my secrets would have come to light, and I would have been—"

"Killed," I finish, understanding exactly where this is going. He would have been executed for crimes he never committed, and I would have been sent off to Soreno with a broken heart and a hatred for the man who raised me. "For so long, I just wanted you to *see* me," I tell him.

"I see you, Carleah, and I promise to continue *seeing* you."

I swallow hard. "You're all I have left." The words leave my lips before I can stop them, an unfiltered declaration of affection I used to fight to keep hidden.

"I know. And I will do what I can to be enough until a time comes when you no longer need me."

～

FORT SLEEPS SOFTLY BESIDE ME, his chest rising and falling with his steady breathing. The sun has long since dipped, the golden shadows it cast disappearing along with it. I've seen nothing that makes me wary we were followed, no crunching branches, or footsteps through the forests.

But the Phantom is close, and the mere sight of it has my nerves frayed. It's the protection cast over Navalis when the world fell apart and the giants retreated to their caverns. And now, we're leaving it all behind to seek help from a man who will likely turn his back on us.

I glance back at Fort. Knowing what lies beyond the Phantom has me even more nervous. Learning all of what Nemoregno stands for, of the fact that it was they who created the soldiers who ransacked my home—I take a deep breath, my hands tightening on Bowman's bow.

It is no longer my family I will be getting vengeance for.

But Fort's mother as well. The moment I have my kingdom back, the second I have an army capable enough, I will be destroying Nemoregno and giving refuge to the innocents who wish to find a new home and a new way of life.

Something moves.

I whirl, arrow already nocked, and take sight of the huge stag standing between two trees mere yards away from where we lay. The horses barely notice, but I do.

And my stomach growls.

With a deep breath, I raise the bow and position the arrow. One shot. I have one arrow and one chance.

So, I take it before the thing can run.

The arrow hits it, and it goes down with a muted thud.

I get up slowly, dagger in hand, and move through the trees. It's lying on its side, the arrow straight through the heart just as Bowman taught me. And even as I feel guilt at taking the thing's life, pride warms me. Because tonight, it is me who will be providing a warm meal for the two of us.

After slinging Bowman's bow over my shoulder, I reach down and grab both back hooves. Then, I begin to pull it slowly and painstakingly toward our encampment.

Fort groans and sits up as I'm pulling the first batch of meat from the mostly flat rock I found and placing in the center of what is now a slightly larger fire.

"What is that smell?" he asks as he shoves the fur aside and comes to kneel on the opposite side of the flames. His gaze widens when he notices the meat. "How long have I been asleep?"

"A few hours, I'd guess."

"And in those few hours, you managed to hunt, kill, dress, and cook a stag?"

I grin at him. "Impressed?"

"More than."

I hold out the leather pouch that had our bread in it and now contains a portion of cooked meat. He takes a piece, sticks it in his mouth, and groans. "Fuck, that's good."

"Yeah?"

He grins, and my heart stumbles at the sight of it. "Oh, yes."

More pride warms my chest as I put more raw meat onto the stone. It sizzles, searing to the surface while I dig into the pouch and eat. The meat is warm and tender with a hint of the winterberries the animal grazed on.

"Apparently, all those times I thought I didn't need to follow you because Bowman had taken over, I should have been paying closer attention." He smiles at me. "What else did he teach you how to do?"

"You pretty much know it now," I reply with a

haunted smile. With each passing day, I miss my brothers more and more. My parents. My people. "He taught me to use a bow, a dagger, and some minor self-defense. He also taught me to track, hunt, clean, and cook an animal just in case I was ever in a position to need to do so." I use the stick I've been using to flip the meat over. "I never thought there would come a day when I didn't have them, you know?"

An owl hoots above, and I smile.

In the midst of such pain.

Such grief.

Such chaos.

Life continues.

Yet more proof that while it's a beautiful tragedy, that my family may have been my entire world, the entire world will not stop now that they are gone.

I close my eyes against the onslaught of tears. Will I ever stop crying? Will I ever be able to face the memories of them without wanting to go back and die alongside them?

"Are you all right?"

"Yes," I reply, opening my eyes to look at him. "I just miss them."

"It's okay to not be all right," he says. "Don't believe that anyone will ever think less of you just because you are not."

"I know they won't. But I also know that crying is not going to get us where we need to go. So when this is over, and I can go home to bury my family, then I will grieve."

"We will succeed," he says. "No matter what we have

to do to get there, I promise that I will deliver you to the steps of your family home."

I smile then add the new meat to the leather pouch before standing and crossing over to sit beside Fort. "I know we will." Though, in my heart, I'm honestly not so sure. It all hinges on Soreno.

Without them, I have no army. And there is no way Fort and I can fight the Tenebris alone.

I lie back on the bedroll and pull the fur up to my chest so I can stare up at the sky.

Fort continues to sit beside me. "Rest now, Carleah, I'll keep watch."

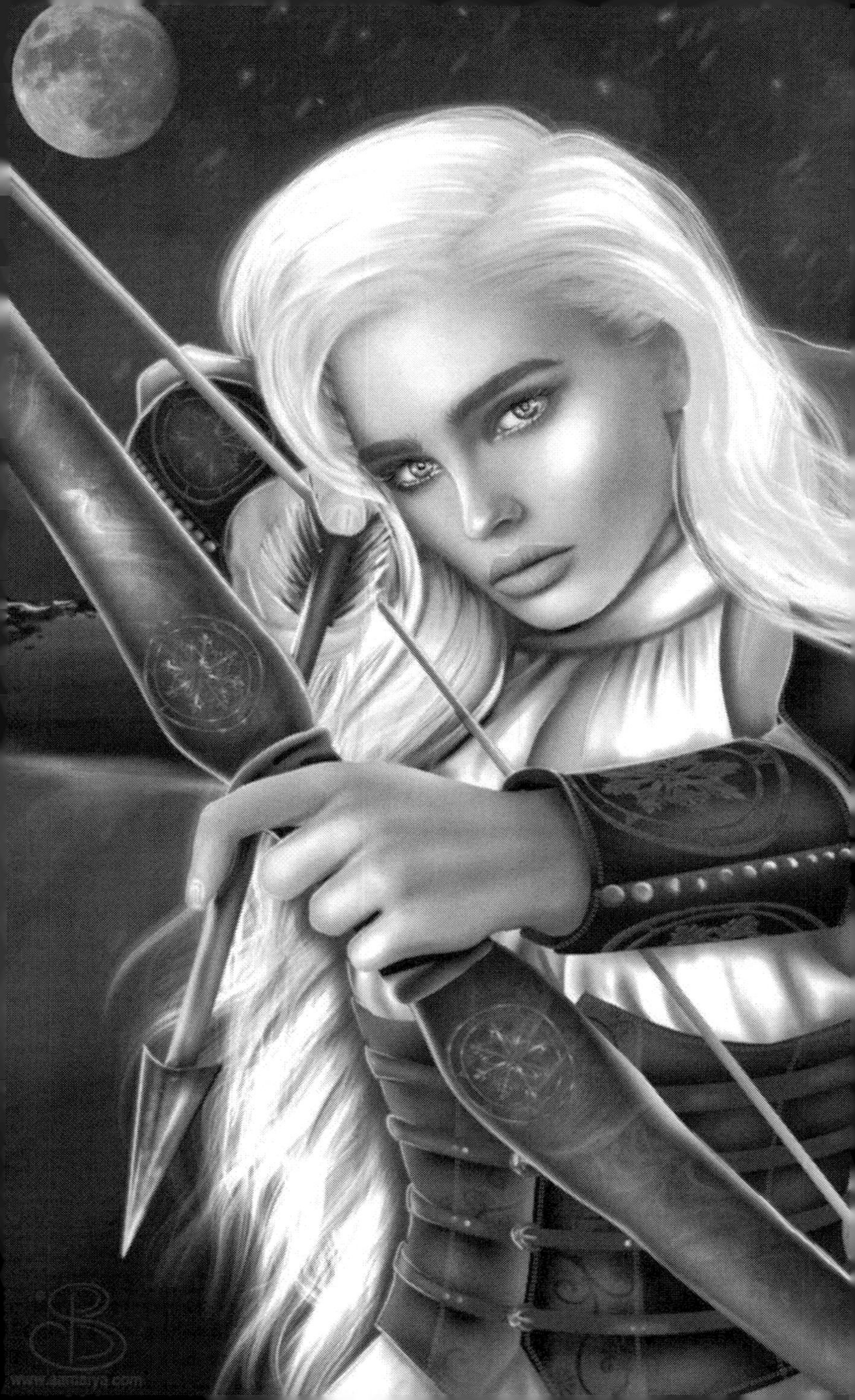

CHAPTER 16
CARLEAH

"Will you tell me what's in there?" I ask as I stare at the Phantom shimmering directly in front of us. Fort reaches into his pack and pulls a long cord of rope.

"Nothing," he replies. "But the danger is real enough."

"Can you truly see nothing?"

Fort secures one side of the rope to my mare's reins. "Nothing."

"How long does it take to cross?"

"I was in there for a week."

"A week?" I choke out. "Of not being able to see anything? You were so young!"

His gaze levels on mine. "It is important that you decide now if you want to turn back. We can hide, try to find our own people to fight. Wait for a supply ship, anything else."

"We don't have time to do that," I remind him. "Even

losing a week in there—" I swallow hard as I look into the thick fog barrier before us. "We will arrive before the ship would."

"This presents more of a risk. Especially once we reach Nemoregno."

"The Cerulean Seas are not safe, either," I say.

"Pirates do not stray this close to the coast," he insists.

I reach out and touch the side of his face. His stubble scrapes against my finger, and even as I try to avoid the shiver that runs through my body, I cannot. Especially when he reaches up and covers my hand with his.

"We will survive this," I tell him.

"Should anything happen and we get separated, you run, Carleah. Understand?"

"If you're asking me to leave you, I won't."

Fort shakes his head. "You need to."

"No. If we die, we die together."

"You are the future of Navalis."

"And I don't want it if it means losing you, too."

He steps closer and rests his forehead against mine. "Please promise me that you will run. You vowed to bring those people to safety."

"I will not leave you behind, Fort. Not even to save my own life."

Fort pulls back, wearing a harsh expression on his face as he secures the rope to his horse's saddle. "It will be easier if we ride together."

"Okay." The thought of him pressed against me when I can see nothing brings me a tinge of relief. Because, for some reason, knowing Fort is there gives me confidence that we're going to make it through.

He's become my lifeline in the midst of death.

My hope when all feels downright hopeless.

I stare at the Phantom. It moves like thick mist, coating the ground and disappearing up into the sky as far as I can see. Every muscle in my body is tense as I consider again what it means to cross it. I will be leaving Navalis behind and entering a realm full of people who breed their women and slaughter for sport.

"Are you—"

I whirl and throw myself at him, flinging both arms around his neck and slamming my mouth to his. Fort's mouth is feverish on mine as he wraps one arm around my body and snakes the other up to the back of my neck.

He pins me to him, kissing me as though his very breath depends on it.

My back hits something solid, so I wrap my legs around his waist, his hard length pressing directly against me. I want him—desperately. But even wanting him as I do, I know we'll likely freeze to death if this goes much further.

So, I pull back and stare into his eyes.

"The first chance we get," he starts. "We're fucking finishing what we started back at that inn."

"Deal."

With nerves dancing in my belly and a heaviness in my chest, I climb onto his gelding, and Fort gets on behind me, one arm banding around my waist while the other holds the reins.

I lean back against him. "The ground changes in there, and if the horses don't sense it—"

I don't need him to finish the sentence to know it would be bad. "Let's go."

"You're sure?" he asks me one more time.

I glance over my shoulder. "Yes."

He guides the gelding forward. The front of the horse passes through the Phantom easily enough with no obvious discomfort, so I am not expecting the pressure that slams into me as we move into it. It repels my presence as though I'm trying to press through a wall. Pain sings through my body, burning in my blood.

"It. Hurts," I grind out.

"A deterrent," Fort says, his tone betraying his own pain. "It gets easier to tolerate the farther in you get."

The heaviness pressing against my chest makes it difficult to breathe, I begin to panic, my hands clenching the reins. "Fort?" I call out. I can feel him behind me, but I cannot hear him. I turn to face him, twisting in my saddle. "Fort?" I scream his name as I lean in closer.

"Easy, Carleah. I'm here." He leans down so I can see his face through the mist. It wraps around him, though, obscuring most of his body and part of his expression.

"I can hardly breathe," I choke out.

My lungs burn; my body aches.

"Lean back against me."

"I can't breathe," I repeat. "It's like something is pressing on my—" I try to suck in a breath, but it's scarcely more than a wheeze. Everything burns, aching with a need I cannot even begin to fathom.

And then—it's gone.

All of it.

The Phantom vanishes, leaving us in a sprawling green paradise, unlike anything I've ever seen.

"What the—" Fort stops the gelding and I stare up at the bright sun. Birds flitter overhead. Somewhere in the distance water crashes down—a waterfall.

I've never seen such beauty, and even though I love the snowy lands of my kingdom, this is magnificent. So much grass, so many bright blooms along the path we're standing on. "Where are we?"

"I don't know," he whispers.

Up ahead, the Phantom shimmers. It sits behind us and on either side, sprawling as far as the eye can see. But this sliver we stand in is bright and green. It makes no sense.

"You sure you were here before?"

"Yes," he whispers, half in awe. "But I never saw it like this." He swings his leg over, and both boots hit the ground. Fort goes completely rigid. He whirls toward me, his gaze never falling on me. It's as though he's looking straight past me. "Carleah!" he calls out.

"I'm right here!" I reach out and touch his shoulder, and he jumps. The gelding jolts away from his movement. But Fort stares up at me now, eyes wide with the panic that has not yet abated.

"You were gone," he says. "The Phantom was back. I don't—what the hell is going on?"

A theory forms in my mind, but I don't want to risk the horse becoming scared and throwing me. So, I swing a leg over and slide off of his back all while keeping my hand firmly on Fort's shoulder. It slides a little once my boots hit the ground, thanks to our height difference, but the contact remains.

"Bear with me," I say. "And don't panic." I remove my hand, and Fort's eyes go wide again. He turns in a slow circle, and I watch his expression morph from fear to confusion.

I touch his arm again, and his gaze clears once more. He turns back toward me. "What is happening?"

I look at where my hand rests against his arm. "I think it's me."

"What?"

"Watch." I remove my hand for a moment then press it back. "The horses must not see the Phantom either." I note the gelding as he drops his head and begins to graze on the grass. "But why me? Why can I see through it now, and you can't?"

"I don't know." Fort's tone is one of awe.

"Maybe because I was born in Navalis?"

He shakes his head. "Alex and Bowman tried to cross it once, and they couldn't see through it either. I had to pull on the rope tied to both of their waists to get them out."

"They tried to cross the Phantom?"

He nods.

"Why?"

"Because they thought they could," he replies.

Realization dawns, and I can't help my small smile. "It was a competition."

"Exactly."

"They were always doing stuff like that." I look around, noting the fragrant flowers, bright sun, and the shimmering of the stream running on our left. "So why can I see through it, and they couldn't?"

"I am not sure," he says. "But we should thank our lucky stars that you can. Because shit's about to be a whole hell of a lot easier. Hopefully." Sweat beads on his brow. "You hot?"

"Yes. Think we can manage to get these off?" I ask, gesturing to our coats.

He reaches up and cups my cheek. "You first."

I release him then shrug out of my jacket as best I can. The moment the weight is off of me, a cool breeze dances over the exposed flesh just over my collarbone and my wrists. I breathe a sigh of relief, drop the coat to the ground, and reach up to cup Fort's face. I have to stand on my tip-toes to maintain the contact.

He shrugs out of his jacket, muscles bulging beneath the thin fabric of his tunic. As soon as he's free of his own jacket, I reach down with one hand and thread my fingers through his before retrieving my coat.

The horses continue grazing, none the wiser to the Phantom surrounding us. Perhaps it's something to do with me being the first-born daughter of a Navalis royal?

"We should continue moving," Fort says. "Just in case this doesn't last long."

I place my coat over the saddle of my mare, still attached to Fort's gelding. He does the same, so I turn to face him.

"You climb on first, and I'll follow." Fort opens his mouth to argue. "I can still see you when we're not touching, Fort, but you will not be able to find the horse."

He hesitates for a moment then pulls me toward the gelding. I keep one hand on him as he climbs on, only releasing him long enough to get on myself. As soon as I'm situated, Fort wraps an arm around my waist, holding on tighter, and I keep my palms pressed to that arm for good measure.

∽

Nightfall comes far too soon, but we're able to find a spot beside a river to rest. After climbing down, Fort takes my hand, lacing our fingers together, as he secures his gelding to a tree. The mare is still tethered to his saddle, so he leaves her for now, though he retrieves our coats and offers them to me. Once he's pulled the fur blanket from the mare's back, we cross over to the stream and lay them all out on the ground.

Hands linked together, we manage to grab some of last night's meat and bread from our saddlebags then return to our jackets where we sit now, eating. My belly full, I lie back and stare up at the bright stars. "It feels strange to not need furs or a jacket."

He chuckles and lies back beside me. "It does. I think I know why you can see and I cannot."

"Why?"

"Because you are pure, Carleah. And pure souls are magic."

"You're pure, too," I insist.

He smiles and shakes his head. "I do not believe I have ever been pure. I was born to be a killer, remember?"

"And what makes you think I am?"

"Because light shines *through* you."

I turn my head to the side to look at him. "I don't know if I believe that. I cannot fathom a reality where a young boy is damned simply because of the blood in his veins."

"Then believe that I am damned for what I've done in my life. I've killed, Carleah. Tortured men for information."

"But you did it to keep Navalis safe."

"I don't think that matters in the bigger picture. Though, I don't regret it." He looks at me. "Because my actions kept you safe. I had a purpose there. Even if I couldn't help but wait for the day someone would discover my secret and the soldiers I trained would come for me."

"That's a horrible way to live." My heart aches for the loneliness that must have brought him.

"It was living, though," he replies. "I had a purpose, and that's all I could have hoped for."

I roll over onto my side then touch his chest with my left hand so I can remove my right and prop my head up on it. "The night before you and Alex left—"

"You mean when you followed me to my room and made it really fucking hard to go?" He arches a brow at me, and heat rushes to my cheeks.

"Yes. Had you thought of me that way before?"

"I told you, Carleah, I've been thinking of getting my hands on you ever since that night by the lake," he replies.

"Then why did you stay away? Even if you didn't think I felt the same, you had to know before you and Alex left. After I came to your room. Why did you let me leave?"

"I went to you," he says. "That night. But Alex was there."

My chest tightens. "You came to my room?"

"I did," he says. "But Alex was just going in, and it was yet another stark reminder that you deserved someone you didn't have to sneak around with. I was never going to be the man you were allowed to have."

"We could have tried." But even as I say it, that final conversation with my father comes to mind, shattering any illusion I might have had for a happily ever after with Fort.

Fort wraps an arm around my waist and pulls me toward him. His lips capture mine, a tender caress that increases with the beat of my heart. I wrap my arms around his neck as he rolls me onto my back and straddles me.

"I would have given anything to taste you," he says softly. "To know what you felt like beneath me."

"We have now," I say. "And tomorrow is not promised." I slide my hands down his back and run my fingers over the soft flesh of his butt. "Please, Fort."

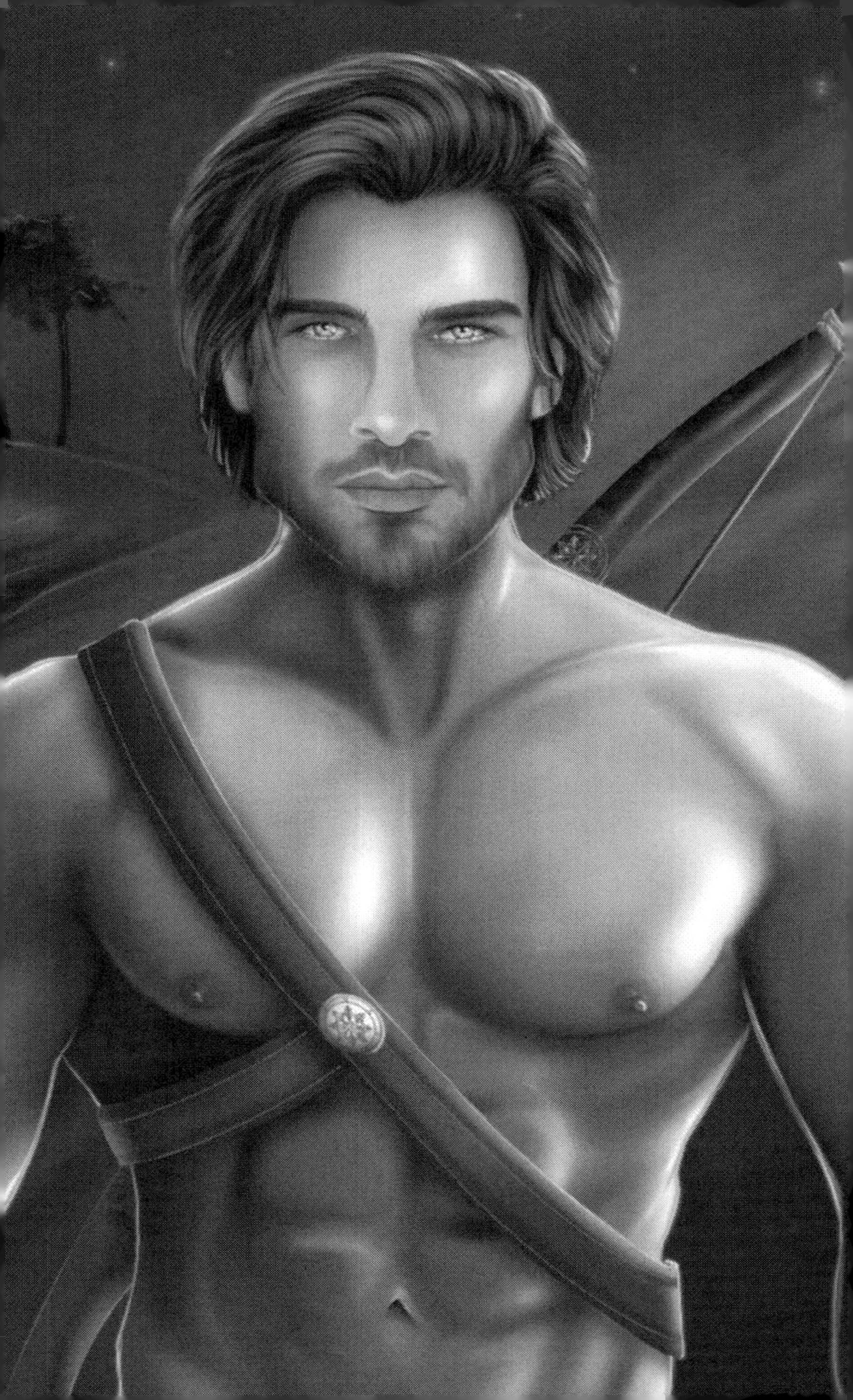

CHAPTER 17
FORT

"Please, Fort," she whispers again. I stare down at her, the bright moon above casting a silvery glow over her features. I'd been so angry with myself for even considering walking down that hall toward her room.

But the feel of her lips against mine, the way her body molded perfectly against me—I'd been unable to get the image of it out of my mind.

And now, here we are, in complete privacy.

Surrounded by a misty veil.

I press my lips against hers. "Tell me what you want, Carleah. Command me, and I'm yours." I lean down, breathing her in. "There's not a damn thing I won't do for you." I glide my lips over her throat, pausing at her throbbing pulse. I press a kiss to it then gently nip her throat. "Whatever you want."

Never, in a million centuries, would I have believed I'd be standing here with her. But ever since I saw her next to that fucking lake. Lips swollen, breathing ragged, touching her is all I've dreamt about. Even if it felt wrong to want someone like that who is not only younger than I am but the daughter of a man who saved me from certain death.

Even now that she's twenty, I still feel like I am robbing her of a future she deserves with someone else. Someone who didn't spend his entire adult life fucking away memories with every willing woman who crossed his path.

"I want you," she whispers.

I don't respond because I can't find the words to describe what I feel for her. Instead, I reach up and pull the tunic from my body. Then, I grip her hands and pull her to her feet. Once she's standing in front of me, lips parted, I swallow hard and release her.

The world goes dark around me, mist closing in until Carleah's palms rest against my bare chest. She grounds me, calling to the ugliness I was born with in my soul. I have never met anyone who quells the bloodlust like Carleah. She makes me want to be a better man.

I grip her wrists and remove her hands from me because I don't want to see the look of pity on her face once she sees the scars I was left with.

After releasing her again, I close my eyes and slip out of my boots and the rest of my clothing until I'm standing before her, completely bared. My heart thunders in my chest, my blood burning with need.

If she is so disgusted by what she sees that she walks away—

Gentle hands caress my leg, brushing over the ugly raised scars left behind by my father's torch. I open my eyes.

Carleah kneels at my feet, her fingers brushing over my damaged flesh. And when she looks up at me, it is not pity I see.

There is no sadness in her harsh blue gaze. Only anger.

"I want to find and kill him for this."

I reach down and pull her to her feet. I capture her lips, stealing every kiss I've long since dreamt about. Carleah lets out a breathless sigh as I let my hands slide down her body and tug the tunic free from her torso.

She pulls back and grins at me. "My turn." Then she removes her hands from my chest and disappears from view.

My pulse thunders.

I remain where I am, completely blind as she removes her clothing. Something hits me in the chest, and instinctively, I reach out and catch her tunic.

My mouth goes dry.

"This is a twisted game you play, Your Highness," I groan.

Her laughter drifts toward me. Then her breath fans over my back. "I find it quite delicious," she says, still not touching me.

I spin and catch her, my arms closing around her body and crushing her toward me. Her flesh warms mine, breasts pressed against my chest. My cock is so fucking hard I can barely stand it, but I'm nowhere near ready for this to end.

With her in my arms, I lay her back on our jackets then lean back enough to take in the sight of her naked body before me. Soft, milky skin, delicious curves, and eyes that steal my breath. I rest a hand over the hollow of her throat then slide it down between her breasts and toward her belly.

"That feels good," she whispers. "That feels so damned good, Fort."

Leaning down, I run my tongue over her pebbled nipple.

A light breeze carries past us, lifting strands of her white hair from her face and sending it dancing away as she arches up. The groan that comes from her throat vibrates straight down to my cock. Most women would be shy at being laid out bare so openly.

But not Carleah. She fucking owns it.

I close my mouth over the taut pink tip of her nipple.

"Yes," she moans.

I draw it into my mouth, sucking, tasting, taking my time with each and every languid stroke. We've been waiting for this moment for so fucking long that the desire to pull her down on top of my cock is near painful.

But fast and hard can come later because right now I want to *savor*.

Every sound.

Every taste.

Every moment of this night...forever.

I release her nipple and pull back to stare into her

glossy eyes. "Are you certain this is what you want?" I ask, holding her bright gaze with my own. If she were to ask me to stop now, I would. Even though it would kill me to do so. Carleah is all that matters to me now.

She's all I have left.

With trembling fingers, she reaches up and cups the sides of my face. "Hell yes," she replies.

"Are you scared?" I ask as I reach up and brush her hair away from her face.

"No," she replies. "Not with you."

I drop my face to hers and gently kiss her lips as my hand slips down and cups her breast. It's full in my hands, and as I run my thumb over her nipple, she lets loose a throaty moan. It drives me fucking wild.

I release her mouth and draw her other nipple into my mouth, sliding my tongue over it as I gently pinch the one I've already tasted between my fingers.

"Yes," she moans.

I release her breasts and slide down her body. Carleah watches me as I grip her thighs and spread her open for me.

"I've dreamt of you like this. Fucking spread out before me, your wet pussy mine for the taking." I lean in closer and press my lips to the inside of her right thigh, letting my hot breath fan over her slick heat as I move to the other side. "I've longed to taste you, to run my tongue over you until you come."

"I—" She trails off as I press my lips to the inside of her other thigh.

"Do you want me to do that?" I ask. "Do you want me

to taste you here?" I take my finger and slide it over her pussy. It's so fucking slick, so hot and wet.

She jerks. "Oh my—yes. Please."

I chuckle. "Your wish is my command, Carleah." I run my tongue over her slit. Her flavor explodes on my tongue, a tangy sweetness that makes my blood boil within my veins.

"Yes!" she cries out and bucks off the ground, so I press her back down with a hand to her lower belly. "Please, Fort," she groans.

I run my tongue back over her again then close around her clit. She moans as I suck it into my mouth, teasing the taut bud with my teeth and tongue. As she's distracted with the pleasure, I bring a finger up and gently press it inside her.

Wet heat surrounds it, and I have to force myself to move slow, to gently press inside her and not lose myself in the passion. She's untouched, so I take my time exploring her body with my mouth, my fingers.

I draw her clit back into my mouth as I press another finger inside her. She bucks up against my hand, her hips thrusting as she grinds against my face.

"Yes. Don't stop. Don't—fuck yes!"

The word *fuck* rolling off of her tongue is like a damned present to me. I don't let up, not even when she comes undone and her release drenches me. I continue pulling at her clit and moving my fingers in and out, drawing out every single ounce of her pleasure. Until she falls slack beneath me. Then, I sit up and slowly remove my fingers, keeping the palm of my hand on her taut stomach. Her blue gaze is shining so damned brightly it nearly illuminates the area around her face.

With her watching, I slip my fingers into my mouth and groan as I suck her release from them. Her lips part, eyes widening.

"That was—" She trails off. "So much better than I ever imagined."

"And just what have you imagined?" I question as I move up her body again. I take her mouth with more passion this time, and as my reward, Carleah nips my bottom lip. Pulling back, I smile down at her. "I am yours, Carleah. Tell me what you want."

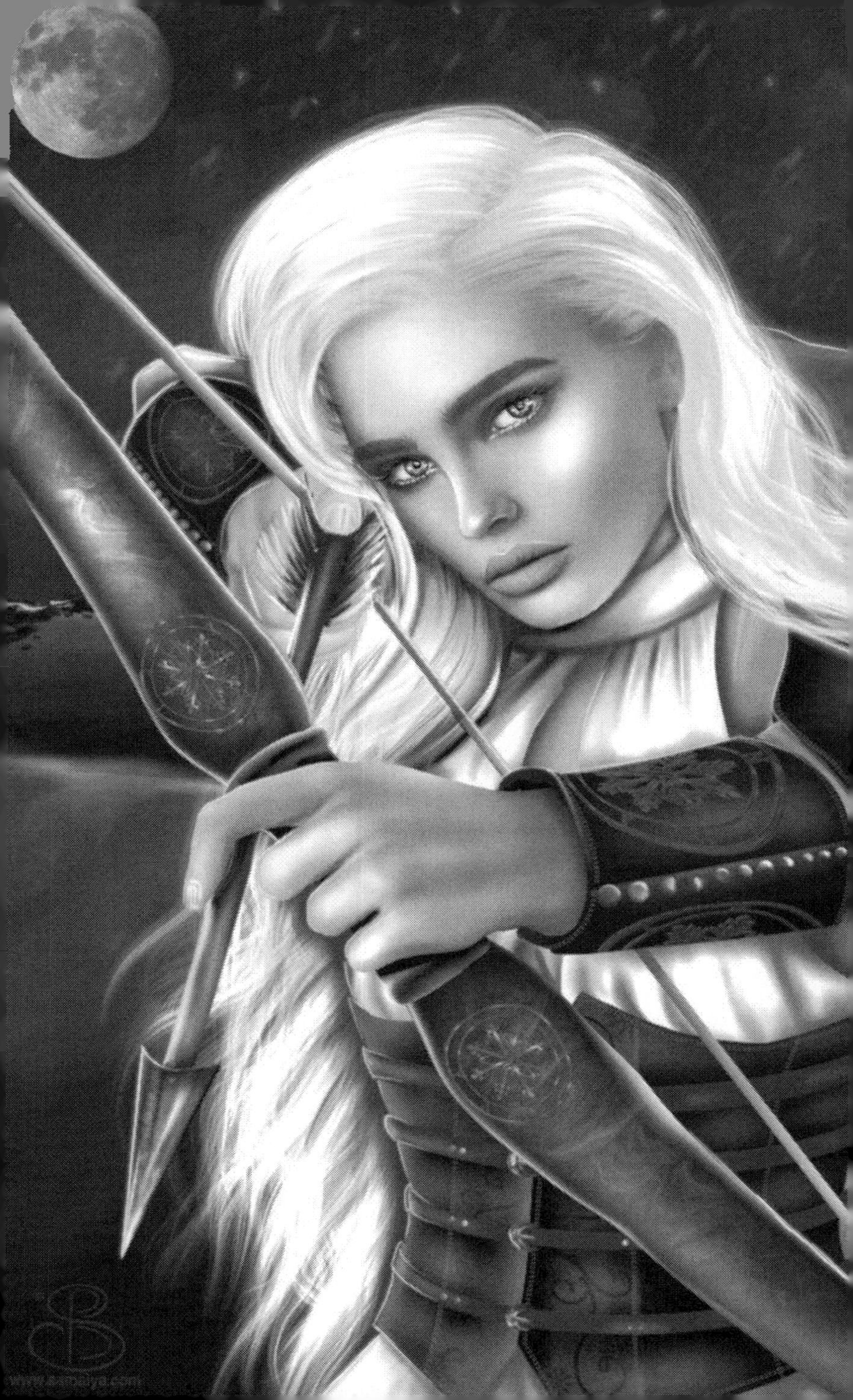

CHAPTER 18
CARLEAH

"*I am yours, Carleah. Tell me what you want.*"

Fort's declaration settles against the fissures of my heart, a bandage to cover the wounds that always haunt me. The throbbing between my legs has eased, but I feel it coming back. A steady thrumming of passion within me.

"I want to touch you."

He grins, and my heart flips. Fort has always been handsome, but right now in the midst of our passion, I've never seen him look so damned good. "As you command." He rolls off of me, careful to keep one hand on me as he lies on his back. "Do what you want."

I get to my knees and stare down at him. His body is muscled from years of training, each line and ridge defined. His expansive torso leads to a deep V on his lower abdomen that seems to point directly at his hard length.

It stands up, looking far larger now that I'm sitting here with him.

I'm a little afraid now, of the pain it will bring, but I do not tell him that. Instead, I reach out and run my palms over his chest. It's warm beneath my hands, and with each new inch explored, I watch Fort's expression.

He stares up at me, gaze never leaving mine. Not even when I reach his hips. Though, then my gaze drops to his length.

Heart hammering, lust burning, I reach out and grip him with my palm. He's far too large for me to completely close my hand around him, but he's silky smooth and hard as granite. I squeeze, and he moans.

"Does that feel good?" I question, unsure if it was pain or pleasure that brought the sound from his throat.

"That feels so fucking good, Carleah." As though demonstrating, he arches up into my hand then falls back to the ground.

I squeeze him again, this time sliding my hand up his shaft.

"Yes," he coos. "More."

My hand glides over his silky flesh, and I feel my own body growing warmer at the idea of it sliding inside of me. I'm desperate to feel it, to have him own me completely, even as the fear that it'll be unbearable sets in.

His eyes are closed, so I take in the sight of his hard length beneath the bright silvery moonlight above. A bead of liquid slips from the slit, so I lean down and run my tongue over it. The salty tang dances on my tongue, and Fort moans.

"Fuck. Carleah. I—"

"Does that feel good?" I ask even as I can see that it does. But I want him to keep talking to me. Because it turns me on.

"Do you have any idea how many times I imagined your mouth on my cock?"

"So you want me to do this?" I question as I run my tongue over the tip of him again.

"Fuck yes," he growls.

I open my mouth and take him inside of me until I nearly gag and tears spring to the corners of my eyes, but Fort growls low and deep again, and the sound of it spurs me on. I grip him with one hand as I work him with my mouth until my jaw is so damned sore I can hardly see straight.

Then, I come off of him and move up his body, straddling him so I'm hovering directly above his dick.

"Anything you want," he tells me. "Take it." Fort snakes a hand around the back of my neck; the other he rests on my hip. Then, he pulls me down and kisses me hard. A passionate frenzy that has my pulse hammering so loud it's all I can hear.

When he releases me, I take a deep breath then slide down on top of him. Pain has me seeing stars, so I freeze, the pressure nearly too much to take.

"Easy," he groans. "Take your time."

After a few heartbeats, I let myself down further. He completely fills me, and when something inside of me gives way, I slide all the way down onto him. "Oh my—" I throw my head back and breathe deeply, remaining completely still as the sting fades, leaving only the pressure.

"You feel so fucking good," he groans. "I—" He trails off, and his lack of speech empowers me.

I draw off of him again then slide back down, the pressure begins to morph into pleasure, so I move a bit faster, gliding off and then back onto him.

Fort's hand leaves the back of my neck, and he grips my breasts with both palms. His calloused thumbs brush over my nipples, sending even more pleasure through me.

"Does it feel good?" he asks.

"Yes," I reply as I move faster. Faster. My release begins to build within me, pressure starting in my lower abdomen. Every muscle in my body tightens in preparation, and I lose myself in the rhythm of our bodies moving together.

For so long, this has been what I wanted.

Fort.

He surrounds me now, his scent, the feel of his hands against my body, the taste of him on my lips—every part of the man is branded onto my flesh—my heart. Never did I truly believe I would get to give him this part of me, get to experience this type of ecstasy with him, but now that I have, I know I can't ever let him go.

I change the rhythm, moving faster now, up and down, up and down, and then—my release consumes me.

"Yes! Fort!" I scream his name into the misty barrier around us.

As I shatter around him, Fort rolls me over onto my back. He raises one of my thighs and drives in even deeper. I gasp, my hands grasping at his arms as he pumps into me. He thrusts his hips, driving harder and deeper inside my body until I'm sure I will shatter.

Then, he pulls out of me and rests back on his knees, one hand on my abdomen, the other pumping his length until he comes, his release spraying onto his palm. Our combined breathing is ragged while my heart races. Fort's gaze finds mine.

"Was that—okay?"

"Was it okay?" he repeats as he stares down at me. "Carleah, that was—amazing. Magnificent. World-shifting. More than fucking okay."

"I've never—" I close my eyes and take a deep breath, relief settling into my bones. "I wanted to make sure it was good for you."

He leans down and captures my lips. I can still taste myself on his tongue, and it warms me to know that a part of me has remained. "You don't worry about me. You are perfect, Carleah. Fucking magnificent. I—"

"Keep fucking moving, you coward," a sharp, unwelcome voice fills our ears. Fort grips his sword, moving like a damned blur until his back is to me, his body blocking mine from the army of men moving through the Phantom.

I pull the fur over my body, my hand closing on the dagger he gave me where it lies directly beside my jacket.

I grip it, keeping it close as they stumble through, each of them with a hand on the man in front of them.

Like Fort when we're not touching, they cannot see, cannot hear, but I recognize their armor plain as day. Crimson soldiers carrying a black banner move past us, unaware that the woman they are after lies mere feet away.

Fort starts to move toward them, but I grip him tighter. I want them dead, too, but they outnumber us. And on the off chance we lose—

"This is fucking miserable," a man groans.

"Did you truly think it would be pleasant, you fucker? But this is the quickest way to Navalis."

"The ships are the quickest way," another grumbles.

"The ships cannot see past the Phantom that has surrounded the damned city since the royal family was gutted like the pigs they are."

Now it's my time to move. I reach for Bowman's arrow and the quiver resting against the tree beside us, but Fort turns and shakes his head. I could kill the man, but then I'm alerting them of our presence.

He remains where he is, between me and the soldiers, as they continue grumbling and moving through the mist.

"Fucking Phantom," another growls.

"We find the little princess bitch, we don't ever have to deal with the shit again," another adds.

"If the legends are true."

Legends.

"She's probably dead by now. I just wish I'd gotten a

look at her before. They say she was quite a looker." The man throws his head back and laughs. "Royal whore."

I swallow hard, ignoring their insults because all I can focus on is their statement over legends and what I have to do with the Phantom. What the hell does that even mean?

By the time the last man has stalked through the Phantom, my adrenaline has waned. There must have been nearly a hundred of them—that we could see. And they're all headed to Navalis.

Looking for me.

Fort turns toward me. "We need to be more fucking careful." He scans my face. "Are you okay?"

"They speak of my family as though they deserved what they got," I reply.

Fort is visibly shaking, his body vibrating with rage. "They're going to all fucking pay," he growls. "Every last one of them will bleed for what they've done."

"What legends do you think they're referring to? The giants?"

He glares after them. "I don't know."

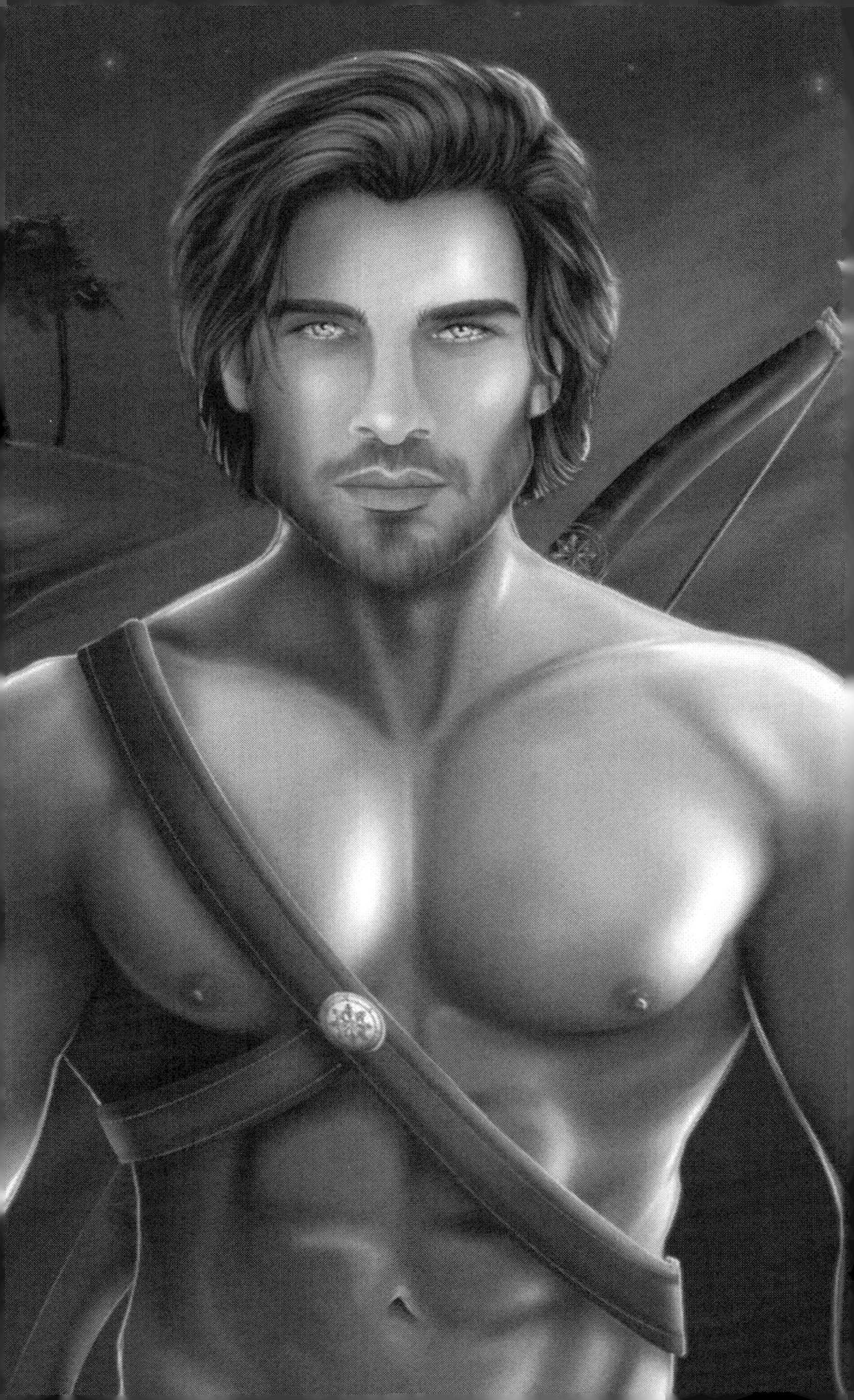

CHAPTER 19
FORT

The moment I open my eyes, my heart begins to race.

Thick, white fog surrounds me. It claws at my throat, at my eyes. "Carleah!" I bellow, scrambling to my feet. All I can picture is those men stumbling on her while she'd been keeping watch. If they took her—I spin in a circle. Afraid to move, to leave, but I need to find her. To touch her.

"I'm here."

I rush forward and slam into a solid body. The moment the contact is made, the fog vanishes, and I get a sight of Carleah as we fall to the ground—me on top of her. My body pins her to the grass. She reaches up and grips the sides of my face as my palms rest on the cool grass on either side of her head.

"You were gone."

"I went to grab water." Her sharp blue gaze narrows. "Are you okay?"

"I thought—" I close my eyes and breathe deeply.

"I'm right here," she whispers. "And I'm sorry I left you."

As my heart begins to slow, I become increasingly aware of the slight body beneath mine. Of my dick between her legs, her breasts pressed against my chest. Lust pounds in my ears. Spurred on by the way her gaze drops to my mouth.

I hunger for her even more now that I've tasted the passion between us. The heat.

I start to lean in, to close the distance—a horse stomps its foot.

It's enough of a distraction to have me pulling away. The men nearly stumbling on us last night while we'd been fucking naked had been enough of a reason to keep some distance until we're somewhere safe.

So even though I want to bury myself in her, I pull her to her feet.

"We should get moving," I say as I lace my fingers with hers. Together, we collect the jackets and blanket. Then, with one hand, I manage to strap all three to the back of our mare. Once the clearing is emptied of our presence, I untie the gelding and climb onto his back.

The Phantom smothers me the moment Carleah's hand leaves mine. But seconds later, she's climbing onto him and sliding back against my body.

"How are you feeling?" I ask as I guide the gelding forward.

"A little sore," she admits. "But otherwise, I feel good.

I've wanted that for so long; it's nearly surreal that—" She chuckles.

"I know what you mean." I press a kiss to the top of her head and she leans back against me. I hate myself a little, for finding such joy amidst her pain. Amidst the loss of her parents, brothers, and people.

But being with Carleah heals something inside of me. A darkness that I've never quite been able to calm. Unfortunately, it's that darkness I must return to and embrace if we're to survive where we're going next. "We need to talk about Nemoregno."

"What about it?"

"There are very few places to hide in Nemoregno. It's flat, barren land, and if we're not careful, we will be spotted quickly by the tribe. By my—"

"Family?" she finishes.

I take a deep breath. "We need to hope my bloodline is dead. No one in power there will show us any mercy, but my father has a petulance for revenge. He'd have me punished and executed for abandoning them."

Carleah turns her head to stare at me, eyes wide with horror. "Are you serious?"

"Deadly. The moment we cross through that Phantom, we will be in immediate danger. We need to move fast and quiet."

She stares back at me a moment then nods. "Okay."

"And—should we be caught—they *cannot* know what you are to me. They cannot know about—" I trail off and cup her cheek. "This. What we have."

Carleah swallows hard. "I understand."

"I will enter Nemoregno first then come and retrieve you once I know that it's safe."

"Fort—"

"No, Carleah. Even setting aside what is between us, my duty to you as my queen is to ensure your safe passage to Soreno. I cannot do that if you don't listen. You can see in the Phantom where others cannot, that gives us an advantage. We're going to use it. You remain here until I come back for you. Promise me." I graze her cheek with my thumb, hating the idea of being separated even though I know it's necessary.

"I don't want to lose you, too. I don't want to be alone, Fort."

"You won't." I press my lips to hers. She relaxes back against me, and I take this moment for all that it is: peace just before carnage. "If we're caught, I need you to trust me. Please, do not offer up any information freely. Let me lead once we cross the Phantom."

"Okay."

I release her, and Carleah settles back against me again. We fall into silence, both of us wrapped in what may be waiting for us just around the corner.

"Tell me something I don't know about you," she asks.

"You know damn near everything."

"Yes. But—what was your mother like?"

I swallow hard. I was so young when she'd been killed, but I still get flashes of her face. Smiling, happy, and then those of her wide-eyed and bled out on the ground.

"Unless it's too painful; you can choose not to answer."

"No, I—my mother worked with leather. It was her trade and something she taught me to do. I can still remember the smell of it tanning, of the oil she used to cure it. She was a kind person and far too fucking good for the cards dealt to her."

"Did she have any other children?"

"Two other boys," I reply. "Both older than me."

"You have brothers?"

"I wouldn't call them that," I reply. "They're fucking assholes. Picture perfect representations of what my father wanted."

"I'm sorry, Fort." Her hand caresses my arm as it bands around her waist.

"We're dealt what we're dealt," I reply.

"That doesn't mean we have to accept those cards. You didn't. You came to Navalis and changed your future."

I want to remind her that I'm going back into Nemoregno, running to the place I was born and fleeing the home I found. But I keep that to myself because our lives are already heavy enough as it is.

Once more, we fall into silence as I run through memories I'd long buried.

"The night of my eighteenth birthday, I dreamt of a winged horse. He was all white, a gorgeous vision against the snowy backdrop."

"You dreamt of a Pegasus?"

"I did."

"Sounds pleasant. They're supposed to be good omens."

"This one wasn't," she replies. Before I can ask why, she continues, "The first couple of dreams were peaceful, but the next one—he was smeared with blood. The ground he stood on was coated in it. And when I tried to approach him, he reared and struck me. That's when I woke. Anyway, I know they're just dreams, but—"

"They sit with you," I finish.

"Exactly. My mother believed I hadn't been sleeping because of the coming wedding, but really, it was the nightmares. They got worse. But I haven't had once since they died." I feel a shudder run through her.

"They were just dreams," I tell her. "Nothing more than your mind likely picking up on what you now know were secrets being kept from you."

"Perhaps. The legends that those Tenebris spoke of last night, though, I can't get them out of my mind. I just cannot fathom why I would be important enough to tear an entire kingdom to the ground."

I'd tell her that I would burn the world to ash for her, but since I don't see how that will help, I keep it to myself. "We will figure it all out, I promise."

She looks over her shoulder to smile, but I use the opportunity to cover her mouth with mine. The gelding continues walking as I cup her cheek, deepening the kiss until she groans against my mouth and melds to my body.

Perfection.

That's what Carleah Rossingol is.

The gelding stops walking, so I break the kiss.

Ahead, the Phantom stops moving, coming to a near-complete stop. Before, the closer we got, the more it moved, but now I can reach out and touch it if I chose.

"Is this it?" Carleah asks.

My nerves might as well be stones in my gut. This is it. The closest I've been to Nemoregno since I left all those years ago. What the hell was I thinking, bringing her here?

"Are you okay?"

"Fine. Ready to get the fuck away from this place." I take a deep breath and climb off of the horse, careful to keep contact with Carleah's leg at all times. She reaches down and takes my hand in hers then slides down off of the gelding.

I've never been someone who backed down from a fight. Someone who ran from danger. But right now, I am fighting a very strong urge to throw Carleah over my shoulder, turn, and sprint back to the Phantom where we can live out our days in constant contact and pure safety.

"Remember what we discussed; give me a few minutes and if I don't return for you, run the other way. Find a ship that will take you to Soreno." I plead with her one last time to turn around, knowing it's futile.

"I'm not leaving you, Fort."

"Carleah. Please. The tribes of Nemoregno are not to be trifled with. They are murderers. Barbarians."

"I'm not running," she replies cooly. "You and I are getting to Soreno. Together."

Exasperated, I try from a different angle with her, "If

I do not make it out, you will not be able to cross Nemoregno. I'm not asking you to stop, just find a different route."

A muscle in her jaw clenches. "Fine."

But I see the lie in her eyes.

"Remember the plan, Carleah. Once I cross, what we shared here and in our past becomes nonexistent for me. But that doesn't mean I don't recall every moment or feel the way that I do." I cup her face once more, my gaze sharing with her what words fail me. Her eyes sparkle, and I lean down and kiss her once again, letting the passion radiate through me. Together, we will reunite her lands and her people. Until then, I'll become the man I was so desperate to forget.

Turing from her, I face the edge of the Phantom and release her hand. Grey mist surrounds me, but I withdraw my blade and take a step forward, then another, moving until I'm emerging on the other side. Nemoregno shimmers into view.

The barren landscape has no grass or living plants of any kind. Dead trees, or rather the trunks and branches, stick up out of cracked, red clay. The mountains behind me are the same red color, the ones far in the distance of Dead Man's Land the only green for miles.

This place is just as dead as I remember it.

Just as barren.

A wasteland of horrible memories and broken truths.

I start to turn back toward the Phantom, but movement catches my eye. Before I can raise my sword, a bola slams into my waist and wraps around me, pinning my arm beneath it. I scramble back, working on freeing myself. *Fuck.*

I trip and go down—hard. My top half falls into the Phantom, and grey mist surrounds me.

Hands cup my face and I stare down into panicked blue eyes.

"Run," I whisper.

"No!" Carleah's hands leave me for a moment. Then she reappears above me as she tries to pull me further in.

A hand closes around my ankle.

"Run!" I whisper loudly as I'm ripped from her. I'm yanked through the mist and pulled into Nemoregno.

"What do we have here?" a man asks as he hovers into view above me. His head blocks the sun from my eyes, giving me a chance to take in the features of not just him but my other attacker. It's then I note the half-sun tattooed on his wrist.

For a moment, my mind goes blank.

It can't be.

Terror ices my veins as I find myself staring up into the eyes of my father. For a brief moment, I am no longer Fort: Head of Navalis Guard. Instead, I'm a terrified child sent to fend for himself, battered, burned, and alone.

Then, cold rationale seeps into my mind, and I remember it's been nearly two decades. This can't be my father. My gaze shifts to the other attacker then back to the one in front of me.

Shit. Not my father. The men have the same amber eyes that he does, though. The same ones I, too, share.

They have the same general build.

And as realization sets in, I feel like a fool for thinking we could slip through Nemoregno unnoticed. I made it five fucking seconds before they found me. I should have known better.

Shifting my cool expression back into place, I glare up at my attacker. "Let me go, Oliver," I demand.

The man narrows his gaze at me. "How the fuck do you know who I am?"

"You don't recognize me?" I question, trying to keep the ball in my court. "And here I've returned. All the way from Navalis." I click my tongue.

"Who the fuck are you?" My middle brother, Duke, steps forward. He narrows his gaze at me while displaying the same tattoo on his wrist.

"I can't believe you don't recognize your brother," I say. "My name is Brax."

They share a look of disbelief.

"Brax is dead," Duke insists as he turns back to me.

"No. I got lost in the Phantom," I lie. "Found myself in Navalis. I wasn't able to get free until recently."

"Lies." Oliver points his blade at me.

"I swear it." I reach down and pull the sleeve of my shirt up to show a scar on the underside of my wrist. I'd cut my mark off, sliced the tattoo of my people from my flesh before the king ever found me. "They removed my mark," I lie.

"It's in the same area as ours," Duke comments.

"Shut the fuck up, asshole," Oliver snaps.

"Our mother's name was Lueann. Our father's name is Yarrow."

"Our mother's name *was?*" Oliver questions. "She's not dead."

I stiffen because I know it's a lie. "She is. I saw her with my own eyes. The night I was shoved through the Phantom. She'd been killed in our home."

"Brax was disfigured," Oliver says with a twisted grin. "Burned. His gaze drops to my groin. "Show us your scars."

Fear claws up my chest. I think of Carleah, likely getting close to losing the fight with her willpower and charging out here. With me on this side of the Phantom, she can't hear a damned thing. Can't see anything beyond the swirling mist.

"I'm not dropping my fucking pants for you out here. Take me back to camp, and I'll show you. We both know that's where you're headed anyway."

The men exchange looks. "Brax?"

"Yes," I say to Duke who studies me with complete and utter fascination, as though I am an apparition.

It's Oliver who looks hesitant to believe. "We take him to father, let him decide." He straightens. "Relieve him of his fucking sword, Duke."

Duke reaches down and slides the sword from my side. Then, Oliver grips my arm and yanks me to my feet. He's ten years older than me, and the years have not been kind to him. Tanned, dried skin covers his face, far too much time beneath the heat of the sun.

Granted, here in Nemoregno, there isn't much choice.

Even as I long to look back, I don't. I keep my attention focused straight ahead as they march me farther and farther away from Carleah. If she rides hard, she can make it back to Navalis and to a supply ship within a week. Once she is aboard, the trip to Soreno will be easy to manage.

She can do it.

I just hope she tries.

Something whizzes past my ear and slams into Duke's chest. He sputters, eyes going wide as blood soaks through his tunic. He falls to the ground, and Oliver roars.

No!

I whirl as Oliver rushes to Duke. Carleah steps from the Phantom, hair covered with the hood of her cloak. The horses walk behind her as she nocks another arrow in her bow. Her eyes are wide as she stares at Oliver. He's still between us, a murderous mass blocking me from what matters most.

She releases another arrow, but Oliver sees this one coming and bats it away. Then, he drops his shoulder and sprints toward her at full speed.

"No! Run!" I sprint toward them, slamming into his back seconds before he can collide with her. "Run, dammit!"

Oliver thrashes beneath me, rolling over and pinning me to the ground. I slam my forehead into his, and pain explodes behind my eyes. He rears back his fist, and I dodge so it slams into the dirt beside me.

Carleah turns to run, but he grabs another bolo and flings it over his shoulder. It slams into her, and she goes down into the dirt—her cloak slipping free from her white hair. Oliver snarls and shoves off of me. I thrash against the bolo pinning my arms to my sides, doing what I can to loosen its hold.

"You fucking bitch!" Olive roars. His hand cracks across her face, and she tries to twist in his hold.

The bolo comes free, and I fling it off of me as I scramble for my sword. But by the time I get it into my hand, he's already raising his own blade.

"Oliver! Wait!" I bellow. "You kill her and Father will have you executed!"

Oliver glares back at me, his gaze murderous. "I think he will be quite pleased that I executed our brother's murderer."

Carleah's gaze widens as she looks to me.

"That is the princess of Navalis," I tell him. "The very reason I was sent into the Phantom in the first place. If you kill her, there will be hell to pay."

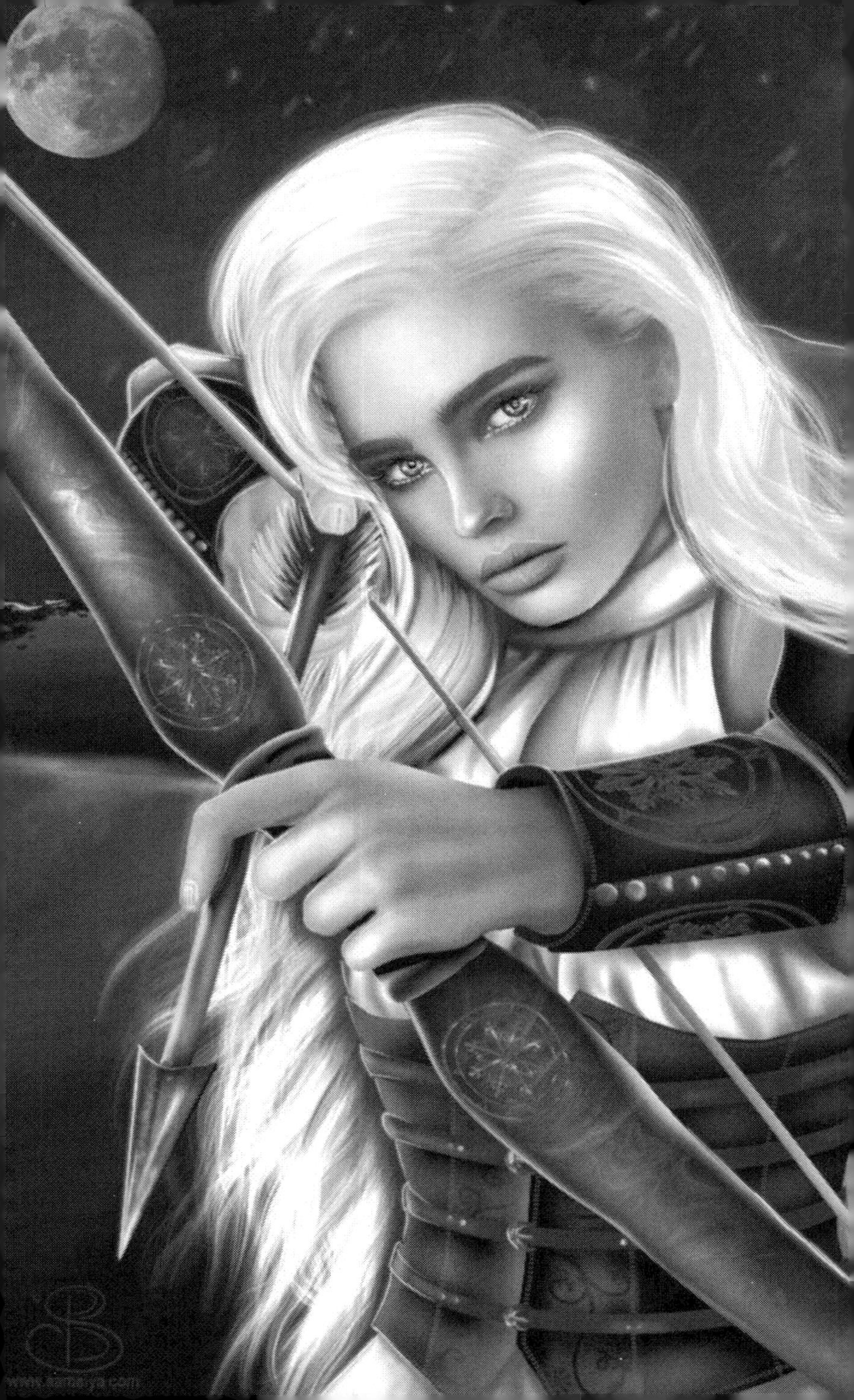

CHAPTER 20
CARLEAH

Brother.

I killed Fort's brother.

The very man he's currently being forced to carry while his other brother holds me by a rope he secured around my throat. It scrapes against my skin, but I barely notice it because my mind is still reeling.

I slaughtered Fort's brother.

Right in front of him. I swallow hard and try to ignore the blood dripping down Fort's back from the dead man he carries.

Oliver walks beside me, and I try to sneak a look over at him. He's a feral version of Fort. The same tall, muscled build though his hair is beginning to grey. It's his eyes that are so different, though. Because in them, I saw no humanity. Just rage. Which, I suppose, given that I'd just killed his brother, is to be expected.

He wears a tan tunic that is belted around his waist with a leather cord, and while he's removed the bolo from me, both of them hang on his waist within easy reach. He holds the horses with his other hand, and they walk slowly behind us.

Oliver confiscated Bowman's bow, which now hangs on his back. He also took great pleasure in searching me, removing the dagger I'd stashed in my boot.

We're weaponless and walking into a place led by a man who sacrificed his youngest son to the Phantom in hopes he would bring me back.

As soon as we crest a small dune straight ahead, I find myself staring down at a village full of women and children. There are no canopies on the trees, no grass on the ground, yet they run barefoot through aisles between tan tents while women—most of them pregnant—watch on, their expressions harsh.

There are no buildings, no houses or solid structures of any kind.

Just tents and red clay.

"This fucking way," Oliver snarls as he yanks on the rope around my neck. I gag, and Fort whirls. "What the hell are you going to do about it?" Oliver snaps. "Go ahead and attack. I'll slit her pretty throat and bury you both before Father ever has to know a fucking thing."

I stiffen, my gaze locking with Fort's. The muscle in his jaw flexes, but he doesn't make a move toward Oliver. He simply turns back around, the man slack on his back, and continues walking.

"How does it feel to return, coward?"

"He is not a coward," I snap.

"Says the murdering cunt," he snaps.

"Watch your fucking mouth," Fort growls back.

"Oh, I'm sorry. Murdering royal *cunt*," he replies.

The villagers stop and stare at us as we pass. Women gape, eyes open, whispering to each other as I pass by. The children watch intently, though there is no joy on their young faces. It makes my heart ache to see such seriousness and brutality.

"What the hell happened?" a man demands as he rushes over. He's larger than the men in Navalis, too, though still not quite as tall as Fort. His gaze hardens when he sees Duke.

"Take the horses and look through the gear. They won't be needing any of it," he snaps. "Weapons come to my tent."

"Understood." He takes the horses and leaves while Oliver continues yanking me forward, half-dragging me until I've passed Fort.

Warriors stroll through the village carrying spears and knives at their belts. They wear their hair longer, some of them boasting braids, others with it loose down past their shoulders. All of them wear the same wary expression, though.

Oliver stops in front of a large tent and gestures inside with his free hand. "After you, *Brother*," he sneers.

Fort freezes a moment, his mask falling a bit before it's firmly in place. He is expressionless, his eyes devoid of all emotion as he steps through the threshold.

Oliver pushes me through the tent flap.

An aged man looks up from where he stands, his hands planted on the desk in front of him. His hair is grey as is his beard. But his eyes, they're the same amber as Fort's. Truthfully, he's an older version of his son. *Sons,* I remind myself. Oliver shares them, too.

But just like Fort's elder brother, his father's eyes lack all humanity. They're hard. The eyes of a murderer.

"What's this then?" he demands, straightening to his full build. He's solid muscle, the tan skin bared by his sleeveless tunic covered in scars.

"You don't recognize the Princess of Navalis?" Oliver demands, shoving me forward. I stumble to my knees, scraping them against the ground.

Fort's father's eyes widen. "Is this true?"

"Yes," Fort answers before I can. He sets Duke's body down and straightens.

Fort's father barely blinks an eye at his dead son. "Who killed him? You?"

"She did," Oliver says. He plants his boot into my back and shoves me forward further.

"I'll fucking kill you," Fort snarls as he rushes forward. Oliver grips me by the hair and yanks my head back. Pain explodes along my scalp, and my throat burns as he presses the sharp edge of a blade against my throat.

"Move and it'll be her last breath."

"Easy, Oliver. Perhaps we should hear them both out."

"She killed Duke!" he bellows.

"And had your brother not had his head up in the clouds, he would have been paying attention." He looks to Oliver. "Leave us."

"Fa—"

"Now."

Oliver throws me forward and steps away, so Fort rushes to my side. He kneels, pulling my face up to see him. "Are you all right?" he questions, though I can see on his face he knows I'm not.

My head is throbbing, my face stinging from Oliver's hit.

Fort gently touches my cheek, and his fingers come away covered in crimson. "I'm sorry," he whispers. "For everything."

"It's not your fault," I tell him. "I'm—"

"Princess, I am quite sorry for the way my son treated you." He bows. "You can accept my deepest apologies. I am Yarrow, leader of the Nemoregno tribe." Yarrow turns his attention to Fort. "So, what the fuck are you doing with the princess of Navalis?" Fort's father demands.

Fort stands, pulling me to my feet with him. Then, with a deep breath, he fully faces his father.

His father freezes in place, eyes narrowing on Fort. I watch the emotions play out on the older man's face. Confusion, disbelief, joy, and anger. Then, after what feels like minutes, he says, "Brax?"

"Hello, Father."

"Where the hell have you been?" he demands.

"You should know," I snap. "You sent your soldiers to Navalis after us."

Yarrow's attention shifts from his son to me, and he grins, a savage smile that contains absolutely no humanity. "Oh, did I?"

"We passed the Tenebris on the way here." No need to tell him that my family is dead if he is unaware.

"And just what are you doing outside of your castle, I wonder?"

"You tasked Brax with stealing me, did you not?" I straighten as he moves around his desk, limping as he does. It's when he's on the other side that I note the wooden leg in place of his real one.

"And what else has Brax told you, Princess?" he crosses his arms.

"Nothing," Fort snaps. "Though, had I realized we would be met with such hostility, I wouldn't have ever left Navalis."

His father grins. "Why did you, then? You've been gone—what—nineteen years now? So why the fuck would you return?"

"I was tasked with bringing her to you. So that's what I've done."

"Yet you armed her." When Fort doesn't immediately respond, he continues. "Otherwise, she wouldn't have been able to kill your brother."

"I didn't know he was your brother," I blurt. Fort doesn't look at me, but Yarrow does, his amber gaze seemingly seeing a hell of a lot more than I want him to.

"Would you have spared his life had you known?" he questions.

I swallow hard. "I would have aimed for something less vital."

Yarrow grins at me. "You have the soul of a fighter, Princess, but the heart of a royal." He sneers the final word, letting me know he meant it as an insult. He turns to Fort. "You care for this princess, do you not?"

"I do," Fort grinds out.

Yarrow throws his head back and laughs. "Have you fallen for her then? Tell me, boy, is it love?"

Fort doesn't reply, though a muscle in his jaw flexes.

"Just like your fucking mother. She was a soft heart, too, and where did it get her?"

Fort's hands clench into fists, and he steps forward.

"Go ahead, *boy*. Go ahead and hit me. One word from me and every man just outside that tent will rush in here, all of them ready to cut you down where you stand. And then where would your princess be?" He steps closer to Fort, their heights an exact match so they are on eye level. "On her fucking back while every man here took their chance at fathering the next bastard son of Navalis."

Fort swings and slams his fist into the side of his father's head. The man stumbles back, and I sprint toward the far wall where I note an axe hanging.

"In here!" Yarrow bellows.

But before I can reach it, Fort grabs and rips me back behind him as half a dozen men—including Oliver—rush inside the tent. All of them glare at him, hatred etched in every line of their expressions.

"You're going to the pit, boy. Live, and I'll even let you be the first one to breed the bitch."

"You can't do this!" I scream as the men rush forward and grip Fort's arms.

Oliver wraps an arm around my throat from behind,

and Fort explodes. He slams his fist into the nearest man, and the warrior goes down like a stone. He hits the ground while Fort plows through the others. He takes a few hits, his lip splitting open in response, but within seconds, all of the men are lying on their backs while he breathes heavily.

His expression is darker than I've ever seen it, his gaze far more murderous. He looks every bit a Tenebris soldier in this moment—no humanity, conditioned to kill.

I slam my boot down on Oliver's foot, and he groans, releasing me just enough that I am able to get out of his hold. But before I can make it even two steps, Yarrow grabs the back of my hair and yanks me toward him.

He presses a cool blade against my heart. "I'll cut it out where she stands," he threatens.

"No. You won't. You need her."

"Do I? Last I heard, Navalis had fallen." Yarrow sticks out his tongue and runs it over the side of my face. It's wet, warm, and makes bile rise up my throat. "She's nothing more than a pretty prize now."

"I'll fucking kill you, I swear it." Fort starts toward him, but Yarrow takes his blade and cuts the front of my tunic open. Humid air hits my breasts, and Fort freezes.

"You go into the pit. Or I'll have them hold you down and make you watch as I tarnish this perfect fucking flesh." He uses the tip of his blade and runs it down the center of my sternum. I don't even breathe, terror running through me as I picture just what he did to Fort all those years ago.

If he's willing to scar his own son, what will he do to me?

"Don't. Please. You can keep me. Just don't hurt her."

"Keep you?" Yarrow throws his head back and laughs. "Boy, I should have fucking thrown you into Dead Man's Land the second you came out of your mother. Then, I should have cut her throat and fed her to the animals, too."

Fort's jaw clenches. "I am stronger than any of your men here. Faster. You need me."

"Do I?" The blade slips over my skin, gliding over my breast until he presses directly above my heart. "Prove it to me. Survive the pit, and I'll let you be the first to breed her. Fail, and you die."

Fort's expression betrays his fear. Not for himself but for what will happen to me if he fails. A heartbeat later, though, his gaze darkens, and for a single moment, it's like looking into the hardened gaze of his father. "Fine."

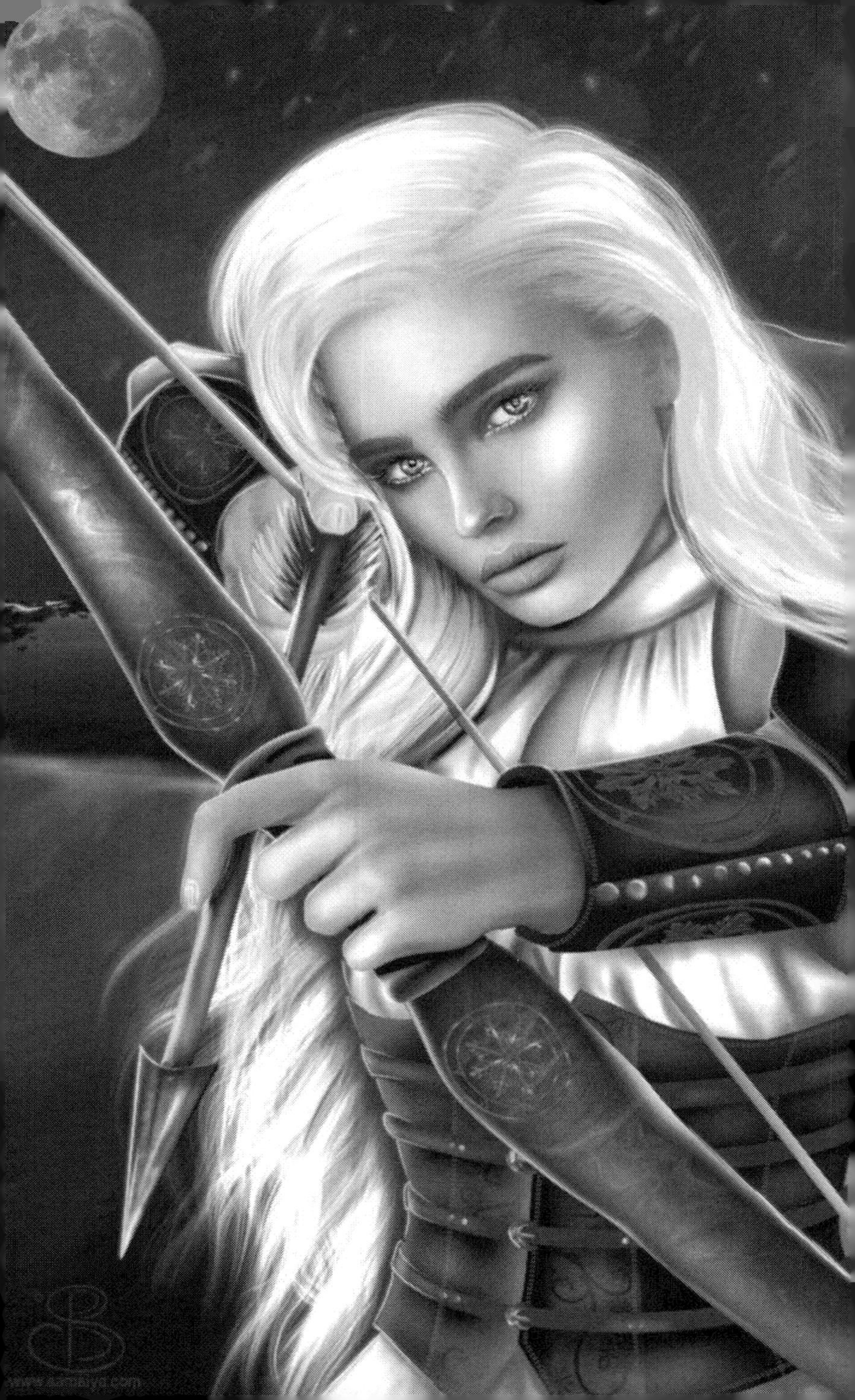

CHAPTER 21
CARLEAH

Hands bound at my front, I sit across from Yarrow as he pours over a piece of parchment on the desk before him. They've forced me to change, stripping me from my riding clothes and putting me in a slip of tanned leather that barely covers my breasts, another around my waist. It falls to my upper thigh, leaving damn near nothing to the imagination.

"You're a fucking monster," I growl.

Yarrow grins at me. "Thank you, Princess. I quite appreciate that reputation."

"How could you slaughter the woman who bore you children?"

Yarrow leans back in his chair. "For you, family is a way of life. You sit in your plush winter wonderland, enjoying the cool weather, game aplenty, winterberries—yes, I know quite a lot about Navalis," he adds. "Yet, you and your people pay no attention to what goes on outside of your walls. At the people whose worlds are crumbling around them. For us, *Princess,* breeding strong warriors is a way of life. Fort's mother was weak. Her offspring was weak."

"Did she not also mother Oliver and Duke?"

"She did," he says. "And clearly, two out of three of her bastard children were not worthy of the name I gave to them as tribal leader."

"You're not worthy to lead anyone," I retort. "Fort is three times the man you are."

He studies me, cocking his head to the side as he does. "You love him, too, don't you?"

I don't answer.

Yarrow's grin spreads. "Well, I'll be damned. My son, a bastard of Nemoregno, has managed to land the one and only daughter of the Navalis royal line. Tell me, has he shown you his scars yet? Did you still spread those pretty legs of yours for him, knowing how damaged he is?"

"Fort is not damaged."

Once again, Yarrow throws his head back and laughs. "So, he has fucked you, then! Damn. And here I thought I could be the first." He shakes his head. "No worries, Princess. I don't mind sharing. And once Brax has succumbed to The Pit, I will take great pleasure in putting sons in you. The fire in your soul will blend well with the fight in mine."

"There's fight, and then there's being a murderer. You're the latter."

He opens his mouth to respond but then shakes his

head and stands. I flinch back as he grips the rope binding my wrists and tugs me to my feet.

I'm terrified of what's to come, but I don't let my fear show.

Because even if he does as he's threatened, even if he takes everything from me, my pride is what will remain. And eventually, I will escape this hellish place then rain hell down upon them.

He all but rips me through the aisle of tents as women stop and look. They watch me with pitied stares, but none of them help. Some hold a hand over their swollen bellies as if they're imagining their own sons and daughters facing a fate such as mine.

A rancid stench hits my nose on the light breeze, and my stomach churns.

The tents part ahead, and Yarrow yanks me toward the ledge of a cliff. He throws me forward, and I fall to my knees beside a huge hole in the ground. *The Pit.* Bones litter the ground below, some partially buried, some still rotting.

Duke's body lies in the center, the freshest of the dead below.

The sides are steep, though a man could scramble up if necessary. Yet, based on the number of dead below and what Fort has told me, the only way they are allowed out is by winning.

"Welcome to The Pit," Yarrow snarls. His hand tightens in my hair. "This is our way of life, Princess. Should Brax perish in there—which, I can assure you, he will—you will become quite familiar with it."

He rips me back, and tears spring to my eyes, the pain in my head throbbing with each tug. Yarrow pulls me closer to another tent then throws me inside. I hit the ground with a heavy thud, landing damn near on my face, thanks to my bound hands.

But he does not follow me in.

Hands go to my arms, but I fight, squirming away from whatever hellish future Yarrow has planned for me. "No!" I kick until the hands flip me onto my back and I find myself staring up into familiar amber eyes. "Fort?" He's bloody, his face bruised.

He begins working at the bindings around my wrists then tosses them to the side and crushes me against his bare chest. "I'm so fucking sorry, Carleah." He holds me to him, one hand caressing my hair, the other holding me to his body. "We never should have come this way. We should have waited—"

"I'm the one that wanted to come this way," I remind him. "So, I'm sorry. I'm so sorry I pushed you to come back to this place."

He pulls back and cups my face. "They're going to kill me," he says. "You need to understand that, and the second you get the chance—you run."

"What? No. Yarrow said—"

"Yarrow will continue sending men after me until they've won. I can promise you that. My fate is sealed. Yours is not. You fucking run, you hear me? As fast as you can. As far as you can. Once you get through Dead Man's Land, Soreno is right over the ridge."

"I'm not leaving you."

"Carleah, you have to." His thumbs brush over my cheeks. "If I can get out, I will find you, but if you get a chance—you fucking run. Promise me."

Emotion claws at my throat. I don't want to leave him. "I don't want to be alone. I can't lose you, Fort."

"You won't." He leans in and presses his lips to mine. It's soft, tender, but weighs with a heavy goodbye. Then, he pulls back and rests his forehead against mine. "I'll be right behind you, I promise."

"The last man who made a promise to me broke it," I say, my throat burning.

"Carleah." He says my name like it's a prayer. "For luck," he whispers, capturing my lips once more. I lose myself in the kiss, in the moment, and bury my hands in his hair as he lifts and crushes me to his body.

His tongue plunges into my mouth and slides against mine. I lean into him as fire blazes in my soul. This is what I have waited for.

This is the passion I craved.

The love I'd read about.

And now, I may very well lose it.

"The odds have never been in our favor," I say. "And still, look how far we've come."

He smiles though it doesn't reach his eyes. "You run, Carleah," he says again. "Run, and I will find you."

Oliver stalks in, destroying our moment. "Time to go," he snarls as he grips me by the arm. Two more men rush forward and grab Fort. We're dragged apart as tears burn in my vision. Nothing will ever be the same. Not after today.

"Survive," I whisper.

Fort swallows hard, and then he's ripped from the tent.

"Let's go, bitch," Oliver growls as he loops a rope around my throat. He drags me toward the opening, and somehow on legs like lead, I manage to remain standing.

Cheers echo loudly from the men who have gathered around the pit, some barely old enough to fight. The women remain silent as they sit away from the action, some pregnant, some holding babes, others emotionless.

Oliver shoves through the crowd, not stopping until we're standing beside where Yarrow sits on a makeshift throne. Fort is already in the pit by the time we reach him, his body coated in dirt from where they must have thrown him down.

"Most of you know that, nineteen years ago, I sent my youngest son into the Phantom to retrieve the Navalis princess," Yarrow bellows. "Well, it seems he has returned!" Cheers erupt. "And while I wish this was a joyous occasion, it is not. Because the dumbass has fallen in love with her!" Boos and laughter fill my ears. Fort turns in a slow circle, studying all of the men waiting at the edge of The Pit.

"Today, we teach him a lesson while she watches, that only the strongest will survive! Should he win—" He trails off, and more laughter fills my ears. My stomach churns with unease as I watch the murderous expressions on the faces of those spectating.

I realize, in this moment, with horrific clarity, that Fort was right.

He won't survive this.

Not unless we get a miracle.

"So who will take him on first?" Yarrow calls out.

Without hesitation, seven men let out deafening shrieks then slide down into the pit. They surround him, and Fort readies himself for their attacks.

"Surely, you're not allowing him to be outnumbered! You fucking cowards!"

Yarrow beams at me as Oliver yanks hard on the rope around my throat. "We cannot make it easy."

"He doesn't stand a chance! And you know it!"

"Do I?" he questions. "Because Brax managed to level six men in my tent less than a few hours ago."

"And you beat him for it!"

He laughs. "No, *they* beat him for it. Fighting outside of The Pit is prohibited. We must have honor somewhere."

"You have no honor," I growl.

The men rush forward, all of them assaulting Fort at once. He takes a blow to the chin, stumbles back, then slams his elbow into the gut of a man trying to sneak up on him. He fights as though he's more than a single being.

Spinning, kicking, fighting with strength that I've only ever witnessed one other time—when we'd been in Miscerico.

"See there is something you do not know about your love, Princess," Yarrow replies.

"And what's that?" I snarl.

"When he was born, he nearly died. He was so small, so weak," he spits the words out as he watches Fort.

I'm unable to tear my gaze from him in The Pit even as Yarrow continues.

"He would have died if not for what I did."

Now, I face the tribal leader. "What did you do?"

He grins. "It is our way, once boys reach fighting age, to inject them with the blood of a giant. We find it makes them grow faster, stronger—"

I can feel the color drain from my face. "Giants are legend."

"So are Tenebris, are they not? Tell me, did you not wonder why he was so much faster than others? Why his senses seem heightened? He received twice the dose as anyone else in Nemoregno because he nearly died as a babe. Pathetic little thing." He shakes his head in disgust. "But now—" He grins, and I turn back to Fort in The Pit.

Four of the men are down, unmoving, their heads bloody.

Fort still moves.

"You inject children with blood?"

"Of a giant."

"And where do you get this blood?" I question. "If what you're saying is true."

He smiles. "You'll discover that soon enough."

Three more men let out battle cries and leap into The Pit. Fort whirls, dropping down and knocking their feet out from under them. He jumps onto one, lifts his head, and slams it into a stone until the man falls silent.

Roars and bellows sound from above as Fort jumps to

his feet, crouching down and facing the remaining five men.

"Tell Duke hi for me," Oliver whispers in my ear, then throws me forward. I fall—straight into The Pit. Rocks scrape me as I roll, my head reeling until I finally reach the bottom.

Men above laugh. I look up as Oliver shrugs toward his father, who glares down at me.

"Carleah!" Fort roars.

I scramble to my feet, still dazed, as a man starts toward me. "Pretty thing," he growls. I scan the area around me, looking for anything I can use. I spot a rock the size of my fist, so I lunge for it.

The man rushes forward at the same time, his hand closing around my wrist at the same time I retrieve the rock from the side of The Pit. I swing as hard as I can, slamming it into the side of his skull.

He stumbles back with a crunch of stone against his temple and releases me. When he straightens again, though, he's snarling, blood streaming down his face. "I will make you pay for that, bitch." He rushes me, and I scramble backward, heart hammering against my ribs.

Fort rushes forward, his shoulder slamming into the man as he takes him to the ground. He drives both thumbs into the man's eyes as he screams, thrashing against Fort's hold. Fort slams his head down into the ground, over and over again, until the man falls silent.

Others charge him.

But Fort is faster.

Stronger.

Just as Yarrow said.

Until—an arrow sings through the air, lodging itself in Fort's abdomen. He stills, and the world seems to stop.

I rush forward, screaming, as another hits him in the side.

And then a shadow looms above.

"Fort!" I scream his name, blood hammering in my veins as I struggle to get to him. The men around me begin to claw their way out of The Pit as Fort goes down to his knees.

But before I can reach him, a hand closes around my arm. I try to yank out of the grip, try to fight my way to Fort, but as I'm lifted from the ground, I note Oliver sliding down into the pit, a blade in his hand.

"No! Fort!"

"Carleah!" he calls out.

Oliver reaches him, and whatever grabbed me, takes off into the sky.

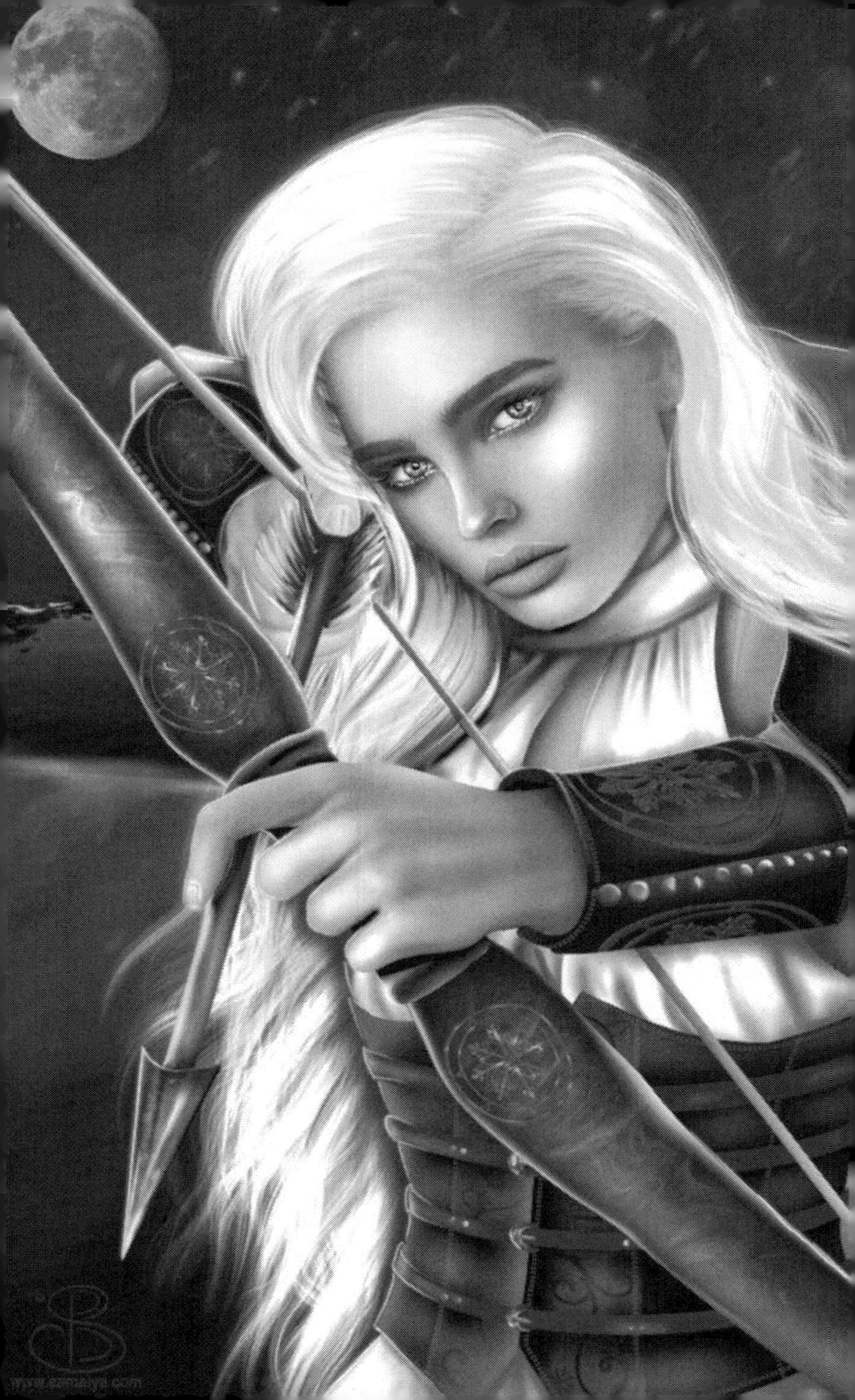

CHAPTER 22
CARLEAH

"Put me down! You have to take me back!" I yell as I thrash against the lap of my abductor. We fly high above the ground, which should be impossible, as are the white legs and hooves that I can see from where I'm draped over the back of what I can only imagine is a Pegasus.

And why wouldn't it be?

The giants and Tenebris are real, so what the hell else is supposed to be legend but is actually living and breathing?

I can't even focus on the fact that I'm draped over the back of a creature I only dreamt about because all I can see—even though we've long since passed over Nemoregno—is Fort with arrows jutting from his body.

"My fate is sealed," he'd told me. *"Yours is not."*

"You have to take me back!"

My stomach plummets as we drop down far too

quickly. All while my abductor keeps his hand firmly on my back.

When the horse lands, my body jolts, and pain radiates through my aching head.

The second I get a chance, though, I throw myself backward onto the ground and start running.

I sprint, pumping my arms as fast as I can in the direction of Nemoregno—or at least where I imagine it is—but I don't make it ten strides before a hand closes around my wrist and pulls me to a stop.

I whirl on my abductor and find myself staring up at a tall, slender man with golden hair, mossy green eyes, and—to my complete and utter shock—pointed ears. "If you go back," he says softly, "You will die, too."

"He wasn't dead," I choke out.

"Carleah." He starts toward me, and I scramble back.

"How do you know my name?"

The man's gaze softens. "I am Lacrae," he says softly as he presses a closed fist to his chest. "And I have been looking for you ever since the fall of Navalis. I am an ally of your family."

I don't believe him even for a second, but Fort's life is on the line. "If you're truly an ally, then you know that the man who was with me—he's the only reason I survived this long. You *have* to take me to him. You have to go get him!"

The man looks past me then offers me a nod. "We will see if he is alive." He reaches out, so I warily take his hand. We rush over and climb onto the back of the white Pegasus then take off into the sky. Wind whips past me, sending my hair flying as Lacrae wraps an arm around my waist and holds me against him.

I fight the urge to pull away because the only man I ever want touching me is currently fighting for his life.

We soar over a small river. Then the ground changes to the red clay of Nemoregno. I peer down into The Pit, and my heart stops. Fort lies on his back atop the men he'd killed. His eyes are frozen open, his torso crusted with blood.

"No!" I scream.

"Quiet, or they will hear us," the man scolds as the horse dips lower. No one in the village comes out to see us, but when he sets me down on the ground and I rush over to Fort, I wish they would.

If only so my body could join his in this fucking pit. His skin is cold. I hold his face in my hands, brushing my thumbs over his cheeks as tears stream down my own. "Please wake up," I whisper. "Please."

But he doesn't move.

Seven arrows just from his chest.

"Fort. I'm so sorry." I brush his matted hair from his face.

"We must go," Lacrae scolds. "Come. Now." He pulls me up, but I still cling to Fort. "He is dead, Carleah, and unless you wish for us to join him—"

Voices call out overhead, so I let Lacrae pull me away from Fort. Away from the only home I had left. I'm not entirely sure when I end up on the back of the horse, but I do, and soon we're soaring off into the sky.

I stare straight ahead, numb inside and out, unable to focus on anything but the breaking of my own heart.

"I am so sorry," Lacrae says. "Had I known how important he was to you, I would have taken him, too."

Fort is dead.

Just like my father. My mother. Alex, Bowman, Diedrich, and Ethan.

Genevieve.

Just like every single person I've ever known in Navalis.

Fort is dead.

∼

HOURS LATER, Lacrae lands on the branch of a massive tree. It's dark outside, so I cannot see anything around us as he pulls me toward a dimly lit hall. I go willingly with him, beyond exhausted as he pulls me up a set of stairs and toward a large wooden door.

He pushes it open, and lanterns illuminate on the walls.

"Stay here. I will get you a healer."

"No," I reply.

"But you are bruised."

"I don't want a healer," I snap.

Lacrae's mouth flattens in a tight line. "Very well. I will leave you for tonight, then. Tomorrow, I will come and explain everything."

I turn away from him without responding, and as soon as the door shuts behind him, I collapse to the ground and cover my face with shaking hands. All I can see is his face, lifeless, staring up at me.

How is this fair?

How is any of this fair?

I push to my feet, anger burning through me, and spin, looking for anything I can destroy. Anything I can break so that maybe I won't feel so fucking useless. I grip the nearest item—a vase on the dresser beside the door—and fling it to the ground.

It shatters, pieces flying everywhere.

I do the same to another.

Then I shatter a glass bottle that sits beside a sunken bathtub. Over and over again, I break items until I'm standing at the epicenter of destruction.

The door opens, and I turn as two women rush in wearing soft green dresses. They don't even blink an eye at the chaos around me.

"Leave me alone!" I scream.

"You must be cleaned so your wounds do not fester."

I look toward the door as a third woman enters. Her hair is the same shining gold as Lacrae's, and she breezes inside wearing a golden gown that hugs her body like a second skin.

"I don't want to be cleaned."

"Because you want to die? Yes, my brother told me of your companion."

"Brother?"

"Lacrae," she replies cooly. "I am Affree, and while he is willing to allow you to make foolish choices, I am not. Clean her," she orders the other two.

I step back. "You will not touch me."

The woman purses her lips and crosses toward me. "I understand you grieve, Princess, for I know all of what you have lost. But letting yourself die out of spite for those who slaughtered your family is letting them be victorious once again." She rests her hand on my shoulder. "If you lie down and die now, you will lose all ability to make their deaths mean something."

"Death is pointless," I snap.

"No, dear girl, it is not." She backs up a step. "Clean her body, dress her wounds, and get her fresh clothing. If she fights, knock her unconscious." She turns and glides out, shutting the door behind her.

The two elven women face off with me, but I do not fight them anymore. If these people truly are allies, then perhaps they have what I need to level Nemoregno to the fucking ground. So, I'll play nice.

For now.

∼

Less than an hour later, I am washed, my injuries dressed, and wearing a white dress that falls to my ankles. A large slit bares my left thigh, and while the fabric is belted around my waist with a leather corset, only two strips of fabric cover my breasts before tying to a collar around my throat.

I'm less exposed than I was but still on display.

There is a knock at the door seconds before it opens. Lacrae steps inside. He is dressed more casually now, with white pants and no shirt. His chest is defined with ridges of muscle though he lacks the bulk and strength that Fort has.

His hair is braided back from his face, his pointed ears on display.

"You are an elf."

"Yes. We all are."

"Elves aren't supposed to be real. Then again, giants, Tenebris, and flying horses are not either."

Lacrae smiles softly. "There is much you do not know, Carleah, and much we must discuss."

I take his offered hand and allow him to pull me toward the door. The second we step outside, I'm bathed in bright light. "I don't—it was dark in there."

"Our warriors often sleep during the day so they may patrol at night. Therefore, the homes within this tree are spelled to remain dark, aside from the lanterns inside."

"It is morning?"

"Yes," he replies.

We're standing on a staircase that winds up the center of a massive tree. Huge branches—far larger than even the halls of my home—extend out, their flat surfaces walkways to colorful homes hanging throughout the tree. They're connected by small bridges made of large leaves.

I gape, unable to tear my gaze from the beauty of what I am seeing.

"Come," Lacrae says softly. "There is much to see."

He pulls me down the winding staircase. As we pass

other elves, they all stop and stare at me, their gazes widening while they whisper to each other.

"Am I the first human you've had here?"

"Yes," he replies. "And no."

"Will you ever answer one of my questions without a riddle?"

"One day, perhaps," he replies with a smile that makes my stomach churn.

We reach the bottom of the tree. Elven men and women stroll happily down an aisle between two rows of buildings. Children laugh happily as they race through, some playing tag, others simply skipping along without a care in the world.

It reminds me of Navalis.

Of the happiness that once resided there.

"Where are we?"

"Elven city," he replies. We continue walking through the village, and I take note of the joy on the faces of everyone we pass. This place is the exact opposite of Nemoregno, a fact that should settle me.

But the numbness in my bones seems to carry through to my emotions as well because I feel nothing but cool detachment.

"Why have you brought me here?"

"The council will tell you."

"Council?" I stop.

"Yes. We have no king here because we serve the kingdom of Navalis. Our council ensures our laws are carried out, and they govern our army."

"How can you serve a kingdom that never knew you existed?"

He smiles though it is haunted. "There was a time when our people lived together," he says sadly. "But that is a story for another day. Come." He reaches for me, but I do not take his hand. I begin walking, though, falling into step beside him as he crosses through the village and toward a massive stone building built directly into the side of a mountain. Pillars flank either side, its façade looming above me.

Lacrae continues walking, and I follow him up the stone steps and through a huge stone archway. Inside, seven elven men and women sit in stone chairs, all of them staring down their pointed noses at me. I recognize Affree instantly, though she pays me no special attention as Lacrae and I stop in front of them. A woman with dark hair, who sits on the far side of the row, pushes thin-rimmed glasses back up her nose as she studies me.

The man beside her—his grey hair cut short to the scalp—looks at me with disdain, a matching expression for the two men and one woman sitting directly to his right.

"Who do you bring us, Lacrae?" a man with a golden collar around his throat asks from where he sits at the opposite end beside a woman with fiery red hair and eyes the color of golden coins.

"Dward, I bring you the future queen of the Third Realm," he announces. "Carleah of Navalis."

"Excuse me?" I demand, turning toward him. He doesn't look my way, though, and no one makes a sound.

Until the man with short grey hair throws his head back and laughs. The others join in, all but Affree. She continues staring at me, her expression as unreadable as the stone around us.

"You claim this ragged thing is the queen of the Third Realm?" the man with the short grey hair scoffs.

"I've been through a lot—" I start.

"You dare speak to me, child?" he demands, standing slowly as he places both hands on the dark wooden table.

If I weren't so damned hollow inside, I might have been intimidated. After all, I've been taught to heed the words of men—or rulers—my entire life.

But this elven man who shouldn't even exist angers me.

"I do dare to speak to you," I sneer. "I am Princess Carleah Rossingol, future Queen of Navalis. And, in the last week, I have lost my entire family to Tenebris soldiers. I have suffered injury, damn near frozen to death, and was chased from the only place I've ever known as home. Then, the one ally I have is captured by a tribe in Nemoregno, and—" I choke on the word. "Slaughtered because Lacrae abandoned him there." I step forward. "So, yes, whoever the hell you are, I *do* dare to speak to you because my family hails from the land of the Giants, and I will *not* be talked down to."

I glare, anger burning through my body like molten lava.

Affree grins at me and begins to clap. She straightens, a wide smile on her face. "My-my-my. A woman who dares silence the great Onemo. If not a queen, then who could she be?"

"Shadow chose her."

Intrigued, Onemo cocks his head to the side to study Lacrae. "You are sure of this?"

Lacrae dips his head in a nod. "We were out scouting, and he went to her despite me urging him in a different direction. It is he who found her, his magic to whom she called."

"Shadow. The Pegasus? What magic?"

"She cannot be the queen. If she were, she would have known what came for her."

"Possibly not," the woman with glasses says. "If she was not taught. Our prophecies have long been forgotten by the humans."

"She believed us to be legend," Lacrae adds without bothering to look my direction. I might as well not even be here.

And that pisses me off further.

"Then why step in at all?" a woman with obsidian hair in tiny curls says. "Why not leave the humans to their own devices? They will destroy each other in time. Then we can retake the realm."

Onemo pinches the bridge of his nose. "Because, Onyx, that is not what the prophecy says."

"The prophecy spoke of a warrior queen, not some child who was recently orphaned," she snaps.

"I am a warrior," I growl.

"Hardly," she scoffs.

"This companion—" Affree eyes me curiously. "What was he to you?"

I swallow past the lump in my throat. "My friend and protector."

She nods then looks past me to Lacrae. "And you left him to his death?"

"He was fighting for sport," he spits out. "It's barbaric."

"He was *not* fighting for sport," I growl. "Fort was forced into that pit by the leader of Nemoregno."

"We recognize no leader of Nemoregno," Onemo scoffs.

"Tell that to Yarrow," I snap. "Because he sure as fuck thinks he's in charge."

Affree comes around the table. She walks in a slow circle around me, and I cannot help but feel as though I have been placed on display. "You have the fight of a queen," she says. "But we do not trust you—yet." She turns to Lacrae. "Keep her under constant guard until the trials are over."

"Guard? You cannot imprison me here!"

"We do not know if you are who we seek. Others have come before you, others who claimed to be what the prophecy called for. And they abducted our people instead."

"You brought me here," I snarl. "Let me leave, and I will happily be back on my way of finding an army to take back my home."

"Not until your trials are over."

"What trials?"

"You will face four," Onemo says as he stands. "Four that will push you to the brink of what you can handle. Once you have passed them all, then we will determine whether or not you are who we are looking for."

Affree touches the side of my face, and I flinch away. Which only seems to amuse her further. "If you are who Lacrae claims, you will have your army."

I straighten. "What do you mean?"

Affree smiles. "The queen of the third realm rules all," she says. "You will have our warriors at your disposal, Princess, and we will help you retake what you have lost. But only if you are who he claims you to be."

A flicker of hope burns within me now. "If I am who you seek, you will help me level Nemoregno."

Her grin spreads, and I get the impression that this is a woman who is far more than what she appears to be. "Gladly, Princess. Once we have, we will prepare you for what is to come. Then, we take back the realm."

"What is to come? War?"

"Not just war." Her golden gaze darkens. "The Awakening."

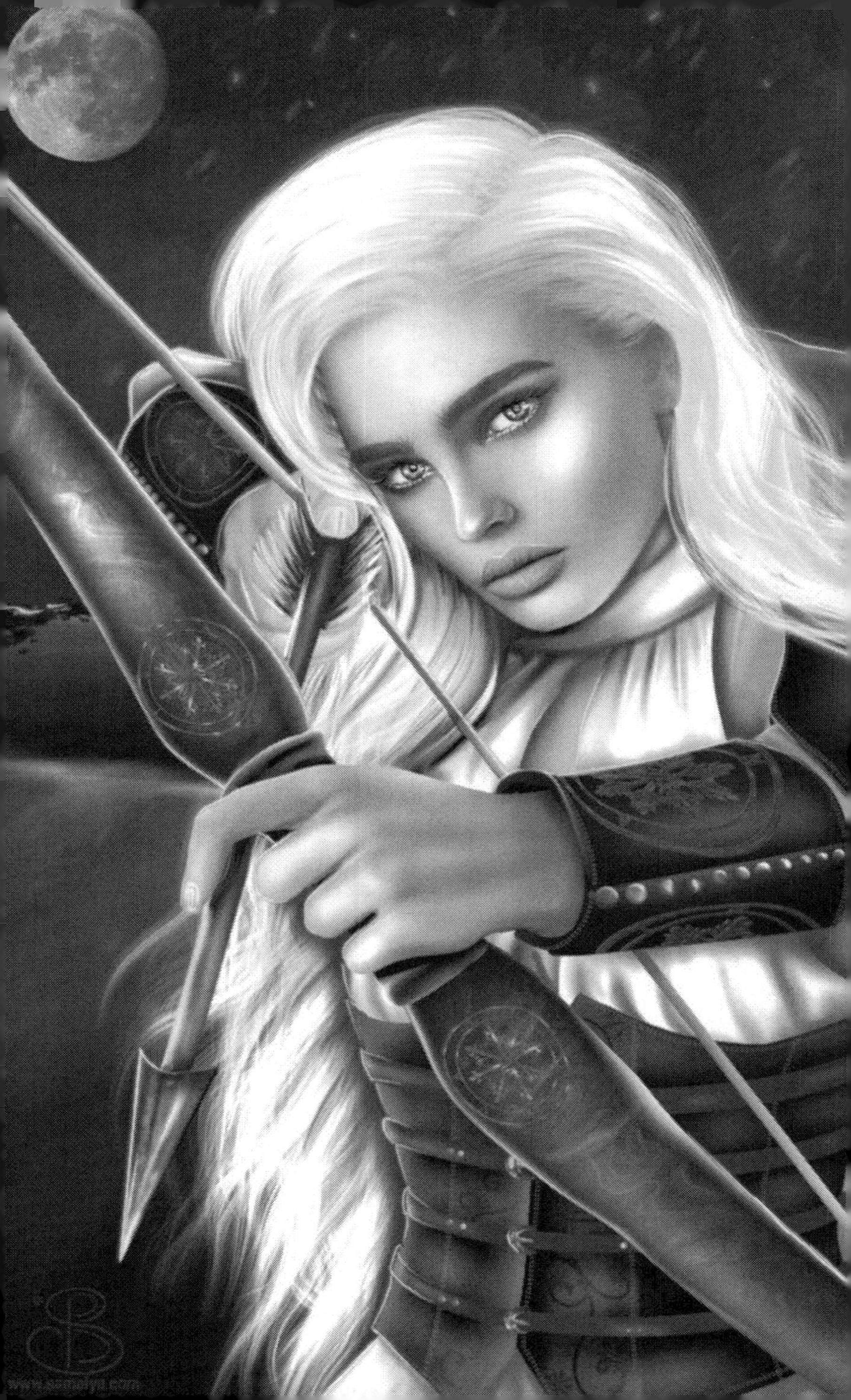

CHAPTER 23
CARLEAH

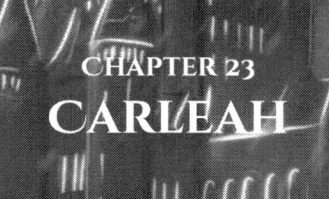

My mind reels with all the new information, but I push it aside as my own curiosity gets the best of me. "Where are we going?" I call back to Lacrae.

We're seated on Shadow as he flies high above the mountains. The fur coat Lacrae gave me is basically useless against the cold wind whipping at me, which makes it even more impressive that the elf is wearing only his long-sleeved, white tunic.

"We need to see how Navalis has fared since the fall," he says.

My blood chills. "We're going back?"

"Yes."

"But, the Tenebris soldiers are still there."

"Perhaps," he replies. "But we will not know for sure until we look. Once we have surveyed the damage, we can plan for retaliation."

The knowledge that he is taking me back to Navalis is

far more nerve-wracking than I thought it would be. After all, ever since we left, the only thing I wanted was to come home. But returning when the deaths of my family are still so new—

Shadow all but plunges down from the clouds. I hold onto his thick mane as he does, only releasing once he's landed smoothly in the snow.

"Get off," Lacrae orders.

But I cannot summon the strength to move. Where the sight of my home once brought me joy, the sight of its high spires of silver and gold, the ornate designs carved over the archway of our door, bring me only fresh pain.

Lacrae grips my arms and tosses me to the snow. "I'm sorry," he says then looks up into the air. Shadow pushes from the ground and I scramble to my feet.

"No! Come back!"

Were they lying? Did the elves just deliver me to the feet of my enemy? Cold sears through my body, freezing the leg bared by the slit in my dress. I scramble to my feet and race toward the nearest tree, hiding myself behind the trunk as I peer into the darkness at my home.

I see no dead.

No bodies or blood.

Which means the Tenebris either cleared them up, or animals came to my home and stole my loved ones. Tears sting my eyes as I move closer to the castle. My boots crunch in the snow, but I move slowly, trying to gradually ease each step so I don't make any unnecessary noise.

I creep forward, inching toward the outer wall. If I can slip inside, I can get a blade, make my way to Soreno, gather an army, and burn Nemoregno and the Elven city to the ground until nothing is left but ash.

Nemoregno killed Fort.

The elves sentenced me to death.

For that, they will all pay.

Someone laughs loudly, and I freeze, my chest constricting. *That laugh.* It's impossible, though. All of— the front door opens and I choke on a sob.

"Listen, you ass, he did not win." Alex steps out onto the porch with Bowman. My brothers look exactly the same as they did before the Tenebris attacked: their white hair cut to their shoulders, their sharp features, and soft blue eyes.

They wear unmarred tunics and dark brown riding pants. As always, Bowman's bow is slung over his shoulder while Alex's blade is secured at his waist.

My chest constricts as I step from the tree and gape at them, unable to tear my gaze away. *What kind of magic is this?*

Both turn to me and stare curiously.

"What are you doing out here, Primrose?" Alex questions, his gaze narrowing on me.

I choke and sprint toward him, wrap both arms around his neck, and crush myself against his chest. I breathe him in and tighten my hold. Pine. My brother always smells like pine.

"Easy, Primrose, or we'll start thinking you did choose a favorite brother."

I pull away only enough to stare at Bowman. But all I can see is his eyes widening as he falls forward, an axe sticking from his back. I grab him and pull him toward me, crushing myself against them both.

Logically, I know this isn't possible. But there's a part of me, a piece of the naïve child I had been, that hopes I've been suffering from little more than a nightmare. Maybe this is when I wake up. When my world goes back to what it was.

"I miss you both so much," I whisper.

"Miss us? We just saw you," Alex says with a laugh. He pushes me back enough to see my face, but I can barely make out his features through the tears streaming down my cheeks. His expression turns serious. "Are you all right? Did someone hurt you?" He cups my cheeks as Bowman looks out into the snow.

"I see no one," Bowman says. "But, what are you wearing?" He glares down at the white dress I wear, at the fur barely covering me. "You cannot be out that way! You'll freeze to death." He pulls my fur closed and tries to guide me to my house.

"Are Mother and Father in there?" I ask. "Ethan and Diedrich?"

"Of course," Alex says. "Seriously, Carleah, are you okay?"

I sniffle and force a smile. Because even if this is some sort of twisted dream, I never want to be the reason for a line to crease between my brother's brows. Never again. "I think perhaps I'm just cold."

"Then let's get you inside. Dinner should be soon."

He guides me into the castle. It's so warm, so welcoming, and my pain grows larger. Our staff smiles at me as they pass.

"Where have you been, girl?" Genevieve demands. "And out like that!" She rushes forward and shakes her finger at me. "How many times do I have to tell you—" I release my brothers and throw my arms around her.

She hesitates a moment before returning the hug. "What is going on? Are you all right?"

"We think she's lost her mind," Bowman jokes.

"Yeah, well, it's no wonder being out in the cold like that. All your brain cells likely froze!" She pulls away. "Your family is waiting for you, girl. Get on in there." But she smiles then moves past us and down the hall toward the kitchen.

The same kitchen where my father was beheaded.

"Come on, Primrose." Alex urges me to begin walking again.

We round the corner into the dining hall, and my father is the first person I see. His greying beard, the smile on his face. "There she is! We have been waiting for you, Carleah." Then, his gaze narrows on me. "Wait, what's wrong?" He looks to my brothers, who hold their hands up.

"Father." I rush toward him, sprinting across the floor and slamming into him. My arms wrap around his neck, and I hold on. My shoulders shake with heavy sobs, but still, I do not let go."

"Are you hurt? What happened?" He pulls me back enough to look at me as my mother crosses toward me.

"Mother,' I choke out, abandoning my father. I embrace my mother, inhaling the scent of flowers as I crush her toward me.

"Easy, Carleah," she coos as she strokes my hair. "Tell us what happened?"

I pull back and sniffle. "Bad dream is all."

"Mother, I tried—"

I whirl on Ethan and Diedrich as they come in. They both stare as I sprint toward them, barely managing to catch me as I wrap my arms around them. "What's this then?" Diedrich questions.

"Primrose is having some sort of mental breakdown," Bowman says.

"No, no." I sniffle and pull away. Then I smile as best I can as I link my arms through theirs and guide them to the table.

We all sit around at our seats. My mother watches me warily as my brothers begin telling us about their days.

Ethan and Diedrich went out hunting and managed to catch the stag we are eating tonight.

Alex trained while Bowman went out and practiced his archery.

The conversation is so normal, so typical of our usual conversations until—Fort stumbles in.

"They're coming," he groans as he falls to the ground.

My entire family jumps up from their seats.

My mother lets loose a scream.

"Did he just speak?" Alex demands as we all rush to Fort. I reach him first, and as I slide to my knees, I note the blood soaking his shirt. Panic fuels the adrenaline in my system as I rip his shirt open.

"Carleah!" my mother scolds.

I stare at the gaping wound. "No. You're not going to die. Not again." I take his tattered shirt and press it to his injury. I apply pressure, pushing down through tears. "Help me!" I scream at my family, but none of them move.

"Sister," Alex says softly. He rests his hand on my shoulder, and I follow his gaze to Fort's face. Lifeless amber eyes are wide open, and a single tear slips down his cheek.

"No!" I scream until my throat is raw. "No! Fort! Wake up! Please wake up." I cup his cheeks with bloody hands. "Please! I need you!"

"We need to go." My brother rips me back, and I let myself be pulled away from Fort. Alex takes my hand and pulls me to my room. "You need to hide."

"No. Let me fight with you. Please. You don't understand. I can fight with you!"

"I understand," he says. "Father is getting Mother to safety, and I need to make sure you're okay. Please just stay here."

He shuts the door behind me, and I scream his name, "Alex! No!" I beat against the door until my fists ache. I rip at the handle as terrified screams echo through the halls of my house. But it does not budge. Alex must have secured it on the other side, so I frantically scan for another route.

I have to save them.

I have to save all of them.

I yank on the door again.

This time, it comes open.

Bodies line the hall, but I step over them carefully because they cannot be saved.

I do not call out.

Do not scream their names.

Because, in my heart, I already know what I'm going to find.

"Where is she?" a man yells.

"You'll never get her," my father growls back.

The slice of a blade.

A body hits the ground.

I run, sprinting as fast as I can into the kitchen, but as soon as I shove through it, prepared to fight until my last breath to save the family I failed the first time around, I stumble into the snow, landing directly beside my mother's body.

"No! Wake up!" I shake her, fear and grief clawing at my chest. "Please wake up!"

When she still doesn't move, I stand, slowly, and cover my mouth with a shaking hand still coated in Fort's blood. The snow is crimson and covered by the bodies of people who were my family.

My friends.

A sea of dead.

And once again, I am the sole survivor.

"Carleah."

I whirl around, prepared for a fight. Lacrae stands in

front of me now, and in the blink of an eye, the world disappears. The snow makes way for sand, and as it disappears, so do the bodies and the imagery of my home.

Tears burn my eyes. My throat is raw, but my emotions are the only thing that remains of the hell I just suffered through.

"What the hell was that?" I demand. I'm standing in the center of a large sand-filled ring. Just outside of the wooden wall surrounding me is a balcony where each of the elven council members sits.

"I am so sorry," Lacrae says as he glares back at Onemo. "That was your first trial."

"Trial. That was fake?"

"Essentially, yes. Though what you suffered through was very real."

"I know it was because I lived it the first time!" I snap. Anger burns through my pain. "And just what the hell were you hoping to see?" I snap. "What exactly did that prove to you?"

"More than you can possibly imagine," Onemo replies as he turns away and steps down off of the platform, disappearing from my view.

I whirl on Lacrae. "Toying with my emotions is bullshit."

"He was simply following orders, Princess," Affree offers.

"How did you do that?" I demand. "How did you twist my mind to believe what it was seeing was real?"

"I am able to use your memories to form temporary

realities," Lacrae replies. "It is how we safely perform the trials as you cannot be injured within them."

"How the hell do I ever know what's real? How can I tell that we're having this conversation?" I demand.

Lacrae reaches forward and pinches the flesh of my arm, and pain radiates on the spot. "That is how. In the augmented reality, you will not feel any pain. Come now," he says. "We must get you rested, for the next trial will take place tomorrow."

But I do not move. "What happens if I am not who you think I am?"

"You are," he replies.

"And if you are wrong? Will you ever allow me to leave this place?"

Lacrae reaches out and brushes his thumb over my cheek. The contact is meant to be soothing, but all it does is unnerve me. "I am not wrong. You are who we seek, and you will have the army you desire."

He turns away and begins walking, the non-answer doing nothing to soothe my nerves. This place may be beautiful, but there's a danger lurking just beneath the surface. I can feel it as easily as I breathe.

"Run, Carleah." Fort's words echo through my mind, and even though a part of me wants to escape this place right now, there's another voice in my mind telling me to stay and see this through.

Because if I am who they claim me to be, then I will have an army to lay waste to Nemoregno and every Tenebris soldier walking the face of this realm.

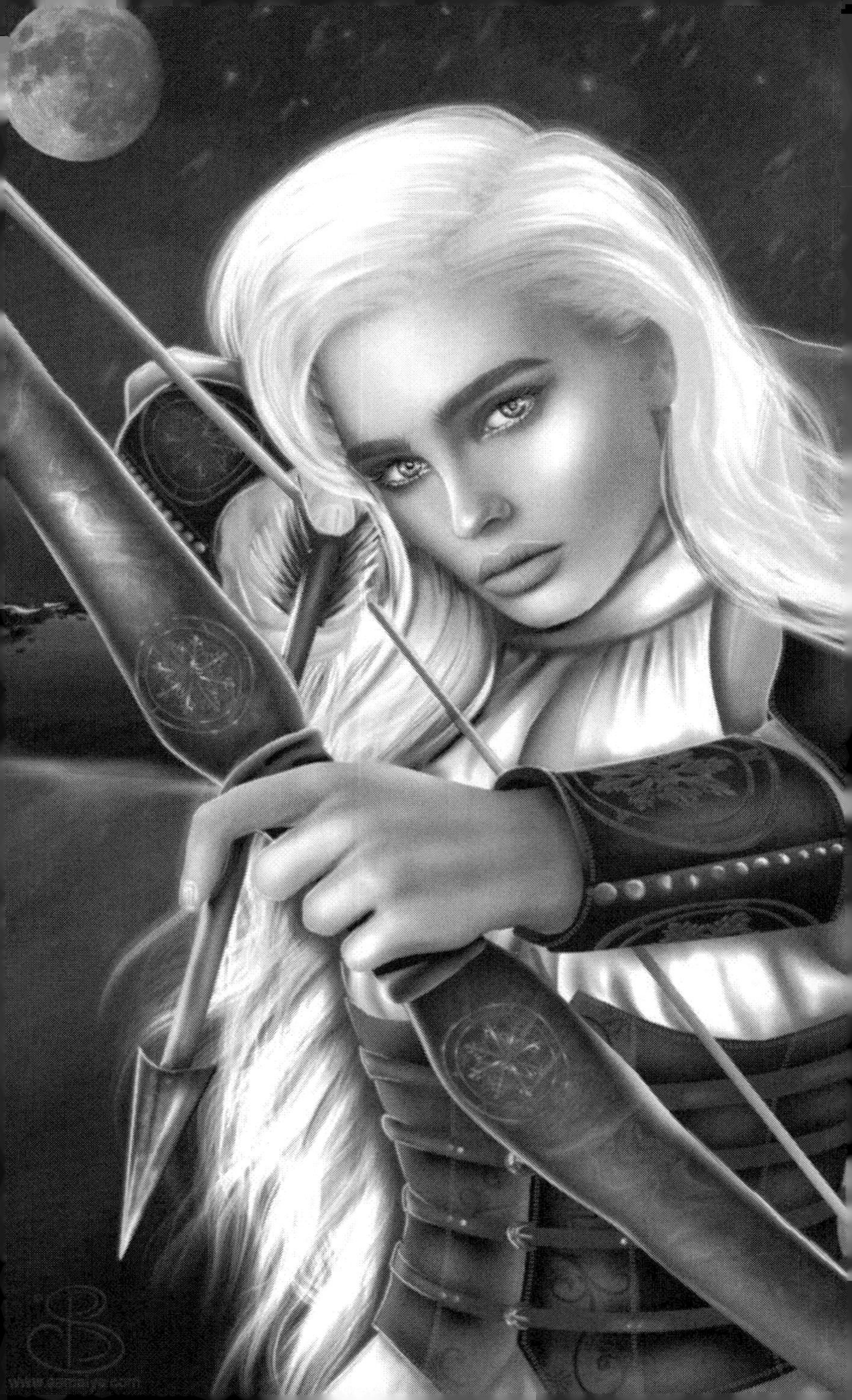

CHAPTER 24
CARLEAH

The door behind me opens, and I jump up from the bed and whirl, my makeshift weapon in hand. A cloaked figure stumbles into my room, and I hold the heavy book up in the air, prepared to strike.

The figure is large, and when they reach up to remove the cloak from their face, I lose my breath.

Fort stares back at me, his face swollen and bruised.

"No. It can't be." I stumble backward. "Stop fucking with me!" I yell.

Fort reaches up and removes Bowman's bow from his shoulder then rushes forward and crushes me against his body so hard it knocks the wind from my lungs. "Fuck, I never thought I'd see you again."

"This isn't real," I whisper. "I saw you. You were dead."

"I'm not dead," Carleah. "He takes my hand and

presses it to his bare chest. The heavy beating of his heart thrums against my palm, but I'd smelled my brother, too. Held them all as though they were still alive.

I stumble backward. "No. It can't be."

"What have they done to you?" he asks. "Carleah. We have to go. We don't have much time." I step back, and pain shoots up through my foot.

"Shit!" I take a seat on the floor, and Fort rushes over to kneel at my side. He takes my foot from me and stares down at it.

Then, he plucks a piece of bloodied glass from it.

Pain burns up into my thigh. I stare at him. "Fort?" I choke out because I *feel*.

And Lacrae told me that in the trials, I won't.

"I told you that I would find you," he replies. "And I didn't break my promise."

I fling myself at him, tackling him to the ground and pressing my lips to his. I cling to Fort like a lifeline as he flips us over and pins me to the ground, his mouth hot and feverish on mine.

He groans against my lips then slows the kiss and pulls away. "We have to go," he says.

"They believe I'm a queen," I tell him as he pulls me to my feet. I keep my weight off of the injured one, though the pain is mild.

"You are."

"No, they believe I'm the queen of the third realm."

Fort's gaze narrows. "That's why they took you?"

I nod. "How did you escape?"

Fort turns. "Later. I wasn't able to get any arrows, I barely got Bowman's bow. So we need to find weapons, and then we need to get the hell out of here." The door bursts open, and Fort shoves me behind him as Lacrae and two elven warriors carrying short blades rush into the room. Affree moves slowly, remaining at the back.

Lacrae lets loose a growl, and I shove forward, coming to stand directly beside Fort. "You never took me back to Nemoregno, did you?" I demand.

A muscle in his sharp jaw tightens, his gaze leveling on me. "No."

"You left him there to die!"

"He was not worth the risk."

"Your Pegasus seems to think I was."

Affree shoves forward now. "Shadow came to you?"

"The large white one that took Carleah? Yeah. He pulled me out of Nemoregno earlier this evening."

"Interesting." Affree grins. "Seems her connection to the creature is stronger than we otherwise thought."

"What the hell does that mean?" I demand.

"Your grief must have sent the creature after this warrior since he sensed it was what would bring you peace. Which is also how you managed to get onto our lands without us knowing."

"Carleah comes with me," Fort snaps. "Or, so help me, I will tear through this fucking city."

"You will do no such thing." Affree waves her hand. "Lower your weapons. He is no threat to her."

"Sister—"

"No, Lacrae. Clearly, he is here to protect her. Is that correct?"

"With my life," Fort growls.

"Then he may stay as our guest. Just as the princess is."

"You mean as your prisoner," I shoot back.

"Not for much longer," she replies. "You've already mastered one trial. What's three more?" Affree moves in closer, stopping right beside Fort. Jealousy churns in my gut as she grins up at him.

"So much power. Strength," she says. "What is your name?"

"Fort."

"Fort," she repeats with a purr of appreciation. "I am Affree of the elven high council."

If he's surprised that she just announced she's an elf, he doesn't show it. "Affree, let us go."

"No," she replies. "You will remain here as long as the princess does."

"And how long is that?"

"Until she proves she is queen or that she is not."

"And if she isn't? What then?" Fort snaps.

Affree grins wickedly, pleasure dancing in her eyes. "I find myself very intrigued by you, and it has been quite some time since I was intrigued by a male." Her gaze drops to his groin. Then she licks her lips and raises it again.

"Back the hell off," I snap as I move in front of Fort. His hand goes to my wrist as though he's prepared to move me but doesn't dare.

Affree's pleasure increases tenfold. "Perhaps he is more to you than your protector." She clicks her tongue. "Time will tell, I suppose. You both may remain here in this room until the trials have been completed. Only then are you allowed to leave. There are herbs beside the tub. Use them to soak your wounds so they do not fester." Affree turns and crosses the room, her dress hugging her body as she does. Once she reaches the door, she looks over her shoulder and says, "Be a good boy, Fort, and perhaps I will let you attend the trials as my guest."

Lacrae offers me a nod then leaves, and the two warriors follow, shutting the door behind them. I hear a lock click into place, sealing Fort and me in this windowless room.

He turns to me, hands going to my arms. "Are you hurt?"

"You are the one she was talking to." I shove the cloak from his shoulders and note the blood crusting his chest and abdomen where I'd seen the arrows strike. "Come, let's get you cleaned up." I tug his hand, pulling him over toward the tub, in search of the herbs. The second I step next to the tub, it begins to fill with water.

I jump back, and it stops.

"What the—" I stare down at the steaming liquid then step forward once more. It begins to fill again, but this time I remain where I am until—in seconds—it is full of steamy, fragrant water.

"That's handy," Fort comments.

"It really is," I reply, turning toward him. "Out of your clothes."

Fort smiles at me. "You've become quite demanding."

I purse my lips and stare up at him. "Your injuries will fester otherwise." Turning away from him, I cross over to the other side of the tub and retrieve a glass container full of dried herbs. After sprinkling some into the water, I turn back around to see Fort, completely naked, standing before me.

Lust hammers in my veins, despite his clear injuries. I study the hard planes of his chest, the defined muscles of his abdomen, and the hard length that hangs between two powerful and scarred thighs.

He's magnificent.

Fort closes the distance between us, his hand snaking around the back of my neck. He pulls me closer and captures my lips as my hands go to his muscled waist. The catch of the collar around my neck comes undone, and the fabric falls forward, my breasts spilling free of the dress.

I moan, arching back to give him access to my throat as he quickly undoes the laces of my leather corset and throws it to the ground. The rest of my dress goes with it, and Fort's hands grip my ass as he lifts and carries me down into the water. It's warm against my flesh, but I can barely feel it, thanks to the heat spreading through me at having Fort's hands on me.

His mouth is on mine.

"I wasn't sure I'd ever see you again," he says as he pulls back to look down into my eyes.

I reach up, emotion clawing at my chest as I cup his face. "I thought you were dead. Lacrae showed me—"

"Showed you?"

"He can manipulate my mind, make me think I'm seeing something that feels real. He showed me you dead, arrows protruding from your body as you lay in The Pit." I run my hands down his chest. "I was going to level Nemoregno to ash as soon as I could for what they'd done to you."

He kisses me deeply, tongue sliding against mine. "You were supposed to stay away from Nemoregno if you ever got the chance to run."

"I don't listen well," I reply as I snake both hands around his neck and cling to his body.

Fort reaches up and pulls my arms from around his neck. His gaze rakes over my body and it burns in response. "I want to wash you," he says softly. "Want to care for you. Because when I'm done, I'm going to fuck you." He kisses my temple.

"Yes," I whisper.

Fort reaches out and retrieves some soap and runs it over my skin. He palms my breasts, sliding his hands over them, then moves between my legs and grips my ass. He washes every inch of me. And when he starts to wash himself, I reach forward and stop him with a hand on his wrist.

"My turn."

Fort grins but offers me the container with fragrant soap. I take it, the floral scent seeping into my lungs as I rub it on my hands and wash away all remnants of Nemoregno from Fort's body. All but the scabbed wounds from the arrows.

"How did these—" I note his shoulder where he'd been injured when Alex was killed. "I completely forgot you were hurt."

"I heal faster than normal men," he replies.

I consider what his father told me about the giant blood, but instead of tainting this moment with thoughts of that bastard, I shove it down.

Tomorrow is soon enough for truths such as that one, as well as facing whatever danger still awaits us. Tonight, I want to love Fort as though we have nothing but time.

Casting a heated gaze over my shoulder at Fort, I move out of the water and retrieve a towel from the rack beside the tub. He follows, grabbing one of his own and drying off.

Before he finishes, though, I cross toward the bed and drop mine then lie back on top of the blankets, completely exposed. "I've brought myself so much pleasure thinking of you," I say.

Fort freezes.

I let my fingers graze over the flesh of my breasts.

"I heard you," he says.

I look at him now. "You did?"

"Up in your room," he says softly. "I'd hear you moaning. Once, you whispered my name."

"Haven't you wondered why his senses are heightened?" The giant's blood.

I should be embarrassed, but honestly, knowing he was listening only fuels the fire in my soul.

"It drove me fucking mad. To know you were up

there and I couldn't have you." He takes a step closer to the bed.

"Did you imagine me?" I question. "Did you picture what I looked like?"

"Every fucking time," he groans.

"Stop," I order.

His dick is hard, his body tense, but he remains rooted in the spot. "You're fucking killing me."

I grin. "Then you're going to want to close your eyes for what comes next."

"Not a fucking chance."

I spread my legs, giving him a full view as I run my fingers down over my belly.

"You're so fucking wet. I can fucking see it from here."

"I am," I say as I run my finger through my wet folds. Pleasure sears me as I do, and I make no attempt to hide it from him.

"Show me how you want me to touch you, Carleah," he orders.

I slide my finger over my clit again, gliding it over my wet heat. Pleasure turns my blood molten. I move faster and faster, every touch pushing me closer and closer to the release I crave nearly as much as I crave his hands on me.

"I want to bury my cock in you," he growls. "I want to fucking drive into you and be the reason you come."

"You've always been the reason I come," I tell him.

That snaps his resolve. He crosses toward me and

kneels on the bed. "I want to taste you as you come. Want to feel you on my face when your release breaks."

"Then do it," I tell him as I spread my legs.

He grins wickedly. "Not like this." Fort rips me up from the bed and sets me on my feet beside it. Then, he lies down and holds out his hand for me. "Sit on my face."

"What?" I choke on the word even as the idea of owning him like that spurs my arousal.

"Trust me, Carleah." I kneel on the bed. "Face the foot of the bed," he orders.

I do then straddle his face. He cups my ass, kneading the muscles there, then slides his hands up and grips my hips. He pulls me down onto his face, and stars explode behind my eyes. "Yes," I moan, gyrating my hips against his face as he fucks me with his tongue.

His cock is hard and directly in front of me, so I lean down and close my lips over the dark pink tip.

He moans, and it vibrates through me, so I suck harder, keeping rhythm with him as he devours me.

"So fucking wet," he growls against me.

My muscles tense as pleasure builds in my core. He sucks on my clit, so I draw his dick further into my mouth, damn near choking on it. The orgasm shatters me into a million tiny, pleasure-fueled pieces.

I come off his dick with a *pop*, but he doesn't let up. He continues tasting me, licking, sucking, taking every ounce of my pleasure down. And when my muscles stop shaking, he lifts me off of him and flips me onto my back.

Both of his hands grip my wrists, and he pins them

above my head beneath one large hand. He drops the other down and caresses my breast.

"You are too fucking good for me. But I'm too damned to care." His hand trails down my thigh, and he lifts it then drives into me. Fort fills me completely, stretching my body, so I cry out. My hands remain pinned above my head as he does just what he promised he'd do—he fucks me.

Hard.

Passionate.

I wrap my legs around him and meet him thrust for thrust, losing myself in the rhythm of our bodies moving together. His hands slide down to my breasts, and he brushes the pads of his thumbs over my nipples. The pleasure building inside of me yet again combusts, and I shatter around him, coming completely and unequivocally undone.

Fort pulls back, leaving my body and pumping himself in his hand.

But I yearn to bring him the same pleasure he brings me.

So I sit up quickly and shove his hand away, replacing it with my own. Then, I lower my head down and take him into my mouth. I can taste my release on my tongue as I suck, drawing him into my mouth and squeezing his shaft with my other hand.

"Fuck, Carleah, I'm going to come. You need to—"

But I move faster. Up and down, doing to him what he's done to me. His hand slips over my ass, and he slides two fingers inside of me, rubbing against the pillowy flesh inside my body. Knowing he's inside my mouth and pussy pushes me into another orgasm.

I shatter around his fingers, drenching him as he comes in my mouth. His dick throbs between my lips as his salty release hits my tongue. He calls out, moaning my name and sliding his fingers out of my body to grip my thigh. I continue working his dick, gripping the shaft with my hand and sliding my mouth over the top of him until he falls completely still.

He sits up, snakes a hand around the back of my head, and pulls me toward him. "I love you, Carleah," he whispers. "You need to know that. I need you to know that. Even if you do not feel the same, believe that I will give the very breath in my chest for you."

I cup his face and press my lips to his. "I love you, too, Fort. With all that I am." The declaration is one I've longed to make for years.

"I am terrified of what this means for us," Fort replies.

I pull back to stroke his face. "Why?"

"It feels an awful lot like we're doomed, doesn't it?" he asks. "The princess of Navalis and a bastard of Nemoregno?"

"We're not doomed," I tell him as I stroke his cheeks. "We're just going to have to fight for it."

"Fighting, I understand," he replies as he brushes a strand of hair from my face.

"You're going to have plenty of time to teach me while we go through these trials," I tell him. "Then again when we are on the road to Soreno."

"You still wish to go to Soreno?"

"If I am this queen they speak of, Affree has assured me that their warriors will fight with me. We will take them to Soreno and request their aid as well. They cannot refuse us if the elves are on our side."

He stares at me. "And if they do?"

"They won't have a choice. Soreno will have to fight, or they will fall just as Nemoregno will."

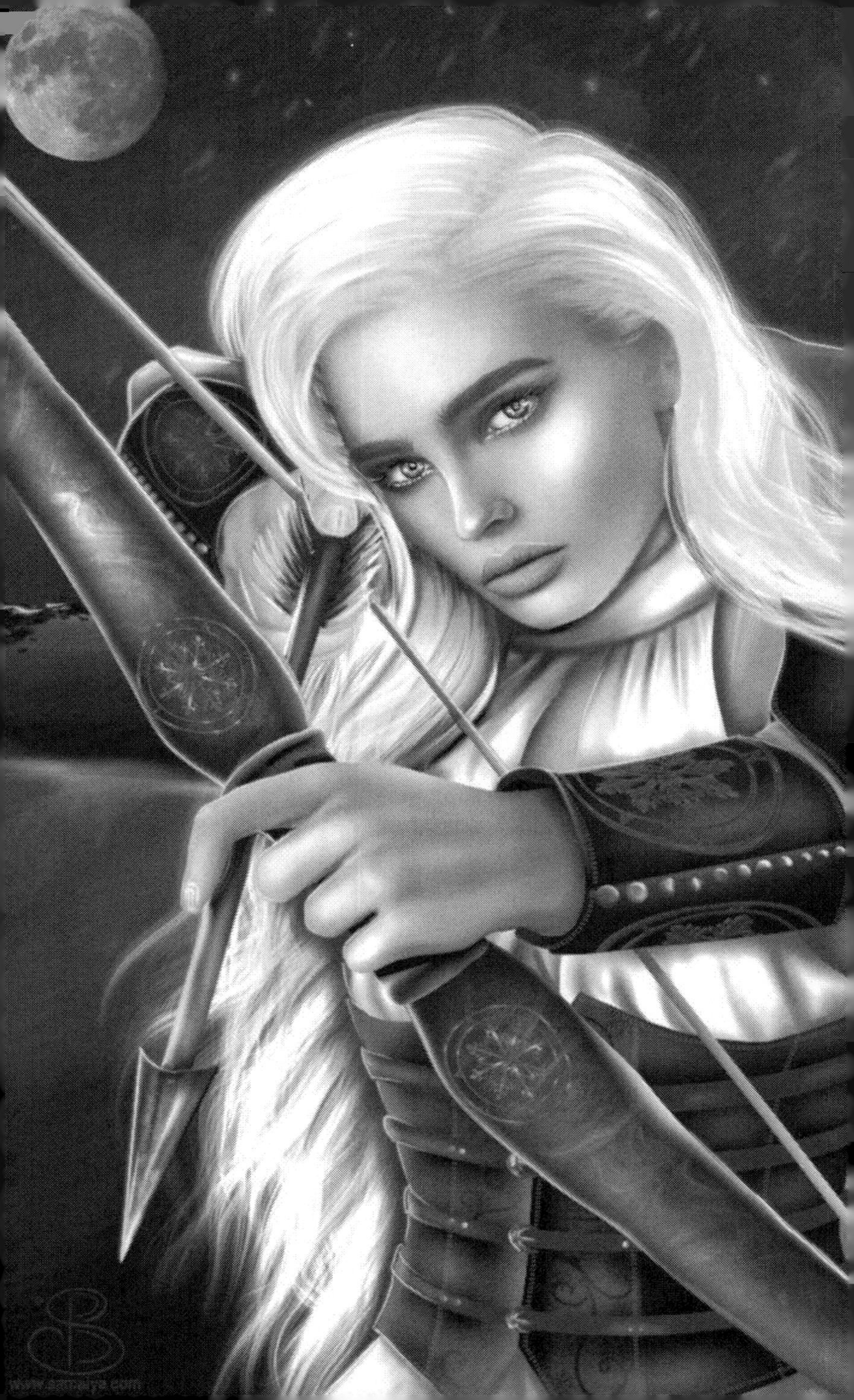

CHAPTER 25
CARLEAH

When I wake, Fort is sitting at the edge of the bed, staring at the door. Whatever herbs we'd used in the bath last night have faded some of Fort's injuries, though the bruises on his face have turned yellow.

I get to my knees and position myself behind him, wrapping both arms around his waist and pressing my lips to his warm back.

"Morning," he grumbles.

"Morning," I reply.

Fort looks over his shoulder at me. "There's a strange sort of peace up here."

"There is," I agree.

Cut off from the rest of the world, Fort and I may be at the mercy of the elves, but we're not running for our lives. Not fighting crimson soldiers or fending off the tribe in Nemoregno. For one night, we'd been able to lose ourselves in each other, and today I feel renewed. Energized.

"You haven't told me how you escaped," I say. "Just that Shadow came for you."

"After you'd been taken, Oliver came into The Pit after me. He meant to kill me while the others were distracted. I beat him to it."

"You killed him?" I don't know why it surprises me, Oliver was horrible, but knowing that Fort has no more brothers—then again, I suppose he never had them the way I did.

"Yes. Yarrow had me ripped from the pit. He pulled the arrows from my body and told me that I'd robbed him of an heir, so death was too easy for me. He tried to break me, but before he could, something distracted them, and they left. I managed to break free of the bindings and slipped beneath the back of the tent. The Pegasus stood just outside. At first, I thought I was hallucinating even though I'd seen it carry you off." He chuckles. "I climbed onto him and asked him to bring me to you. Not that I actually thought he'd be able to understand me. When he landed just outside of the tree, I stole a cloak and watched, waiting to see you."

"How did you find my room?"

"Luck, I suppose. I caught sight of you walking beside that elf—Lacrae—and followed. I had to wait quite a while to get in here, though, because there were so many elves around. Once they started retreating to their homes, I snuck through."

My heart aches for the pain he suffered. Fort pulls

away from me then turns and leans down onto the bed. "I promised I would find you."

"I'm so glad you did."

He kisses me deeply.

"What were you thinking of?" I ask when he releases me and takes a seat on the bed beside me.

"Your family. I think of them often."

"You do?" I don't know why, but the fact that he misses them too makes me feel less alone.

"Always. I loved your family, Carleah. They were the closest thing I had to one."

"They thought of you as a son." I smile, recalling the moment my father learned of my affection for the man sitting beside me. "My father caught me watching you one day."

Fort arches a brow. "Oh?"

I nod. "I was hidden behind the smoke shed outside, watching you train in the ring. I believe I'd been sixteen at the time?" I laugh. "Anyway, he snuck up behind me. Scared me half to death." The memory of it makes me smile. "He did not tease me for it, which I was grateful for. But he did tell me to ensure my mother never caught me lurking."

Fort grins at me. "She would have been furious."

"Yes. But only after the betrothal was announced. Everything changed between us then. It became more about preparing me for a marriage I didn't want."

Fort cups my cheek. "The day you announced your betrothal, I considered returning to Nemoregno."

"What? Why?"

"So they would put me out of my fucking misery." He releases me and looks straight ahead. "I'll never forget the way you looked standing beside that fucking worm, his hand in yours. You'd looked so miserable, and he was the happiest man in the fucking realm."

"I was miserable. I tried so hard to want him the way everyone wanted me to, and maybe I would have if it weren't for you." I shake my head. "No, I don't think that's true. But you gave me a fantasy that he would never live up to."

Someone knocks on the door, pulling us from our thoughts.

"Who is it?" Fort demands.

"Lacrae."

Fort looks over at me and the fact that I'm wearing nothing. "If he comes in now, I'll kill him."

I smile. "Don't come in!"

There's a pause, then Lacrae calls back, "Please get ready for the day. We have much to discuss."

***

Fort and I dress quickly. He slips back into his pants and boots. Though, with no tunic, his chest is bare. I can all but feel Affree's gaze on him, but I shove the jealousy down as I tie the collar around my neck.

We open the door, and I'm not at all shocked to see Lacrae standing there, arms crossed. "Princess," he greets then looks past me at Fort. "Barbarian." He throws a white tunic at Fort. "Can't have you frightening the locals."

Fort grins and slips the shirt over his head. "Better?" he asks, sarcasm lacing his tone.

"Hardly." Lacrae smiles at me. "Did you sleep well?"

"You don't get to treat me as though we're friends," I snap. "Not after what you did."

Lacrae's expression falls. "I am truly sorry, Princess. I wish I could take back my actions, but what I did was out of fear for your life."

"You lied to me. Manipulated me into thinking the one person I had left in this world had been stolen from me."

Lacrae bows his head. "Please let me make it up to you."

"You can't," I reply. "But I am happy to move on with my trials so we can get past all of this."

I can see the hurt on his face, but I feel no guilt in putting it there. He lied to me. Robbed me of hope. And I will never be able to fully trust him.

"I understand. Regardless, I was hoping you might accompany me somewhere. I have something I wish to show you."

"Fine."

He dips his head in a nod and begins walking. I remain beside him while Fort walks directly behind me.

"Have you eaten?"

"No."

"We should remedy that first, then," he says with a smile and veers off to the right, across a large branch that heads into a blue house built into the tree. It's fascinating, stunning, but I don't let it show that I think so.

I keep my expression neutral because I get the impression Lacrae is trying to impress me on some level.

We step into a room full of tables that are overloaded with fresh fruits and vegetables. Lacrae leads us to a table near a row of windows then takes his seat and gestures for us to take ours. I sit beside Fort on the bench, and his hand goes to my knee beneath the table.

"Eat. Please." Lacrae reaches out and plucks some grapes from the tray and begins to eat in silence.

I do the same, choosing plump, purple grapes. The sweet flavor nearly makes me groan as it slips down the back of my throat. Since they do not grow in the winter, the only time we'd get any was when they came through on the supply ships.

They were a treat and always one of my favorites.

Fort is more cautious, taking a few grapes for himself and eating slowly.

"How much do you know of your own people's history, Carleah?"

"All of it. My mother made sure I understood," I reply as I pluck another grape into my mouth.

"Enlighten me," he says.

"In the beginning, the realm was one solid land mass governed by the king of Navalis. Giants stood as our greatest protectors. They ensured our safety and were loyal to the king. When a war broke out between Navalis and the men who sought to overthrow the king, the giants were so angered that they used their extreme strength to break the realm into multiple parts, allowing the men to have their own kingdoms while protecting Navalis."

Lacrae's gaze never strays from my face. "And what happened to these protectors? To these giants?"

Something in his tone sets me on edge. Fort gently increases the pressure on my knee, letting me know he picked up on something, too.

I clear my throat. "They retreated to a mountain range."

"The Land of the Sleeping Giants," the elf says.

"Yes. The Phantom appeared not too long after, a barrier between us and the rest of the realm." I look out through the window, scanning the land and taking in the sheer beauty of the green hills. "I always believed it to be stories, though. Mere legends told to frighten young children."

Lacrae chuckles. "We do not need stories to do that when history is frightening enough. Though your account is entirely wrong."

I glare at him. "Excuse me?"

"Do not take offense, Carleah, for I mean none. It is no surprise, really. History is oftentimes flawed because those who ensure its recording are also seeking to tell the tale of their own heroics."

"Then you enlighten me," I snap.

Fort's thumb strokes my knee tenderly.

Lacrae is not the least bit bothered by my tone. "The giants were not peacekeepers," he says. "They were enforcers. Merciless warriors who killed for coin. The realm was broken by their strength—yes—but it was a way to divide us. To ensure we could not work together to defeat them."

"Enforcers?" I choke out. "You cannot be serious."

Lacrae's expression morphs from the handsome elf to something far more sinister. "I am deadly serious, Princess."

"And how do you know this isn't your history merely having been re-written? Why are you so quick to assume ours is flawed?" Fort questions.

"Because I do not need history to teach me of my past," he replies as he meets Fort's gaze. "I was there." He reaches toward me with his hand. "If you will allow me, I can show you."

I stare at his outstretched palm. "Show me?"

"Yes. The same way we pull your memories for the trials, I can show you mine."

"And how do we know these memories are not altered for your own gain?" Fort demands.

"I cannot alter memories unless I am in the ring. That is the only place with enough magic woven into the land itself that I can craft an alternate reality entirely." He turns to me. "I assure you, Princess, I will only show you the truth."

"That's a large declaration for a man who lied to me the first time we met."

"I know. But—I need you to see. Please."

I consider his offer. If I don't let him show me what he claims to be his memories, I know I will regret it because I'll be consistently wondering. But if I do let him, how the hell do I know he's being honest?

I take his hand, and Lacrae smiles softly. "You will need to take her hand," he tells Fort. I offer it to him, and he lifts his hand from my knee to thread his fingers through mine.

Lacrae closes his eyes, and the wind picks up as we plummet into his mind.

∽

THE WORLD around me is white.

It is cold, though I cannot feel it.

Beside me, Lacrae holds my hand, his fingers threaded through mine. Fort is on my other side, his hand tight on mine.

I turn my attention from him to the area around us, my gaze landing on the castle of Navalis. It's smaller, though, just the main structure that was built well before my father's time. Warriors stand outside wearing white and golden armor, their sunlit hair a near match to the elf beside me.

I look at him. "We were allies?"

His gaze is deeply saddened as he studies the scene. "We were friends, Carleah. Your people and mine fought and lived beside one another. Come." He pulls me toward the castle though, as we approach, no one pays us any attention.

"Can they not see us?"

"Not this time. I am not manipulating a memory but

merely showing you one as it played out. That is how you know it is real. If they can see you, it is a fallacy."

I pocket that information for later as we make our way inside the castle. A fire roars in the hearth as a woman sits in front of it, brushing the short, white hair of her son. "I'm frightened, Mother," he says softly, voice wavering.

"Do not be afraid, Viktor. We are protected here." She glances over her shoulder, and I follow her gaze, mine locking on another version of Lacrae. His expression is haunted, burdened, but he watches them with a longing affection.

"Who was she to you?" Fort questions.

"A friend," he replies, though I get the impression she was much more.

"There you are." A man rushes through the front door. His golden hair is pulled back and braided down his back, showcasing two pointed ears.

He kneels. "My son, are you all right?"

The little boy launches himself into the arms of his father.

"Son?" I ask.

Lacrae nods even as his counterpart forces his attention away from the scene, moving toward the stairs instead. "As I said, we lived together. Your ancestors are descendants of both elves and humans."

I gape at him, unsure how to feel. "I have elven blood?"

He nods. "More so than you should. The line was so

diluted, though your eyes—" He shakes his head as he stares at me. "I've never seen such eyes on a human."

I look over at Fort, who's nodding in agreement. "I've always said they were unique."

Lacrae nods though he doesn't elaborate. "Come. There is much to see, and my energy will wane soon." Still holding my hand, he tugs me toward the stairs. We take the narrow passage up, following the memory version of him, and I reach out to trail my fingers along the wall.

The stone should have been cool beneath my touch, but I feel nothing.

We make our way down the hall and toward the study. My chest constricts, the muscles in my stomach twisting into knots because I half expect my own father to be seated behind his large desk.

Instead, we walk into a room I barely recognize. The desk stands, but there are very few books on the shelves, no tapestries on the wall. It lacks the warmth I attributed to this space, and it makes me miss my father even more.

The man behind the desk doesn't bother to look up at us upon our arrival, though his grey brows are furrowed as he glares down at the map in front of him.

Long, grey hair is tied behind his neck while a simple golden crown adorns his head. "You have news for me?" memory Lacrae says.

"Father."

We turn as a white-haired man rushes into the room. His blue eyes are sharp, his face clean-shaven, and for a moment, I am struck with an image of Alex rushing into Father's study the night before he left for good.

Now, the king looks up, though his attention is on the man, not the elf. "What is it, Ky?"

"The giants are nearing our southern border. They will be here momentarily."

"Son of a bitch," the king grumbles. "We should have had more time." He looks to Lacrae. "Have you any word from your kind? Any idea how we stop their assault?"

Lacrae shakes his head. "They are working on a spell, but the weaving of it takes time. We must hold them off. Send as many of our troops as we can to—"

"The giants have obliterated our armies," Ky insists. "We must run."

"And go where?" Lacrae demands. "Where will we go?"

"Anywhere but here."

"There is nowhere else. If Navalis falls, there will be no way to defeat the giants. Which means the entire realm will fall to their mercy."

"We're already at their mercy!" Ky bellows.

Lacrae steps forward. "It is not lost yet." He grips the man's arm. "Ky, you must retain your hope. Otherwise, we *will* lose."

Ky's gaze darkens, remorse and pain etched into every line. "Lacrae, we have already lost."

Present day snaps around me as I'm ripped from the memory. Lacrae's cheeks are pink, his eyes a duller shade of gold, but his attention is still very much on mine as he withdraws his hand. Fort, however, continues to hold onto me.

"Why did you stop?" I ask.

"It takes a great amount of strength to hold a memory that long. We will need to do this in steps." He stands. "There is much I wish to show you."

"Your people and mine were friends," I say cautiously. "Does that mean we are related?"

Lacrae nearly chokes on his laugh. "Are all humans related?"

"Well, no—"

"All elves are not. Rest assured, Princess, our lines do not cross." He winks at me, and my stomach churns.

Beside me, Fort lets out a growl.

"I didn't mean it like that."Lacrae smiles. "And why would you?" He looks to Fort. "If your warrior is so much more than just your protection?" He doesn't wait for me to respond before turning and leaving the room.

Fort and I follow cautiously, letting him lead us higher into the tree and onto a flat platform near the top. Wind whips past us here though it does not knock us over. I stare out at the sea of clouds, noting the dips and different shades. We're so high up, so far into the tree that I can see all the way to the ice-capped mountains of Navalis.

My chest tightens.

Lacrae lets out a shrill whistle.

"What are you—"

"Shh," he whispers. "Listen."

So, I do. The wind begins to pick up moments before the heavy flapping of wings fills my ears. A dozen horses rise from the clouds, their wings outstretched as they circle us and land on the platform.

I stare, completely and totally overwhelmed by their beauty.

In varying shades of ebony charcoal, black, and brown, the creatures stand, their massive, feathered wings folded at both sides.

"Oh my." And then, a white horse steps forward. The others part for it, and it drops its head. I stretch out my hand, palm first, and he presses his huge nose against it, breathing me in and letting his hot breath warm my hand. "You are incredible," I whisper as I reach forward and run my hand along his long face.

"This is Shadow," Lacrae tells me. "He is a king in his own right, and he is who chose you."

I touch him softly, and he moves toward me, nuzzling me with his face. "Hello, Shadow. Thank you for bringing Fort back to me."

The horse backs away enough that I can make out his bright golden gaze.

"Once you pass your trials and are the proven queen, he will be yours. Though, I believe he already recognizes you as his."

"A creature such as this belongs only to himself."

Shadow drops his head and nuzzles me again, his hot

breath fanning over my abdomen. I can feel it through the thin fabric of my dress and smile.

"I would say he appreciates that response."

Fort walks forward and rests his hand on the massive horse's neck. "Thank you," he says softly.

Shadow turns toward him and drops his head. After he snorts, he backs away, spins, then takes to the sky. The other horses do the same, following him through the clouds until I can no longer see them.

"Your connection to Shadow will continue to grow," Lacrae tells me. "It is said that the queen of the Third Realm and the king of beasts will be as one in mind. Your thoughts will become his own, and you will understand him in turn."

"They are magnificent. I never knew such creatures existed." I stare after them.

"There is much your history failed to mention, Carleah, and I will be telling you all of it before the finalization of your fourth trial."

I look over at Fort, who's eyeing Lacrae as though he's imagining what would happen should he throw the elf over the side. And honestly? I can't say I'd blame him if he did.

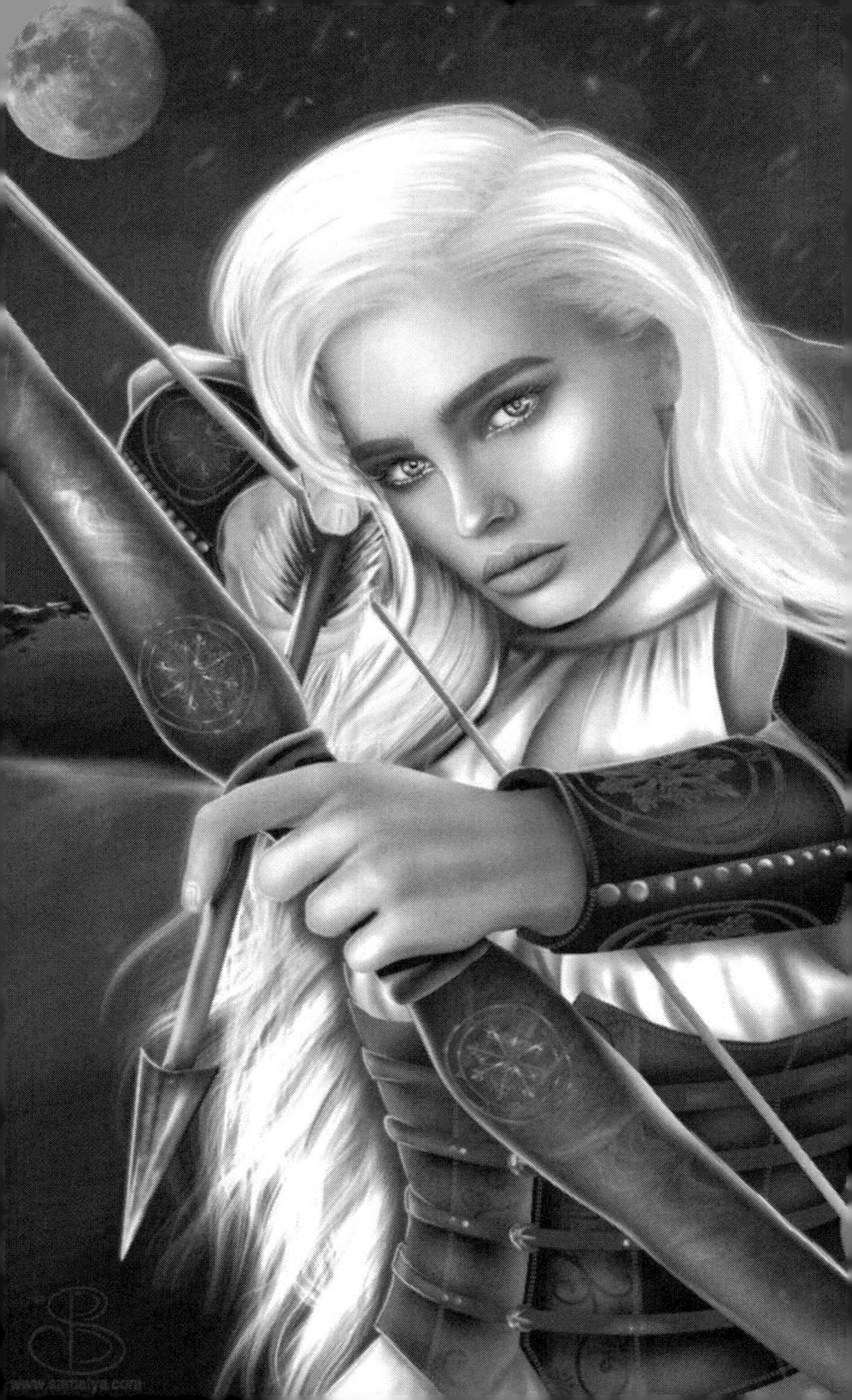

CHAPTER 26
CARLEAH

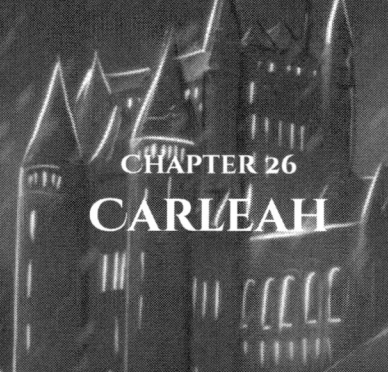

Fort was gone when I woke, and because of that, I'm less than relaxed as I walk beside Affree and Lacrae and through the village.

According to them, we are on our way to see him since he has been training with the elven army all morning. An army that they claim will one day be mine to lead.

And how strange is that? Calreah Rossingol, Warrior Queen of the Third Realm. I would laugh if it all weren't so damned heavy.

All around me, elves move with purpose.

Shopkeepers tend to their wares while those purchasing them haggle prices or hand over coin. Children race through the streets, laughing loudly without a care in the entire world. It reminds me of home.

Of a land where peace reigned.

If only it would always remain that way. But if the ugliness of war reached even my lands, I cannot imagine this place will remain untouched forever. Especially if the Tenebris are looking to wake the giants. If they are truly the monsters Lacrae claims, they will decimate this realm.

"What do you see?" Affree questions.

"People."

"Not just people," she replies as she gestures with both arms. "Happy, joyful, peaceful people."

For now. "Yes."

"I hear your cynicism, Carleah, and that will not bode well for the second trial."

"And just when is this second trial going to happen?" I question.

"When you are ready," she replies.

"Isn't the entire point of these trials to push me to my breaking point?"

She throws her head back and laughs like it's all a big, damned joke and they didn't assault me with images of my dead family mere days ago. "The first one is, yes. But the second trial is to test who you are as a person." Her gaze levels on mine. "So, Carleah Rossingol, who are you?"

"A princess," I reply.

"There was not a hint of certainty in that response." Affree clicks her tongue.

"I was born a princess," I reply. "It's all I've ever known."

"But it is not *who you are*. Your title is that of a princess, yet the fire in your soul is not."

"I want to fight," I say. "To be taken seriously."

She stops walking, so I do as well. "My dear girl, you are a fighter. You begged to fight back in that first trial."

"Yet I couldn't save them. Again."

She purses her lips. "This is why we do not use memories of past loved ones lost so violently in the first trial. It sets one up for failure because there is *never* a chance of victory. Those you love are already gone."

Her words hit harder than they should have. Maybe it's the lack of sleep or the feeling that Fort and I are simply waiting around for another attack.

"Tell me of that night."

"Excuse me?" She speaks as though we are old friends, like I should tell her all of my secrets, but there's not a damned person aside from Fort I trust.

"Tell me what happened when your family was killed."

"It's not something I feel like talking about."

"I wish to know what led the princess of Navalis to our door."

"Lacrae kidnapping me led us here."

Beside me, Lacrae chuckles. "Because you both were doing so well for yourselves when Shadow and I found you."

The soft cries of a child draw my attention from them, and I turn to see an elven girl curled in a corner between two tents, her knees drawn up to her chest. The pale green dress she wears is splattered with various fruits, and the sight of her pain grates against my already angry heart.

I start toward her.

"Leave her, Carleah. We have things to discuss."

I turn and glare at the elven councilwoman. "She is hurting."

"She is embarrassed, that is hardly the same as pain."

"You are wrong. Feel free to continue walking, but I will not stand idly by and do nothing." I turn my back to Affree and Lacrae, and cross the distance. Once I've reached the small elven girl, I kneel in front of her. "What makes you cry?"

She looks up at me through tear-stained golden eyes. "The other children called me names. They threw fruit at me."

I brush golden hair behind her pointed ear. "It is not right for them to call you names. May I ask what they said?"

Sniffling, she pulls the sleeve of her dress up to reveal two large pink splotches on her otherwise pale flesh. "They do not have these, but I was born with them."

"Oh, honey." I reach out and smooth the tips of my fingers over her birth marks. "These make you unique."

"Unique is another word for weird."

I gasp. "It is not. I like to think I am unique, too."

"You do not have pointed ears." She reaches up and touches her fingers to the top of my rounded ear.

"I do not. See, I am different, too."

"Are you the same as other humans?"

I lean in closer. "Can I tell you a secret?"

She nods, her eyes growing wider. "My brothers all had pale blue eyes. But as I got older, mine got far brighter than theirs. They were very jealous." I laugh easily now, thinking of Alex, Bowman, Diedrich, and Ethan.

"Did they call you names?"

I take a seat beside her, brushing my white skirt beneath me. "Not to be mean," I tell her truthfully. "But they did call me Primrose because, when I was a child, maybe two or three years old, I wandered off. No one knew where to find me, but my oldest brother, Alex, found me wandering in a primrose patch. The name stuck." I reach out and brush the pad of my thumb over her cheek to clear a tear from her face.

"I do not like being different." She sniffles.

"It's hard," I admit, feeling the little girl's pain. "But I promise that, when you get older, you will like standing out. It's those who are different that change the world."

She sniffles then takes a deep breath.

"My mother would tell me that it's okay to cry as long as you stand again."

"I like that." She smiles, showing a missing front tooth.

"Are you ready to stand?" I offer her my hand and she takes it. Together, we push off the ground and straighten.

"I am Hollie."

"My name is Carleah. It is a pleasure to meet you."

The little girl surges forward and wraps her arms around me then pulls back. "Will I see you again?"

"I certainly hope so. Ignore the ugly words, Hollie. They are just jealous of the joy in your soul. Do not let them have it."

"I won't. Promise." She beams at me.

Something crunches to our left.

I turn my head as a massive feline steps through the tents. With glowing green eyes, it watches us. Its body is at least the size of a horse, it's claws large enough to slaughter a grown man with one swipe.

People around us scream, but the little girl remains frozen in fear.

"Lacrae!" I yell.

He does not answer, and I am too afraid to turn my back to look for him in the crowd of panicking elves.

"Come, Hollie. We must go." I tug on her arm, panic clawing at my chest. It smothers me now, pulsating through my veins alongside the adrenaline.

The thing moves closer.

"Come on!"

She doesn't move.

The cat lets loose a roar then races toward us. I grab Hollie and spin, dropping down to my knees and hovering over the shaking little girl as the cat leaps toward us.

And then—the world around me disappears.

I straighten only to find myself standing in the center of the arena, sand around my feet. A light wind whips at my hair, sending the granules flying all around me. When I look up at the elves watching me from stands above the pit, my gaze finds Fort.

He stares down at me, his hands white knuckling the wooden bar separating us. A golden collar sits around his neck. Affree stands just behind him, and the wide smile on her face makes it clear enough that I passed their test.

And if it didn't do the trick, the scowl on Onemo's would have told me as much.

Relief burns through me even as the seeds of mistrust sprout anew. I thought I'd woken alone this morning, so if they are this good at manipulating my mind, what more is false?

Either way, it's another trial gone. And I, for one, am looking forward to the fact that I am one step closer to taking back my home.

Two down. Two to go.

～

"What was the purpose of that?" I ask Lacrae as he walks beside me. We move up the spiral staircase in the center of the tree.

"The trial of compassion and sacrifice," he replies. "Are you willing to show compassion when it is needed? Are you willing to sacrifice your life to save an innocent? You passed both."

"I want to know how you got us out of the room without our knowledge," I demand. "And where Fort is."

"On his way back to your room," he replies. "As for the how, I'm afraid I cannot tell you that until the completion of the trials." He gestures for me to enter a room to the right, so I do, though I don't make it far before my feet become rooted in the spot.

Around me, bodies gyrate together, completely

unashamed at their nakedness. Some elves watch the public display, gently pleasuring themselves as they do, while others partake.

"Umm, what is happening?"

Lacrae chuckles. "Rest assured, Princess, this is not our final destination. Onyx," he calls out.

The councilwoman with ebony hair raises her hand as a man moves between her legs. "What is it, Lacrae? If you are not here to join, I am uninterested."

"I need your key to the Hall of History."

She groans and shoves the man away from her. I note his disappointment. "Very well." She stands, full breasts swaying as she walks. Then she bends down and retrieves her robe before tossing it to him. "Take what you need." She looks to me, a slow smile spreading over her face. "You look fascinated, Princess. Shall you stay and watch? Perhaps we can fetch your warrior as well?"

"No," I reply quickly.

Onyx grins. "Humans always were rather prudish."

"Not prudish," I reply, "Just uninterested."

"Uninterested in anyone but your human?"

"Yes."

"I appreciate your honesty." Then, she reaches out and brushes a finger down Lacrae's jaw. "Feel free to come back later."

He laughs. "I am afraid that I, too, am uninterested. Thank you." He holds up the golden key then takes my hand and pulls me back toward the door.

"What was that?"

"The door was unlocked. I assumed she would not be tending to her needs so openly."

"That is not unusual?"

"Not at all," he replies. "Most elves have more than one lover."

"And they just all—get together like that?"

His laugh does not relax me in the slightest. "Some choose to have sex together while others prefer intimacy. I am one of those who prefer the latter." He leans in. "Sharing has never been something I was good at." When I don't respond, he pulls away. "Come, there is much to show you."

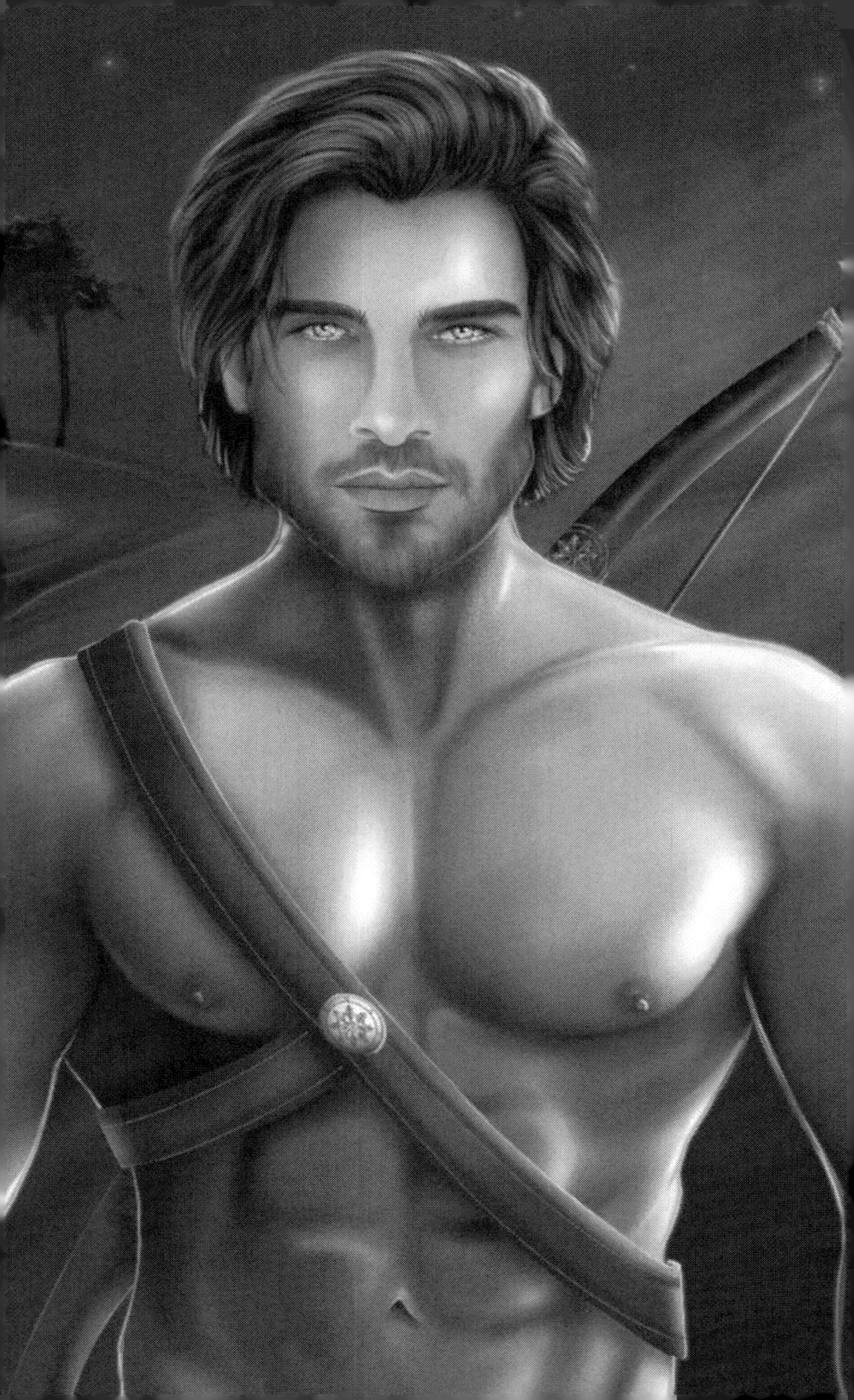

CHAPTER 27
FORT

Watching Carleah walk away with Lacrae has me tightening my hold on the bar separating me from the arena. So fucking close, and yet she might as well be miles away from me. Her hair had flown around her face, a white curtain that shielded her expression as he leaned down and spoke to her. As he reached out and touched her.

Even though they've already left, I can still see them there.

Him stroking the soft strands of her hair.

"Jealousy is a fantastic color on you, warrior."

I don't even spare Affree a look. "I have nothing to be jealous of."

"No?" She laughs. "My brother has quite a reputation," she says. "Carleah would be quite pleased with him."

"Seems a strange thing for you to know," I growl.

Affree comes to stand beside me. "Does it? Are

humans truly so off put by pleasure that they do not find pride in the tender reputations of their family?"

"No. It's fucking weird where I come from." I turn toward her. "Can I go back to my room now?" The need to be close to Carleah triples. When I'd woken this morning, only to find Carleah gone and me wearing a golden collar around my fucking neck, I'd been furious.

But anytime I tried to break free, the damned thing shocked me like a bolt of lightning.

"I wonder what you are thinking of," Affree coos as she takes my hand. "Come." She pulls me toward the exit. We climb the steps of the tree, moving from where the arena sits at the base and up to the cells which reside at the very top.

But before we make it even halfway up, Affree drags me off to the right and onto a hallway that leads toward a door. "Where the hell are we going?"

"You are going to join me for tea."

"No. I'm not."

She arches a brow. "If you are in a rush to get back to Carleah, rest assured my brother has not returned her to her room. If I understand things, they were going to join Onyx in her private chambers for some—entertainment." She pops the 't', her gaze traveling down my body.

"Take me back to our room."

She smiles. "You do not have a choice, Fort. Enjoy a mug of tea with me. Then I shall return you to your room where you can stare at Carleah until your eyes fall out if that's what you so choose." She pulls me, but I dig my heels in.

"I'm not going any fucking where with you. Take me back. Now."

Affree releases my hand and crosses her arms. "You must make everything so difficult."

"Tends to be a side effect when you imprison someone."

"Imprisoned?" She arches a brow. "You are not a prisoner here."

"Great. Then let me go."

"Once we determine that Carleah is who we believe, we will do just that."

"And if she's not?" When Affree doesn't answer, I nod. "Exactly. I know what happens should she not pass your fucking tests. You forced her here because a damned horse chose her, and now you won't let us go."

"Shadow is not a damned horse," she replies, her tone taking on a dangerous edge. "He is ancient, older than even our race, and prophecy says it is he who will carry the Warrior Queen to victory."

"A prophecy," I scoff. "So you're risking our lives on a legend."

"A *legend?*" she snaps. "Do you have any idea the history that this realm carries? The bloodstain that taints each and every race?"

"I know plenty of history."

"No. You do not. Not the truth, anyway. Perhaps you should ask Carleah? Lacrae has shown her the truth, after all."

A muscle in my jaw tightens. "Giants and prophecies are mere stories told to children to make them fearful of the dark."

"Are they?" she questions, her expression turning murderous. "Because I was there, Fort. When the giants were brought to their knees by sheer will of a broken king and my own brother's resilience. I stood upon the mountain and watched that cavern sealed off. And I can assure you, warrior, it is not a fallacy." She looks past me and orders, "Do it."

Before I can ask what 'it' is, pain shoots through my neck. I drop to my knees, hands gripping the collar as I try to pry it from my skin. Exhaustion is a sudden plague, a darkness trying to pull me under.

Affree shakes her head though my vision blurs so her expression fades in the next second. "So stubborn."

I fall forward, and my world goes dark.

∽

PAIN BRINGS me to the surface.

Pain in my neck. My throat. My head.

I sit up slowly, vision still a blur. Blinking rapidly, I manage to clear it, only to find myself staring at golden bars. I shoot up from the ground and turn in a circle, panic clawing at me. I'm surrounded by golden rods that arch up over my head like some kind of large bird cage.

My chest is bare, though thankfully, I still wear my pants and boots.

"So delicious to look at. I knew you would be." Affree

stalks in from behind a floral partition wearing nothing more than a sheer robe. It bares her entire body to me, so I quickly avert my gaze.

"What the fuck am I doing here?"

She crosses the room and climbs onto a large bed where she drops the sheer dress she wears and climbs beneath the covers. I keep my gaze firmly on the wall, refusing to give her the satisfaction of looking anywhere near her.

"Loyal, too. How refreshing."

"Why. Am. I. Here?"

"We need Carleah on edge for the next trial. So, you are here until she passes it."

I grip the bars and shake them. "Let me the fuck out!"

Affree grins. "Oh, dear warrior. All you do is turn me on when you behave so animalistic. I could make all of this go away, you know. I could let you out, but you must do something in return for me."

"What?" I demand, fearing I already know the answer.

She throws the blankets off of her body. "Touch me. The way you touch her." She runs the tips of her fingers down her throat, but I don't follow them as they trail down.

"Not a chance in hell."

"No?" she grins. "Even if I were to let you fuck me right now?"

I don't even dignify her with a response, just turn and walk toward the back of the cage.

"Perhaps you want to listen to me then?" She gasps. "Yes. That feels *good*, Fort."

"I swear if any harm comes to her, I will burn this fucking place to the ground," I growl, my back still turned to her.

"Fort. Yes. Just like that," is all she says in response.

The door opens, and I turn as two elven men with bare chests and cloths dangling over their cocks stroll in.

"You both are late," she snaps.

"Sorry, mistress." The one closest to her bed removes his cloth and steps forward, gripping her by the legs and pulling her toward him. He kneels and buries his face between her legs. She cries out in pleasure as the other leans over her and shoves his cock into her mouth with such force she damn near chokes on it.

I turn away again, wishing like hell I was anywhere else as I grip the bars, tugging on them. I'm not at all surprised to feel how fucking sturdy they are. Carleah is safe here as long as they believe she is this queen they seek.

So, that in mind, I focus only on my plan to get us the hell out of here, all while trying desperately to ignore the sounds of slapping skin behind me.

Fucking elves.

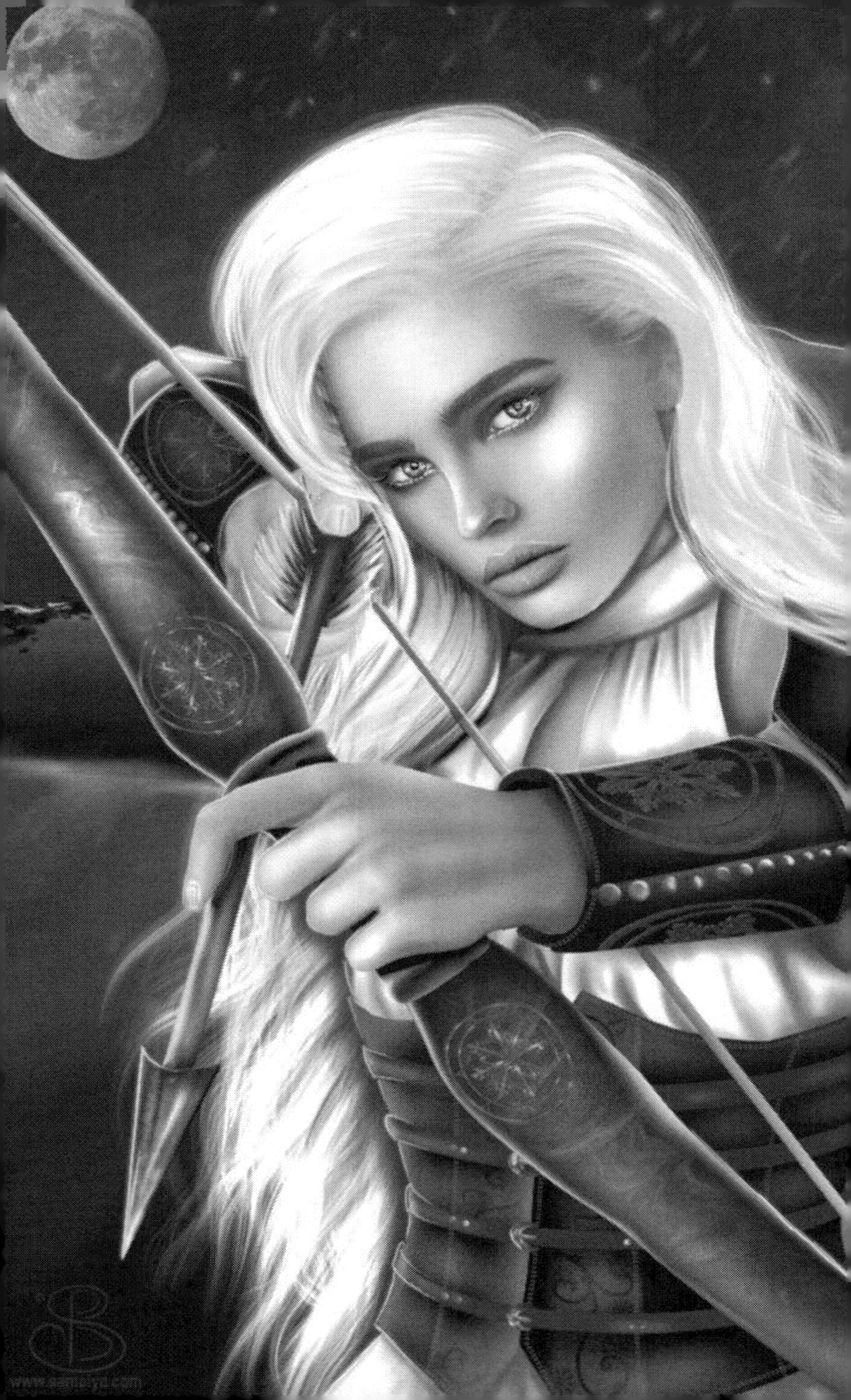

CHAPTER 28
CARLEAH

The Hall of History is the largest collection of books and scrolls I have ever seen. It's nearly impossible to avert my eyes from the stacks as we pass them, even as Lacrae continues pulling me deeper inside.

"How much is here?"

"The history of the entire realm," he replies. "Every battle, great war, or enemy."

"Elves are immortal, are they not? Why do you feel the need to write everything down?"

He grins. "Elves are immortal, yes, but we can be killed. And because of our immortality, we understand the vast importance of knowledge. History, as I told you, is easily manipulated by those with a short lifespan."

"I would think it to be the opposite."

Lacrae releases me once we reach a pile of colorful pillows. He drops down on a blue one and gestures for me to sit atop a golden pillow directly across from him. I do. "Elves have no reason to manipulate history."

"And why is that?"

"We are truth seekers by nature."

"Unburdened by human emotion?"

Lacrae grins. "Hardly. If anything, we feel far more deeply than humans are capable." He gets a look in his eye that borders on affection and has me squirming in my seat.

"Let's get this over with, I want to get back to Fort."

"Always so quick to return to the warrior. Rest assured, Princess, my sister is keeping him company."

My blood chills even as jealousy turns to an inferno inside of me. "She has a fondness for him."

Lacrae throws his head back and laughs. "My sister has a fondness for all she cannot have. I doubt your warrior will give her the time of day." He reaches out, and I place my hands in his.

～

Wind whips at my hair and dress as I stand beside Lacrae on a snow-capped mountain.

"You cannot be serious!" The memory version of Lacrae is mere feet away, his face reddened by anger as he argues with the king. "You would abandon your people?"

"I have bled for my people!" he roars. "And what have your kind done for us?"

"Besides fight this war alongside you?" Lacrae yells back.

"The giants will be here in mere hours, and you expect me to allow my son to lead them into the mountain?"

"They crave the blood of a royal," Lacrae replies. "If I could do it, I would."

"My son is not bait."

Lacrae stares at him. "If I could carry this burden for you, old friend, I would," he repeats as he places his hand on the king's arm.

"You call me old friend, yet I fear you do not understand the meaning of that word." The king's tone is harsh, but his expression is no longer angry. It is fear that drives him now. Fear for his son and for his kingdom.

"You and Ky are the only royals left standing. You cannot do this because Ky is not yet prepared for what it means to be a king."

"Ky is my only heir," the king replies, a tear slipping from his cheek. "To risk him is to risk the entire kingdom."

"To risk *you* is to risk the kingdom," Lacrae insists.

But even I see the flaw in his logic. The king can no longer produce an heir, which means—

"You speak to me of duty. Of sacrifice. Yet you are unwilling to let me sacrifice myself even though we both know it's the right choice."

Beside me, Lacrae stiffens. I steal a glance at him, shocked to see he's just as immersed in this memory as I am. His expression is twisted with pain—loss—making it clear how this memory plays out.

The memory of Lacrae closes his eyes. "You are my dearest friend, Harlow."

"I know." The king clasps the elf on the shoulder. "Which is one of the many reasons it must be me." He reaches up and lifts the crown from his head, offering it to Lacrae. "You must give this to Ky."

But Lacrae does not take it. "You are sacrificing your life."

"I am saving the kingdom."

∼

I'M PULLED from the memory, and Lacrae removes his hand from mine. A single tear slips down his cheek. "I apologize for my display," he says. "I have not visited that memory in quite some time."

"He was your friend."

Lacrae dips his head. "Harlow was an amazing king. When it came time to train him to fight, it was I who was tasked with it. We grew close as brothers. There was a time when I believed he and Affree would marry."

"Seriously?" I gape at him and he smiles.

"She did not wish to settle down, but he adored her. Harlow ended up marrying a human woman, which is where your line became diluted. Previously, kings would marry an elf who drank the water of mortality once she'd birthed their children."

I gape at him. How can things like this be real?

Giants, elves, waters of mortality? It all breathes fiction. "Water of mortality?"

"Most elves who fell in love with humans did not wish to watch them die. Since we do not possess the magic to make other souls immortal, a water was spelled that would strip the immortality, effectively making the elf age and die as a human would."

"That's romantic."

He grins. "I find it to be so as well." Lacrae stands and moves toward a far shelf, so I follow. Once he reaches it, he stops and retrieves a scroll from the lowest shelf then offers it to me.

"What is this?"

"Your family lineage."

"You tracked it?" I unroll it, placing it upon the table. At the top, Harlow's name is scrawled in ink. Below his, Ky's. Which then travels to three sons. I continue following down the line past all of the sons born to Navalis royalty until I reach my father's name. He, like Ky, was an only child.

Beneath his name, scrawled in elegant ink, is Alex, Bowman, Dierdrech, Ethan, and Carleah. Tears burn in the corners of my eyes as I run my finger over the names of my brothers.

"You could not see us, Carleah, but we elves have been watching Navalis."

I look up at him. "Then why weren't you there to save it?" I demand. "Why did you allow my family to be slaughtered? If we are the descendants of your friend, why let them die?"

His golden gaze darkens. "Because I was called back. There was a disturbance in the Land of Giants. We were worried they were awakening, but when we arrived, it was simply an animal who had gotten inside and alerted the wards. By the time I got back to Navalis, everyone was dead, and you were gone." He swallows hard. "If I could have saved them, I would have, Carleah. You must believe me."

I narrow my gaze on his. "Did Shadow truly choose me? Or am I merely the ancestor of your friend whom you saved out of nostalgia?"

Lacrae reaches out to brush a strand of my hair back over my shoulder. I step back, and instead of persisting, he lets his hands fall. "Shadow chose you. I thought you dead, too. We'd been out scouting for the Tenebris when he'd sensed your presence. And it wasn't until he found you in that damned pit that I realized who you were. I believe, Carleah of Navalis, that you are the one true queen of this realm. That you will lead us to peace unlike any we've ever known."

"How can you be sure?" I move away from him.

"Because you are the first-born daughter of Navalis in over two millennia, and that has to mean something. And Carleah, you must believe in yourself for the remainder of these trials. They will only get more difficult."

"If you are so sure, then why do I need to prove myself?"

"Because the others do not see you as I do. And worst of all, you do not see yourself as a queen. These trials are meant to push you to the limits of your mental prowess, bravery, compassion, and strength. Not just so we can see it but so *you* can understand." He touches my arm. "I understand that you are uninterested in me the way I see you, but I beg of you, Carleah, see yourself through my eyes. Through the eyes of your warrior."

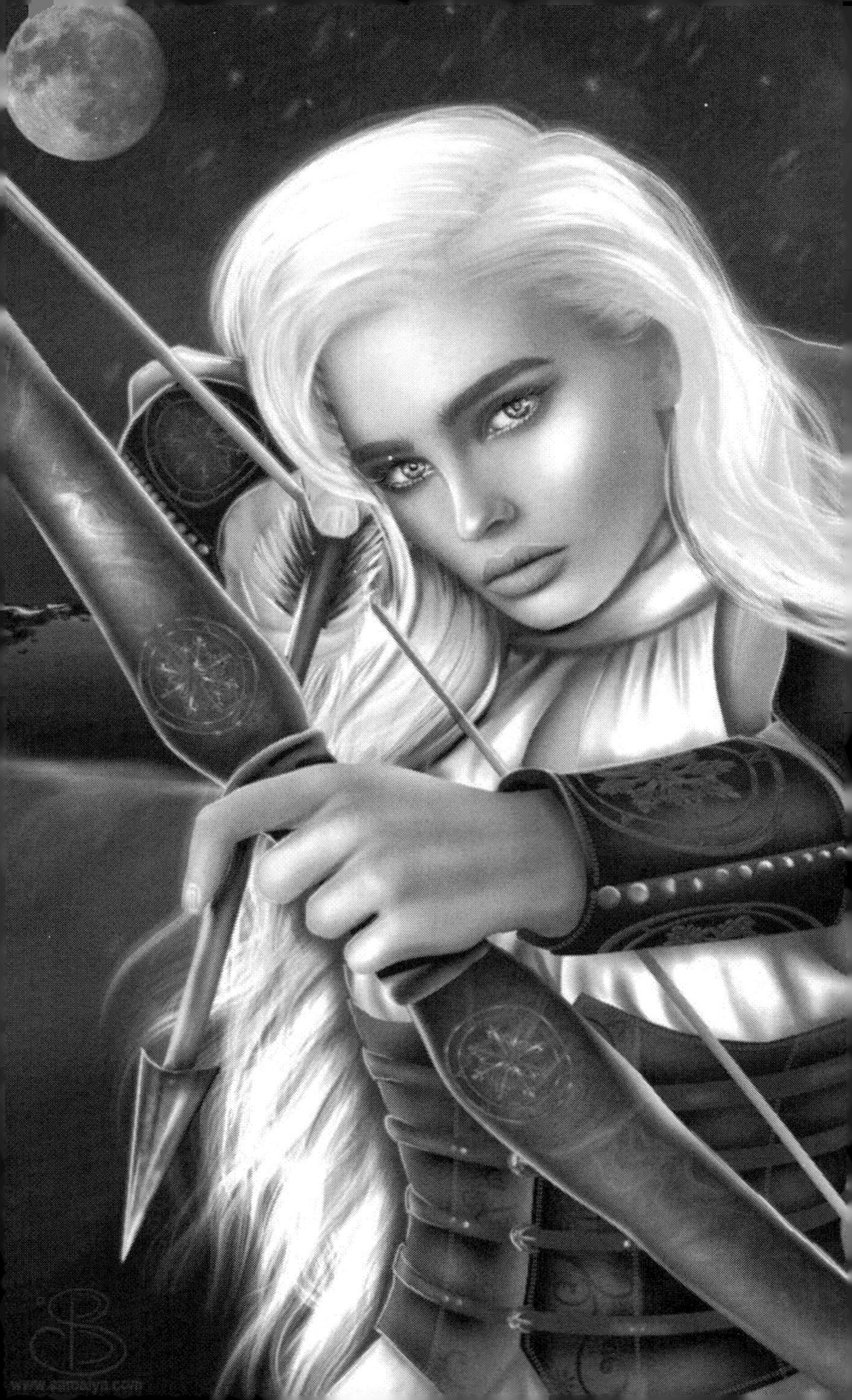

CHAPTER 29
CARLEAH

Two days after Lacrae brought me back to my room, and I still haven't seen Fort.

I've screamed.

Thrown things.

Tried to escape.

Beat against my door when it wouldn't open.

And nothing has happened. No one has shown.

Instead, I've remained here, completely and utterly alone. I sit on the bed now, a broken table leg in my hand. I'm peeling pieces of the wood off, trying to shape it strategically and sharpen it best I can so I have something to use when they *do* finally come for me.

I'm done waiting. Done with these ridiculous tests. And as far as I'm concerned, these damned elves can continue to hide up here in these mountains while I save the realm from the Tenebris—prophesied warrior queen or not.

And so help them if they hurt Fort.

My eyes burn with the lack of sleep, my lids growing heavier with every passing moment, but I don't dare sleep. I need to be alert when they come for me. Only then will I be able to fight my way out of this damned prison.

Only then can I find my way to Fort.

Something scrapes against my door, and I whirl on it, holding my makeshift spear up.

I'm starving, the tray of food they gave me after the second trial the only one they've given me in the last couple of days. Even it sits by the door, partially uneaten. They haven't collected it, and I've survived by drinking water from the basin that consistently refills near my mirror.

A mirror I am afraid to look into because, the last time I did, I nearly didn't recognize the woman that was looking back at me. I was raised to be refined. A princess. The woman in the mirror is a wildling. A creature who has lost everything.

There was a part of me who wondered if this wasn't just another illusion.

But when nights turned to days and days to nights, I knew it couldn't be. The time moves far too slowly. So, either something is wrong and they forgot I am up here alone, or they took him from me as punishment.

Onemo's face comes to mind. Did he do this? Another way to torment me?

My door slides open, and I jump, spear in hand. When no one immediately comes through, I move toward it, my bare feet padding silently against the wooden floor. I peek out, seeing no one climbing up or down the stairs.

Strange.

I start down, knowing if I need answers, the council is where I will find them. So I descend, taking the steps slowly while hugging the large trunk of the elven tree. I cling to the spear like a lifeline, holding it close to my body.

There are no sounds. Only complete silence and a light breeze that raises the hair from my shoulders. The scene is not peaceful in the least, though.

"Fort!" I call out as I reach the first platform beneath our room. I'm expecting elves to glare up at me. Instead, I'm met with a deserted room. "Hello!" I call out, not at all caring if someone hears me. My heart pounds in my chest as I descend faster. The village—surely there are people in the village. And the council will be in their hall just beyond that.

They can tell me where to find Fort.

But even as I think it, I worry that our time has run out before it has even begun. How many times now have we been close to death? It's bound to catch up sooner or later.

I reach the bottom of the stairs with a heavy heart and a twisted gut.

There is no movement here. The tents are abandoned, the grounds completely and totally barren as far as I can see. It's as if everyone just left. "Hello!" I call out. "Fort!" I scream his name, fear smothering me. "Fort!"

A branch breaks.

Something crunches beneath my foot, and I still, letting my gaze drop to the ground. Fissures begin spreading like ice on a lake. I freeze because I know all too well what happens if you move, thanks to a terrifying afternoon and a frozen pond.

But my stillness means nothing.

The cracks begin to spread, the crackling echoes of ground breaking absolutely deafening. I try to jump out of the way, but the entire thing caves in, and I fall. I hit more ground with a heavy thud. Groaning, I try to roll over, but something bites into my wrist.

I rip my arm free only to be grabbed again.

I thrash, scrambling to break free from the thorny vines shooting up from the sand around me. Above my head, the open ground remains, a gaping hole that swallowed me.

"Help!" I scream.

Another grabs my other wrist.

Then two latch onto my ankles.

Pain burns through me, yet more fear because it shouldn't hurt, right? Didn't Lacrae say in the alternate reality, I wouldn't feel pain?

"Help me!" I thrash, desperately seeking freedom, but it's no use. The hold they have on me is far too strong. Still, I'm not one to give up. I yank my wrist, uncaring that the thorns tear at my flesh.

My back stings as whatever is beneath me scratches at my flesh. "Help!" I scream again, yet no one comes. "Fort! Lacrae!" I scream, begging someone—anyone to come to my rescue.

The pain lessens as the vines release me and seep into the sand beneath me. But, before I can get my bearings, the ground begins to open, and I slide down with it. I try to climb, grasping at sand as I fall closer and closer to the epicenter of my demise.

My body weight shifts as I'm pulled down, losing any grip I had. "Help! Please!" Sand closes around me, sucking me down, down. My fingers claw at nothing, my long-forgotten spear disappearing beneath the surface. "Help me! Please!"

Panic races through me, my stomach pitting because I realize, on some carnal level, that this is how I die. This is the moment that I—"Help!" I scream again, but it's the last sound I make as the ground closes in around me.

Sand seeps into my mouth.

My lungs.

I cannot kick my feet, cannot grip at anything. I'm completely helpless as the ground swallows me whole.

A hand closes around mine.

It rips me from the dirt, though I cannot see thanks to the granules burning my eyes. Arms band around me, holding me against a strong chest. "Easy. I have you."

Fort.

Lungs burning, I heave, bile and sand splattering the ground.

"What the fuck was that?" Fort demands. "She nearly fucking died!"

"Someone has something to explain," Lacrae snarls.

"I can't see," I manage.

"Easy." Soft air blows against my face moments before tender fingers brush against my eyelashes.

I try to blink, opening my eyes slowly. My vision is blurry at first, but a heartbeat later, Fort's face swims into view. I throw my arms around his neck and cling to him. "Where were you?"

"It's a long story," he growls, but there's something in his tone that tells me it is not an overly pleasant one.

"The test needed to be pure. Your involvement in her preparation would have skewed the results," Lacrae insists.

"And what results are those?" Fort demands. "How fast she could die? Tell me, *elf*, did you get your fucking answer?"

"That shouldn't have happened," Lacrae insists then looks down at me. "Bring her to the healer."

Strong arms lift me, and Fort begins walking.

"What happened?" I choke out.

"We're going to find out," Fort promises. "Someone fucked something up."

"Your test was not secure," Lacrae tells me. "My sister and the others are already trying to determine what happened. The simulation should have ended, but for some reason—" he shakes his head. "I don't know who would have such magic to open the ground like that. It's —troublesome."

"Let me have some time alone with Onemo. I'll get to the fucking bottom of it."

Lacrae glares at Fort. "He is a councilman. He would not tamper with the test."

"No? You so fucking sure about that? Because, according to your sister, this is the first trial he has overseen himself."

"It hurt," I tell them. "The pain was real. You told me it wouldn't be."

"Given the punctures on your wrists and ankles, I imagine it did," Lacrae retorts. We climb the stairs ascending into the tree, but we only go up one landing before Lacrae is leading us through a golden door.

A woman with golden robes and silver hair turns toward us. "Yes?"

"She was injured. See to it she is cared for." Lacrae looks at me one final time then turns and leaves the room.

"Set her down," she orders.

Fort sets me on a table and stands beside me as the woman comes forward. Her silver hair is braided over her shoulder, and her golden eyes are framed with soft wrinkles. There's a scar on her lip, a divide that has long since healed but does not dilute her elegant beauty.

Even with as much pain as I am in, I can appreciate her soft gaze.

"What happened?" she asks.

"The ground ate me," I rasp.

The woman's eyes narrow, and she looks to Fort, who nods.

"It was during the third trial," he explains. "It swallowed her whole."

"Hmm." She holds her hand up to my forehead and closes her eyes. Then, she guides her hand down over my arms, belly, legs, and feet. Moments pass by, and the pain fades. I watch in complete fascination as my flesh knits back together beneath her palms. Moments tick by, and finally, she pulls her hand back. "She will heal. Though she could use a dip in her bathing pools."

"How did you—"

"I am a healer, my dear," she replies with a smile. "There are herbs in your room, yes?"

"Yes," Fort answers.

"Those will ease some of the aches that I cannot reach with my magic. Her body will be sore tomorrow, her muscles strained, but soak each night, and that will ease it."

"Thank you," I say as Fort helps me to my feet.

"Of course, Your Highness." We leave the room and find Lacrae standing just outside, talking in hushed tones to an elven warrior, who offers him a nod then turns to leave. Lacrae faces us. "Come, I will see you back to your rooms."

"I'm not going back into that room," I told him. "I want a new one. With a fucking window."

Lacrae studies me.

"I don't care what you threaten or what you say. You left me locked in that damned room for two days. I'm not going back just so you can do it again."

He shakes his head angrily. "I told them this would happen should you two be separated. Rest assured, Princess, I am not going to take you back to that room," he promises. "Please, come." Holding out a hand, he gestures toward the large tree.

I look to Fort, though he doesn't tear his gaze from Lacrae.

"Please, trust me."

"None of you have given us any reason to trust you," Fort snaps.

Lacrae's gaze does not leave mine. "How am I to lie to you again if I wish to win your favor?"

Fort stiffens beside me.

"You will not win my favor," I tell him. "I thought I made that clear."

Lacrae looks to Fort. "I rather enjoy a challenge."

Fort's body begins to vibrate with his rage, tremors shooting straight through him. I tighten my hold on his hand.

"Unless you want Fort to rip you apart and redecorate your damned tree, I suggest you cut the shit, Lacrae."

The elf grins then continues walking again.

I pull Fort along, carefully studying the area around us for any sign that something is off. But, aside from more elven warriors than normal, I see none.

Lacrae leads us further up the tree, but instead of guiding us up past our original room, he moves in the opposite direction and begins climbing a second set of stairs. I follow next with Fort directly behind me. Legs shaking, I damn near fall backward, but Fort presses a hand to my lower back, the constant presence that keeps me moving.

A few minutes pass by in complete silence until we reach a hallway carved atop a huge branch. Lacrae walks across the polished surface without fear, so I follow, though I pay close attention to either side of me. One gust of wind and I'd fall right off the side.

He stops just outside the door and gestures to a clear glass square just outside and to the right of the door. "You two are the only ones permitted to open *or* seal this door. From the outside *and* inside. Press your hand against it," he tells Fort.

Warily, Fort steps forward and presses his palm to the panel.

It slides open.

Lacrae snaps his fingers, and Fort's golden collar falls to the ground where the elf bends to retrieve it. "Enjoy your evening. We will speak again in the morning when I have answers for you both." He offers Fort and me a nod, then turns and leaves, golden collar in hand.

Fort moves into the room first, and I follow. It's at least three times the size of our previous room. The far wall is wide open, though we can see nothing but clouds beyond it. There are no mountain tops, no other rooms, just a sea of white that reminds me so much of the snow at home it makes my heart ache.

A large four-poster bed sits on one wall, its intricate frame carved from dark wood.

White sheets adorn the surface while a silver fur blanket lies across the edge of the bed. Sitting atop the blanket is Bowman's bow. Relief warms me, so I turn and study the rest of the room.

There's a chest of drawers on another wall, and carved into the very floor of the tree is a sunken bathtub large enough for at least four Forts. The one in our previous room was good-sized, but this is massive. Nearly the size of half of our room before.

I turn to Fort and tip my face up to look at him, my gaze landing on a red ring around his throat. "What happened?" I rush forward as fast as I can and reach up to press the tips of my fingers to just above his injury.

"The fucking collar fought me as I was trying to get to you."

"It hurt you?"

He nods. "I'm okay now."

"Could it have killed you?"

"Probably," he replies. "But I'm not going to stand by and watch you die."

I let out a deep breath because I would have done exactly the same had the roles been reversed. "Where have you been the last two days?"

A muscle in his jaw tightens. "You really do not wish to hear about it."

"I do. It was likely more eventful than mine." I try to smile, but my body aches. I roll my shoulders. Fort takes notice and crosses over toward the bath. He steps up beside it, and the water begins to fill.

"I was in a cage in Affree's room."

Angry jealousy sears me. "They put you in a *cage*?"

He clenches his jaw. "Oh yes. Fucking assholes. The collar knocked me out, and when I woke up, I was in a damned cage."

"In Affree's room."

Something shifts in his gaze. "Not by choice," he says carefully.

"Did she—never mind. I don't need to know." I drop my face.

Fort leaves the side of the bath and presses his fingers beneath my chin before tilting it up. "She tried. Though I imagine the two elves she had pleasuring her every night did not care much for my presence in her room."

I scrunch my nose. "She made you watch?"

"Again, she tried. I turned my back, though not before I saw things I will never unsee." A shiver runs through him, and it's the disgust in his expression that eases my anger—for now.

"Fucking elves," I say.

"Fucking elves," he replies with a smile. "Those were my sentiments exactly." He leans down and presses his lips to mine. "But it gave me time to think."

"About?"

"How the hell we're going to get out of here."

"You don't think I'll pass the final trial?"

"I do," he replies. "But just in case, and on the off chance they are lying and choose not to let us go, I have a plan."

"What plan?"

"We use your connection with Shadow. If we can get to him, then surely, he will help us escape, right? He came for me when they chose not to. That must mean his loyalty is to you. So all we have to do is get to the platform and call for him."

The plan is risky. But it's far simpler than fighting our way through the elven army. "Okay," I say. "If they do not let us go, we run."

Fort presses his lips to mine again then pulls away.

"How many days has it been since I saw you last?" I ask.

"Two," he replies. "They moved you to the arena this morning."

"I don't understand how I didn't realize it was a vision. I stayed awake for the entirety of the two days, waiting for you. Unless I drifted off without realizing?"

"I'm not sure, Carleah. They carried you into the arena unconscious. Then, when the ground fucking swallowed you—I thought you dead. Everyone was screaming. Lacrae and I jumped into the arena first, but it damn near took us out, too. It was as though the ground was alive. I've never seen anything like it."

Dread settles in my gut. "I'm ready to leave. These trials can go to hell."

"We will." He looks from me to the bath that is now full of steaming water. "Do you wish to bathe?"

"I really do." I turn back to the tub.

He moves back. "Then let's get you into the water." He crosses over to a shelf similar to the one in our previous room, and retrieves a glass jar full of dried herbs. After pouring some into the water, he places it back, then moves around to my back.

Strong fingers remove the collar at my throat, followed by the leather corset, until finally, my dress falls to the ground. Fort hisses. "Your back is scratched. The healer missed it."

"I'll be fine."

"The water is going to sting."

"I've suffered worse." I turn back to him. "Bathe with me?"

"Abso-fucking-lutely." Fort steps in closer, cups my face, and presses his lips to mine. It's a tender caress, a whisper that soothes my soul in ways I am learning only he can.

I wrap my arms around his waist and break the kiss to lean against his chest.

The steady beating of his heart against my ear eases the rest of my frayed nerves and helps calm the storm inside of me.

∼

FORT'S FINGERS trace lazy lines over my side. He lies on his side behind me while my cheek rests against his muscled arm.

I roll over so I can face him. The soft light of lanterns on the walls cast a soft glow over his handsome face. Reaching out, I run my hand over his stubbled cheek, and he closes his eyes, inhaling deeply. "Do you believe that first memory Lacrae showed us?"

Fort considers. "I don't care for the elf, but I cannot see what him lying about the true history of the realm would gain him,"

"After the second trial, he showed me a new memory."

"What about?"

I explain it to him in detail, the arguing between Lacrae and Harlow, the way he was fighting with the king about sacrificing himself.

"If what he's saying is true, then the giants were no friend to Navalis," I tell him. "They were the enemy of the realm. And the elves worked with us to imprison them, though I am still unsure how."

"Do you believe him?"

"My father didn't. He believed the giants were good."

"I didn't ask you what your father believed," Fort says softly. "You are your own person, Carleah. What do *you* believe?"

"I believe that, although I hate Lacrae for lying to me about you, he has no reason to continue doing so." Fort doesn't respond, so I continue, "The others? I wouldn't trust them as far as I could throw them. But Lacrae cared deeply for my ancestor, Harlow. They were close friends, and as far as I can tell, Harlow sacrificed himself to draw the giants into the caves."

Fort shakes his head and stares down at me. "Affree mentioned something about the bloodstain on this realm and how the history did not portray the truth." He sighs. "Do you believe your father knew the truth?"

"No. I think the history was altered," I say, somewhat mirroring Lacrae's words once again. "Though I am not sure why. I cannot understand reasoning that would justify making them out to be our allies when they were indeed merciless warriors."

"Likely because they didn't want enemies seeking to control the giants," he says.

I sit up. "What?"

"If your enemies knew the giants were imprisoned by Navalis and not there by choice, it would have been tempting to use them against your people."

The blood drains from my face. "You're right," I whisper. How did I not see that before?

"It's strategy," he replies.

I grin at him then reach up and pull him down on top of me. "Strategy from my brilliant soldier."

Fort grins down at me, his dark eyes shining in the low light. "Your brilliant soldier?"

"If you'll be mine," I reply as I weave my arms around his neck.

"Until I draw my last breath, Carleah, I will be yours." He leans down and presses his lips to mine.

"There's something else," I say, pulling back and sitting up so I can face him. "Something I've been keeping from you."

"What is it?"

"I should have told you before, but I couldn't find the right time, and then—" I sigh. "I'm making excuses. Your father told me that, when the boys of Nemoregno become old enough, they are injected with the blood of a giant. He didn't tell me where they got this blood but said it's why they are so much stronger and faster than other men. The men who father these children were injected, which makes the line only stronger the larger it gets." Fort watches me carefully, though he does not speak. "He told me, that when you were a baby you nearly died. To save you, they injected you with the blood. Then, they did it again after you'd come of fighting age."

"You're telling me they injected me twice?"

I nod. "That's why you're so much stronger than the others. Even those from Nemoregno."

He shakes his head. "I should have known."

"Did you know about the blood?"

"I knew that we received our Tenebris mark." He holds out his wrist and shows me a raised scar. "It's a half-moon tattoo that is inked into our skin. But I don't recall ever receiving an injection aside from it."

I reach out and brush my finger over the raised skin. "I bet they dipped the tattoo needles in it. I bet that's how they put it into your blood." I shake my head angrily. "They're using giant blood to breed Tenebris soldiers."

"Does that horrify you?" he questions. "Is that why you kept it from me?"

"No," I reply instantly. "Not at all. I was so wrapped up in everything else going on that I forgot. I'm sorry. It was not my intention to keep it from you."

"Considering I lied about not being able to speak for nineteen years, we can call it even."

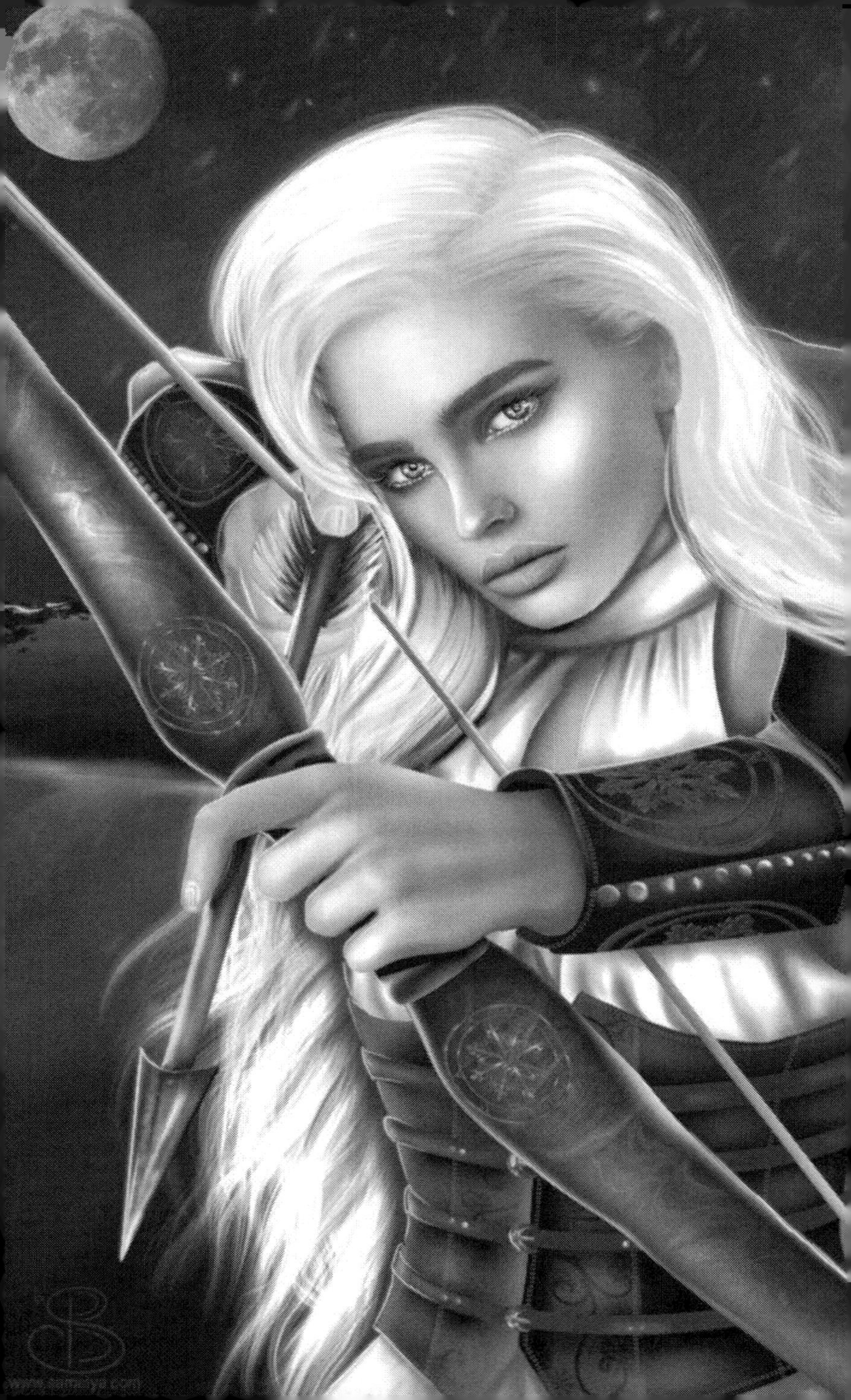

CHAPTER 30
CARLEAH

"You slept well in your new room?" I glance over at Lacrae. Fort walks on my other side, his dark hair such a contrast with the elf's lighter strands that it feels as though I'm walking between night and day.

"Yes. Thank you."

"You should have been allotted better chambers the moment we brought you here. In my opinion," he replies with a smile.

We move across a thick branch toward the Hall of History.

"We appreciate the change in scenery," I tell him. My body is sore, just as the healer warned it would be, but I'm alive and one step closer to my army and my freedom.

Lacrae slips a key into the lock and shoves the door open. It slides easily enough, and I move past him inside.

"This room contains the entire history of the realm," I tell Fort. "From those born within it to the battles fought."

"You have genealogy here?"

Lacrae nods. "Among other things."

I note the strange look both men share, though it's not entirely unexpected. Fort does not trust Lacrae, and I am fairly certain the elf feels the same way about him.

Taking Fort's hand in mine, I move farther inside and retrieve the same scroll Lacrae showed me the last time we were in here. I unroll it and show it to him. His gaze travels over the entries, stopping when he sees my name alongside my brothers'.

"How do you know so much about the realm if you've stayed hidden up here all this time?" Fort questions.

"We stay hidden," Lacrae replies. "But not entirely unaware. Very little took place over the millennia that we did not document and place in this room."

"How did you seal the giants in the mountain?" I question, pulling his attention back to mine.

"That is what I will show you today," he says as he takes my hand. Fort lets loose a low growl though he follows closely, and Lacrae completely ignores him. "After that, I shall teach you of the different creatures living within the realm so that you may be better prepared for what awaits you beyond these walls."

Hope blossoms in my chest. "You are still planning to let us go?"

Lacrae turns to me. "Of course. Did you think we would hold you prisoner?"

"I wonder what would have given her that idea," Fort comments.

Lacrae glares at him. "We have every intention of letting you go, Carleah, when the time is right."

"And when will that be?"

"When the trials are over," he replies.

"What if I fail the final one?"

"You will not fail, Carleah. Of that, I am certain." He starts to take my hand again, but Fort grabs it first. Lacrae chuckles then continues toward the pile of pillows. He takes his seat and holds out his hand.

Fort drops down beside me, taking my hand in his as I slip mine into Lacrae's.

∿

THE WORLD IS white once more, thick snow blanketing the ground as large flakes continue to fall. It warms my heart to see the snow, which makes me realize just how much I miss home.

Not that it will ever be the same even when I do return.

Just ahead, memory Lacrae stands, his sword at the ready.

A man groans.

"Stay down," Lacrae snaps.

My gaze falls to the man lying just behind him, and dread coils in my belly. *Harlow.* Blood stains his tunic, and both hands are coated in crimson. "I need to get inside."

"You need to remain still until I know the threat is—" A man bursts from behind a tree. Crimson armor glints in the sunlight, and my heart hammers.

They were here? Even back then, they were a part of this?

The man brings his blade down, swinging with ferocity, but it is met with Lacrae's in return. They fight, metal clashing with metal, until Lacrae's blade slices across the man's neck. He falls to the snow.

Lacrae whirls on Harlow. "You told me the tribes were not a threat!"

"I didn't realize they would be!"

"Did you not meet with their leader?" Another man in crimson rushes out. He swings his blade, but Lacrae is faster. He spins and drives his dagger backward and into the man's throat.

"I was assured of their neutrality." The king coughs, blood splattering the corners of his mouth.

"They lied to you, you old fool!" Lacrae rushes forward and grabs him by his armor. "Can you walk?" I can feel the panic rolling off of Lacrae, see the desperation in his gaze.

"I can try."

Lacrae rips Harlow from the ground and settles him on his feet. The king sways, but Lacrae holds him on his feet though he mutters something I do not understand. "Come, I will take you inside."

"And if you don't make it out?"

"Then we die together," Lacrae snaps.

I look over at Fort, who is watching the scene

intently, his gaze trained on Harlow. My attention shifts to Lacrae, and I'm surprised to see him not watching the memory but rather focused entirely on Fort.

The scenery shimmers around us and shifts, and soon we're standing in the center of a large cavern. Huge rocks jut up from the earth, firelight dancing off of them from the torch in Harlow's hands. He sits on the ground, leaning against stone, his face pale.

"Tell me what they told you," Lacrae demands. "Tell me of the prophecy."

Harlow sucks in a breath. "The daughter of ice will seek refuge with the son of flame," he manages.

"What the bloody hell does that mean?"

"I do not know," he rasps, words growing faint. "But they believe that the daughter of ice is—" He sucks in a ragged breath. "From Navalis."

"Daughter of ice. There are no daughters born of the royal line in Navalis."

"It's. Just. What. They. Said." The king coughs again.

"What else?" When the king doesn't answer, Lacrae tosses his torch to the ground and grips his tunic, shaking him. "What else!" he roars.

The king's eyes flutter open. "The son of flame will use her for the power she possesses," he whispers. "And then, he will destroy our kingdom," he chokes out. "Because he is the one who can control the giants."

∼

I RIP my hand from Lacrae's, leaving the memory in a blur of color. I push to my feet, mind reeling.

The daughter of ice will seek refuge with the son of flame.

"That was quite dangerous," Lacrae says. "Pulling your hand from mine in a memory."

I turn toward him. "What did all of that mean? The prophecy."

Fort doesn't speak. He merely stands beside me, arms crossed, as though he can't decide whether to throttle Lacrae or demand his own answers.

"The tribal leader managed to capture a Weaver. It is from her the words of the prophecy were spoken."

"A weaver?"

"Of destiny," he replies. "There is only ever one in existence, and she hides far above all the realms, watching and waiting for all to come to pass. She knows all of the present, past, and future."

"And the tribes? Are those the same ones from Nemoregno?"

Lacrae looks to Fort. "Yes. As your warrior knows quite well, don't you?"

"You know, then?" Fort asks.

"As I said," the elf replies, "there is very little that takes place in this realm that we are unaware of."

"If you're referring to where Fort comes from, I already know, too."

"You realize that he comes from the same tribes that murdered your family?" he looks genuinely shocked.

"Yes. Because he told me."

"And you still accepted him? Still allowed him in your

bed? You're knowingly sleeping with the enemy?" he demands.

Fort starts forward, but I beat him to it and slam my hand into Lacrae's chest. "Here's my question to you: Why tell me now? If you've supposedly known all this time, why pick today if not of your own jealousy?"

Lacrae's jaw tightens. "I thought you should know the truth about him and then—"

"Then, what? I would choose you? I don't even know you, and the only thing you know about me is that I am descendant of one of your old friends. Your connection with me is entirely built off a past that I had nothing to do with. Fort has stood by my side every single step of the way. He has fought for me. Bled for me. And I've no doubt that, if it came down to it, he'd die for me, too, yet instead of actually helping me prepare for this supposed Great Awakening I'm going to face, you're trying to plant seeds of doubt in my mind. Seeds that will *never* take root."

Lacrae swallows hard. "I care for you, and I do not understand it either."

"Then you better find a way to cope with that because it's not my—" The door opens, and a dozen elven warriors rush in. "What the hell is this?" I ask. Fort rips me behind him.

"Why are you here?" Lacrae questions.

"I sent them." Onemo steps forward. 'Thank you for the confirmation, Lacrae, I've had my suspicions of this warrior, and here we are with an enemy amidst us all this time." His sick, twisted smile makes my stomach churn. I move around in front of Fort.

"He is not your enemy."

"He is the son of our enemy. And I imagine, under the right circumstances, he can give us information on how to find the Tenebris training encampment."

"I have no fucking clue where it is," Fort snarls.

"And I do not believe a single word out of your mouth."

Lacrae moves in front of us. "This is not necessary, Onemo."

"It is absolutely necessary," Onemo snaps. "Grab him."

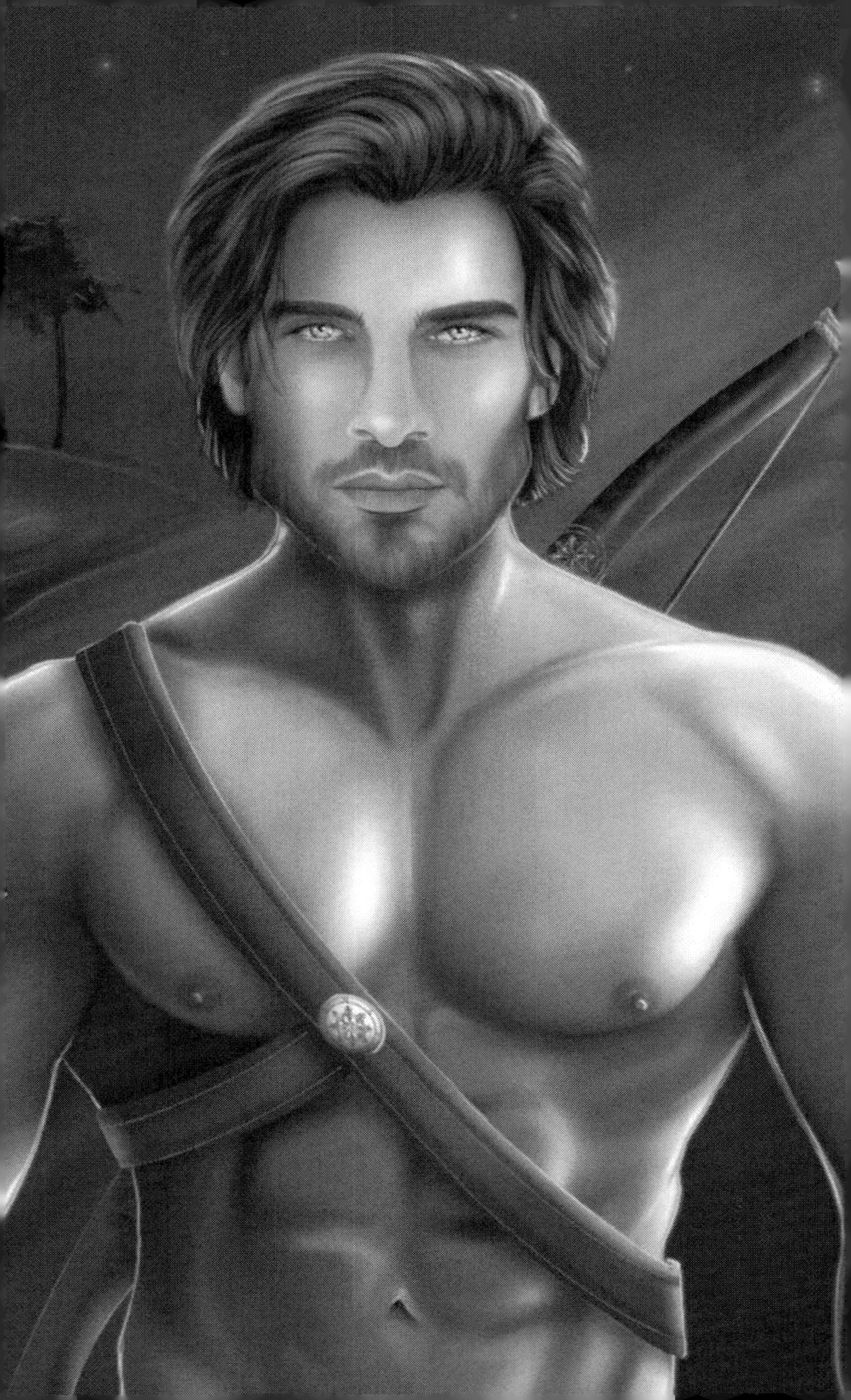

CHAPTER 31
FORT

"Information has come to light," Onemo starts, wearing a scowl on his face. "That we feel needs to be addressed."

I sit in a chair across from the council while Carleah sits beside me, her hands bound. Her knuckles are red, just as mine are, from the fight that led us to this damned council chamber.

Lacrae folds his arms behind his back and steps forward. "I only just informed them. If you give them time to process—"

"There is no time to process," Onemo snaps. "The crimson soldiers have been spotted."

Dread coils in my belly. "You need to let us leave, then. We need to get Carleah somewhere safe."

"Carleah has not been cleared to leave yet," Onema says. "And given what we now know of your history, you will not be permitted to leave the sanctuary of this place."

"You cannot keep me prisoner," I growl.

"And we will not allow you to awaken the giants," Onemo retorts.

"I'm not awakening any-fucking-thing." I turn to Lacrae. "You seriously believe that I'm the one in the prophecy?"

"We know that Carleah is the daughter of ice. Given your relationship and your place of birth, it seems only logical to deem you as the son of flame."

I gape at him. "Never in a million fucking years would I harm Carleah."

"How can we believe you when the blood of our enemies runs rampant through your veins?"

"You have no idea who he is," Carleah snaps. She tugs at her restraints.

Affree clears her throat. "You are both born of prophecy, and despite what has taken place, your destinies are intertwined." She turns to Onemo. "You do not need to imprison the warrior," she says. "His loyalty to Carleah is enough to keep him from doing anything that would harm her."

"Loyalty?" Onemo snorts. "He's a fucking Tenebris sent to capture her as an infant."

"I was a child," I reply. "Sent on an impossible mission, which I abandoned the second I reached Navalis. If you all were watching, then you know I never reported anything back. I was never anything but an ally to the royal family. I loved them as my own. Just as I love Carleah. There is nothing I wouldn't do to keep her safe and nothing I would ever do to harm her."

Onemo shakes his head. 'You expect us to believe the word of a liar. You are the son of our enemy," he says it again as though repeating it over and over again will make it the truth.

"He is *my* enemy as well." I snarl.

"You have no idea what Yarrow did to Fort back in Nemoregno," Carleah growls. "He beat him then sent him to die in a pit."

"All a good show, I'm sure," Onemo replies cooly.

Frustration burns in my veins.

"There is only one way to solve this." A councilwoman whose name I do not know stands and slides her glasses further up her nose. "Trial of Truth."

Affree's gaze widens, but a slow grin spreads over her face. "He must agree for that to work."

"If he has nothing to hide, why would he not?" Lacrae adds.

"What is the Trial of Truth?" I question.

"We will give you a tonic that is immensely painful, and you will be asked questions. Under its influence, you cannot lie."

"Painful?" Carleah chokes out.

"I'll do it," I say quickly. I don't give two shits what anyone in this fucking place—Carleah aside—thinks of me. But she is willing to die at my side, and I am not going to allow her to walk through the flames with me. So if proving my loyalty to them means making things easier for her, then I'll do it ten times over.

"It is incredibly painful," Affree confirms. "The tonic

will attack every nerve in your body and will not wear off for nearly a full day."

"I don't care. If this is what I have to do to prove myself, I will do it."

"Are you sure?" Carleah questions.

"Yes."

"Then we shall see where you stand when this is over," Onemo says. "Should you fail, we will execute you. Even if it means killing you both."

―

"This is going to be uncomfortable," Lacrae says as he tightens the leather straps around my arms. The chair is hard beneath me and sturdy enough that, even with my arms and legs bound to it, I cannot make it move.

I'm trapped in this place, surrounded by my enemies.

Carleah remains in the corner where they forced her to stand. Two elven warriors flank her, but I can see her studying every movement before us, searching for a weak spot. She wants to break free, to break me free.

But this is the quickest way to gain both because I know, without a doubt, I am not who they think I am.

Affree glides over the floor in a white gown that is damn near see-through. She stops in front of me with a vial of bright red liquid in her hand. "Once you take this into your body, there is no getting it out. It must run its course, no matter how much you beg for mercy."

"Understood."

With a smile that borders on regret, she starts to lift it to my lips but pauses. "Carleah?"

"What?"

"Come here."

Carleah doesn't argue as she crosses the floor. Affree hands her the vial.

"You will give him the tonic."

Carleah looks down at it then moves in close enough that I can smell the floral fragrance drifting from her skin. The fingers of her free hands touch my chin as she presses the glass vial to my lips.

"I'm so sorry," she whispers.

"Don't be," I reply.

She tips the glass vial up, and I stare up into her eyes as I down every last drop of the bitter tonic.

Carleah pulls away and all but tosses the vial back at Affree, who appears rather amused with herself now. She doesn't move away from me, though.

"How long until—" Violent pain shoots through my body. I groan, clenching my teeth to keep from yelling. Every single muscle in my body clenches to the point of agony. My stomach rolls, bile churning, but even that is nothing compared to the blinding pain like daggers in my skull.

"Focus on my voice, warrior," Affree calls out.

"Fuck, this—fuck!" I try to pull my hands free so I can claw my fucking eyes out, but they do not move. The pain—the blinding agony is too fucking much. My gaze finds Carleah. Her eyes are full of tears, her lips parted.

And it's the sight of her that has me choking down my pain as best I can.

I am doing this for her safety.

Her security.

And our future.

"Can you hear me, warrior?" Affree questions.

"I hear you," I growl.

"Fantastic. Let us get started then, shall we?"

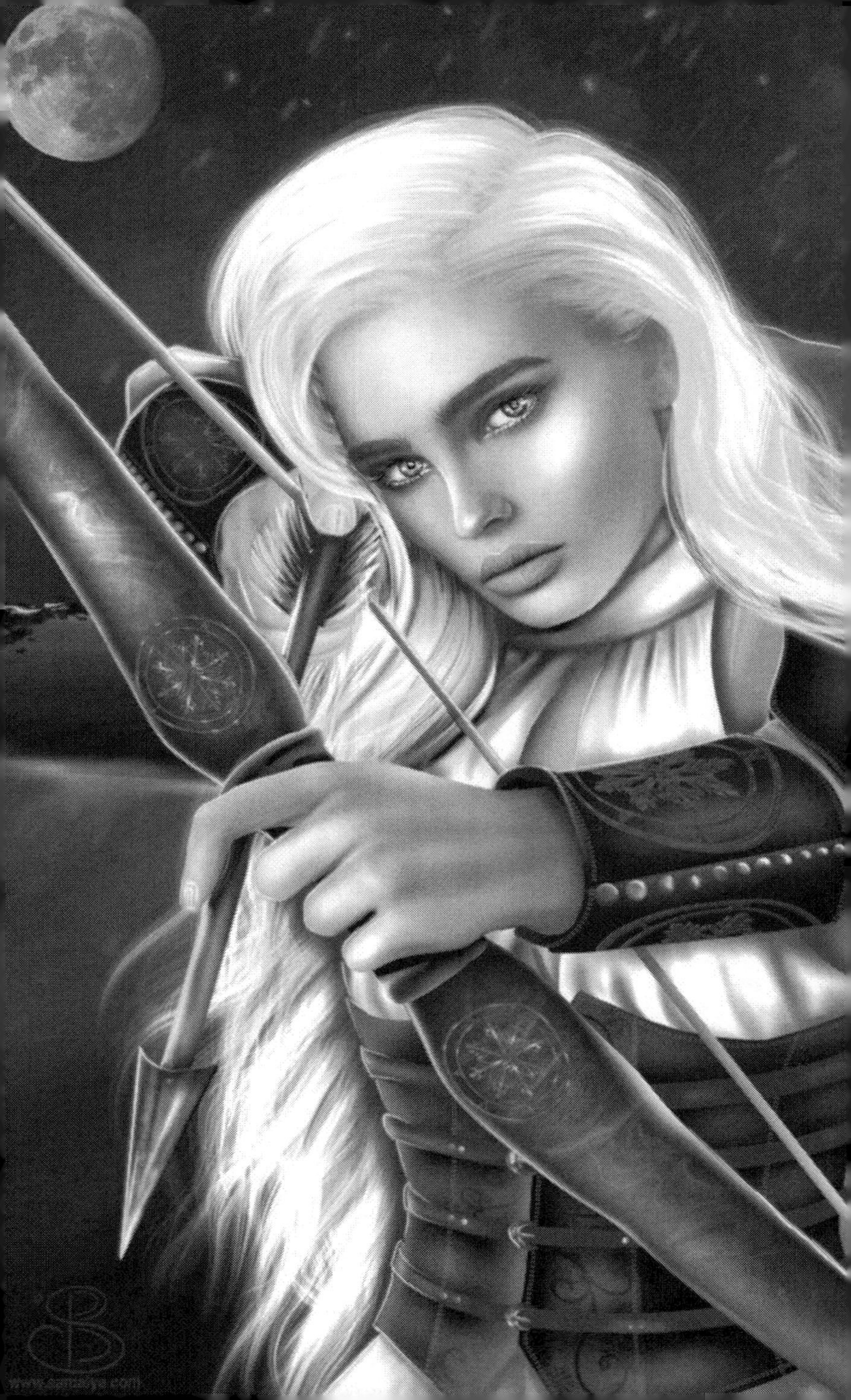

CHAPTER 32
CARLEAH

Fort writhes in his seat, the cords in his throat more defined now than ever before. His face is red, his expression contorted in pain. My stomach might as well be full of rocks as I stand here watching.

I want to kill everyone in this room for making him suffer, and that bloodlust surprises me.

I clench my hands into fists and glare at Lacrae, who avoids eye contact with me at all costs. It's the first smart thing the elf has done since we met.

"Were you born of a tribe in Nemeregno?"

"Yes," he growls.

"Is your father leader of that tribe?"

"Yes."

Affree begins to pace as Fort sucks in a breath. "Were you sent to Navalis by your father?"

"I was," he growls. "After he tortured me and slaughtered my mother."

"Tortured you how?"

"No," I snap. All gazes shift to me. "You do not get to ask him that."

"We can ask him whatever we deem necessary," Onemo says flatly.

"Not that. I know what happened to him, but you do not need that information."

"All information is required by this council."

"Not that." I clench my hands into fists. Lacrae crosses over and touches my arm, I glare down at it. "Remove your hand from me before I find a way to cut it off."

He pulls back.

"It's okay," Fort gasps. "He had me burned in front of my mother."

"Burned you where?" Onemo asks.

I look to Affree, hoping that the affection I've noticed she carries for Fort will extend here, too. Unfortunately, it does not. "I see no burn marks on you," she says.

"Between my legs," he growls. "On the insides of my thighs."

Even Lacrae looks horrified by the confession.

"Why were you burned?"

"Because I didn't wish to fight in The Pit," he chokes out.

"And what is The Pit?" Affree asks.

Fort sucks in a pained breath. "Where boys and men prove their strength. I was to fight for the *privilege* of going into Navalis."

"You won, then?"

"I never fought," he wheezes. "My mother told me I didn't have to. She was killed after watching me punished. Then, my father sent me into the Phantom anyway."

"You did not wish to go to Navalis?" Onemo asks.

"No."

"Did you know of the prophecy? Before today?" Affree clarifies.

Fort shifts his dark gaze to mine. "No. We are not taught history where I come from. It is merely about surviving and training fighters."

"And the Tenebris?" Onemo questions. "Do you know where they train?"

"No," he rasps.

"But you are aware of their connection to your people?"

"Yes."

"Do you know how they are made?"

His gaze darts to mine. He knows because I told him. And now it will look as though he understands more than he truly does. "Yes."

"Tell us."

"Giant blood."

Gasps fill the room, and the council members share looks of shock and disgust.

"He only knows that because I told him last night."

Onemo rolls his eyes. "And how did you know?"

"His fa—Yarrow told me when I was being held captive. He told me that is why Tenebris soldiers are so strong."

"So you have been tainted with the blood of a giant," Onemo sneers. "Even worse than I thought."

"Fort is clean," I say quickly. "He was sent away before he was injected with the blood."

"Why would we believe you?" Onemo demands. "You would say anything to save him."

"Give me that tonic," I bluff. "I'll tell you the damned truth, too." I step closer to the councilman. "I swear to you, though, should you harm Fort, I will tear you apart until there is nothing left of you." I growl the threat, meaning every single weighted word.

"You threaten me?"

"It's not a threat; it's a promise."

"There is a much simpler way to end this peacefully." Affree crosses back to Fort. "Do you have any interest in controlling the giants now that you know the truth?"

"No," he growls. "I want nothing to do with any fucking prophecy. I just want to keep Carleah safe."

Affree turns to Onemo. "Is there anything else you wish to know?"

He stands. "Why are you here? In this city?"

"Carleah," he growls.

"And should Carleah fail the final trial and be put to death, what will you do?"

Lacrae and Affree both whirl on him, but neither interrupts.

Fort's body goes completely rigid. "I will slaughter every single one of you until this entire fucking place is bathed in elven blood."

Onemo's grin spreads, and his intentions become

clear as day. He's purposely taunting us. This has nothing to do with getting to the truth and everything to do with getting rid of both Fort and me.

"Lock him up," he orders the guards.

"No!" I yell, rushing forward. "You set him up!"

"He is a threat to our people," Onemo tells me.

"The only threat I see is you," I retort. "Maybe we should give you the tonic and ask about my last trial? About who tampered with it?"

The councilman pales slightly, and Affree looks at her brother. "Is it possible?" she questions.

"Possible?" Onemo scoffs. "I had nothing to do with that!"

"It is, Sister," Lacrae replies.

Onemo's face reddens, and he slams both hands onto the table. "I will not be subjected to this type of treatment! I refuse!"

"As is your right," Affree says softly. "But you will understand if we must detain you."

"She is using this as a distraction!" Onemo roars, his finger pointed at me.

I glare right back. "I have had everything that ever mattered stripped from me. I have no reason to speak mistruths. You, however, have made your disdain for me evident since the beginning."

"You would turn against me!"

"We will ensure the integrity of the final trial remains intact," Onyx comments as she waves two elven warriors from the door. They rush in and grab Onemo.

"You will all pay for this!" he bellows as he's dragged from the room.

Fort groans.

"I think we've heard enough," Affree says. "Take him back to his room."

Lacrae crosses over and undoes the leather binding Fort to the chair. Then, he loops one of Fort's arms around his shoulders and helps him from the chamber.

We reach our room in minutes, and Lacrae drops Fort onto the bed. "Are you all right?"

"You lied to me, too," I tell him. "The only difference between the two of you is that he told me the truth because he cared, not because of some twisted form of jealousy."

Lacrae's gaze hardens, but he nods. "I am sorry for keeping it from you for as long as I did. I am sorry for everything."

"Go."

The elf dips his head and leaves, the door sliding closed behind him. Fort groans on the bed and rolls to his side, curling in on himself as he does. Sweat beads on his forehead, so I cross over to the wash basin and retrieve a clean cloth.

"Are you okay?" I whisper as I run the cloth over his forehead.

"Fine," he replies, though his tone is sharp—pained.

"I'm so sorry for all you have suffered since we met."

Fort forces a smile. "It's been worth every moment. I love you," he whispers. "Carleah of Navalis." His lids flutter closed, and he falls still. This whole Trial of Truth feels like a massive distraction when compared to everything else we face.

Fort is loyal—something he has proven over and over again.

Yet, they insist he is not, that he is this son of flame from the prophecy and will destroy me in the end.

Lacrae's memory plays out in my mind once again.

"Tell me of the prophecy."

Harlow sucks in a breath. "The daughter of ice will seek refuge with the son of flame," he manages.

"What the bloody hell does that mean?"

"I do not know," he rasps, words growing faint. "But they believe that the daughter of ice is—" He sucks in a ragged breath. "From Navalis."

"Daughter of ice. There are no daughters born of the royal line in Navalis."

"It's. Just. What. They. Said." The king coughs again.

"What else?" When the king doesn't answer, Lacrae tosses his torch to the ground and grips his tunic, shaking him. "What else!" he roars.

The king's eyes flutter open. "The son of flame will use her for the power she possesses," he whispers. "And then, he will destroy our kingdom," he chokes out. "Because he is the one who can control the giants."

The son of flame will destroy our kingdom. I take in the angle of Fort's jaw, the sharpness of his features. *He will use the daughter of ice.* Even knowing what I do now about his past, the idea that he would destroy me and a kingdom is a fallacy.

There's no world in which the man before me would

allow any harm to come to those who do not deserve it. Will he kill? Yes. I've seen him do it. But not for power. Which leads me to believe that, either the prophecy is wrong about him, or I am not the daughter of ice they were hoping for.

Because Fort cannot be the son of flame.

I reach out and brush a strand of hair from his face.

I forgave him the moment he told me the truth.

Alex forgave him, too.

And while I refuse to condemn him for treason he never committed, I cannot trust the elves to do the same. Even though this damned interrogation is over, tonight merely convinced me that I cannot trust these elves to let us go.

"Fort?" When he doesn't answer, I lean in and whisper, "I love you, too."

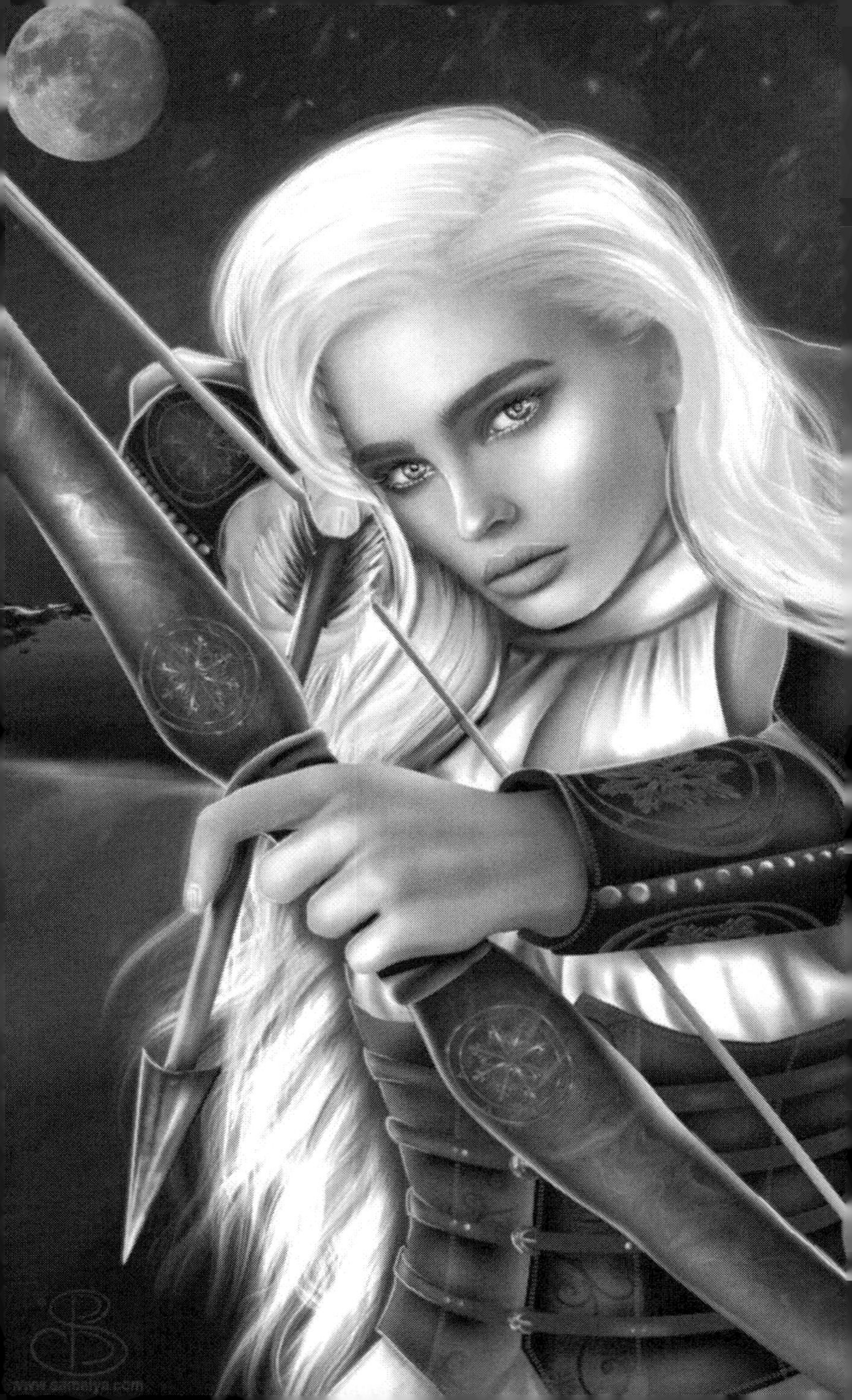

CHAPTER 33
CARLEAH

I sit up and stretch. The bed beside me is completely empty, so I immediately scan the room for signs of Fort. His back is to me as he sits in the pool of water, his head hung low. Given that it's light outside, I hope that means the tonic has begun to wear off, so I swing my legs over the edge and climb out of bed.

"Fort?" I come around to the stairs.

His face is pale, his chin pressed against his chest. He doesn't move.

Panic sends my pulse racing and I rush into the water. "Fort?"

He blinks slowly and raises his head to look at me.

I breathe a sigh of relief. "Has it worn off?"

"Not entirely." He shifts and winces.

"I hate that they made you take that tonic."

. . .

He looks up at me, his eyes so damned beautiful I want to drown in them. "There is nothing I won't do for you. But you should truly begin re-thinking your alliances," he says softly.

"What the hell does that mean?"

"You should have condemned me for what my people did to your family. You should have hated me the moment you discovered just who I was."

"It's not your fault. None of it was your fault."

"I have giant blood in my veins," he says. "Blood of monsters who literally tore the realm apart."

"You are not a Tenebris."

"But I am," he insists. "Aside from the fact that I grew up in Navalis, I am a soldier of the army who stole your home. Who murdered your family. My loyalty is with you, but my blood is theirs."

I close the distance between us, the water lapping at the dress on my body. "I don't give a shit what anyone else thinks, Fort. You are *mine*. Do you understand me? Regardless of what blood is in your veins, you belong to *me*."

He sighs.

"Do you truly believe you are not the son of flame?" I question.

"I can't be," he replies.

"Why?"

He looks up at me now, eyes amber fire. "Because I won't do anything that will hurt you!" he roars. He winces, the force of his words clearly bringing him pain.

I move in closer to rest my hand on his chest. His

flesh is hot beneath my touch, his body quivering. "And this is why I refuse to condemn you, Fort. You are the only person in this entire realm I trust with my life. The only one I want at my side. It doesn't matter where you come from. Nothing and no one else matters but us."

"I never wanted this," he says. "Between us. I have spent the last two years in agony because I knew I wasn't good enough for you."

Even as I know loving him will likely be my damnation, I move in closer and press my lips to his. "I will not walk away from the last shard of joy I have ever had in my life," I whisper against his lips.

"Your touch is agony."

I start to pull away, but Fort grips me and pulls me back in. "Never stop."

My heart hammers in my chest as I slide my hands over his expansive chest. Fort shivers beneath my touch. "This hurts?"

He nods.

"You don't want me to stop?"

Fort shakes his head.

"Is it because you think you deserve the pain?"

"Yes."

My heart aches for him, for the truths he so plainly speaks now, but I pull my hand away. "I won't be your punishment, Fort."

"Why not? I do deserve it."

I close my eyes, recalling the scars on the insides of his thighs. From a young age, this man was taught that, when he acted out or did something against what his father wanted, he could expect to be tortured.

Which, I realize now, is exactly what he's looking at me for.

"I am not your father, Fort. I will never punish you."

He shivers, a tremor running through his body. "I'm cold," he says. "Will you help me to the bed?"

"Yes."

After helping him to the bed and settling him back against the covers, I move toward the magical barrier separating us from the elements. Per usual, there is nothing but cloud cover visible just outside, but I can imagine the way it looked when Lacrae had taken me up to the landing where we'd seen the Pegasus.

Snow-capped mountain ranges and grassy hills.

I wrap my arms around myself and try to imagine what my father would advise in a moment like this. He was a man of peace and mercy, not blood and war.

Yet, I recall him telling me that he had killed before. That he had spilled blood for our allies. Is it possible that, to be a king of mercy, you must also be a man of war?

For so long, I truly believed that there could be no peace if there was war on the horizon. But now I see that the constant threat of war is what keeps the peace. "I'm sorry, Father," I whisper. "I understand now."

The tree jolts, and I fall backward, adrenaline pulsing through my system.

I whirl as a heavy thud hits the ground behind me.

"Carleah!" Fort calls out.

"I'm here!" I rush over to him as he's trying to stand. "We need to get you dressed." I retrieve his pants and boots as something else shakes the tree. The barrier snaps and disappears, so wind rushes into our room.

"They're here," he says. "The crimson soldiers have found us."

"Not yet," I tell him.

I help him dress quickly then pull him to his feet. The door to our room slides open, and I throw up a hand as Lacrae rushes in, carrying a quiver full of arrows.

"This is my apology. Your brother's quiver. I stole it back from Nemoregno after I first saw it in your memory. Forgive me for not giving it to you until now. The others did not wish you to be armed, and since Fort brought back the bow—"

I want to point out that he continues doing shit that needs my forgiveness, but I'm so grateful to see another item of my brother's that I keep it to myself and run my fingers over the smooth leather side. "Thank you."

He dips his head then reaches behind and removes the quiver from his back before offering it to me. "We need to fight. The Tenebris are here."

He reaches into his pocket and offers Fort a vial of clear liquid.

"What the hell is that?"

"The antidote," Lacrae says with a haunted smile.

"You have one? You said—"

"Affree said we didn't have one," he corrects. "Because if you were to have known that we had relief, the pain wouldn't have been as intimidating. You needed to be willing to suffer in order for them to believe you were telling the truth."

"That's sadistic," I reply though, even as Fort didn't deserve it, I see their logic. The reasoning behind it. If someone believes they can get relief as soon as it's over, they're more likely to just push through it. But Fort offered to take that pain, to bear that burden for a full day and night. That alone speaks volumes.

Fort doesn't hesitate before biting the cork and ripping it off then downing the liquid. Seconds tick by, but within a matter of a few heartbeats, he's standing on his own. "Thank you."

"Do not thank me yet. Wait until you survive." He reaches behind him once more and withdraws a blade before offering it to Fort. Then, he turns to me. "You have your bow?"

"Yes."

"Good." He rushes across the tree, stumbling when it shakes again. Outside, the screams are near deafening. "Call him."

"Who?" I ask even as a voice in my head calls out, *Shadow*. Before Lacrae can answer, the flapping of wings fills my ears as a massive white animal emerges from the clouds. He tucks his wings and glides into our room then bows his head.

"Wonderful." He rushes toward me. "You will ride Shadow. Let him guide you as you use the bow."

"She can't ride and—" Fort stops himself then turns to me. "Can you?"

I shove the surprise that I simply thought of him and Shadow appeared aside, and focus on surviving. "I will."

His hand snakes around the back of my neck, and he yanks me toward him, claiming my lips in a heated kiss that stirs my blood even as it feels a hell of a lot like a goodbye. When he pulls away, he stares down at me. "For luck."

Then, he steps back.

"Good luck, Carleah," Lacrae offers before dipping his head and rushing out the door.

Fort gives me one final look before following the elf.

I turn to Shadow. "Shall we?"

The massive horse drops his head, and I climb on, my heart in my throat. I reach up and retrieve an arrow before burying my free hand in his long mane. He steps toward the edge, and I bite back a choked scream as he leaps and dives from the room.

My seat is firm, my thighs gripping his muscled body as he drops down. The moment we break free of the clouds, I see the chaos in the streets of the otherwise peaceful elven city, and I feel the first tendrils of bloodlust surging through my system.

Men in crimson race through the streets, their blood-coated blades swinging freely at men, women, and children.

Without a second thought, I release Shadow's mane, ready an arrow, then send it flying into the throat of a soldier preparing to cut down a woman and her child.

He falls to the ground, but before his body even hits

the dirt, I've readied another arrow. In my mind, Bowman is here with me, guiding every single one of them to their mark.

I catch sight of Fort and Lacrae fighting a group of soldiers. They remain back-to-back, and Fort fights with the same revere I saw so many times when he'd been training. His body is one with his blade, an impressive sight to behold.

A soldier charges to him from the side, so I let loose another arrow.

It hits the man in the eye, and blood oozes as he drops to the ground.

Fort glances up at me and nods.

Shadow climbs back up into the sky before diving down again. Soldiers surround the council. Affree holds a blade out, though even from where I am, I can see it shaking.

I fire an arrow at the closest man.

He falls.

Then I let loose another. And another. The men whirl on me and snarl.

"There she is!" one calls.

"Get her! Focus on the girl!"

Shadow climbs, but from the clouds emerges a creature that makes my blood run cold. A giant with jet-black hair down to its waist and dark eyes steps out, his snarling grin aimed directly at me.

"Up, Shadow!" I roar.

The horse climbs, but pain explodes from my shoulder, and I lose my grip on the horse. I fall backward, off of Shadow's strong back, and plummet toward the ground below.

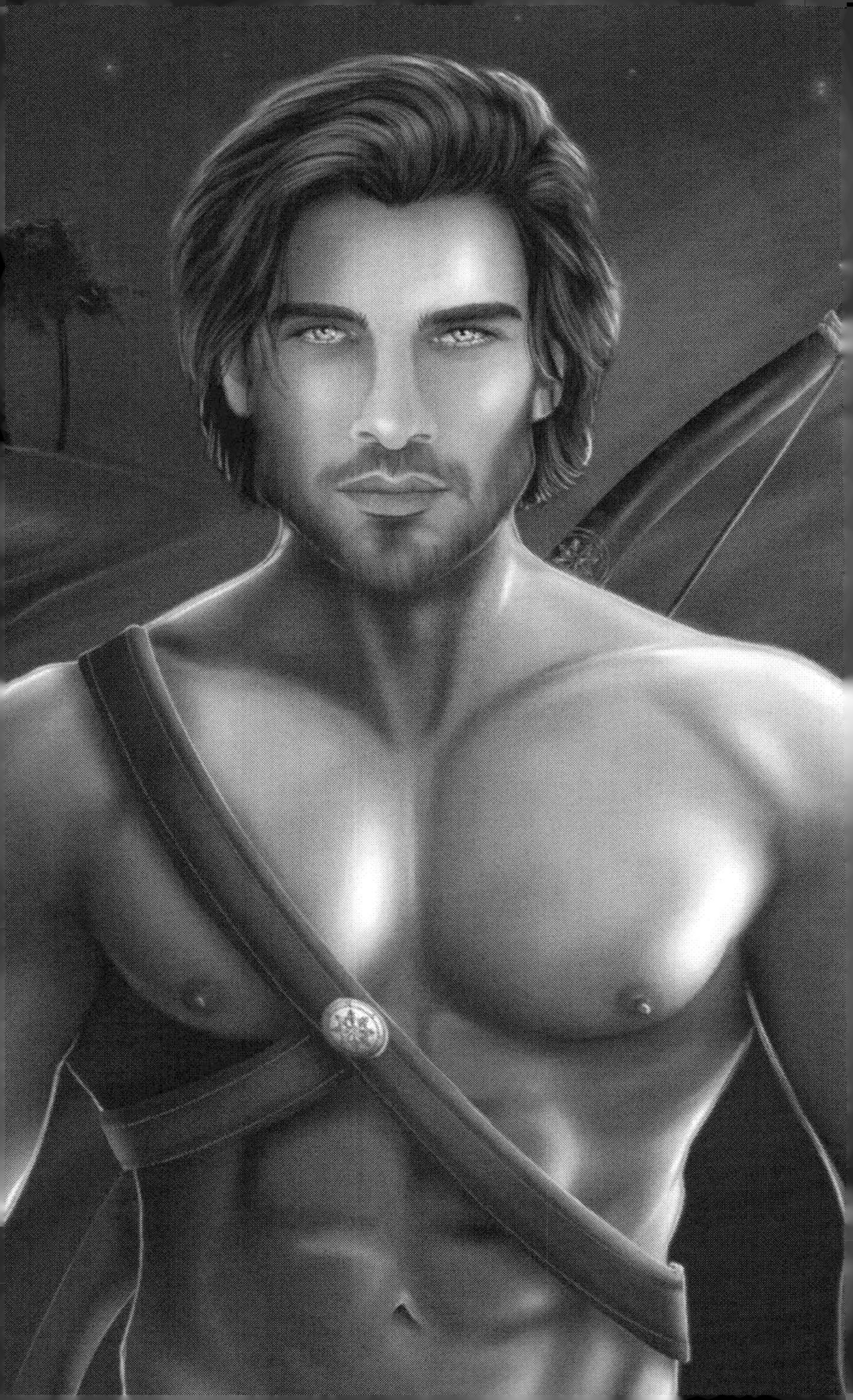

CHAPTER 34
FORT

Carleah's scream rips through the early morning, and I whirl as she falls from the back of Shadow, an arrow through her chest.

"Carleah!" I bellow, sprinting toward her just in time to see a massive hand jut out from the clouds and grab her. "No!" I leap over bodies, dodging blades in my desperate attempt to get to her.

The horse lets loose a cry as it swoops into the clouds after her.

"Carleah!"

"What is it?" Lacrae yells as he matches my pace.

"Something grabbed her!"

He bounds after me, the two of us racing through the bloodied streets. I burst through the cloud cover as the massive creatures brings Carleah closer to its face and snarls. She squirms in its hold, fighting to break free.

"Giant," Lacrae whispers. "Impossible."

"Aren't they all locked in a fucking cave?" I demand.

"They're supposed to be."

"Daggers. Do you have any?"

He nods and hands me his sword before reaching behind his back and withdrawing two silver daggers.

"Take this." I hand him my sword, palm both daggers, and sprint toward the giant. His gaze entirely on Carleah, he doesn't even see me coming. I jump onto a wagon and leap, driving both blades into the creature's thigh.

He roars and spins, trying to find me, and it takes every bit of strength I have to cling to him. I pull one dagger out and drive it into his flesh then repeat the action with the other, all while he spins in a circle, holding onto Carleah.

Either he drops her to get me, or he falls back and crushes me.

But I don't let the odds stop me.

I continue using the daggers until I reach his shirt, then, I let one fall, stick the other between my teeth, and use the fabric of his clothes to climb his massive body.

"Put her down!" Lacrae roars, distracting the thing.

It lets loose a roar and stomps a foot at the elf, who barely manages to avoid being squished.

Carleah screams in pain.

I reach his shoulder and stare down at her. Her bright blue eyes are set in a pale face, and the front of her dress is saturated in her blood. The arrow is not in her chest as I thought, though, but through her shoulder.

Which bodes well for both of us.

I launch myself onto the creature's neck and bring

my blade down into his eye socket. Then, I twist. He roars, a deafening bellow that shakes the very ground. Carleah tries to break free, but the thing maintains its hold, so I rip the dagger out and drive it into his other.

He drops her and she falls—I jump, leaping from the giant and diving toward her. She's mere inches from me, but the ground is coming fast.

Carleah reaches for me, and I grip the tips of her fingers before pulling her against my body and spinning us just in time to slam into the ground. I await pain—death—but neither come.

Carleah shivers against me, her body trembling.

I open my eyes and find myself staring out at the council. Lacrae is beside me, covered in sweat and dirt. He reaches down and pulls Carleah to her feet then offers me his other hand.

"You had no right," he growls.

Affree completely ignores him and turns to Fort. "You fought well, warrior."

"That was a test?" Carleah hisses. "Another damned trial?" Her tunic is still coated in blood, the arrow jutting from her body.

"Most of it was," Affree says. "The arrow is quite real. Though our archer did miss your heart as he assured us he would."

Fury saturates my blood. "You fucking shot her?"

"She would have suspected it was a trial, and for the final one, we needed her to believe it was real. We needed to know what all three of you would do and whether or not you would sacrifice yourself to save her."

"Could you not have just asked me when I was under the influence of the fucking tonic?" I demand.

"Yes," she replies. "But there are many who truly believe they are willing to give their lives for those they love, yet when it comes down to it, they choose their own selves."

"I will choose Carleah every time."

"As we now know." Affree steps down from the stands and makes her way into the arena. "We are quite pleased with the results of this test."

"You are my sister!" Lacrae roars. "And you plunged me into a trial without my knowledge?"

"It has become clear to this council that you have taken an affection toward the woman, Brother. We wished to know how deep that emotion ran."

Carleah sways on her feet. "Can we yell at each other later and get the arrow out of me now?"

"Yes. Of course." Affree snaps her fingers, and the same healer who'd tended to her after the third trial rushes over.

"This will hurt, dear."

I pull Carleah against me, holding her still as the woman snaps the head from the arrow and rips the shaft from her flesh. She groans, but as soon as the arrow is free from her, the healer places her hands over the wound, and I watch it knit back together before my very eyes.

"It takes quite a bit of strength from me," the healer says when she catches me staring.

I swallow hard as Carleah pulls away and rolls her

shoulder. "The pain is gone."

"Good." Affree claps her hands then turns. "Well, Onemo? Did you see all you wanted to?"

"Onemo?" Lacrae growls.

All three of us whirl on the elderly elven man who steps into view, holding a cloth-covered object in his hands. He smiles and crosses toward us. "I did."

"What the hell is he doing here?" I demand.

"All three of you did quite well," he says. "And your suspicions of me prove that you can see well beyond what is in front of you." The elf grins at me. "Your intuition is impressive."

"I don't understand." Carleah looks from him to Affree.

"Your third trial was not tampered with," Affree says.

"What?" Lacrae steps forward. "You told me it was. You assured me it was not done on purpose?"

Affree groans. "Your emotions would have clouded your ability to see how important it was that we test both her resilience and the intentions of the man *you* informed us was born of our enemy. He ran to her aid, which meant—"

"You lied to me. Over and over again," Lacrae shakes his head angrily.

"Doesn't feel great, does it?" Carleah questions.

He looks to her, his expression hardening. His affection has been clear to me since the first moment we met. But I didn't believe it to be anything real until right now.

"This will not be forgiven, Affree," Lacrae snaps then marches from the field.

"Now that this ridiculous display is over." Onemo reaches up and begins to unwrap the package in his arms.

"Ridiculous display?" Carleah snarls. "You're toying with people's emotions, and you're calling it a ridiculous display?"

Onemo glares at her, his expression hardening. "Do not patronize me, girl. I have been alive longer than your great, great, great grandfathers. Your ancestors have died while I have remained, watching men fight and kill each other over land that was never theirs to begin with. Before we dare move forward, we needed to know that you were the one we had sought all these years."

"According to your prophecy, I was," Carleah snaps. "Daughter of ice? I'm the only royal daughter born in Navalis."

"Prophecies have been misinterpreted before," he says. "And this is no light burden that is resting on your shoulders." With one final pointed glare, he looks back down and removes the canvas covering from the thing in his arms.

Carleah gasps, and I stare down at the clear, crystal blade in his hand. Made entirely of ice or crystal—I cannot be sure—the blade is absolutely stunning. "What is that?"

"The Blade of Ice," he replies. "It is the only thing that can kill a giant."

"It looks so fragile," she says as she takes a step closer, completely enamored by the thing. "Yet it calls to me."

"Take it," he urges. "Take it, and know that you are the Queen of our Realm. Our hero. Our champion."

Carleah reaches out and touches the blade. The wind around us picks up, whipping past her as the blade solidifies in her hand. Silver drips over the blade, covering it and climbing up the hilt, which turns a deep gold.

Her gaze is transfixed on it, and as soon as the sword has solidified in her hands, Carleah's eyes begin to blaze a hypnotizing blue.

Power.

Carleah Rossingol of Navalis is the Warrior Queen of the Third Realm.

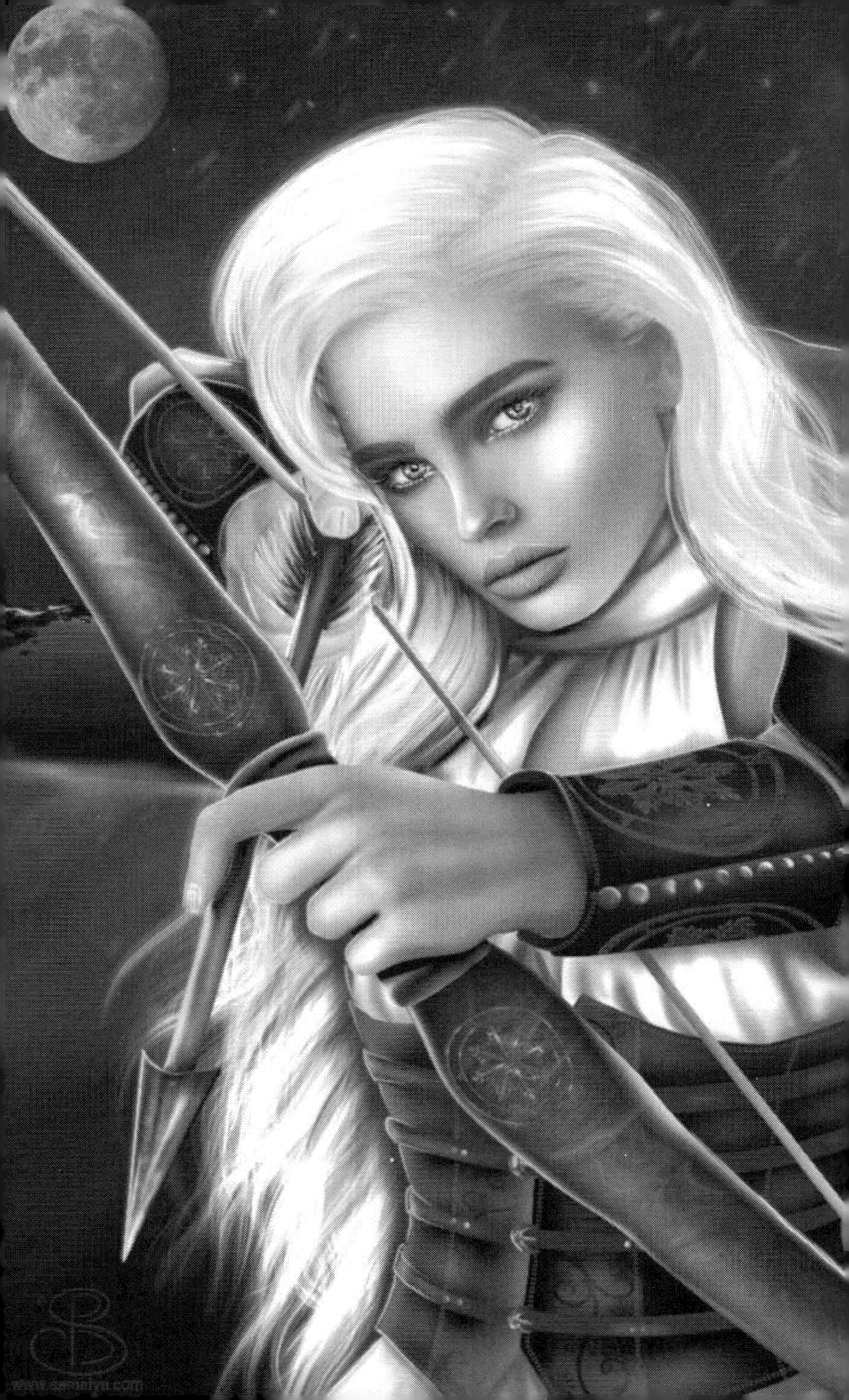

CHAPTER 35
CARLEAH

Lanterns light up the elven village. Children's laughter fills my ears as they race down the aisle on the opposite side of the long table that has been placed directly in the center of town. I sit beside Fort as elves offer me their congratulations and allegiance.

It's a strange feeling.

I know I should be proud. After all, the trials are over.

I passed.

I have my army.

However, this lingering weight in my gut makes it impossible to appreciate and enjoy the celebration. My family never believed I'd be anything more than a queen who stands beside her king. And now I'm expected to be *the* queen.

Why the hell does it feel so bittersweet when all I wanted was to be seen as more than I was?

Fort sits beside me, holding an ale in his hand as he

watches the people around us. Even Onemo and the other council members are laughing joyfully across from us. Everyone is having a good time...except us.

Have we seen too much to ever really enjoy life again?

"Carleah," Fort says, his hand sliding over my lower back. I turn to him, and he offers a nod at an elven woman standing across from us.

I plaster an apologetic smile on my face. "I'm so sorry. I'm exhausted."

"As you should be, my queen." She bows her head. "I merely wanted to present you with this gift." She holds out a crown made of flowers and green ivy. I take the delicate gift then place it on my head. The woman beams at me. "It looks lovely on you, as I knew it would."

"Thank you so much—"

"Bess," she finishes.

"Bess." I smile. "I will cherish it."

With a beaming grin, she turns and rushes back into the crowd. They dance to a band playing happy tunes.

"What is on your mind?" Fort asks, his voice low enough that only I can hear him.

"That I used to love parties," I reply. "And now, I cannot summon up a single ounce of joy."

"You've suffered tremendously," he reminds me. "It's going to take time to get back to some semblance of who you were."

"That's just it, though," I tell him. "I don't know that I want to be who I was before. She was naïve, weak, and the realm needs me to be strong. Impervious."

"You do not need to be impervious to pain in order to

be a good leader, Carleah," he says softly. "And you are strong. Look at all you've faced. The loss of your family, trudging through Navalis with Tenebris hunting you. The attack at Miscerico. Nemoregno. The elven trials." He takes a drink of his ale. "You're so much stronger than anyone I've ever known."

I turn to him, eyes misting. "Then why don't I feel it? Why does all of this feel like misplaced hope?"

Fort takes my hand in his. "It's not misplaced. But you now carry the weight of the realm, Carleah. You just need to remember that you do not shoulder that burden alone."

I recall wishing I could carry the weight of his darkness on my shoulders. How ironic that he now offers to carry mine.

"You do not celebrate?" Lacrae questions as he plops down on the bench across from us.

"We're tired," I tell him.

Fort merely lifts his mug and drinks.

Lacrae watches the both of us. "I would like to apologize, one final time, for the part I have played in your misery. I am hoping that we might all be friends."

Fort snorts.

A grin toys at the corners of my mouth. "Perhaps one day," I tell Lacrae. "When I no longer feel like slamming my fist into your jaw."

To my surprise, the elf smiles. "Most of my closest friends long to hit me from time to time. Harlow was the same way."

"Don't hold your breath for me, elf," Fort says.

Lacrae's grin spreads. "One day, we will fight side-by-side, warrior."

A woman with bright red hair rushes over and tugs on Lacrae. He allows himself to be pulled from the seat then rushes into the crowd and begins to dance with her.

"For someone so old, he sure as hell doesn't seem to understand when something is a lost cause."

I lean against Fort, and he wraps an arm around my shoulders, pressing a kiss to my temple. "Do you think my brothers would ever believe this?"

"Ethan, yes. But the others?" Fort laughs. "They would believe you'd lost your mind."

I smile as I recall the morning that feels like lifetimes ago when I found Ethan's nose buried in *A History of Elves*. "Ethan believed in magic," I tell him. "In the legends. Diedrich, too, I think. Though he'd never admit it."

"Your entire family would be incredibly proud of you," Fort says.

I pull away to look at him. "My mother would be horrified."

Fort grins. "And you would enjoy every moment of it, wouldn't you?"

With fairy lights dancing around us, I lean in and press my lips to Fort's. His hand slips into the back of my hair, and he holds me to him.

After that horrific night when Navalis fell, I never thought I would find my way again. A part of me wished I'd died back in Navalis so that I could be reunited with those I lost. But with Fort at my side, I continued putting one foot in front of the other, and eventually, I crawled my way free of the darkness smothering me.

It took losing everything for me to find my own strength.

And while I wish I could bring my family back, I no longer feel like I am searching for my destiny. I've found it.

With Fort at my side, I am going to destroy the Tenebris.

I am going to bring peace back to the realm and take back my home. Or I will die trying.

Fort tears away from me and jumps up, ripping me from my seat and shoving me behind him.

Someone screams.

He falls backward into my lap, and I stare down at the shaft of an arrow sticking out of his chest.

"Fort!" I scream.

All around me, chaos breaks.

Soldiers leap from the shadows, crimson armor glinting in the light.

"Please! You have to get up!" I try to tug him to his feet.

"Go," he chokes out. The color of his skin is already beginning to fade, but I refuse to let him go.

"No. I'm not leaving you!" I pull Bowman's bow and quiver from where it sits beside me, nock an arrow, and fire at a soldier rushing us—blade drawn.

Elven warriors pour into the center of town, momentarily taking the attention of the Tenebris. I grab Fort and try to slip one of his arms over my shoulders, but his weight is too great. He goes down.

Then, in a blur of movement, Lacrae is there, lifting him from the ground and wrapping one of Fort's muscled arms around his shoulders.

"Please. You have to get him inside. Get him help."

"Carleah—" Fort chokes out as his eyes begin to droop.

"Go!" I scream at Lacrae. He hesitates a moment but turns and moves as quickly as he can with Fort at his side.

I nock an arrow and scan, looking for a clear target. I spot a soldier rushing for Onemo and Affree, so I fire. It sails through the air and slams into his throat, taking him straight to the ground.

I ready another arrow, feeling the pressure before I send it singing through the air at another soldier. The blade at my waist is useless to me now, because my knowledge of fighting with a sword is limited.

But the bow—that I understand quite well.

And, in this moment, I breathe deeply, focusing only on the task at hand.

The elven warriors continue beating back the crimson warriors, though they lose some of their own as well. However, no matter how fast the enemy is, the elves are faster. They spin and fight, moving even faster than Fort.

Fort.

I try not to think about him. Try not to worry that I'll never see him again because that will only lead to a distraction. Instead, I focus on not allowing this elven paradise to face the same fate as Navalis.

Then, I couldn't fight.

Now, I can.

A crimson soldier turns his murderous gaze on me and attacks, sprinting toward me at full speed. I fire an arrow, but he dodges to the side, gaining more on me at every second. I rip my blade free and swing, sending every bit of power I can into the strike.

He raises his blade as well.

They clash together.

And his crumbles to ash.

His dark eyes go wide, and I grin, using his momentary distraction to drive the blade of ice straight into his throat. He coughs and sputters, falling back to the ground in a heavy thump. Adrenaline pumping through my system, I rush forward, swinging my blade and decimating the enemy's steel.

Once again, he gapes at it in shock.

"That's right, asshole," I growl. I drive my blade straight into his heart, right through his armor plate. It dissipates, turning to ash on the breeze just as his blade did.

Feeling powerful for the first time in my life, I attack, moving with speed I didn't know I had. Between my blade and the elves, we manage to beat the Tenebris back, though the ground is littered with the bodies of the dead.

Elves and Tenebris alike.

"What the hell was that?" Affree demands as she rushes forward. "How did they get past the scouts?"

"We don't know, but that was merely a small company," a female warrior elf says. "There will likely be more coming."

Affree turns to me. "You need to leave," she says. "You and Fort need to begin rallying the realm behind you if we are to succeed."

"He's been shot. Where did Lacrae take him?"

"He would have taken him back to the tree. I'll get the healer and meet you there." She gathers her skirts and sprints in the opposite direction, so I race through the streets, the dead a blur in my vision as I make my way back to Fort.

I find him in the room we share.

Fort lays still on the bed, Lacrae applying pressure to his wound, though his expression is grim.

"Is he—" I rush to his side.

"Alive," Fort chokes out.

"You better not die on me," I tell him. "I swear, if you do, I will find a way to bring you back so I can kill you myself." Tears burn in the corners of my eyes.

Affree sprints in. "The healer is dead."

Hope deflates in my chest.

She crosses over toward us and studies the arrow that Lacrae ripped from Fort's chest. "Let me see the wound," she orders. Lacrae removes the pressure and tears Fort's tunic. "Shit."

"What is it?" But before she can answer me, I look down and note the black lines snaking from his injury.

"Poison?" I choke out. "How do we fix him? Get another healer."

"We don't have another one here," she says.

"Then herbs! Do something!"

She purses her lips. "He needs a healer to pull the toxin from his veins, or it will pollute his body before claiming his life. There is an elven healer who resides with the dwarves in the caverns of Dead Man's Land. You stand a chance of getting there quickly, but only if you leave now."

"I can take him," Lacrae offers.

"Absolutely not," I snap.

"You cannot hold him on Shadow," Lacrae says.

"Then you come with us. You help me save him. Please."

Lacrae dips his head in a nod. "Of course."

"Let me get some herbs; they may help to slow the toxin down." Affree rushes over toward the bathtub and pulls the glass jar from the shelf. After opening the lid and dipping it into the water basin near the mirror, she crosses the room in three long strides.

I grab it from her and apply the paste to Fort's injury. Then, I reach down and tear part of my dress to wrap it around as a makeshift bandage.

Affree reaches up and withdraws a pin from her hair. It's a Pegasus with a crown of ivy leaves. "Offer the healer this. She will heal him. She owes me a debt."

Fort groans.

I stroke the dark hair from his forehead, trying like hell not to see him pale and lifeless like all the others I loved. Am I cursed? Is that what this ridiculous prophecy is? All those I love have to die?

"Get to Dead Man's Land," Affree says as she rushes toward the transparent wall and presses her hand to the clear barrier. After uttering a muffled word, it drops, and wind whips into the room.

Before she even has the chance to whistle, the thundering of wings fills my ears seconds before Shadow tucks his wings into his sides and lands in the room. He bows down.

"Come. Quickly." Lacrae lifts Fort and carries him toward Shadow while I retrieve the blade and Bowman's bow.

I climb onto Shadow's back, and Lacrae helps Fort on behind me. Then, he climbs on after him and wraps both arms around Fort to keep him steady. "Stay safe, Sister."

Affree's eyes mist. "You do the same, Brother. Ride fast, Your Highness," she tells me. "The dwarves also have an impressive army, and should you make them understand what is happening, I have faith they will join our fight."

"And if they don't?" I ask.

"You had better hope they do," she replies. "From there, you need to seek out the king of Soreno as well as the Siren King. Shadow and Lacrae will show you the way. Trust them to guide you." She offers us a nod. "Be wary, Queen Carleah, for the perils that await you outside of these mountains are great. Trust that your army will be preparing for your return. We stand with you. Always."

Pride and hope swirl in my chest even as fear for Fort grows heavy. "Thank you. Let's go, Shadow." I urge him forward, and the horse turns then runs toward the opening. He dives out, wings spreading, and we fly over the elven village.

As we do, I note the cheers carrying up to my ears.

Shadow doesn't slow beneath the weight of the three of us as we fly through the clouds high above the mountains. Hours pass by in a blur while I keep my eye on the ground below, scanning for any sign that more Tenebris are closing in on the elves.

I see nothing.

Dawn begins to break, casting the world in bright rays of gold and orange.

"How is he?" I call back.

"Alive," Fort chokes out.

"I'm keeping him steady," Lacrae calls to me.

"Getting rather handsy, elf," Fort tries to joke, but it ends on a wheeze that only increases my fear.

Shadow dives down closer to the ground just as we're passing the last of the cliffs. It's then I note an army marching in the morning sun, their white banners high, a golden sigil that will forever be burned into my mind.

Because it is the sigil of my family.

My home.

"Fort," I choke out.

"I see them," he agrees.

I know it in my heart, and yet—"Lower," I tell Shadow. "I have to see," I tell him.

"I know," he replies.

"Be wary, Carleah," Lacrae warns.

Shadow dives down, and the men scramble back, their weapons being ripped from their sheaths. Their white and golden armor is dirty and crusted with blood, their faces wide as they stare at me.

The Pegasus lands, but I remain where I am.

That is until a man pushes through from the back.

White hair. Soft blue eyes.

My chest tightens, tears burning in my vision because I know what I am seeing cannot be true...can it?

"Bowman?"

A Quick Note

Thank you so much for reading! This series is one of my all time favorites, and I cannot wait for you to see what's next!

Keep reading for an extended preview of what's to come in Fall of an Empire!

FALL OF AN EMPIRE
CARLEAH

Bowman is *alive*.

Living. Breathing. Walking. Laughing. It seems so surreal still that my brother sits across from me now, a hunk of bread in his hand as he tells Lacrae the story of his and Alex's last hunting trip. A stag got the drop on them and nearly took my eldest brother out. Would have if it weren't for Fort stepping in at the right moment.

Fort.

My gaze drifts to the closed tent where the man I love sleeps. Luckily, the healer who saved my brother is still with him, and she managed to purge Fort's body of the poison. But the damage to his system was far greater than we knew, and she'd been forced to put him into a deep sleep so his body could heal itself.

It could take days for him to wake, she'd said.

I close my eyes and take a deep breath, shoving that

from my mind. It can't be days before he's back on his feet. We don't have that much time.

According to Bowman, the Tenebris have been raiding all of Navalis. Torching villages and ransacking the homes of those who lived outside of the city. If we don't get to Soreno and gain our army, there will be no home left to save.

"Carleah?"

I meet my brother's gaze. "Yes?"

"Are you all right? You look as though you're in an entirely different realm over there."

Forcing a smile, I stir the hot stew I've yet to take a bite of. "I'm sorry, Brother, I was considering our next steps."

If he were my father or our eldest brother, Bowman undoubtedly would have told me not to think of such things. But instead of that, he simply nods. "What do you propose we do?"

I set the stew aside. "I think we need to divide our attention. You go to Soreno and convince Patrick to aid us while I take Fort north to the dwarven kingdom."

"But Fort is on the mend. We don't need another healer."

"No, but they have an army, Bowman. And I have this gut feeling that we're going to need every able body in the realm in order to defeat what's coming."

He considers my words, his blue gaze darkening as he processes them. "I don't want to split up again. We lost so much time. The pain of believing I'd lost everyone—"

"Is something I know quite well, Brother." I smile at

him. "But we will have all the time in the world once this war is over and you're seated on the throne."

"I don't want anything coming between us again, Carleah."

"Nothing ever will," I assure him.

"Not that this sibling bonding moment isn't wonderful, but what of me?" Lacrae's tone is annoyed at best. "You didn't mention me in your plan."

"I think you need to return to the elves and do whatever it takes to convince them to send their army now."

"My sister will not go for that. Not when our forest is still at risk."

"You better make her go for it, Lacrae," I tell him. "Because we're going to need the elves and dwarves to join us in order to make a show of an army large enough to force the Tenebris to retreat."

"My sister told you to unite the entire realm," Lacrae reminds me. "And you're forgetting some."

I sigh because I know who he's referring to. His sister made a point to mention the Siren King before I ever left their haven. "The sirens have a reputation for slaughtering outsiders. We shouldn't go to them unless we have to." While I may not have believed the stories of their hostility toward strangers to be true before, I'd also believed the sirens themselves to be merely legend.

I had once believed the elves and dwarves to be legends as well. Now, I cannot help but take every legend as fact until proven otherwise.

"You are their queen," Lacrae reminds me.

"So you say. They may not agree."

"So says the Blade of Ice," he retorts.

"Blade of Ice?" Bowman all but whispers it.

"The elves believe I am Queen of the Third Realm," I tell him as I reach for the blade sheathed at my back. I pull it free, and the metal glints in the fire between us. "This is the Blade of Ice."

Bowman all but lunges to his feet and moves around the fire to my side. He reaches out, and I offer him the sword. But the moment he touches it, the metal and steel give way to clear ice. "Amazing."

"Why are you surprised?" Lacrae questions. "You've always known who she was."

Shock turns my blood cold. "You knew about it?"

Bowman glares at the elf, a hardness in his eyes I've only ever seen in my father. For a moment, he's all I can see. "We all did," he replies, though he doesn't elaborate.

I pull the blade in closer. "You had better start talking, Bowman."

He runs a hand through his white hair. "Lacrae believed that you were the prophesied queen the realm had been waiting on. So when you were born, he brought the blade in a case made of wood. While I wasn't there for the initial meeting, I know Father was furious at what Lacrae insinuated and refused to let you anywhere near the sword until we'd all held it." He swallows hard. "Alex was first. He grabbed the hilt, and the thing remained cool as ice in his hands. Same with me, Dierdrech, and Ethan."

"Did he let me near it?" I demand, hanging onto every single word he's saying.

"Yes."

"And it solidified?"

The answer is betrayed in his eyes before he ever speaks a word. "Yes."

The wind is all but knocked from my lungs as I realize what this means. Not only did Lacrae lie to me, but my entire family kept this massive secret from me. And, they were planning to marry me off instead of letting me fulfill the destiny that was laid out for me since before I was born.

I jump to my feet.

How twisted is that? They *knew* I was meant for more and were still going to let me settle for a life with Patrick.

"You all knew? Is this some kind of cruel joke?"

Bowman stands, too. "Why do you think I made it a point to train you all those years? That I treated you as more than a prized cow to be married off."

My glare turns molten. "Prized cow?" I growl.

"I'm sorry. That's not what I meant. What I meant was—"

"I know what you meant. I should be thanking you for training me even though you were more than willing to let me be married off, despite who legend said I was. I always longed for a life bigger than what you all planned for me, and this entire time, I had it. You just wouldn't let me live it."

"I couldn't tell you. And your marriage to Patrick had nothing to do with your destiny. If anything, it only made you more valuable for securing an alliance."

"More valuable." I shake my head. "As though my

value was for nothing more than what's between my legs."

Bowman pales. "You know good and damn well that's not true!"

"Do I?" I roar back as I sheathe the blade and go toe-to-toe with the man I thought had been my only true ally growing up. Now, I see him for what he is: a liar just like the rest of them. And that guts me.

"I swore an oath to our father not to speak of it again after that day. We all did. And if we'd broken it—"

"You were going to let me marry a man I didn't love and hide away from my one chance to put the pieces of our realm back together!"

"We all have to do things we don't want to do!" he yells. "That is the cost of being a royal."

His choice of words stops me cold. "I'm not marrying Patrick."

Bowman takes a deep breath. "Yes. You are. That is as much a part of your destiny as that damned blade is."

"No."

"Carleah, you have no choice. You were betrothed well before the fall of Navalis, and we need that alliance now more than ever."

Hot tears fill my eyes at the sting of his betrayal. "I will not marry him. You cannot make me."

"Carleah," he starts, his anger deflating. "I know all too well about doing what you don't want to for the good of the kingdom. But these are our burdens. You must marry Patrick. Father promised him your hand, and as King of Navalis, I need to follow through on that promise."

"King of Navalis." I shake my head and step back from him. "You should be better than him; instead you're picking up the reins right where he left off."

"I'm sorry, Carleah."

"So am I. But I'm not marrying Patrick. When Fort is healed, he and I are leaving. And there's not a damned thing you can do about it."

"Fort's loyalty is to the crown, Carleah. He will obey my orders."

I laugh, but there is no humor in it. "Fort's loyalty stopped being to the crown when we fell in love. He will not allow this to happen. And neither will I."

"Love?" Bowman steps toward me. "Did he—have you—"

"Had sex? Oh yes. So if your plan hinges on me being untouched, well, that ship has already sailed."

Bowman's cheeks turn crimson. "That son of a bitch—"

"It was as much my idea as his. Hell, it was more my idea. But the fact still stands. I want to be with Fort. I *will* be with Fort."

"Carleah. What you are saying would put us at odds with Soreno in a time where our very survival relies on their mercy. Can you not think of anyone but yourself?"

"Anyone but myself—"

"Yes!" he interrupts. "It was always what Carleah wanted. What Carleah felt she deserved! Neither of us wants to be where we are right now, but there's not a damned thing we can do that will change it. Not desire. Not love. Not what you believe you deserve. Our only hope is to get to Soreno and hope they offer us aid—even as you've strayed from your damned promise to their future king."

"You cannot force me to marry him."

"I am your king," he snaps. "And I can."

"I am a queen, dammit!"

"Yet, you sit on no throne," he snaps. "I am a king by birth; you are one that was created by legend. But when you marry Patrick, you will be a true queen."

I rear back and slam my fist into his jaw. Bowman stumbles back, and three guards rush forward. Even as I prepare to fight them all—and likely lose—my brother throws a hand up, dismissing them.

"Always behaving like an immature child, Carleah. I would have thought the life experiences over the past few months would have hardened you to reality."

"You are not my brother," I say. "I would have expected this from father. Alex. But never you."

"We are products of the trauma we face," he replies cooly. "I am merely stepping up into my place."

"We are *not* products of the trauma we face," I snap. "But rather how we choose to move forward. You are choosing this path whether you believe it or not. And no matter what you say, I will not let you drag me down with you."

I turn on my heel, but Lacrae steps into my path.

"Carleah—"

"Get out of my way, Lacrae," I warn. "You just

continue lying to me, and I have no patience for whatever nonsense comes from your silver tongue next." I shove past him and head off into the dark.

Shadow falls into step beside me, the horse seemingly appearing from nowhere. Which, I suppose, solves the mystery of his name. My chest is heavy, my breathing ragged as the claws of panic close in around me.

I'm honestly not even sure why. It's not as if I've ever had control over my own destiny. But I'd truly believed that Bowman would stand beside me. That it would matter what I wanted. I am not a prize to be handed over, dammit.

"It was always what Carleah wanted."

Was I truly that childish? Am I being that childish now? Is it nothing more than an impossible dream to believe I might get to be happy with the man I want versus a man I do not wish to spend a single moment with?

I stop beside a pond that glistens beneath the bright moonlight above. Shadow drops his head to drink, so I take a seat at the water's edge and stare down at my dim reflection. Bright blue eyes. Snow white hair.

I am a Navalis Royal. There is no denying that. And I wouldn't want to even if I could. I'm proud of the blood that runs through my veins. I only wish my bloodline didn't come with shackles around my wrists.

A light breeze lifts strands of my hair as Shadow drops down beside me and lays his massive head in my lap. I run my hand over his soft hair, letting the repetitive movement calm me down even as the tears still threaten to fall.

"None of this is fair," I tell him. "On one hand, I understand where Bowman is coming from. He *is* king, and we do need Soreno to back us if we are to reclaim Navalis. But can I truly give up everything I've found with Fort for the good of the kingdom?"

Feeling more alone than I have since Navalis fell, I stare out over the water and try to concoct some scenario where what I want and what I need to do align.

Unfortunately, as I've learned over the past few weeks, nothing is fair in this life. And even as I don't want to accept it, I am learning that sometimes being a royal means setting aside what you want for what you must do.

I only wish doing what I must didn't mean sacrificing Fort.

Keep reading Fall of an Empire today!

Fall of an Empire

A warrior princess. A man infected with giant blood. A shadow hunting them both.

I won the trial...now it's time for war.

As the first daughter born to a Navalis in centuries, it was my duty to marry a king and secure an alliance for my kingdom. But that all changed when my empire crumbled beneath the steel of our enemy.

It was the man I've been secretly in love with for years who saved my life, and he who still stands at my side, a blade ready to strike down any who come against me.

But not all enemies can be seen.

Not all enemies can bleed.

Ever since I touched the Blade of Ice, I've been haunted by visions of a shadowy figure. He promises me passion should I succumb and death to all I hold dear if I refuse.

Passion.

Death.

As we fight our way toward a once-ally in hopes of gaining his favor in this fight, I am yet again faced with a choice:

love or duty?

Get your copy of Fall of an Empire and keep reading!

WHISKEY THIEF

If chatting books, sharing stories, and seeing sneak peeks of all the things sounds fun to you, come join my Facebook group! Jessica's Whiskey Thieves is where I hang out when I'm not writing or spending time on my Patreon, and it's such a great, supportive group of readers!

Sound like your cup of coffee? Then come hang with us!

ALSO BY JESSICA WAYNE

IMMORTAL VICES AND VIRTUES WORLD

Welcome to the circus. Enter if you dare.

Slay Me

Protect Me

FAE WAR CHRONICLES

Ember is dying.

But as she will soon discover, some fates are worse than death.

Accidental Fae

Cursed Fae

Fire Fae

VAMPIRE HUNTRESS CHRONICLES

She's spent her entire life eradicating the immortals. Now, she finds herself protecting one.

Witch Hunter: FREE READ

Blood Hunt

Blood Captive

Blood Cure

REJECTED WITCH CHRONICLES

She's in love with the man who murdered her. Complicated? You don't know the half of it.

CURSE OF THE WITCH

BLOOD OF THE WITCH

RISE OF THE WITCH

DARK WITCH CHRONICLES

She sacrificed her soul to save those she loves. Now, he must fight to help her get it back, or risk losing her forever.

BLOOD MAGIC

BLOOD BOND

BLOOD UNION

SIREN'S BLOOD CHRONICLES

He's a fae prince in love with a siren.

But they're both too broken to see what's right in front of them.

Rescued by the Fae

Healed by the Fae

MATED BY MIDNIGHT

Barbarian. Beast. Murderer? One thing's for sure, nothing is as it seems in this crazy town.

MIDNIGHT CURSED

MIDNIGHT HUNTED

MIDNIGHT BOUND

ACCIDENTAL ALCHEMY

My job is to keep the things inside these supernatural books from coming out…unfortunately, I suck at it.

DRAGON UNLEASHED

SHADOW CURSED

He can have her body. But never her heart.

Savage Wolf

Fractured Magic

Stolen Mate

BLADE OF ICE

Rise of a Warrior

Fall of an Empire

Birth of a Queen

CAMBREXIAN REALM

The realm's deadliest assassin has met her match.

The Last Ward: FREE READ

Warrior Of Magick

Guardian Of Magick

Shades Of Magick

RISE OF THE PHOENIX

Ana has spent her entire life at the clutches of her enemy. Now, it's time for war.

Birth of the Phoenix

Death of the Phoenix

Vengeance of the Phoenix

Tears of the Phoenix

Rise of the Phoenix

Tethered

Sometimes, our dreams do come true. The trouble is, our nightmares can as well.

Tethered Souls

Collateral Damage

For more information, visit www.jessicawayne.com

About Jessica Wayne

USA Today bestselling author Jessica Wayne was only seventeen when she wrote her first full-length novel. Titled *One Lovers Ill Will (A book that never saw the light of day.)*, it was at that moment she realized she wanted to be a full-time author.

Life had other plans, though. After spending seven years in the Army, Jessica finally had the time to push forward with that dream.

Now, a wife and mother of three, Jessica spends her days crafting worlds in which anything is possible.

She runs on coffee, and if you ever catch her wearing matching socks, it's probably because she grabbed them in the dark.

She is a believer of dragons, unicorns, and the power of love, so each of her stories contain one of those elements (and in some cases all three).

You can usually find her in her Facebook group, Jessica's Whiskey Thieves, or keep in touch by subscribing to her newsletter via her website: www.jessicawayne.com.

- amazon.com/Jessica-Wayne/e/B01MQ1OH4O
- tiktok.com/authorjessicawayne
- patreon.com/authorjessicawayne
- facebook.com/AuthorJessicaWayne
- x.com/jessmccauthor
- instagram.com/authorjessicawayne
- bookbub.com/authors/jessica-wayne

Made in the USA
Columbia, SC
06 August 2024